Praise for the novels of Paula Treick DeBoard

"Emotionally powerful from beginning to end,
Paula Treick DeBoard's novel *The Fragile World* chronicles
the heartbreaking dissolution of a family after tragic loss.
Exquisitely told, this bold and moving story is a study in grief
and the transforming power of love. Absolutely unforgettable."
—Heather Gudenkauf, *New York Times* bestselling author
of *The Weight of Silence*

"A heart-stopping series of events drives *The Fragile World*,
as Paula Treick DeBoard skillfully alternates between
a father and daughter dealing with tragic loss.
The result is a gripping read, but one that delivers,
by the book's end, a beautiful reminder of the resilience of love."
—Karen Brown, author of *The Longings of Wayward Girls*

"A coming-of-age tale about a family in crisis expertly told by
Ms. DeBoard. *The Fragile World* examines how profound loss
changes all who are forced to come to terms with it.
Touching and compelling, it will move you."
—Lesley Kagen, *New York Times* bestselling author of
Whistling in the Dark and *The Resurrection of Tess Blessing.*

"Assured storytelling propels DeBoard's first novel.... What most
compels is the observant Kirsten's account of how a small town
and a family disintegrate under the weight of the tragedy."
—*Publishers Weekly* on *The Mourning Hours*

"Rich and evocative...compelling."
—*RT Book Reviews* on *The Mourning Hours*

Also by Paula Treick DeBoard

THE MOURNING HOURS

the fragile world
PAULA TREICK DeBOARD

MIRA

ISBN-13: 978-0-7783-1676-3

The Fragile World   DEC 1 9 2014

Copyright © 2014 by Paula Treick DeBoard

First printing: November 2014
10 9 8 7 6 5 4 3 2 1

For my parents, who taught me that a journey of a thousand miles begins with a single packed-to-the-gills station wagon.

the fragile world

The only thing we have to fear is fear itself.
—Franklin D. Roosevelt

Also, blenders.
—Olivia Kaufman

prologue

Olivia

In the beginning there was Daniel. He was the only child my parents ever needed, because he was perfect. His first word was *magnet* and, the story goes, he said it while looking at the refrigerator, where my mother had spelled out D-A-N-I-E-L in brightly colored letters. Other kids might have memorized the stories their parents read to them from the Little Golden Books, but my mother always swore that Daniel was actually reading, even though he wasn't three years old yet. By the time he was five and still belted into a child seat in the back of Mom's car, he was already reading every sign on the road: City Limit and Closing Sale and Fresh Donuts. His early teachers strongly suggested that he skip grades, and if my parents hadn't worried about his size—smallish—and his sociability—shyish—he would probably have been one of those kids who make the news when they graduate from university at age twelve.

When he was six years old, Mom enrolled Daniel in piano lessons, since he had taken to singing road signs as they drove and later banging out the tunes on the kitchen table with his fork and spoon. Prompted by the sight of the golden arches, he would launch into "Two all-beef patties, special sauce, lettuce, cheese…" and he could produce, on demand, the exact jingle that matched every car dealership in the greater Sacramento area. When I was born—and just for a moment, let's pause to consider why, exactly, my parents would want another child when surely they had everything a parent could want in Daniel—he was already on his way to becoming a musical prodigy.

Physically, our lives revolved around Daniel and his music. Our funky, turn-of-the-last-century house near downtown Sacramento was crammed full with musical instruments—the upright piano in the living room, the drum set at the top of the stairs, his guitar propped against one wall or another. I was convinced that he was the only person on earth who could make a recorder look cool.

When Daniel was in the seventh grade, Mom picked me up from kindergarten one afternoon and drove me across town to his middle school auditorium for the annual talent show. The other kids were truly kids—they performed bright, cheery dance routines in spangly costumes, they lip-synced to pop songs, they executed strange karate routines that involved a lot of posturing and choppy air kicks. Daniel was the last one to take the stage, no doubt because the organizers knew he was the best. He announced that he was playing "Flight of the Bumblebee" by Rimsky-Korsakov and the entire gym went quiet with the opening notes. His fingers flew confidently over the keys; if he was intimidated in any way by hundreds of eyes on him, it didn't show. Mom had tried to convince him earlier that day to bring the sheet music as a backup, but Daniel had only tapped his head with one finger, meaning *It's all up here.* It was the first time I realized that Daniel was really great, something special.

What a disappointment I must have been, must still be. I took three years of piano lessons and barely advanced beyond the "early learner books." I remember one song, played with my right thumb on middle C and my right index finger on D. *See the bear, on two feet, begging for a bite to eat.* All I had to do was toggle my fingers between the two keys, and yet somehow I couldn't help but hit adjacent keys or lose the simple beat, giving up in a frustrated squash of all my fingers against the keys at once. Inside, a voice was saying, regular as a metronome: *Don't mess up. Get it right. Play the notes.* It didn't seem hard—but somehow I couldn't do it.

On the day of what would be my last lesson, Mom arrived at my teacher's house as I was fumbling my way through a simple scale I'd spent hours practicing. I'd been biting my lip in deep concentration, but when I saw her listening in the doorway, I burst into tears.

"It's okay," she said as we drove home, my tears finally drying against my cheeks. "You know, I'm not a musical person, and your father isn't, either. We're all talented in different ways. I don't want you to feel bad about this, all right?"

But I did feel bad. Not because I had any illusions about my musical ability—even as a third grader, I understood that the awkward clunking sounds I made at the piano were never going to evolve into the effortless music Daniel made. It hurt me, though, to think that my mother had given up on me so early, that she had accepted my lack of talent so easily. I might have resented the hell out of her for it later on, but at that moment, I wanted her to fight for me—or at least give the slightest acknowledgment that I was worth fighting for, even if it was a lie. Something like: "Olivia, you have hidden potential...."

But no. I was an eight-year-old failure.

As he got older, Daniel seemed to float through our lives on his way from one practice or event to another—concert band, musical ensemble, pep band, a steel drum band that met before school, a band that jammed for hours in our garage after school. He was a member of the youth symphony orchestra; he played piano for the spring musical his junior and senior years. Colleges fell over themselves with scholarship offers— on top of everything else, Daniel had maintained a 4.3 grade point average throughout high school. Basically, he was that one-in-a-million kid, the one who participated in everything and volunteered for everything and did a fan-*freaking*-tastic job at everything. His face—pale beneath a shock of dark hair— appeared dozens of times in his high school yearbooks, the margins crammed with notes from friends and phone numbers from hopeful admirers.

Sometimes I thought his success would have been easier to take if Daniel had been an asshole, some mean-spirited genius who could only look down his nose at everyone else. But the thing was—he was so damn nice. He was the best big brother you could have. He never once told me to go away because I was bothering him. He never once told me that I sucked at the piano or worse, showered me with pity. He made up silly songs for me every year as a birthday present, and when he got his license, he once spent an entire Saturday afternoon driving me around Sacramento in search of the best sno-cone. When he went away to Oberlin, he sent emails that were just for me, separate from the ones he sent to Dad and Mom, filled with jokes and links to funny things he'd found online, like penguins bowling and dogs chasing their tails. He liked to set cat videos to his own music, little things he composed for a joke and that I thought were genius.

Basically, I worshipped him. And as bad as I felt for disappointing Dad and Mom, I never once felt that I had disappointed Daniel. You just couldn't feel bad about yourself around him, because he didn't have that effect on people.

In the beginning, there was Daniel.

Until one day, there wasn't.

The obituary in *The Sacramento Bee,* written by Aunt Judy when neither of my parents was up to the task, left out everything interesting and reduced my brother to the barest of facts: Daniel Owen Kaufman was predeceased by both his paternal and maternal grandparents. He is survived by his immediate family, parents Curtis and Kathleen Kaufman and sister Olivia. He is also survived by an uncle and aunt, Jeff and Judy Eberle, cousin, Chelsey, and friends throughout the Sacramento and Oberlin, Ohio, areas.

Survived, when you think about it, is a funny term. *Survived* implies that we were there on the sinking ship, that somehow we got on the lifeboat, but Daniel didn't. *Survived* suggests that we were pulled from the wreckage of the collapsed building, but Daniel wasn't. *Survived* also means we kept on living—and I'm not sure that's true.

Oh, we were still alive in the biological sense of hearts beating and lungs inflating. Dad kept on showing up at Rio Americano High, where he had taught physics for so long that he was almost an institution unto himself. Mom, who had been a buyer for an antiques dealer before branching into her own furniture restoration business, threw herself into her work with a passion that bordered on mania. And me—I guess you could say that I kept going, too. I was still living and breathing and getting decent scores on my homework. I still basically *looked* like a normal kid. But nothing ever *felt* right.

Somehow, as the years passed, Daniel was still there. Not in some weird, spiritual way, as if his ghost were haunting our upstairs hallway or his profile had appeared on a moldy tortilla, but in the hold that he had over me—every memory of my childhood had Daniel in it, hovering at the edges like an orb sneaking into the background of a photo. Moving forward— *moving past the incident,* as our family therapist had said in her nice-nice way, as if everything bad could be covered over with a euphemism—was like stepping into a vacuum, a World Without Daniel, a blank space, an empty room. Some people, I heard, kept phone messages from their dead loved ones, replaying them for a dose of comfort, a reassurance of immortality. Mom's way of keeping Daniel alive was to say his name as much as possible, to bring him into conversations like that old saying I'd learned about Jesus, *the silent guest at every meal.* Seeing a notice in the paper about a soloist in a holiday concert, she'd say "That name sounds familiar. I wonder if that's the younger sister of what's-her-name, the one who used to play clarinet with Daniel?" Cleaning out our junk drawer: "This must be the missing piece to Daniel's little gadget, that little thingamajig that he used to spin around on the patio...." For no reason at all: "Remember when we rode the cable cars to the wharf and Daniel..."

Yes, Mom. I remember. We know.

Dad and I, by tacit consent, mentioned his name less and less, until we stopped saying it at all. The space Daniel had occupied was now a silent void, a sort of musical black hole that we tried to fill with the television, with random chitchat about things that didn't matter at all. It was as if Daniel had taken with him all the arias and sonatas and symphonies, all the pianissimos and fortes, all the beauty and improvisation.

Dad and I kept our silence because it was too hard—it was shitty, frankly—to acknowledge that Daniel had ever existed, because then we had to remind ourselves that he didn't exist anymore, that he was, and would always be, dead.

olivia

October 29, 2008

When the phone rings after midnight, it's never
good news.

The sound was startling, echoing off our wood
floors and banging around in the hallway, but in the strange
way that sounds penetrate sleep, it seemed as if the ringing
came from deep underwater. Or maybe I was the one underwater, swimming to the top of my dream, and suddenly
bursting through. I jerked upward, head foggy, propping myself up on my elbows.

Dad had picked up the phone, and from down the hall I
could hear him repeating, "What? What...? *What?*" as if he
were talking to a foreign telemarketer, someone trying to sell
an upgraded something or other—except he wasn't cursing
and hanging up, which was Dad's standard fare for unsolic-
ited phone calls.

Then I heard Mom's voice demanding, "Who is it, Curtis?
Who is it?" Her voice, although sleep-tinged, was panicky.

Dad was still on the line, now whispering, "I don't understand...." and I figured we could safely rule out both telemar-

keters and drunken prank calls from Dad's physics students. My room was just across the hall, and by this time I was fully awake, struggling out of a tangle of sheets and comforter. This was made more difficult by the presence of Heidi, our ancient basset hound, who was upside down next to me, her legs splayed open, her mammoth chest rising and falling with sleep. Heidi had never been the most diligent watchdog, it was true—the mailman held no interest for her, although she could hear a crumb drop in the kitchen from anywhere in the house—but she had recently passed into the stage of life where even an earsplitting telephone ring and raised voices were not cause for concern. "Move, Heidi," I ordered, nudging against the resisting bulk of her body.

A small amount of time had passed—ten seconds? Fifteen? Thirty? But between the first ring of the phone and the time I stood in the doorway of my parents' bedroom, I had the sense that my life had already changed.

One minute I had been in dreamland, my only worry the pre-algebra test I had the next day in fifth period with Mr. Heinman, who was notorious for asking questions that had nothing to do with our notes or assignments. In the back of my mind, I was also thinking about the Halloween dance on Friday—the first dance of my seventh-grade year. Simple stuff. The kind of thing you have the luxury to think about when the rest of life is going well, when your life isn't hinging on a middle-of-the-night phone call.

Mom had switched her bedside light on, and both of my parents were sitting up, looking rumpled and older than they did during the daytime. Dad's hair was sticking up in strange tufts, and his glasses, which always rested on his nightstand within arm's reach, had been perched lopsidedly on his face. "But how?" he was saying now. "I don't understand how. I mean, *how?*"

Mom was holding a throw pillow and was either knead-
ing or throttling it in her hands. "It's not, it's not, it's not,"
she kept saying. When I was younger, I used to thank God
for the food I was about to eat and say *Now I lay me down to
sleep* at night, but this might have been the closest thing to a
prayer I'd ever heard from my mom. She just wasn't the sort of
person who prayed, at least not on a regular or official basis. I
figured she didn't want to bother God with it unless the situation was really hopeless.

"Curtis," Mom pleaded, and he swallowed hard, trying to
say something. But he didn't seem to be able to get the words
out, so instead he nodded. Just once.

Mom moaned. I slipped onto the bed next to her and buried my face in her hair. She smelled of wood shavings and
varnish, a smell that was as reassuring to me as the smell of
flour and sugar probably was to other kids.

Then Dad asked, his voice thin and drifting, like a helium
balloon that had slipped away, "What do we do now? I mean,
what do people do?" He was speaking just as much to the person on the other end of the receiver as to us, or, it seemed, to
the universe as a whole.

Mom was squeezing me as though she was holding on to
me for dear life. Mine or hers, I couldn't have said.

Then Dad said, "Okay, I will," and hung up the phone.

The three of us sat very still for a long moment. Whatever
was said next, I knew, would change everything. It was the
last semi-normal moment of my life, and then we would all
live miserably ever after.

Mom asked, "What happened to Daniel?" Her eyes gleamed
wetly in the glow of Dad's bedside lamp.

I wished she hadn't asked that, because once my brother's
name was out there, it was no longer possible that it could be
someone else. If she had mentioned another name, I was sure,

then maybe this late-night call could be about some other person, someone else's brother.

But of all the people in the world—billions of them, more people than any one single person could ever meet even if that was a person's life goal; of all the people in big cities and small towns, in countries where it was too hot or too cold year-round; of all the men, women and children, even those who were so old that the *Guinness Book of World Records* had them on some kind of short-list, and even the tiniest of infants in neonatal units, hooked up to tubes and complicated computer systems—out of all these people, it was my brother, Daniel, who was dead.

curtis

After the phone call, Kathleen stayed in bed with Olivia. I could hear them there, crying, comforting each other. I should have been there with them—I know that now, I knew that then. But I couldn't. I needed, in the fiercest way, to be alone. Not just in our house, but in the world. I needed the whole world to just stop—moving, thinking, talking.

I paced between the living room and the kitchen, picking things up and putting them down, staring at them stupidly as though they were foreign objects, things that didn't belong in my home. A picture of our family—from a time that already seemed distant, back when there had been four of us, all alive and healthy—in a silver frame that said *Family Forever* in a fancy script. A booklet of fabric swatches from one of Kathleen's projects. The swatches were in shades of blue, and each was labeled with a different name: Ocean, Marina, Infinity, Reflection, Tidal Pool. I thumbed through them, thinking how pointless and trivial it was that someone had given names to these different shades of blue, that something so irrelevant could possibly matter in a world where my son was dead. Everything was pointless, I thought. Everything was nonsensical and ludicrous.

Suddenly my legs felt insubstantial, not quite up to the task of supporting my body. I reached for the door frame for balance, nearly tripping over Heidi, our two-ton basset. She looked up at me, confused, expectant.

"Not yet," I told her. "It's not time." The sky beyond our front porch light was a deep, middle-of-the-night black.

She thumped her thick tail and cocked her head, as if she were trying to understand.

"Go back to sleep," I ordered, nudging her with my shoe.

When she didn't budge, I snapped, "Fine, then," and opened the front door, ushering Heidi into the night. She stepped onto the porch and turned, watching me. "This is what you wanted," I told her, and closed the door too hard.

Kathleen came in a moment later, red-eyed, hair sleep-tousled. Her face was shiny from tears and snot that had been wiped haphazardly from her nose. "Was that the door? Did you go outside?"

I didn't answer.

She stepped past me and opened the door. Heidi was waiting on the porch, her jowls hanging. Kathleen turned to me, her face crumpled with grief and something else—doubt. In me.

"What's going on, Curtis? Do you want her to wander off or something?"

"I wasn't thinking," I said—a lie. I was thinking that Daniel was dead, and nothing in the world mattered. Let the dog go. Forget the color swatches. Get rid of the smiling family portrait that sat on the edge of a painted side table, mocking me. And the piano. Jesus, the piano. It had taken a Herculean effort to get the piano up our porch steps, only to learn that our front doorway wasn't wide enough to accommodate it. It had gone back down the steps, around the side of the house, up another set of stairs and through the French doors. So much careful effort. Now I thought: *Burn it. Get it out of my sight.*

Safely inside now, Heidi butted her head against Kathleen's legs affectionately. Kathleen reached out a hand to me and said, "We have to keep our heads, Curtis. We have to be strong."

I stared at her, feeling dizzy and unbalanced. It was puzzling that she was here, like seeing a familiar face in the middle of a nightmare. It wouldn't have been hard to take her hand, to fall into her embrace, to wrap my arms around her waist while she wrapped hers around my neck. But I couldn't do it. I couldn't move forward, couldn't take the one step and then another that it would require of me.

Behind us I heard sniffling and turned around. Olivia stood in the doorway to the living room, impossibly tiny, hugging a blanket around her body.

"I'm supposed to call him back," I said. "The sergeant. After I talked to you, he said I should...." And I stepped past them, leaving them there in the living room like two lost little planets, out of orbit, out of sync.

My fingers, thick and unfamiliar, fumbled with the phone. In those awful moments while I waited for the call to be answered, the dial tone buzzing in my ears, I allowed myself to hope that maybe, somehow, it was all a mistake.

But the voice on the other end was the same I'd heard not fifteen minutes earlier. "Sergeant Springer," he said.

I cleared my throat. "Curtis Kaufman."

He laid bare the facts, based on an investigation that was several hours old at this point—hours during which I'd watched David Letterman with Kathleen, and then we'd made love with the particular quiet that comes from having a twelve-year-old asleep down the hall. *Impossible.* Meanwhile Daniel had been motionless on the pavement. Someone from the pizza parlor had come outside, hearing the crash, and glimpsed the truck as it drove away. It hadn't been hard to identify—a commercial truck, a small town. The suspect had been asleep already by the time he was apprehended.

"Asleep?" I demanded. "Was he drunk?"

He'd passed a breathalyzer; a blood draw had been taken later at the station. There were no other details at this time, Sergeant Springer said, but he would be in touch. He gave me his direct line, his personal assurance that—

"Wait." I couldn't let him hang up. I reached for a yellow legal pad, turned to a fresh page. There was something I needed to know. "Tell me his name. I want to know his name."

The sergeant hesitated. "At this stage in the investigation…"

"His name," I repeated. The voice that came out of me was surprisingly low, almost a growl. It didn't sound anything like me. I was the soft-spoken voice in the back of the room at faculty meetings; I wasn't a teacher who yelled or threatened. I was the calmer parent on the rare occasions when Daniel or Olivia needed discipline. But this new voice had authority; it was intimidating. It reminded me, in an alarming way, of my father.

The sergeant gave a small sigh, a gesture of hopelessness or maybe regret. "Robert Saenz. That's his name."

"Spell that for me," I ordered. In the middle of a clean page I wrote ROBERT SAENZ, and then I drew a box around it, digging the pen deeper and deeper, a trench of dark lines and grooves, until the ink bled through the page.

olivia

I wanted to know everything.

Dad had spent most of the night in his office making phone calls. When he finally joined Mom and me in the living room, he was carrying a yellow legal pad full of notes that he refused to show me. Dad had a scientific mind-set, and I wondered if he had been trying to add things up, to find the flaw in the logic, so that somehow Daniel wouldn't be dead.

"I'm practically a teenager," I told him from the window where I had been looking out at our street. The neighbors were still sleeping; none of them knew yet. It was almost morning by then, although not according to my standards. Our cuckoo clock had clucked four-thirty, and the sky outside was beginning a slow shift from black to purple. I'd been twelve for less than a month, but that was too old to be shooed away from adult conversations. "Dad," I said, so sharply that he looked directly at me, then down again at his legal pad. "I'm not a child."

He slumped onto the couch like a deadweight, hair still flattened on one side from his pillow. Mom, perched on a chair across from him, was out of tears for the moment. She asked, "What did you find out?"

Dad looked at me for a long beat, and I stared him down.

"All right," he said softly. While he talked, he kept his gaze on the carpet, as if it were suddenly the most interesting carpet he'd ever seen. And even though I'd wanted to hear it all, I found that the only way I could handle the details was to leave the window and sit on Mom's lap with her arms wrapped around my waist—exactly like a child.

As Dad spoke, I re-created the scene in my own mind. I was good at that—visualizing scenarios. Daniel had met friends for pizza after a late-night practice session. It was after one when he left the restaurant, with snow starting to fall. He would have been bundled up in the coat Mom bought him online after a fruitless search of California stores for appropriate Ohio winter wear. He would have been wearing a knitted hat, pulled low over his ears. Maybe with his ears covered and his head down, he didn't hear the truck behind him, barreling down a side street and swerving, taking the corner too fast. Maybe he was replaying music in his head—an aria, a sonata. The truck hit a metal speed limit sign, uprooting it from its concrete base and sending it through the air, as unexpected and deadly as a meteor dropping from the sky. The sign came crashing down on an oblivious Daniel, and just like that, my brother had died. Dad enunciated carefully: a blunt force injury to the head.

"An accident," Mom insisted, rubbing her knuckles back and forth, a little roughly, over the ridge of my vertebrae. "Just a freak thing."

Dad looked at her for a long moment but said nothing.

A freak thing. I turned the phrase over in my mind, but couldn't find comfort there. Was it any better that a random, horrible thing had killed my brother, rather than something orderly and prearranged?

"What about the driver?" I asked, my mind reeling, imagining that panic behind the wheel, the out-of-control moment that couldn't be taken back.

Dad swallowed, loosening the words caught in his throat. "He left the scene, but he's in police custody."

"You mean…what? Like a hit-and-run?"

"Someone from the restaurant heard the crash and saw him driving off. It's a small town, you know. Not that difficult to track him down."

"He just left Daniel there?" I shuddered, closing my eyes as though that would block out the image that was forming in my mind: my brother, my only brother, my sweet and funny and talented brother, lying bloody and alone in the street, and the man who was responsible for it driving off as if nothing had happened. A thought occurred to me. "Was he drunk? The driver, I mean."

Dad said, "I don't know." I thought his voice sounded strange, but I couldn't have said how. Everything was strange right then. We were sitting in the living room, where we only sat when we had company, in the middle of the night, talking about how Daniel had died. There was no normal anymore.

"It was an accident," Mom repeated, her voice dissolving into tears.

Dad flipped a page on his legal pad and then looked at his hand distractedly, as if he didn't know where it had come from, or how it connected to the rest of his body. Then he stood and left the room. A moment later we heard his office door close.

Mom was sobbing now, her head pressed against my back. She tightened her arms around my waist and held on. I closed my eyes. *An accident. A freak thing. A blunt force injury to the head.* This time it had been Daniel in that wrong place at that wrong time, but it could have been anyone: my father, my mother, any one of the seven billion people in the world or even me.

curtis

The only way I could handle Daniel's death was to work my way through the facts, to build a massive to-do list and check off the items one by one. And so, I became the detail man.

By the time it was five o'clock in Sacramento and eight o'clock in Ohio, I was on the phone to the Oberlin switchboard, then passed upward in the chain until I was talking to a director of housing, a dean of student enrollment. I talked to a funeral home in Ohio, a funeral home in Sacramento. I called my school secretary at home, before she'd left for work. I called Olivia's school, reporting her absence. I looked online for flights from Sacramento to Cleveland. I filled pages on the yellow legal pad with my notes. Money—there was an astounding amount involved—dates, times, names, phone numbers, confirmation numbers.

I was vaguely aware of Kathleen on her cell phone making the personal calls—to her brother and sister-in-law in Omaha, to our mutual friends, to the parents of Daniel's friends and bandmates from one group or another. I was glad to have the impersonal tasks; I couldn't bear to be the one to give this news.

At one point, I heard Kathleen running a bath. Beneath

the sound of the water rushing in the old claw-foot tub, there was another sound—low, keening—that I realized was Olivia, crying.

I paced back and forth, four steps each way, the length of my office, a glorified closet beneath the stairs that I'd claimed as my own when we bought the house. I wished I could pace right out of my body, leaving it behind. Was this what madness felt like? I wanted to be there, right at that moment, with Daniel's body. I wanted it to be last week, or last summer when we were all together, or two years from now when this hurt wasn't new. I wanted it to be the moment before the truck took the corner too fast, hitting the speed limit sign. I wanted to grab Daniel's arm and yank him back to safety.

Kathleen knocked once and opened the door, and we stared at each other.

"We have to figure out what to do…" I began, but she stopped me by stepping forward, falling into my arms before I was aware that I had reached out to hold her. I tried again. "About the arrangements…"

"Shh, shh. Just hold me. We can talk about that in a moment."

I kissed the top of her head, my lips cool and dry, as if they'd been sculpted out of marble. From nowhere came the line from a poem in a humanities class I'd taken with Kathleen, so many years ago. *Lips that would kiss form prayers to broken stone.* Why had it stayed with me, dormant all these years, only to come back now?

After a few minutes, I let my arms go slack, slithered out of her embrace. "When you're ready to think about it, I've got some information about plane tickets."

She stared at me. "Plane tickets?"

"It makes more sense to take a mid-morning flight, since

we'll have to connect somewhere along the way, probably in Chicago."

"Tickets?" she repeated.

"To get Daniel," I said. "To bring home his…" I hated Kathleen for a sharp moment, for not filling in the blank, for making me say it. "His remains."

"You were thinking we would all go?"

"Of course."

Kathleen shook her head. "I don't think… I mean, Olivia can't possibly go." She said this with such certainty, as if it were the sort of common sense thing every parent should know.

"I suppose she could stay with one of her friends. With Kendra, maybe," I suggested.

Kathleen's stare had turned incredulous. "Leave her alone, you mean? When her brother has just died?"

I rubbed my face, letting this sink in. Maybe because of grief and general sleeplessness, my skin had started to feel like a rubber mask, stiff hairs sprouting haphazardly in anticipation of a morning shave. Someone had to go to Oberlin, to attend to the dozens of things that seemed impossible, at that moment, to attend to. It was the worst possible trip in the world, and one I couldn't imagine taking alone. But that, I realized, was exactly what was going to happen. "You won't come with me, then?"

"Curtis, I can't."

It was just a small conversation, just a few words, but a fault line had opened up between us. I was on the side with Daniel, charged with protecting him, with bringing him home. I went back to my laptop to book a single flight, and Kathleen left the room, shutting the door behind her.

olivia

By noon, it seemed that everyone knew—our friends, our neighbors, even a reporter from *The Sacramento Bee* who wanted a "human element" to accompany her article. Daniel had been no stranger to the local news outlets, which had all printed pictures or run footage of him from one concert or another, receiving one award or another. *Local hero...musical prodigy...*

When I stepped onto the front porch that afternoon to get the mail, I found half a dozen cards tucked up underneath our doormat. Mom and I opened them together, read them silently and started a stack on the sofa table. Later that evening, she went outside and returned with a basket of corn bread and honey butter. Our house was under the surveillance of a small army of sympathizers and well-wishers, people who loved us but couldn't bear to actually encounter us. And I didn't blame them one bit.

That night Kendra, my best friend since fourth grade, called. I took the cordless extension into my bedroom and closed the door and sat cross-legged on the floor, feeling small and strange.

"I heard about your brother," she said. "I'm sorry."

"Thanks," I said. We let the quiet between us stretch for minutes, and then I said, "I think I have to go."

"I'm sorry," she blurted again.

"I know."

"Are you still going to go to the dance?"

It took me a long moment to figure out what she was talking about. And then I remembered: the Halloween dance, our matching costumes. Mom had made us our dresses, and Kendra's mom had bought our matching wigs. We were going as the dead twins from *The Shining*.

"Um, no," I said.

"Do you think that maybe I could borrow your costume for someone else? I was thinking maybe Jenna, from our homeroom? I mean if you're sure you're not going...."

"Whatever," I said, my throat tight, and hung up.

It was the loneliest I'd ever felt in my life.

In the hallway, I paused outside my parents' bedroom, listening to their voices. They weren't arguing, exactly. Dad was packing—he'd be in Oberlin for two nights and back again on Sunday. Meanwhile, Mom was in charge of the arrangements for Daniel's memorial service, which would be on Monday.

"I just can't imagine that we won't have a headstone for Daniel," Mom was saying.

"We can have a headstone. Of course we can. We can have whatever you want."

"But his body won't be there!"

"No, it won't."

I braced myself with an arm against the door frame.

"I just never pictured..." Mom said, her voice trailing off.

"It's the right thing to do, Kath. There's an incredible expense associated with shipping a body—and besides, it's not Daniel anymore. He's gone."

"It just doesn't feel right. And how will we know? How will we absolutely know?"

"How will we know what?"

"When we get the—Daniel's—remains, how will we know those are *his* remains? I mean, you read those things about funeral homes...."

"Kath," Dad was trying to calm her.

"I mean it!" Mom's voice had risen to a hysterical pitch, which I probably would have heard without eavesdropping. "I've been thinking all day, maybe they mixed something up. Maybe it wasn't Daniel who died, after all. Do you know, I kept calling his phone and leaving messages? I was thinking maybe he would pick up and say it was some kind of stupid mistake—"

I remembered the times I'd seen Mom on the phone, dialing, listening and hanging up. I began to feel sick.

"They found his wallet in his pocket," Dad pointed out.

"Right! And I could just imagine Daniel saying, 'Oh, yeah, I lent my wallet to this guy from my dorm....'"

"Kathleen," Dad said, "you're being—"

"What? What am I being?"

They were quiet for a long moment, and then Mom said, "I know. I know exactly what I'm being. I don't think I know how else to be right now." She flung open their door and stepped into the hallway.

Startled, I stepped back, whispering, "I'm sorry."

What else was there to be but sorry?

curtis

The trip to Oberlin was endless—the drive to the airport, the hassles of TSA screening, the agony of being wedged into a middle seat with nothing to do but think. Even when I closed my eyes, I saw Daniel—at six, at ten, at sixteen, at nineteen…at twenty-five, an age he would never be.

When I'd successfully forced Daniel from my thoughts for a few moments, I remembered again the name I'd written on my notepad: Robert Saenz. It was like swallowing a mouthful of dirt; thinking of him brought a lingering grit, a foul taste. He'd driven home while Daniel lay dying. "Careless, so careless," Kathleen had bawled into my shoulder. But it seemed now that *careless* was the absolute wrong word. Careless was forgetting to throw the sheets in the dryer, or not picking up the promised gallon of milk on the way home from work. It wasn't driving away with my son dying on the side of the road. I must have fallen asleep grinding my teeth, because I woke in Chicago with a sore jaw. My first thought was: *Robert Saenz, you bastard.*

The scheduled two-hour layover in Chicago grew to four hours, thanks to a weather delay. I watched as a cargo train wobbled by in the gray slanting rain, and uniformed personnel hoisted luggage indiscriminately into the hold. I strained, trying to spot my bag, which was black and therefore indistinguishable from dozens of other black bags. I hadn't been to Chicago in close to thirty years, but the airport version of the city wasn't one I would have recognized, anyway— steel-beamed ceilings, black-and-white checked floor tiles, deep-dish pizza, a preponderance of Cubs and Bears paraphernalia. The Chicago of my childhood had been my father, the cramped house with the nicotine-stained walls, the accordion closet door that had been thin protection against his rages.

Daniel's death had brought my father back to me as a real person, rather than an abstract part of my past, buried alive in a time I rarely revisited. I hadn't called him twenty years ago, when Kathleen was pregnant, and I hadn't called nineteen years ago when Daniel was born, or seven years later when Olivia came along. Why ruin our happiness with his condescension? Later, when Daniel performed at Carnegie Hall, when Oberlin called with a full-ride scholarship offer, I'd wanted to rub his face in it: Look what my son has done. Look how well I've done, away from you all these years. But there had been the promise to Kathleen, and I'd never picked up the phone.

I was tempted to call him now, to hurt him with Daniel's loss. Impossible idea—my father couldn't begin to feel the loss of the grandson he'd never known. It was yet another defeat for me—even my effort to deprive him of his grandchildren would spare my father pain, in the end. Escaping to the bathroom, I drove my fist once, hard, into the metal door.

It was dark by the time I checked into the Oberlin Inn, the only hotel in town. It might have been late in Ohio, but it was only seven o'clock Sacramento time, too early for sleep. I flicked idly through the channels, then grabbed my coat.

On the sidewalk in front of the hotel, students passed in hurried clusters, their heads covered. I crossed North Main Street and circled Tappan Square, ending up before Oberlin's monument to the Underground Railroad, a set of railroad tracks rising to the sky.

Daniel had first mentioned Oberlin at the beginning of his junior year, when college seemed impossibly distant. "It's famous for its music conservatory," he had gushed, producing one glossy brochure after another. That fall it had been Oberlin this, Oberlin that. In the spring he'd flown out for a college visit, and then there was the admissions process, the gathering of transcripts and letters of recommendation, the seventeen drafts of Daniel's personal statement. I'd driven him to his audition in San Francisco and paced anxiously outside the conservatory. During the hour-and-a-half drive to his audition he'd been quietly nervous; on the return drive, he was exuberant. "I nailed it," he'd said over and over, reliving every second for me. Finally, there was the acceptance letter, a scholarship offer and dozens of phone calls about housing. Oberlin had seemed to me to be larger than life—it was all of life, as far as Daniel was concerned.

It had been somewhat surprising to discover that the town of Oberlin was *tiny*. Kathleen and I, on our one visit, had rented a car and marked out the parameters of the town in just a few circles. The main streets bisected at the college, which loomed large and official—museum, concert halls, the conservatory with *more than two hundred grand pianos,* Daniel had informed us—next to the rest of the town, which had relatively few amenities. We had taken Daniel out for Chinese at a restaurant a block from campus. In our spin around town, he pointed out the bowling alley, an archaic-looking video rental store, the self-serve Laundromat and a used book store.

Now, my hat pulled low over my ears, I headed in th[e] [di]rection of the gas station and pizza parlor on the outskirts of town. It was here that Daniel Kaufman was walking down the sidewalk, hunched against the cold for the hike back to campus. It was here that Robert Saenz had taken a corner too quickly, clipping the 35 mph sign.

It wasn't hard for me to find the exact spot. Less than two days after Daniel's death, the area was still roped off with yellow police tape. I circled the perimeter, hands balled into fists in the pockets of my jeans. Two students walked past me, darting into the street to avoid the police tape, then stepping back onto the sidewalk. I waited for them to say something, to acknowledge that a person had died right here, a person they had possibly even taken a class or shared a pitcher with, but the only scrap of conversation I caught had to do with a party that weekend. I crossed over the police tape, half expecting someone from the pizza parlor to stop me. Snow had covered the sidewalk, but still I could see where the concrete had been disturbed, where a speed limit sign had been uprooted. I stood there until I had no feeling in my ears or cheeks, watching cars slip by on their way in and out of town. I wanted to yell at each driver to slow down, to acknowledge what they were passing: *This is where my son died! Daniel Owen Kaufman died right here! He was my son, and he deserves your respect, you dirty sons of bitches*. I was furious with them and disappointed in myself. This patch of cement didn't feel like hallowed ground. Instead of a connection with Daniel, I felt only anger, slow and determined.

The next morning at the Oberlin P.D., I was shown into a room with green walls and a concrete floor, a table flanked by two chairs. An interrogation room? Had Robert Saenz sat in this very chair, still groggy from sleep? Sergeant Springer had a face to match his gravelly voice—deeply lined, ruddy in a way that suggested permanent sunburn—and a no-nonsense handshake. "I've done some digging," he said, passing me a manila folder.

Inside was Robert Saenz—face-forward first, then in profile. In the way that a hard life can pack on years, he looked much older than forty-one, older even than me. I was reminded of my father, prematurely aged with the help of Jim Beam and Johnnie Walker, with Wild Turkey and bottles of blue wine that looked like antifreeze. Robert Saenz had dark curly hair that hit his collar, and bloodshot, slightly bulging eyes that looked out with a vacant stare. In profile he had a double chin, a layer of stubble. His eyes held nothing—not regret or anger or surprise. Nothing.

"Keep reading," the sergeant said.

I set the picture aside and continued slowly, fanning out the pages as I went. In 2003, Robert Saenz had caused a fatal accident in North Carolina, when his truck had jackknifed on a freeway, and an oncoming car, unable to avoid him in time, had crashed. The driver—a thirty-two-year-old Mary Kay saleswoman—had been killed instantly. Her infant son, in the backseat, had both legs crushed on impact. Robert Saenz had been above the legal limit. I was gripping the edges of the folder so hard, my hands were beginning to cramp.

"Pled down to a misdemeanor," Sergeant Springer said. "Did a couple of years, paid a fine, had his license revoked. But that was five years ago, you understand. In North Carolina. Looks like he's been in Oberlin for a year or so, driving for a company owned by his brother."

"He did a couple of years," I echoed numbly. He'd killed a woman, and he'd been set free to kill Daniel. I sat very still, thoughts swimming. Sergeant Springer continued, but I only half heard him: *waiting on the results of the blood draw…charges will be brought…a bail hearing…*

This was probably meant to be reassuring—there was a legal process, and it was in capable hands. But I heard something else: Robert Saenz, that low-life piece of shit, could go free again.

Sergeant Springer led me to the pathology lab, where Daniel's body was waiting to be identified. Kathleen had been insistent on this point. *We have to know for sure. How can we not know?* The deputy coroner, Dr. Kline, showed me to a sterile room where a body lay on a gurney, covered by a heavy piece of plastic. The scene was sickly surreal, like walking into a script of one of the thousands of crime dramas I'd watched over the years.

Dr. Kline looked at me, asking a wordless question. There was no way to be ready, not now or in a hundred years, but I nodded. He pulled back the tarp.

It wasn't Daniel—it was an awful, horror movie caricature of who Daniel had been. It was a face I wouldn't have known in a million years, his skull a concave thing, a grotesque mask. If it hadn't been suggested to me that this was Daniel, I might not have come to the conclusion on my own. This was no more my son than it was a bad prop in a haunted house.

Kathleen should be here, I thought. She would have known Daniel's shoulders and chest, despite the gaping Y of the autopsy incision, the thick stitches of the sort that had made Frankenstein's monster so grotesque. Kathleen had marveled over our children's bodies as they grew, thrilling that Olivia had *the cutest buns in that bathing suit,* that the moles on Daniel's shoulder resembled a specific constellation, where I saw only a scattershot of stars.

It wasn't until I saw the scar on the abdomen that I truly recognized Daniel's body—a small sickle, pale pink beneath his navel. Daniel's appendix had burst when he was nine years old, late on a Saturday night after a recital. He must have been in pain the entire day, the E.R. doctor told us, but it wasn't until we were in the car afterward that he mentioned it, cautiously, as if testing the waters. *I think something is wrong with my stomach.* He'd gone into surgery just in time, ending up with an overnight stay in the hospital and a week's worth of antibiotics rather than anything more serious.

"It's him," I choked, biting back the memory.

When I turned away, Dr. Kline replaced the plastic tarp and peeled off a pair of gloves, dropping them into a wastebasket. He disappeared for a moment and returned with a transparent garbage bag, the red handles tied together at the top. The bag was labeled with a simple tag: PERSONAL PROPERTY— DANIEL KAUFFMAN. I homed in on that extra F in our last name, feeling it like a slap in the face. *Get the spelling right!* I screamed inside my head. *It matters.*

As we walked to the door, the plastic bag knocking between us, Dr. Kline laid a hand on my shoulder. It was hard to pull away from this offer of human comfort.

I went to a café for lunch but left without ordering. Food had lost its appeal.

That afternoon I met the dean of students at Daniel's dorm. Daniel's roommate had separated the belongings for me, folding everything on top of the bare mattress—clothes, sheets, the tartan plaid comforter Kathleen had picked out for him. I held a flannel shirt to my nose, inhaled the faintest whiff of pot. It was surprising to see how meager the pile was— textbooks, coffee mugs, his laptop, toiletries, the black bow tie he'd worn for performances. Kathleen would have had a plan for everything. She would have talked about packing and shipping and receipts and reimbursements, so that somehow everything that had been Daniel's could live forever. I didn't have the stomach for it. In the end, I took what I could carry, and the dean promised to donate the rest to Goodwill.

On the way back to the hotel, a boy ran past me in a red cape, his underwear outside his jeans, and a girl followed in a pointy witch hat and thigh-high boots. Little orange buckets dangled from their wrists. Of course: Halloween. I looked around, noticing the small clusters of ghosts and goblins and cartoon characters on the sidewalks, the fake cobwebs spanning bushes, the jack-o-lanterns on front porches. This was what normal life was like, but there was no more normal life for the Kaufmans.

Back at the Oberlin Inn, I sat on the closed toilet seat and opened the bag from the coroner gingerly, setting its contents one by one on the tiled bathroom floor. Daniel's black Converse—the exact style he'd worn and replaced and worn and replaced since junior high. I had a pair, too. Somewhere there was photographic evidence of Daniel and me in black T-shirts, blue jeans and matching shoes. I fished Daniel's key ring out of the bag. Four keys—one to our house, marked by a drop of red nail polish, Kathleen's doing. The other keys must have been to his dorm, his practice rooms, the places where he had lived his life without me.

I opened his wallet to the photo on his California driver's license, taken when Daniel was sixteen. He looked so young, his shoulders impossibly narrow, hair closely cropped on the sides and spiky in the front. Then, Daniel's Oberlin ID: a goofy half smile, hair grown almost to his shoulders. He hardly looked like the same kid, but I knew both versions of him, and many more. I pulled out the other cards, then returned each carefully to its spot. An electronic passkey. His Sacramento Public Library card, well worn. A punch card to a local sandwich shop with three holes.

In the pocket, I counted four wrinkled one-dollar bills and peeled apart a few stuck-together pictures. Daniel's senior prom photo, his arm around a girl whose name was lost to me now. A years-old family snapshot we'd taken in Yosemite when Daniel was in junior high and Olivia was in elementary school, in her braided ponytail years. Kathleen was in the middle, an arm around each of them, her normally pale legs and shoulders pink from the sun. I had taken the picture—we were on the trail to Vernal Falls, far from another human who could have snapped the photo for us. Kathleen had sent out copies with our Christmas cards that year, along with a joke about me being camera-shy. I turned the photo over, suddenly aching to see Kathleen's writing on the back, but it was Daniel's scrawl I found: *The Fam, 2004.*

The Fam. Minus one.

Carefully, I slid that picture into my own wallet.

In the morning, I picked up the cardboard box with Daniel's remains from the funeral home, thanking the manager for her rush. "Please sign for the cremains," she said, prompting me to address a stack of forms. I blinked at her stupidly. *This is my son we're talking about. Don't give me some made-up word I don't even want to know.*

During my return flights—Cleveland to Chicago, Chicago to Sacramento—I clutched the box to me as if I had been charged with the safekeeping of a carton of eggs. This was *Daniel,* I reminded myself, over and over, feeling the weight of his ashes, insubstantial, lighter than he'd been that first night in the hospital, wrapped in a receiving blanket. I wished the box could be a hundred pounds, a thousand. I wanted to feel the physical burden of his weight, as I had when I'd hoisted his two-year-old self onto my shoulders for an evening walk around the block.

The box accompanied me through security gates, where the funeral home paperwork was scrutinized by a half-dozen harried TSA personnel. It came with me into the restroom stall at O'Hare, into a newsstand where I purchased a box of

Milk Duds and a *Scientific American*. Even when I was seated on the plane, I found I couldn't release my grip. This was the last thing I could do for Daniel. I could make sure he made it home.

olivia

We made it through the memorial service—the tributes, the crying, the video slide show Mom had compiled to show the highlights of Daniel's life. The whole time, I felt anxious and edgy, panic rising in me like puke at the back of my throat. Mom gave me the keys, and I escaped the weepy reception line to spend a half hour in the backseat of her Volvo, sick and warm in the afternoon sun. Daniel's friends exited the funeral home in sad little clumps, and I couldn't stop myself from thinking: *Be careful. Watch where you walk. Drive safely.*

Then Dad and Mom were there, discussing plans to drive Uncle Jeff and Aunt Judy to the airport in the morning. Mom turned her key in the ignition, the engine caught and the radio programming sprang to life in the middle of an announcer's sentence.

And then it happened.

All of a sudden the world blurred in front of me, everything going too fast, all the colors running together—*blueskygreengrassgraycement.*

Dad adjusted the passenger-side visor, and Mom began to back out of the parking lot. Without even knowing what I was doing, much less why I was doing it, I reached over the seat and grabbed her arm as she maneuvered the gear shift.

"Holy—Liv! What?" she demanded, slamming on her brakes, the car jolting forward at the sudden stop.

"What is it?" Dad asked, half turning.

I opened my mouth to say something, but I couldn't. Everything inside me felt liquid all of a sudden, as if my organs and bones had disappeared and I had become a child's squishy toy. I wanted to unlock the door and bolt from the car, but I couldn't move.

Dad was staring at me curiously.

Mom put a hand on my forehead. "Are you sick?"

"I—don't know," I stammered, sinking back into my seat.

Mom slid the gearshift to Drive and maneuvered us into the parking space we had just vacated. "Do you need a bag or something?"

I took a deep breath, trying for calm. My body was turning solid again, but slowly. I didn't trust it. I reached out a hand, surprised I could still move. My leg bone was connected to my thigh bone and so on—which meant my parts were still in working order.

"You okay now?" Dad asked, and I nodded numbly.

You're not dying. You're okay, I reassured myself. But it felt as if something were gripping me around my insides and squeezing.

"Better use a plastic bag in case," Mom said, and Dad began digging around under his seat. He came up empty-handed.

"No, I'm okay," I mumbled, although it must have been obvious that I wasn't.

"Look, I'm just going to get us home." Mom backed up again, slower this time.

"Talk to me, Olivia," Dad said, unbuckling his seat belt to reach around. With one hand, he dug into the backseat pocket and came up, victorious, with a crumpled paper bag from Starbucks.

Mom exited the parking lot, took one turn and then another, merged onto a busy street. All the other cars seemed far too close to ours, mere feet away, hurtling along at unsafe speeds. What was keeping them in their own lanes, exactly? What was a lane except a painted line, a mere suggestion for social order?

I gripped the door handle more tightly, leaning into the turns. I was braced for it; I was ready. If Mom's Volvo slid off the road, I was going to see it coming. And if Dad and Mom and I all died in a sudden, fiery crash, I was going to see that coming, too.

My breathing sounded funny, like the time I fell in soccer practice and had the wind knocked out of me. I picked up the Starbucks bag Dad had given me and blew into it weakly. It smelled like a pumpkin scone.

"What's going on, Liv? Talk to me," Mom demanded, looking at me again in the rearview mirror.

"Watch the road," I croaked weakly, but my words were trapped in the paper bag.

Dad, who still hadn't refastened his seat belt, turned again, examining me like a specimen pinned to the wall. Hadn't he seen a gazillion public service announcements about buckling up? Didn't he know that buckling up saved lives?

"You're okay, Liv. We're almost home," Mom called.

"She's not okay," Dad said sharply. "She's a mess back here." He gripped my knee with his hand. "Just take it slowly, Olivia. Concentrate on taking a deep breath, holding it for a few seconds and then exhaling."

I glanced out the window and saw the row of utility poles lining the street. My vision blurred, and my thoughts began racing again. How long had those poles been there? What was the average life expectancy of a city utility pole before, one day, it just crashed to the ground?

Breathe, I ordered myself. The bag inflated and deflated, fast at first and then more slowly. It helped if I closed my eyes, imagined myself safe in my room. By the time we arrived home, I was exhausted. It was hard work trying not to be terrified.

We sat in the driveway for a long moment. Dad and Mom exchanged a glance, and then I felt Mom's eyes on me in the rearview mirror. Her irises were bright blue from crying, the whites of her eyes streaked a veiny red.

"I'm sorry," I croaked, balling up the paper bag in my hand. I didn't want to be a problem, especially since we were in the midst of other, bigger problems. As we walked into the house, my fears began to dissolve like magic, like a bit of dandelion fluff in a breeze. But somehow I knew they'd be waiting for me the moment I was expected to step outside again.

How stupid I'd been before, how naive I'd been to walk through my life unaware of the dangers that were everywhere, around every single corner. I would notice them now, I promised myself. For Daniel's sake, I would always be on the alert.

curtis

Time passed, more slowly than I could have imagined, faster than I would have dreamed. Every time I walked through the living room I saw the little box on top of our fireplace mantel. Kathleen had mentioned buying an urn, and we'd each promised to look online, but hadn't. Add Daniel's *cremains* to the list of things we didn't discuss.

It was a relief to go back to work, to slide back into my regular school schedule—the bells ringing, students shuffling in and hurrying out, meetings before and after school, the emails and paperwork, the endless, reassuring cycle of lessons to be planned and papers to be graded.

I began leaving for school earlier and earlier, while Kathleen and Olivia were still asleep. I was the second car in the lot, behind the janitor. Somehow it was easier to think there, when my classroom was quiet and there was work to be done. At home, I couldn't escape the way things had changed. Olivia had panic attacks that could be brought on, seemingly, by nothing—the paperboy passing on his bike, the coffee grinder running in the kitchen. Kathleen, determined not to mope at home, was attempting to fill our lives with fun things. She actually used this word, as if Olivia and I were two-year-olds who had to be coaxed into a trip to the grocery store. "Come on, it will be *fun!*" She made big, elaborate meals, found movies for us to watch together, proposed a family night that fell flat when Olivia realized all of our board games required four players.

At night when we lay in bed, staring at opposite sides of the room, she would dive into the pep talks that I'd begun to dread.

"Please, try, Curtis."

And: "You need to do this for me. You need to make an effort."

Her concern soon changed to disappointment, and eventually, to disgust.

"I can't believe you won't do this for me."

"I'm not there yet," I admitted.

We slept in the same bed, but it might as well have been split in two—her side, mine, like Lucy and Ricky Ricardo in their twin beds, a nightstand between them. The truth was that I wanted to reach for her, that night and the next and the next, but I couldn't make myself cross the invisible barrier between us. The days and nights became a meaningless blur, as if some anesthesiologist had forgotten to let up on the ether, and, beneath its fog, we lay deadened and numb. We slept less than three feet apart, curled on our separate sides. I could hear her quiet breaths, the occasional sniffle, a stifled sob held back even in sleep. In my mind, I reached out a hand, touching her shoulder, her waist, the ridge of spine, the skin I knew better than my own. But in actuality, I couldn't do it. I couldn't bridge the gulf. I didn't want to open up to her, or have her open up to me. Wouldn't the doubling of misery have been more than we could bear, collectively?

In my saner moments I realized we were running some kind of course, and Kathleen was way ahead, flying through those stages of grief. I heard her on the phone with her friends, referring to what had happened to Daniel as "the accident," as if it were a completely random thing, a hard fact of life that she had accepted.

But I couldn't accept it. A lightning strike on a clear day—that was a random thing. In my mind there was a deliberateness to Daniel's death, a reckless calculation in the act of getting behind the wheel, in taking a corner too fast, clipping a sign, driving away and crawling into bed as if nothing had happened. It didn't feel random. It felt purposeful. It felt premeditated.

Still, I couldn't tell her: You're wrong. I couldn't say: This was no accident. I just couldn't bring her down there with me, to the place where I nurtured a long-buried, simmering anger. If Kathleen could find comfort in randomness, in silly clichés offered by shallow people and greeting cards, then so be it. I would take comfort in what was real. I would take comfort in my anger.

Eventually, the tox screen for Robert Saenz came back positive for amphetamines—an upper, speed. I'd learned this from the Oberlin P.D., after daily phone calls made from my classroom before school. He'd been denied bail; charges were being amended. *What does this mean?* I persisted. What kind of punishment would he get? Jail time? Prison? Could I do anything—write letters, testify?

Eventually, Sergeant Springer passed me off to the D.A.'s office, to an A.D.A. named Derick Jones, who gave me information so sparingly, it might have been drops from a leaky faucet. He had probably been schooled—*don't make any promises.* He talked about "precedent" and the possibility of a plea bargain, a reduced sentence. Robert Saenz might get anywhere from ten to fifteen years; it might be reduced to seven if he pled down.

Seven years? Seven fucking years? It was a joke. It was a nightmare.

And then that February, as I was leaving Arden Fair Mall where I'd been picking out a new pair of work shoes, I saw him. I recognized him immediately as he cut in front of me, hands shoved into his pockets. I noted the same curly hair, the flabby jowls, and walked faster, looking for the dead, blank expression in his eyes. I was just going to see. I was just going to get a closer look. With each step, I felt a pressure building up in my ears, my head like the volcano Olivia and I had worked on for her sixth-grade science project.

I was even with him when he turned his head, startled at my proximity—and up close, he looked nothing at all like Robert Saenz, who was, of course, locked up awaiting trial. "Sorry," I mumbled, head down, hurrying past the man.

I sat for a while in the Explorer, my hands shaking on the steering wheel. What was I thinking? Of course it wasn't him. And what would I have done if it was? I was armed only with my key ring and my rage. Would I have gone after him with my fists, throwing the not insignificant weight of my body on him, kicking him, getting my hands around his neck? I felt sick with the possibilities.

I'd promised to be home by eight, but I was too worked up to face Kathleen and Olivia. Instead, I found a restaurant near the mall, and I made my way straight for the bar. After the first few overpriced drinks, I didn't even think about them. The display on my cell phone lit up with Kathleen's number four times, but I didn't pick up. I rolled the highball glass between my hands, wondering how far I would have gone and how much I would have to drink to forget what I might have done. Was that why my father drank, to forget his daily faults? To dull the pain from the things he had done?

At ten-thirty, the bartender cut me off. I wasn't used to the hard stuff. Kathleen and I never had more than a bottle of wine in the cabinet above our refrigerator; a single glass at dinner had always been my limit. Now I staggered coming off the bar stool. "Want me to call you a cab?" the bartender asked, not meeting my eye. He was just a kid—or not a kid, but not all that much older than Daniel would have been.

Kathleen picked me up. She was tight-lipped on the way home, her body tense with anger. When she did speak, it was in fuming bursts. "This is what you do? This is your answer to our problems? Do you think drinking worked out well for your father?"

I couldn't answer; it was taking all my concentration not to vomit. A light rain was falling, and I focused on the slight swishing of the tires on the damp streets.

"Just tell me," Kathleen said when she pulled into our driveway. "Is this the way it's going to be?"

"I don't know how it's going to be," I said, not looking at her. It was the most honest I'd been with her in a long time.

I spent most of that night in the bathroom, sleeping on the bath mat, a towel under my head so I could be close to the toilet. In the morning I called for a substitute. Kathleen moved around the house, ignoring me, making coffee, talking cheerfully to Olivia, hurrying her out to the car without saying goodbye.

I stayed in bed for most of the day, long after the effects of the alcohol had worn off. I wouldn't tell Kathleen what I'd really been thinking, I *couldn't*. I'd gone too far on my own. I didn't want to scare her with the vision of the monster I'd become for those few minutes. Worse, if it had been Saenz in that parking lot, I knew that I would have killed him, one way or another—and I couldn't find a way to feel bad about that.

olivia

At the beginning of spring, when Daniel had been dead for six months, Mom announced that we were going to see a family therapist. She looked desperately tired, as if she hadn't slept in weeks—which maybe she hadn't. It must have been exhausting, doing nice things for Dad and me and then having to point out that she'd done them, since we never noticed on our own. *I made that Alfredo sauce you love....* *I replaced the button on that shirt cuff.* We thanked her, and five minutes later we had forgotten all about it and were back to our ungrateful selves.

We let her drag us into the meeting with the family therapist, Dr. Fisher, although we attended only once as an actual *family*—what was left of it, anyway, now that we were down to only three. Dr. Fisher had a sunny office that overlooked a small courtyard, and although the furniture was basically industrial gray, there were little pops of color everywhere— yellow throw pillows, a vase practically choked with pink and purple hydrangeas, an orange sunset on one wall.

It went just about how I figured it would go: Dr. Fisher asked some questions, and Mom answered them. Dad looked at his hands, and I looked out the window at the courtyard, trying to assess the level of danger present in two gingko trees and a shallow fountain. Dr. Fisher could have been anyone's grandma; she was pleasantly white-haired, wore a floaty skirt and long cardigan, and had the patience of the world's best kindergarten teacher.

Mom had commandeered the session, rambling on and on about communication and how she feared we would turn out if we simply couldn't start talking again.

"And, Curtis? What would you like to say?" Dr. Fisher asked when Mom paused for a breath.

"Well, I—I would have to say that I agree," Dad blurted, caught off guard. I noticed that his shirttail had come untucked, that there was a small streak of mustard on his pants.

I glanced at Mom and caught her at the end of an eye roll. She gave a forced laugh. "You see, this is what I'm—"

"Yes, but why do you feel there's a lack of communication, Curtis?" Dr. Fisher probed, and Mom sat back.

It took Dad a very long time to respond. "I couldn't say, exactly."

"Olivia," Dr. Fisher said, turning to me after a beat. "Let's hear from you."

I know what I should have said—about my panic attacks, and how much I missed Daniel every time I passed the closed door to his bedroom. I should have said that I was miserable and I was afraid of making my parents miserable—but these were very real things, and too awful to say with my parents staring at me. Mom kept nodding her encouragement, looking so hopeful that I knew whatever I said would absolutely crush her. Dad seemed surprised to realize that I was in the room, too.

"I don't know," I whispered.

Mom's laugh this time was painful and sharp, like glass breaking into jagged pieces. "I mean, you read stories about families that break up when a single bad thing happens to them, and you think, that will never be my family. But it's getting to the point.... Oh, I don't know. I don't know." She leaned forward, head in her hands.

Dad and I looked at Dr. Fisher, waiting.

"Well," she said, smiling at us kindly. I wondered if she ever came right out and said to someone, *There's really no helping you.* "This is a very normal reaction for families who have experienced a sudden loss. It can be terribly difficult to express feelings openly. What I'm going to suggest are some one-on-one appointments for the time being, so that I can help each of you articulate your feelings. And then we'll meet again as a group. In the meantime, I'd like to suggest a few activities that you can do together."

Mom looked up, brightening. This was just her thing— a to-do list. Give her a thousand tasks, and she would tackle them all.

For the rest of the summer, I visited Dr. Fisher every week, not having any other choice. Mom went to her sessions and reported on them over dinner, determined to model "good communication" for us. As far as I could tell, Dad went only twice on his own; whatever was said in his sessions stayed there. Or maybe he said nothing at all and only stared alternately at his shoes or his car in the parking lot. Mom worked her way through a family togetherness checklist, insisting that we plan meals, visit the Youth Symphony Orchestra to make a donation in Daniel's memory and spend at least one weekend night together doing something new—even if it was just wandering through a Pier 1, where we immediately branched off on our own and gathered again at the cash register. The week before school began, we took a vacation to Coronado, which involved a long drive from Sacramento to San Diego, nights in hotels with dubious cleanliness, a tour of the island on rented bikes and a long drive home. Somehow when Mom coaxed me into the trip, she'd neglected to mention the word "island," and I had a full-on panic attack on the bridge, with Mom holding on to my head while I breathed into a Subway bag that had contained, ten minutes earlier, Dad's pastrami sandwich.

The morning we left the island, Mom crushed a pill and slipped it into my yogurt, so Dad basically had to carry me to the car, wedge me into my seat and wrangle with my seat belt. I hardly remembered anything about the trip, but the photographic evidence was stored on Mom's camera—a dozen or so pictures where none of us was exactly smiling, even though Coronado was beautiful. Despite my worrying—or maybe because of it?—nothing horrible had happened, after all. The bridge didn't collapse, the island didn't suddenly sink into the Pacific and, although I'd seen a shocking special news report about how rarely hotel bedding was washed, we didn't take home a single bedbug.

When we finally arrived home, Mom dumped the contents of our suitcases into the washing machine and announced that she was going to bed for the night and didn't want to be disturbed. It was four-thirty in the afternoon.

After that, she stopped seeing Dr. Fisher herself, but kept dropping me off for my appointments. And Dr. Fisher *was* helping me—it was her idea for me to find a new "coping mechanism" since I'd been more or less refusing to take my anxiety pills since the Coronado debacle. "Why don't we do this?" she suggested, although I was pretty sure there would be no *we* involved. "Why don't we keep a record of these things you're afraid of? If you write them down during the week, we can discuss each fear at our next session."

This turned out to be a fabulous suggestion. In a week, I filled ten pages, single-spaced. Dr. Fisher's eyes widened in surprise at first, but as she kept reading, I had the distinct feeling that she was trying very hard not to laugh.

"Hair dryers?" she asked, looking up.

"Because hair could get caught in the little vents," I explained.

"Right. That *could* happen. Has it happened to you, with a hair dryer in your home?"

"Not yet."

"Okay. What about this one—open-toed shoes?"

"Because toes can get caught in escalators." Anticipating her next question, I added, "It didn't happen to me, but I heard about it happening to someone else, a cousin of a girl who was in my homeroom last year."

"Fairly rare, though, I would think," Dr. Fisher said, closing my notebook. "And I notice you have escalators on the list, as well."

I nodded.

"It would seem to me that the escalator is relatively benign, though—provided one is wearing close-toed shoes, of course," Dr. Fisher qualified quickly. "But I would think, compared to elevators—"

I shuddered. "Elevators are in a class unto themselves. The sudden plummeting, the claustrophobia…"

"Whereas with an escalator, if it stops working, you simply walk the rest of the way."

"In that case, you might as well just take the stairs," I pointed out. "Or, better yet, just stay on the ground floor."

Dr. Fisher smiled, the skin around her eyes crinkling. "Well! Okay. That's definitely a good start, then, Olivia. I think the next step might be for us to begin sorting through these fears, putting them into categories." I must have looked puzzled, because she explained, "You know—like things that have happened to you before, or are likely to happen, versus things that are not at all likely to happen—that kind of thing."

I agreed to think about it, although I didn't see the value in this. It didn't particularly matter what category things were in—I was equally scared of everything. But I kept writing fears down, filling one notebook and starting another. During the day I carried it in my backpack, sealed in a jumbo-sized Ziploc bag so it wouldn't fall victim to a leaking pen or a spilled water bottle. At night, I kept the notebook on the floor next to my bed, in case something new came to me while I should have been sleeping.

Dad began referring to the notebook as my Fear Journal.

Mom called it my security blanket.

And it did give me security—enough, at least, that I had stopped taking medication completely by the time I entered eighth grade. I kept a single pill with me, wrapped in a ball of cellophane at the bottom of my backpack for an emergency situation, like a shooter on campus or an unannounced field trip. The busier I was with my classes and the more obsessed I grew with writing things down, the less I saw Dr. Fisher, until one day it occurred to me that I hadn't seen her in months.

It had been a good idea—family therapy. But my family had approached it like a ride on a merry-go-round in the world's saddest theme park, until one by one, we'd all simply flung ourselves off.

curtis

I can't say I didn't see it coming. The trouble was that it had been coming for so long, it never seemed real—like a tsunami, where the waters recede and you watch them go, go, go, but remain unprepared for the reversal, for the sudden, gushing onslaught.

Kathleen had been talking to her brother in Omaha, making arrangements about the house where she'd grown up, which had been sitting vacant. She had reconnected with one of her best friends from high school, Stella something-or-other, who was divorced, living again in Omaha and hoping to open an upscale boutique furniture store. Kathleen had researched the local high schools for Olivia; she had found a family physician, a veterinarian.

I know this because she told me. I'd been coming to bed later and later at night, but still Kathleen was awake, stubbornly waiting for me, propped up by pillows, scribbling items on a to-do list. There was something triumphant about this, something smug: *See—I'm doing the work. I'm putting in the effort.*

I laughed at first. Back to Omaha?

"It makes sense," she had insisted. "It's exactly what we need."

"It's exactly what *you* need," I countered, but there wasn't much heat behind my words. I couldn't summon the energy to be bitter. I'd been building up a wall between us, one giant rock upon another. Dr. Fisher had told me as much. "If you keep this up, you'll get what you seem to want—to be alone," she told me on our second counseling session, and I had agreed, thanked her and never returned.

"You're right," Kathleen admitted. "It is exactly what I need."

"That's it, then?" I asked, gesturing to her list, noticing that just about everything had been checked off.

"Curtis, listen to me. You can be part of this change. It's not too late."

Wasn't it? I turned away, loosening the belt on my khakis. Everything felt too late. We'd heard the news, finally, more than a year after Daniel died. There would be no trial; Robert Saenz had agreed to seven years in exchange for his plea to involuntary manslaughter. I'd imagined myself addressing a judge, a jury, showing the world how wonderful Daniel had been, but I'd never had the chance. That too was gone.

"I can't keep having this conversation with you," Kathleen hissed. "Daniel is dead! Nothing you do is going to make him not be dead!"

I stared at her, remembering how the Lorain County A.D.A. had said the same thing to me, essentially. "I hope you can put this behind you, Mr. Kaufman, and begin to move forward." In other words: *We're done. It's over.* It was done and over for Kathleen, but it wasn't over for me.

Kathleen lowered her voice, softening with a visible effort. "This is it, Curtis. This is the moment where you have to make a decision. This is where you say 'Yes, we're going to stay together as a family,' or 'No, I'm going to go my own way.'"

The words were there, hanging in front of me like lines on

a cue card: *We're married. We're a family. We need to stay together.*
But I couldn't say them. Whatever fight was in me had shrunk
like a helium balloon three days after a party. If the roles had
been reversed, how long would I have stuck it out? She was
right; it would be better for Kathleen and Olivia in Omaha.
It probably would have been better for them in Timbuktu.

Kathleen was done waiting for a response. She pulled her
knees to her chest, looking small and far away. "I don't know
you anymore, Curtis. I don't know who you are. You're not
the same person...."

"No," I agreed. "I don't think I am."

Kathleen snapped off the light. In the dark she whispered,
"I would give you all the time in the world if I believed it
would change something."

"I don't blame you for leaving," I told her. "I don't blame
you at all."

That night I slept with my arm over her body, breathing in
the woodsy scent of sawdust and a pungent, chemical smell I
couldn't place. Paint thinner? Varnish? She'd been on an almost manic streak, finishing projects for clients. Touching her
was the closest I could come to saying I was sorry, and the
best way I could manage to say goodbye.

We sat down with Olivia on the last Saturday of July, with
the start of school looming only weeks away. Olivia must have
known something was up; she sat in the turquoise armchair
across from the gold patterned couch—when had we acquired
these things?—and stared first at Kathleen, then at me.

"What is it?" Olivia demanded, her voice flat. We were
coming off an eight-day heat wave, and it was already warm
at ten o'clock. The windows were open, but one of us, Kathleen or me, would soon get up to close them when the air
conditioner kicked on. It would be me, I realized. Kathleen
had one foot out the door; she had all but packed her bags.

"Olivia," Kathleen began, twisting the wedding ring on her finger, the tiny, paltry stone I'd been able to afford all those years ago. How much longer until she stopped wearing it? Would she slide off her ring the minute she pulled away from the curb? Would I slide off mine?

"Just say it," Olivia hissed. Her hair was fastened around her head in a random arrangement of bobby pins, so that she looked like some long-necked, exotic bird. Her forehead was shiny with sweat.

Kathleen looked at me, and I nodded back to her. *Go ahead.* I knew I was being an asshole; I knew that if this were taped and later played back, I would not see myself as the sympathetic character. But I figured that the person who was leaving should be the person to explain, and the person who was being left could sit righteously silent—even if it were his fault.

Kathleen swallowed hard and began, "Your father and I have been talking, and we think that it would be best for now if we took a little break."

"A little break," Olivia echoed.

"You know that we've talked about making some changes, and some really great opportunities have opened up in Omaha. You know that friend I've been talking to, the one who is planning to open a store in the spring?" When no one said anything, she plunged bravely on. "It's really sort of a dream situation for me, and I figure that once we're settled in—"

"Wait. Who are you talking about? Who's *we*?"

Kathleen bit her lip and said, "You and me, Liv. The two of us would go out there to begin with, and then your father, if he decides to, would join us."

Olivia's eyes shot to me. "Dad's staying here?"

"I'm under contract to start the school year in a few weeks," I explained, although of course this was no explanation at all, and Olivia was no dummy. There were teaching jobs in

Omaha, and the school district wouldn't have held my feet to
the fire over my contract.

Olivia asked, "Is this really happening?"

"Honey." Kathleen leaned forward, a curly lock of hair
tumbling over her forehead. "I didn't think this would be
that big of a shock to you. We've talked about starting over."

"*You've* talked. You said *you* wanted to start over."

"We talked about us starting over," Kathleen insisted,
wounded. "And that includes your father. He just can't come
with us now."

Olivia shook her head. "Mom, seriously. I'm not moving
to Omaha. I'm starting high school in a few weeks. I can't go
somewhere where I don't know anyone."

Kathleen put a hand on Olivia's arm, and Olivia pulled
back, out of her reach.

"Sweetie," Kathleen tried again. "I know this isn't exactly
what you hoped for, but I know you're going to love it in
Omaha. It really is the best thing for us right now."

"No, Mom. I'm not going to Omaha."

"Honey. Everything's arranged."

"And I'm not going to leave Dad behind, either. I'm not
going to do it."

I flinched. It was striking how adult Olivia sounded, un-
afraid and unwavering. And then it hit me—she sounded just
like Daniel.

"Olivia, your father is choosing—"

"I don't care, Mom. You're choosing, too. And now I'm
choosing. I'm staying here." Her body was tense, trembling.

"Oh, Liv, come here," Kathleen said, but Olivia took one
step out of the turquoise armchair and tumbled right into
my lap.

I felt this strange, triumphant rush go through me, like a
powerful jolt of déjà vu—picking Daniel up in the hospital,

freshly swaddled; lifting a crying Olivia out of her crib, watching in awe as her sobs settled, her breathing slowed, became even. I hadn't wanted it to be this way, but Olivia was almost fourteen now, and maybe that was old enough to make a decision for herself.

Over Olivia's shoulder, Kathleen glared at me. *Say something.*

That was all I had to do—say the words. *Olivia, you can't stay here with me. You need to go with your mother.*

"Dad?" Olivia asked into my shoulder. "I can stay here with you, right? You want me to stay here, don't you?"

Olivia would keep me sane, I thought. And I would keep her sane, get rid of her endless fears once and for all.

"Of course, honey," I said, and next to me, Kathleen dropped her head into her hands.

I promised myself right then that I would try to put it behind me—if not for my sake, then for Olivia's. I would let Daniel go. I would accept the fact that Robert Saenz was in prison, locked away, one orange jumpsuit among thousands of other orange jumpsuits. I could do this for Olivia. I had to.

A week later, Kathleen backed out of our driveway, her Volvo packed to the gills. I wasn't absolutely sure until that very moment, watching the brake lights as she slowed for the yield sign at the end of our street, that she was serious.

From that moment on, it was just Olivia and me.

olivia

April 26, 2013

It was a fairly normal day at Rio Americano—at least, what had become normal for me. I'd gone through the motions of note-taking in my American History class, worked the problems in precalculus, and then ditched P.E. for the fourteenth time this semester to sit in the last stall of the D wing girls' restroom and do absolutely nothing. The bathroom was public-industrial gross, with huge wheels of single-ply toilet paper bolted to the wall and graffiti etched into the stall doors—swearwords and gang signs and the names of girls who were sluts, courtesy of the girls whose boyfriends had been stolen. Every now and then someone would enter, and I heard a series of electronic beeps; public school bathrooms in this century seemed to be used solely as a quiet place for sending uninterrupted text messages. For the fourteenth time that semester, I was sitting cross-legged on top of my backpack, which sat on top of a floor that, even when freshly mopped, was as sanitary as a petri dish.

Still, it was a million times better than being in P.E., which had become my nemesis and the focal point of my fears: the rushed, awkward changing of clothes in the locker room, shivering in short sleeves while I did the world's slowest jog around the turf, being picked last for a team and then ignored by my teammates, ducking when one sort of ball or other zoomed toward my head, trying to avoid Ms. Ryan, the whistle-tooting P.E. teacher who was determined to make an athlete out of me. *"Kaufman!"* She would boom in that teacher-projection voice from across the length of a football field, and I'd wish I could melt into a little puddle and evaporate, like the Wicked Witch of the West.

It was infinitely better to sit on a bacteria-laden public restroom floor.

I shifted so I could dig into my backpack for my Fear Journal, the twentieth or so version of the book I'd used since Daniel died. The others, dense with my hasty scribbles, were stacked on a shelf in my bedroom. It was comforting to know that they were there, that my fears had been recorded and catalogued and preserved for posterity. I opened my latest notebook and wrote in black ink the new fear that had occurred to me that morning during American History: *Getting hit in the head by a falling 80s-era ceiling tile.* Underneath it I had scrawled this explanation: *If I got hit in the head with a ceiling tile and passed out, someone would call my dad in his classroom, and he wouldn't be able to take it, so he would probably have a heart attack. And then when I came to, I would be an orphan. (Or as good as.)*

I put a little asterisk by this fear, because it was way more terrifying to me than some of my other fears, such as *bugs that look like sticks,* and also way more likely to actually affect me, since there was a full month left of school, and I sat underneath those industrial ceiling tile rectangles for approximately six hours a day, and it only made sense that at some point, one of them would fall. This was the sort of fact I should bring up in my statistics class—which was both the most fascinating and

horrifying class I had ever taken. But that would mean raising my hand and contributing, and this was something Olivia
Kaufman simply did *not* do. The bug that looked like a stick
was something I'd seen in a natural history museum during a
forced field trip to the Bay Area, so it might not even live in
Sacramento. But the ceiling tile…this was a very real worry.
Maybe it could be mentioned in an anonymous note addressed
to the school board?

I was considering this—a private, philanthropic act that
would be far more beneficial to my fellow students than, say,
a new vending machine outside the cafeteria—when I heard
my name over the intercom and froze, pen in hand.

"Olivia Kaufman, please report to the office. Olivia
Kaufman, to the office, please."

Shit. I looked around reflexively, as if I'd been spotted in
a crowd. Had Ms. Ryan reported me? This was possible, but
not part of what seemed to be the unwritten agreement that
governed my life at Rio. Basically, the other teachers and staff
members seemed to treat my dad and me with equal parts pity
and protection—they pitied us because Daniel was dead; they
became protective when my mother left almost three years
ago. And recently, our dog had died—our beloved Heidi—
and I'd written a poem about her for my English class, forever securing the sympathy of my teacher and her lunchroom
buddies. Ms. Ryan had agreed not to talk to my dad about my
failing grade in P.E. as long as I talked to my guidance counselor about my "options" for next year. And my dad, caught
up in his own turmoil, seemed a much happier person for not
being bothered with the truth of it all.

I'd agreed to see the guidance counselor, but I'd never made
the appointment. I knew exactly what Mr. Merrill would say
when I took a seat in his office that was more or less the size
of the bathroom stall I was currently wedged into. He would

tap a few keys, pull up a file, frown at me and say "Are you really failing P.E. for the second time? You know that's going to put you twenty credits behind, don't you? You do realize that you'll be spending your senior year in not one, but two P.E. classes, and that it's going to be nearly impossible for you to fill out any college applications?"

I knew what he would say, because I'd already had the conversation with myself a few hundred times. No—I wasn't going to visit Mr. Merrill and talk about my "options" when there really weren't any. And although I'd survived almost three years of scrutiny from teachers who had known and loved Daniel, I wasn't in any hurry to have our differences made any more obvious. Daniel had applied for universities across the country, been accepted everywhere, had received a full-ride offer from Oberlin and a $1,000 scholarship from the teachers' union. It was becoming glaringly obvious that I'd be lucky to graduate high school, much less go on to any kind of college. But, really—I was okay with that, too.

How could I possibly move away from home and into some kind of dorm situation? College represented a host of new fears. I would have been scared to live on anything other than the first floor, since I was scared of both heights—specifically, falling from them—and depths—specifically, falling into them. Hundreds of reckless students holding knives in the cafeteria meant that violence was possible at every meal, and fires could be started by lit candles in dorm rooms. Besides, I would be absolutely alone without my dad—a very legitimate fear for someone who lost her brother and then, sort of, her mother, and then, finally, her dog.

Even the thought of attending community college freaked me out. I'd have to drive myself there or depend on public transportation, either of which could go wrong in dozens of ways. I had accepted the necessity of riding shotgun in Dad's

Explorer to and from school, to and from the grocery store or Target or the pizza place on J Street, but I refused under any circumstances to ride in a bus. How in the world could a bus, with no seat belts and a rather loosely formed seating structure, be any kind of safe? And forget about driving myself anywhere. Dad had cajoled and tried to bribe me into a driver's training course, but I professed profound disinterest in this particular rite of passage. "I'm not always going to drive you everywhere you want to go," he'd said, which was kind of funny, because I didn't particularly want to go anywhere. In response, I'd said, "I'll walk. It's healthier, anyway." But no safer, I reminded myself bitterly. Daniel had been walking, after all.

Dad had said that he might as well put me into a padded room, and I know he said this out of frustration, to show me how ridiculous I was being, but I pounced on the idea.

"You could get me padded walls for my next birthday," I'd suggested. "But soft padding, like a couch cushion. Nothing hard like a gymnastics mat."

The memory of this conversation brought a smile to my lips, and I was just about to relax because clearly I'd imagined the page from the office, when the voice came over the intercom again, more insistent this time: "Olivia Kaufman, to the office, *please.*"

I tucked my notebook into my backpack and slowly did the zipper. The jig was up. Ms. Ryan had reported me, and the entire office staff—and maybe even my father—was likely waiting to ambush me in some kind of intervention. My repeated P.E. failures were probably being discussed right now. I took a deep breath and hoisted myself from the floor to a standing position.

The last thing I wanted was to face a hallway crowded with students. If there had been a tunnel from the D-wing girls' bathroom to the outside world, I would have taken it—even if that would be the sum of all my fears: a dark, tight-fitting, possibly rat-infested and ultimately unknown place. But there was no tunnel, no secret hatch.

Right then the exterior bathroom door swung open and big, clumping footsteps approached. I instinctively shrunk back, closer to the toilet seat than I preferred to stand. Underneath the stall door, I caught a glimpse of a pair of black Doc Martens with pink skull-and-crossbones laces. They belonged to a senior named Kara, one of the Visigoths, the group I loosely associated with when I associated at all. Despite what the name implied, the Visigoths weren't a nomadic tribe of warriors, but more of a group that wore all black and scorned our Abercrombie & Fitch-clad classmates. I wouldn't have called Kara a friend—after Daniel died and Mom left, I'd basically stopped being friends with everyone, especially people who had two-parent homes and happy, well-adjusted siblings. But Kara was decent.

"Olivia?" she whispered. "Are you in there?"

"Yeah," I admitted, coming out of the corner. I slid the lock on the stall door and opened it about an inch, as if to peer at a stranger standing on my doorstep. "What's going on?"

Kara bit her lip and brushed a spiky black piece of hair out of her eyes. "Umm, Olivia...it's your dad."

curtis

The letter had come three days before. It was just by chance that I'd grabbed the mail that day instead of Olivia. I had spotted the return address—Elyria, Ohio—and immediately tucked the letter into my back pocket, letting my shirttail hang loose over it. I read it in the bathroom, and again in the bedroom, door locked; later I shredded the envelope. When Olivia went to bed, I taped the letter to the back of a framed art print in the living room, a place she would never look. I wanted to keep the letter in case I needed to remind myself of the details—but already I'd memorized every single word, beginning with *It is my duty to inform you that...*

I didn't tell Olivia about the letter, like I hadn't told her about the parole hearing and the letter I'd written myself, on Daniel's behalf.

In the years since Kathleen left, I'd prided myself on my business-as-usual approach to our lives. The size of our family had been reduced by half, but Olivia and I hadn't fallen apart. We had more or less maintained a normal life. We folded our laundry, although somewhat haphazardly; we did the dishes vigorously each Saturday, and let them pile up in the sink on the days between; we made a weekly trip to Target for toilet paper and Q-tips and the half-dozen other things we always, suddenly needed. If Kathleen had popped in unannounced, she might have been alarmed by the stack of unsorted mail by the front door, but she wouldn't have found a complete disaster. Not that Kathleen would have popped in unannounced; she had scheduled visits for two weeks during each of the past two summers, and she'd begged Olivia to fly out for every holiday in between. "As *if,*" Olivia had said on each occasion, unmoved by statistics about air travel being safer than car travel and by my patient lessons on lift, weight, thrust and drag.

Olivia and I had kept on going simply because that was what we had to do—but we'd had a sort of strange fun doing it. I'd thrown myself into the part wholeheartedly; I'd been proud that none of it, not even for a second, had felt like a chore.

And then, on Tuesday, I'd received the letter. *Pursuant to criminal law… regulations regarding prison overcrowding and mandates for prisoner behavior…* Robert Saenz had somehow managed to behave himself in prison, completing a sobriety program and an anger-management course, and the state of Ohio was willing to take a chance on him.

Since learning this, every movement I made required a conscious effort. I taught my classes, attended a science department meeting, made a not-bad ziti with Olivia and fell asleep each night with the television on, waking at random hours to the enthusiastic sales pitches of infomercials. I was now fully informed about revolutionary skin care products, microwave egg poachers and a new food chopper that promised to chop food faster than any other food chopper in the history of food choppers.

You have to keep going, I ordered myself. Just put one foot in front of the other. Just keep moving.

Since Kathleen left, I hadn't allowed myself to wallow.

There simply wasn't time. Maybe if I'd been alone, eating TV dinners and repeating yesterday's clothes. But Olivia and I had a life to navigate together. If she had a cold, I was the one who bought cough syrup and gathered her used Kleenex. If she had a quiz, I peppered her with review questions. If she had a panic attack—more and more rare, but still possible—I tried to talk her through it. If she wanted to watch long stretches of Hitchcock-fest on AMC, then that's what we did, with Olivia writing things down in her Fear Journal as she went: *birds, heights, dizziness, strangers on trains, trains....*

Days had passed without me thinking about Robert Saenz at all. When he was locked up, living in the hell of his own making, Saenz hadn't deserved another minute of my time.

But I woke up on Friday morning with a tight feeling in my chest. Not "call the ambulance" tight, but uncomfortable enough that I had to steady myself against the bathroom counter for a long moment, until I could pull it together. Robert Saenz's face swam in front of me, all fleshy chin and dead eyes. Dr. Fisher would have called what happened next a "break—" comfortable, padded-chair speak for going bat-shit crazy.

"You all right?" Olivia had asked me on the way to school, gripping on to the door handle the way she always did, like our route was one of hairpin curves, rather than a fairly straight shot.

"Of course."

"You don't look all right."

I glanced at myself in the rearview mirror. "What do I look like?"

"I don't know. You look sort of gray."

I gave what I hoped was a convincing smile. "Like the Tin Man?"

Olivia frowned. "Not exactly. More like you've got a case of rickets or something."

"I think you mean scurvy. That's the Vitamin C deficiency. But I don't know if it actually turns you gray."

"Great. Then you have some kind of undiagnosed illness that no one has been able to name yet. Thanks, Dad. Major consolation." She dug in her backpack and came up with her journal.

Ordinarily, I would have had another joke at the ready. Olivia and I had developed, in these past, lonely years, a sort of Abbott and Costello routine with each other, as if everything were a joke, as if our problems were basically just ways of trying out new material on each other. Some days I suggested we take our show on the road. But now I turned on the radio, raising the volume a few notches to drown out the words in my head: *After serving sixty-three percent of his court-ordered sentence...*

First period physical science was a blur: take roll, collect papers, write key terms on board. Then my second period physics students arrived with noisy enthusiasm: it was Egg Drop Day, our annual competition to drop raw eggs in carefully constructed cages from the cafeteria roof to the ground fifteen feet below. Ordinarily, it was one of my favorite teaching days of the year. I had been known to greet my students in a white T-shirt with a smear of fresh yolk across the front. It was a new shirt every year, and I'd embellished it with a Sharpie: "Oops" one year, "Your Egg is My Breakfast" another. This year I'd forgotten.

I pretended to marvel at my students' creations: eggs in toothpick cages, eggs riding in Styrofoam canoes, eggs dressed as babies in cotton diapers. We walked en masse to the cafeteria and the class split into teams. I monitored the dropping of eggs from the roof while Alex, my Berkeley-bound T.A., judged their landing from the ground.

The competition moved along on schedule: the preliminary rounds with the heartbreak of early elimination, the tense drops during the semifinals and at last, a face-off between my two best students that ended with a dramatic finish as one egg came free of its wrapping during descent and hit the ground with a sudden stain of yolk. With all the screaming and cheering and congratulatory crowd-surfing, it might have been the pep rally before the first football game.

"All right—we clean up, and everyone heads back inside. Bell's about to ring," I called down, shielding my eyes from the bright, piercing blue of the sky. The few students who remained on the roof were vowing revenge, if life should ever allow them another Egg Drop Day. One by one they went down the staircase to the lower level of the cafeteria, past the hair-netted ladies wielding massive stainless steel serving spoons, and wandered in the general direction of my classroom. I should have been right behind them, picking up the last scraps of their trash, giving the losing team a gentle goading. That's what I'd done every other time in the history of Egg Drop Day, but today I lingered on the roof, watching my students descend the staircase and emerge from the cafeteria into the asphalt parking lot below.

There was no reason in the world for me to stay on that roof one more minute, but I couldn't make myself go. I tracked my students as they crossed the lot and rounded the administration building. My room was at the northern corner of the science wing. There, I imagined, they would wait, still joking around at first and then growing antsy as they waited for me to appear.

After a few minutes, Alex came around the corner of the administration building and started toward the cafeteria. Halfway there, he spotted me on the roof. Shielding his eyes with the flat of his hand, he called up to me, "You all right up there, Mr. K?"

"I'm fine, Alex," I called down.

He came closer, considering this. "You need help with anything?"

"Not at all," I said. I dug in my pocket and pulled out the massive wad of keys I'd been carrying around for my entire teaching career. "Hey. You want to let them into my room?"

"What? Really?"

I dangled the keys before me and then flung them over the side. They fell much less elegantly than my students' eggs had fallen, just a straight shot down. Alex made a quick dive and retrieved them. He grinned, pleased with his catch, and stared up at me again, puzzled.

"Go on." I waved him away. He smiled uncertainly but complied, stopping once to look back at me before disappearing out of sight.

I stayed at the edge of the roof, which was basically flat, with only the slightest peak in the center. In all my years of Egg Drop Day, I had never noticed how I could see the entire campus from this vantage. I'd spent most of my life—twenty-eight years now—teaching here. The campus had changed in that time, of course—a new gym had been constructed, and the football field had been upgraded with million-dollar artificial turf. Portable classroom buildings stretched into the horizon. The school had computer labs now, whiteboards and ceiling-mounted projectors, security cameras and automatic-flush toilets. The kids dressed differently, sure, but they were still kids—still teenagers with the same sorts of problems: love and dating and friendship and grades and finding themselves and hating their parents and figuring out their futures. Only now they all had cell phones, omnipresent as an extra limb. If I squinted my eyes and strained into the distance, I could see students on the soccer field. Olivia had P.E. this year, although I couldn't remember her schedule. Was she the girl chasing down the ball, her dark ponytail bobbing? No—Olivia probably wasn't the running type. But it was comforting to believe that she was out there somewhere, doing what the rest of her classmates were doing, being a normal kid.

It weighed on me that I wasn't giving Olivia the same shot at a great life that I'd given Daniel. That *we* had given Daniel— because Kathleen had been part of that pact, too. Olivia had turned into this wise-beyond-her-years kid, funny and quirky and far too well-behaved to pass as a normal high school student. Sometimes it seemed that she was tiptoeing through life in order not to disturb me, in order to make up for the fact that Daniel had died. She deserved better, and when I was honest with myself, I knew it. She would have been better off going with Kathleen to Omaha, even if it had meant going kicking and screaming, or half-drugged on medication that wouldn't have worn off until she got to the Rockies and there was no way back.

That could still happen, I realized.

Olivia could still go to Omaha. She could still get that shot at a better life.

I felt again the strange tightness in my chest and lowered myself to a sitting position, allowing my legs to hang weightlessly over the edge of the roof. It felt good to just sit down for a minute. There wasn't a huge rush. My students would have packed up their things by now, and I could still stand up, head down the stairs, out the cafeteria door, and be back to my classroom before the tardy bell rang.

And then I remembered the letter, that itch I'd had to consciously remind myself not to scratch all week. *Robert Edward Saenz has been paroled from this facility effective on this day, the 15th of April, 2013.*

Distantly, I was aware of the bell ringing and students

swarming out of classrooms. They looked not like ants, exactly, but like some type of laboratory experiment, their bodies squat and foreshortened. It was beautiful how they all blended together, this mass of color and energy. I squinted into the sunlight. Was Olivia, wearing her ubiquitous head-to-toe black, one of them?

"Hey!" someone called, pointing up to the roof of the cafeteria, at me.

A few students stopped to look.

"It's Mr. K!"

"What are you doing up there, Mr. K?"

"Is this for Egg Drop Day? Throw me an egg, Mr. K!"

I gave them a polite wave but didn't answer. Most of the students glanced at me and kept walking, but a small crowd had begun to gather below. I recognized Alex among them, my key ring in his right hand. He was such a conscientious kid; he'd probably fended off my incoming class at the door and locked up before returning to find me.

"Mr. Kaufman!" someone called, and I focused in on Candace Silva, the principal's secretary, waving her hands over her head in such an exaggerated way that she might have been signaling to an incoming aircraft. Everything about Candace Silva was exaggerated, from her very pink cardigans to her candy-themed office cubicle, which had always made me slightly dizzy, in an overindulged way.

"You have class!" she called to me now. "Mr. Kaufman! Curtis! You need to come down now!"

I will, I thought. *I'll come down in a minute.*

"Are you sick? Do you need me to call you a substitute?"

"No," I whispered, which of course she couldn't hear. Everything seemed to be moving farther and farther away—the buildings on campus, the horizon, the distant hum of the freeway. On the ground below, one of the kids called my name, but all noise had dissolved into a drone. I saw Alex step forward uncertainly, handing my key ring to Candace.

"Curtis? Do you hear me? You just stay right there! You don't need to move a muscle! I'm going to take care of this!" I watched as she began walking back to the office rapidly, and then broke into a near-run after a few steps, her heels clattering. In all the years we'd known each other, I had never seen Candace Silva run.

I was dimly aware that more time had passed and that what was happening was not normal, but I didn't seem to be able to prevent it. Standing up was out of the question, an act of superhuman strength and resolve. I shielded my eyes and looked out farther, at the horizon, a distant place where sky met land. The whole world was so tiny, so fragile, just waiting to be crushed by a giant footstep.

Over the intercom I heard Olivia's name paged, and I thought distractedly, *How nice. Everyone else must love Olivia, too.*

The campus security squad—two burly guys in their twenties who intimidated even the staff members—arrived and hustled the students below back to class. The only students who remained, I realized, were *mine,* the students who should have been sitting in my third-period class. I recognized a group of boys who perennially sat in the rear of the room, and smiled to see that they were kicking a hacky-sack in a circle, and not looking up at me at all. Then Candace was back, pointing and gesturing frantically to Bill Meyers, Rio's principal for the last decade. Bill waved an arm at me, and I raised mine in a weak salute.

I heard Olivia's name being paged again, and I thought: *Liv.* I should get up now, just for Liv. I could feel the sun beating down on my head, where every day I combed fewer and fewer hairs. Olivia thought I had rickets, but maybe this was simply a case of sunstroke. Kathleen would take care of me.

She would press a cold washcloth to my face and keep refilling a glass of ice water. I would be feeling better by the time Daniel and Olivia got home from school.

"Curtis," a voice behind me said, and I turned around to see Bill Meyers, holding out a hand to help me to my feet. "Let's get out of here, okay?"

So I stood, light-headed and unsteady. Bill took firm hold of me until we were well away from the edge of the roof. Then he held out his hand in a wide, strangely formal gesture and said, "After you." I led the way across the roof, to the open door and down the stairs, past the serving ladies, the skin of their foreheads pinched tight by gray hairnets. They stared at me, bewildered.

A few of my students were still gathered on the sidewalk below, although it must have been well into third period by now. Why weren't they in class? The hacky-sack guys stopped when they saw me, the sack hitting the ground with a soft, beanbag *ploop*. Candace Silva was still there, too, chewing on a lacquered fingernail. On the outskirts of the group, which was just about where I could always find her, stood Olivia, weighted down by her massive backpack. I waved at her as Bill Meyers and I passed, his hand on my elbow.

"Everything's okay!" he boomed heartily. "Back to class now."

"Dad?" Olivia's eyes were huge, her face even paler than normal.

I took a step in her direction, but Bill clamped a hand on my shoulder. "Curtis, maybe we should have a little talk first."

"Okay," I agreed. "I'll see you in a bit, Olivia."

She nodded slowly.

I felt a sudden longing for the cot in the nurse's office, but Bill steered me out to the parking lot, straight to my dusty green Explorer. From his pocket he produced the ring of keys I'd tossed from the roof.

"Get in," he said. There had been some warmth in his voice when we were on the roof, as if we were two friends who had bumped into each other at a coffee shop. Now he was coolly efficient. "Passenger side, Curtis. I'm driving."

olivia

By fourth period, everyone knew. I took my seat in Spanish, feeling sick and anxious, and listened to the gossip of my classmates.

"Did you see Mr. K just totally lose it?"

"I was sure he was gonna jump or something."

"If he jumped, I bet we'd get a sub until the end of the year."

I gritted my teeth. They were just stupid things said by stupid kids who had never experienced a tragedy beyond what they'd seen on television. I checked my cell phone for the dozenth time since Dad had left campus with Mr. Meyers. Wasn't he going to call me? Didn't someone want to tell me what was going on?

A guy in the back of the room said, "Seriously, the guy must be a total wacko. The school cafeteria? Couldn't he find like, a bridge or something?" and I almost screamed at him. *Shut up! Don't you know that's my dad?* To be fair, maybe he didn't. It was a school of sixteen-hundred students, and I had perfected the art of being off the radar.

But I didn't have to listen to this. I shoved my Spanish notebook in my backpack and left class just as the bell was ringing, before my teacher had logged off whatever important email she was sending from her computer.

On my way to the office, I passed the science wing. A cute blonde girl who must have been just out of college was Dad's substitute. The lights had been dimmed in his room, and I recognized a *Nova* episode on the white projector screen.

Mrs. Silva didn't seem too surprised when I entered the office, although she clearly had no idea what she was supposed to do with me.

"I just want my dad," I said, fighting very hard not to cry. "He's not answering his phone."

"I'm sure he's fine, dear. Mr. Meyers is with him."

"But how am I supposed to get home?" We lived several miles away from campus—a trip I'd never made on foot.

Mrs. Silva smiled at me patiently, like I was an idiot. "You know it's still several hours before the end of the school day. Shouldn't you be in fourth period now?"

"Would you go back to class if everyone in the whole school was talking about how your father almost jumped from the roof of the cafeteria?"

We stared at each other for a long moment over a jar of hard candy on the lip of Mrs. Silva's cubicle.

"I could call your mom," she offered finally, her voice rising at the end in a subtle question mark. But of course, she knew my mom was in Omaha, and that wasn't going to solve my immediate problem.

"I would prefer to call her later," I said icily.

"Okay. Why don't you just have a seat for a minute, and I'll see what I can find out?"

I plunked myself into one of the chairs outside Mr. Meyers's empty office and listened while Mrs. Silva left several discreet voice mail messages. At one point I heard her say "I would really appreciate some guidance on what to do here once you've handled the situation." Great. Dad was *the situation*. He was probably going to lose his job, which meant that we would lose our house and have to live on the streets with our heap of multicolored furniture. Or worse—we'd have to move to Omaha.

I pulled out my journal and added this fear to today's growing list. I could feel Mrs. Silva's eyes on me and had the unnerving feeling that she could see what I was writing from ten feet away. I wrote that down, too.

Every few minutes a staff member wandered through looking for one form or another. Some shot me sympathetic glances— *Oh, you poor kid*. I tried to communicate back to them telepathically—*Help me out here. I need to find my dad*. But they retrieved whatever they were looking for and moved on quickly, not wanting to get involved.

Finally, after a hushed phone call that obviously concerned me and/or my dad, Mrs. Silva said sweetly, "Olivia, I think you can go ahead and wait in the library until the end of the day. Mr. Meyers is going to stay with your dad until then, and I'll be bringing you home. Would that be okay?"

No, it wasn't okay. I wanted to see my dad right now, right this second. It was completely horrible to have no options, to be at the mercy of the school bell and an adult who was probably only pretending to care about me. But at least some plan was forming, my dad was apparently still alive, and he hadn't completely forgotten about me. I bit back my sarcasm and whispered a grateful, "Okay."

For the rest of the day I sat in a molded plastic chair in the library, adding pages of new worries to my Fear Journal— things that had seemed highly unlikely that morning, but seemed incredibly likely now. *I'm afraid of my dad cracking up. I'm afraid of my dad doing strange things. I'm afraid my dad doesn't have enough to live for. I'm afraid I'm not enough.*

And I thought about my mom. We talked every week, sometimes several times a week, mostly about little things that meant nothing at all—how I'd done on my stats quiz, what Dad and I had eaten for dinner, which of the self-absorbed borderline mental cases had been eliminated from one reality show or another that week. It was hard for me to tell her things that really mattered. It didn't seem entirely fair that she should get an all-access pass to my life when she had made the decision to leave. Every single time we talked, she mentioned me coming to Omaha, like the constant mention would wear me down. "I'm fine here," I insisted. "Dad and I are doing fine." Then she would be quiet for a long time, and I could picture her in my grandparents' old house, which Daniel and I had visited for Christmas when we were kids. Sometimes she didn't seem to be that far away, after all. Other times, like now, Omaha might as well have been Mars.

I had my cell phone, so I could have called her right then. No matter how busy she was at the store or in her workshop, Mom would have dropped everything to be on the first flight out of Omaha. She would have been in Sacramento late tonight or early tomorrow morning, and then she could be in charge. She could ask Dad what the hell he'd been doing on that roof and why in the world he hadn't come down. She could do the adult thing—take charge—and I could go back to being a self-absorbed sixteen-year-old.

But I didn't call her. After everything Dad and I had been through, it didn't seem right to throw him under the bus. I figured I owed him that much. He'd taken care of me. Taking care of him seemed like the least I could do.

curtis

It was almost like waking out of a dream, or rising out of the haze of anesthesia. One moment I'd been on the roof of the school cafeteria, trying to gather the momentum to make my way downstairs, and the next I was a passenger in my own SUV and Bill Meyers was behind the wheel.

Bill was an old-school principal, over sixty-five but so far not even hinting at retirement. I'd been a teacher on his interview panel ten years ago; since then, he'd been my evaluator and sometimes friend. We hadn't always seen eye to eye, and more than once as the chair of the science department I'd been in his office, sitting across the heavy mahogany desk, with Bill in his fancy leather executive chair, the sort of chair that principals had and teachers didn't.

Since Daniel died, our relationship had deteriorated—my fault, of course. He'd been at Daniel's memorial service, a handshake in the long reception line afterward. Once or twice since then he'd mentioned Daniel's name to me, and I'd recoiled, stung. At most we exchanged a few minutes of chitchat in the hall between classes, cordial rather than companionable. So it was surreal to show him into my home, to take a seat on the gold couch while he putzed around in the kitchen, opening and closing cupboards in search of a box of tea that I wasn't sure existed. When he finally produced some Earl Grey, I was sure it was something Kathleen had purchased years ago and hadn't been used since. Did tea have an expiration date? I wasn't sure.

By this time I was feeling more myself, which is to say, incredibly embarrassed about the entire thing. Bill had already referred to it twice, gravely, as an "incident," and I realized that the "Mr. K on the Cafeteria Roof" episode would be the stuff of school legend, like the time Janet Young, a ninety-pound English teacher, had separated two basketball players who suddenly realized they had the same girlfriend. It would be all over the school by now. For all I knew, one of my more enterprising students had captured the entire scene—such as it was—on a video that was even now making the rounds of the internet.

For the first time, I thought about Olivia and how pale she'd looked when I'd passed her. *Oh, God. Liv.*

"I'm feeling better already," I told Bill, taking the too-warm mug of tea and shifting it awkwardly from hand to hand.

He lowered his lanky, six-three frame into a turquoise armchair, one of Kathleen's "reclamations" that had been on the side of the road one day and reupholstered, refinished and situated in our house the next. Our entire house was a riot of Kathleen's color choices that—it occurred to me only now, as Bill's eyes roved over the decor—not everyone might appreciate. The Meyers house was probably done in complete neutrals, like sand and stone and khaki and beige.

"Curtis, we've known each other a long time now, haven't we?"

It sounded like the opening line of a rehearsed speech. I nodded.

"I knew you before your son died. Before Kathleen left. Right?"

I nodded again, bristling. *Rub it in, why don't you?*

"I remember a time when you were larger than life on that campus. You were involved, you know? You were department chair. You were excited about trying new things. Kids looked up to you, right? But it's been a while since those days, hasn't it?"

These seemed like rhetorical questions, so I took a sip of tea, and remembered why the box of Earl Grey had gone untouched since Kathleen left. I hated Earl Grey. Earl Grey was Kathleen's tea, not mine.

"Now I see you walk around campus, and it's like you're not even there, except physically. Students call your name, and sometimes you don't even react. You haven't returned a single email all year, and sometimes when I pop in to see you after school, you're just sitting behind your desk staring at nothing."

I flinched at each of his statements. It was like getting a glimpse into my private file, seeing all the evidence that had been amassed against me.

"Now, I'm not trying to downplay in any way what you've been through, Curt. I can't say I would handle this situation any better than you've done, but I think it's time you faced certain realities. You're not giving one hundred percent—" He raised a hand to cut off my protest. "It's true. You're not giving one hundred percent to your students, to yourself or to Olivia."

I set the mug on the trunk that served as our coffee table. I must have set it down harder than I thought, because some tea splashed over the side, and Bill reached forward, dabbing at the spill with a napkin. It was an old steamer trunk, transportation stickers still affixed to the side. Olivia, her stocking feet on its surface, had once wondered out loud if it had belonged to someone from the Titanic, if somehow a trunk had survived but its owner had not. *Impossible,* I'd said. *But it's an old trunk, anyway,* she had pointed out. *The owner is probably dead, shipwreck or otherwise.*

"Don't bring Olivia into this," I said now, a note of warning in my voice. Maybe he was right about things at school, but that didn't mean he knew a thing about Olivia and me.

Bill raised his hand again, as if I were a dog who needed to heel. "It's only because I like you and respect you that I can say this, Curt. But Olivia's floundering, too."

"What do you mean? She's doing fine."

"She's failing P.E. I talked to Jessie Ryan only yesterday, and she says Olivia has missed at least a dozen classes since January."

I shook my head. "She's only been sick once this entire semester."

"Well, she's not *sick.* She's skipping class, Curtis. Hanging out in the bathroom, the library... We all know she's bright. We're all rooting for her, and that's why Jessie came to me, to figure out how we can help her. You must have seen it. She's lonely. You never see her talking to another kid."

"Wait," I said. "You might be right about P.E. I don't know. I'll talk to her today and get to the bottom of things. But Olivia is not lonely. She has that group of friends." I didn't add, *the ones who wear all black and call themselves the Visigoths, the ones who scare the hell out of me half the time.*

"She eats her lunch in the library."

"Sometimes," I felt myself being too defensive, but couldn't stop it. "She eats there sometimes."

"Every day," Bill countered.

I closed my eyes, fighting off a sudden stab of pain. Olivia, eating alone in the library, taking a listless bite of the egg salad sandwich she'd made the night before, peeling a mozzarella stick in tidy, industrious strokes. "I'll talk to her," I said. "And Monday, when I'm back at school—"

"Let's talk about that, too," Bill said. He leaned forward in the chair, a hand on each of his knees. Dress slacks, a button-down shirt, a sports coat with leather patches on the elbows—that was part of his style. No khakis and polo shirts for this man, ever.

Here it comes, I thought. Maybe I'd been waiting for it. Maybe I'd known since the moment Bill Meyers had appeared on the cafeteria roof. He was going to do it—he was going to release me, quickly and painlessly as pulling off a Band-Aid.

But instead, Bill laid out a rationale over the next hour or so, and everything he said made perfect sense. I *was* struggling. I *wasn't* giving one hundred percent. The state testing—that grasping, insatiable god all public school teachers worshipped—was over, the year was winding down. It was nearly May, so I could limp through the last month of the school year, doing right by no one. I could keep going through the motions. But it wasn't fair to my students. It wasn't fair to my own sense of integrity. I stiffened again when he mentioned that it wasn't fair to Olivia—but I was starting to see that he was right. What was Olivia doing at this very moment? Probably freaking out about what I'd done.

On the other hand, Bill pointed out—I did have plenty of sick leave accrued. I'd taken two weeks when Daniel died, and the odd day here and there during my annual bout with laryngitis, but I had more than enough days banked to take the whole rest of the year. I could start fresh in the fall, and my job would be waiting for me.

As for Olivia, Bill continued—something could probably be worked out if we wanted to take a little time off. Independent study packets, an incomplete that could be amended later, a summer class at a community college to fulfill the P.E.

requirement. There were options; it just required a little creative thinking. "She's a good kid," he said. "She's going to come through one way or another."

Of course, I thought. Of course she'll come through.

Then Bill said, "Forget about school," with a little flick of his wrist as if school had no significance at all. "Forget about students and responsibilities to the job. For now, just forget about all of that. What you need is to figure out what you really want to happen in your life, Curt. What is it that Curtis Kaufman needs to do right now, more than anything else in the world? What's going to be the best thing for Curtis Kaufman and his family?"

His question startled me, even though it was one I'd been considering in a subconscious way, all week.

My eyes flicked to the print on the wall. It was a vintage Jefferson Airplane poster, hand-lettered. Kathleen had found it at a store near Haight-Ashbury on a trip to San Francisco early in our marriage, then mounted and framed it. It had hung in our first apartment, and later in the two-bedroom house we'd rented until Olivia was born, when we'd offered our meager savings for the down payment on this house, which Kathleen had dubbed the "funky fixer-upper" and I'd fondly referred to as "the money pit." I'd half expected Kathleen to take the frame off the wall when she went, but maybe it was more significant that she'd simply left it behind.

And maybe it was significant that behind that particular frame I'd taped the letter from the Lorain County D.A. *Although we understand that such a notification is not welcome to families of victims…*

"Curt? Are you listening? It's important to rediscover your purpose. I know that must sound like a bunch of New Age bullshit, but—"

"No, you're right," I said. The tightness in my chest, which had been there all day, was releasing, like the loosening grip of a blood pressure cuff.

My *purpose*.

One single act could set everything right, reestablish the balance in our lives.

Deep down, of course, I had known this all along.

I needed to kill Robert Saenz.

olivia

At 3:15 p.m., Mrs. Silva and I got into her little red Volkswagen Beetle and navigated our way through Sacramento. I tried very hard not to grab on to the door handle every time we turned, and it seemed that she was trying very hard not to appear annoyed with the situation—angling the A/C vent directly toward me, turning the radio station to something fast and upbeat. It was a relief to see Dad's SUV in the driveway, to feel for a second that everything might be normal. We parked on the street, and Mrs. Silva followed a few feet behind me. I was shaking as I let myself in the front door, not sure what I would find inside.

Mr. Meyers met me in the entryway, stooping to avoid our overhead light fixture. "Hey, Olivia. I think your dad is going to be fine, but just in case, I'm going to leave this with you, okay?" He passed me a slip of paper with a phone number and his name printed in block letters: BILL MEYERS—HOME.

I folded the paper and pushed it deep into a pocket. It was uncomfortable and strange enough to have my school principal in our home—I couldn't imagine calling him at his.

"You're all right now, Curt?" Mr. Meyers asked, and from the couch Dad said, "You bet, Bill."

"Dad?" I let my backpack slide to the floor and studied him. He looked normal—not unfocused like he'd looked coming down from the cafeteria roof, and not grayish like he'd looked only this morning on our way to school. He actually looked *good,* healthy and smiling, as though he'd been home all afternoon doing shots of wheatgrass infused with extra vitamin C.

He patted the couch. "Come here, Liv."

I sank down next to him, leaning my head automatically into his shoulder, something I hadn't done in a long time. My head must have grown, because it wasn't the comfortable fit I used to remember.

"Hey…hey. Don't cry."

I was about to protest that I wasn't crying, that I was freaked out since my father had been sitting on the roof of the cafeteria, thank you very much, but I wasn't going to cry about it. And then I realized that my shoulders were heaving, and my breath was coming out funny, and that Dad, as usual, was right.

Outside, a car started; Mrs. Silva and Mr. Meyers had left. This made me a little worried, and then it worried me that I was worried—because being with Dad should have been the least worrisome thing in the world.

I pulled away and looked at him. "What happened?"

"Really, it was nothing. I just felt like I needed to take a little break." There was something I didn't trust about his face. It was exactly the way I'd look if someone had a gun to my back and was telling me to smile or else.

"In the middle of the school day. On the cafeteria roof."

Dad pulled me close again. "Everything's fine now, Liv. There's something I want to tell you."

I groaned. Whatever followed this statement wasn't going to be good. Cue Daniel telling me he was going to college halfway across the country, but we would talk every week. Cue Dad announcing that the guy responsible for Daniel's death had worked out a plea bargain. Cue Mom telling me she had something to talk about, and then moving to Omaha. I braced myself as if I were preparing for a slap to the face or a punch to the gut. Maybe it was worse than I thought—maybe Dad had had a stroke or been diagnosed with brain cancer or any one of the awful diseases you could find on medical websites.

But what he said was, "Love."

It took me a minute, and then I realized he was playing this game we'd made up when I was just a kid and had trouble falling asleep at night. It went like this: The first person said the word "love," and the second person said a word that started with "e" like "elephant," and the first person said a word that started with "t", and so on and so on, with the last letter of one word spawning the first letter of the next. It used to make me feel happy and silly, and then somehow in the middle of thinking of the next word, I'd fall asleep. Now it seemed ridiculous. Shouldn't we be doing something other than playing games?

"Come on, Liv," Dad prompted. "Love."

I shook my head. "Empty."

He gave me a hesitant smile. "Yield."

"I really don't feel like playing a game, Dad."

"One more. Yield."

I sighed. "Danger."

"Real," he said, touching his chest and then holding his hand out to me, as if we were practicing sign language together.

"Dad," I groaned. "What's going on?"

"Okay," he said. "Okay, I know this is all a little weird. But I'm completely serious. What would you say to taking a little trip with your old man?"

I blinked. Earlier I thought he was about to take a header from the cafeteria roof. Now he wanted to take me on a trip.

I chose my words carefully. "First, I would say that the phrase *old man* has always disturbed me for reasons I don't fully understand. Then I would say that we're almost out of milk, and if this little trip includes a stop at a grocery store, I'm all for it."

Dad chuckled. "No, not to the grocery store. I mean a real trip. A voyage."

Well, this was new. A *voyage?* "Does this involve a boat?" I demanded, trying to keep the panic out of my voice. I was going to have to call Mom for sure. There were probably five hundred water-related entries in my Fear Journals. "You know I'm afraid of boats and sharks and currents and rogue waves and—"

"No boats, I promise. Voyage is the wrong word, then. I'm talking about a road trip. You, me and the open road." He paced to the windows, whirled around, paced back. It surprised me how young he looked, how goofy. *Like his old self,* I thought, and then out of nowhere: *Like when Daniel was alive.* But he looked a bit manic, too.

"A road trip? Dad, are you sure you're okay? I'm serious. Do you need me to, um, be a supportive passenger while you drive yourself to the doctor or something?"

He laughed a bigger-than-genuine laugh that was not at all reassuring.

I can't take this, I thought. One member of my family was gone forever, another lived a few thousand miles away and now my last remaining family member was cracking up—on the cafeteria roof one minute, on the couch talking about a voyage the next. I had to call Mom. This was definitely more than I could handle by myself.

"Don't you want to know where we're going?"

I wasn't sure *we* should be going anywhere, unless maybe it was to some kind of "hospital" for a little "rest." But they would have to take me, too, because I wasn't going to survive for a second on my own. "Okay," I said, slowly, preparing to hear him suggest the wilds of Alaska or a hot spring in Arizona, the sort of place that couldn't be found on a map. "Where are we going?"

His grin was so big it threatened to split his face in two. "We're going to Reno, to Salt Lake City, to Cheyenne…and, *drumroll, please*…to Omaha."

"Omaha? You mean, to Mom?" I tried to say it neutrally, to keep the emotion out of my voice. This was a surprise, and not an unwelcome one. Maybe Dad had come to the conclusion himself that he was cracking up. Maybe Mom and I could get him some professional help.

"Aren't you excited?"

"Dad, talk to me. Did you just get fired?"

"Fired? No. Of course not."

"So what were you and Mr. Meyers doing all afternoon?"

"Just talking, Liv. He helped me figure something out."

"He helped you figure out that you need to go to Omaha," I clarified.

"I know, it's sudden. But look—I have an entire plan worked out. We'll take a few days to get things situated around here, and then we'll hit the road."

I groaned. "Dad, seriously. We have another month of school."

"That's what Mr. Meyers and I figured out. I can take some sick leave—I've got more than enough to spare. And we'll talk to your counselor about independent study for you, just to the end of the semester. Don't worry." Leaning down, he put a hand on my shoulder, and I felt his warmth burning through my sweatshirt.

And then I froze, imagining that conversation with Mr. Merrill. "Dad, there's something—"

He stopped me. "I know all about your P.E. class, and it's okay. We'll get it all figured out."

I sat back on the couch, about to cry for the zillionth time today. What in the world was going on? I was failing P.E. for the second time, and I wasn't even going to get yelled at? "Dad, come on. Why are we going to Omaha?"

"Olivia, I just—I feel like it's time."

"Time for what? For us to be together again, you and me and Mom?"

"Of course." He didn't even blink.

He's lying, I knew instantly. Fantastic. My father was lying to me.

"Does Mom know about this?"

"Well. Not yet."

I groaned. "And how long…?"

"Oh, four or five days, and then we'll be there."

"That's not what I meant."

But Dad was pretending not to hear me. When I stood and tried to move past him, he caught me in a big, spin-in-a-circle hug that felt phony, too. He felt like a different version of my dad than the one I'd been living with for the past few years, as if a stranger had bought a mask of Dad's face and borrowed one of his polo shirts. When he put me down, he was red with excitement. "This is the right thing," he whispered. "I know it."

I didn't believe that for a second.

But I would have been the shittiest daughter in the world to say so.

curtis

Olivia was sharp; I could feel her watching me that weekend, waiting for me to slip up, or trying to catch me off guard with her questions. But I'd made up my mind. This was the right thing, the best, the only thing. Kathleen and Olivia would be together, Saenz would be dead, and I would finally, finally have done right by Daniel.

"So, we're seriously doing this?" Olivia asked me the next morning, after I called *The Sacramento Bee* to put our newspaper on hold.

"You're not backing out, are you?" I asked.

She glared at me. "I don't really see that as an option."

I hauled down two suitcases from a shelf in the garage, where they had aged disgracefully since our disastrous trip to Coronado, acquiring a layer of dust and more than a few spiderwebs. It took a half hour of cleaning with damp cloths before Olivia would consider either suitcase as a viable option. Then she stood before her open closet doors, hands on her skinny hips.

I sighed. "What's wrong now?"

"It's impossible to pack without knowing exactly how long I'm going to be gone," she announced.

I laughed. "Are you kidding me? I know exactly what you're going to pack. Black pants, black shirts, black sweatshirts, black socks and black boots. Can't be that difficult." It was basically her uniform, as much as khaki pants and polo shirts were mine. I wasn't sure when it had started, exactly, or where all the clothes had come from—but one morning at breakfast a couple of years ago, I realized that I was the parent of a teenage daughter who wore only black.

She glared at me. "But how many black shirts, exactly?"

"What does it matter? It's not like there are no washing machines in Omaha." It was better, I figured, to be vague than to tell an outright lie. Telling the truth was out of the question.

There were dozens of small details to figure out, and several major ones. It was almost thrilling to have a plan, to have a specific goal that was further than a day or two ahead, the way we'd been existing since Kathleen left. I had installed a massive whiteboard in the front entryway, and each night Olivia and I had crossed off our completed chores and added new ones. *Buy cereal, take the trash out, pay phone and cable, run sprinkler in backyard.* Now I was thinking beyond today, beyond this week.

I didn't find a chance to break away until Sunday night. Olivia had insisted on coming along on all the errands I devised—an oil change, a trip to Target for a few travel necessities, a stop at the ATM. This wasn't that unusual—Olivia didn't typically like to be left at home, where she was convinced that all sorts of things could go wrong, like a burglar who assumed the house was empty if there wasn't a car in the driveway, or a carbon monoxide leak that she couldn't smell. So I had to wait until she started a load of laundry to say "Why don't I just grab dinner?"

"Can't you wait a bit? Twenty minutes?"

"Well, I was thinking In-and-Out. You know how that drive-thru line always takes forever."

Olivia frowned. "I could stop the washer."

"Don't bother," I said, grabbing my keys before she could jump into action. "I'll be back before you know it."

I did go to In-and-Out, and the line was wrapped around the restaurant and through the parking lot, so at least that wasn't a lie. But while I waited, I made the phone call Olivia absolutely couldn't overhear. "Pick up, pick up," I pleaded. It was a long shot; it was Plan A, but there wasn't a Plan B yet.

"Yeah?" The voice on the other end was suspicious. *One of those conspiracy nuts,* Kathleen had always said, back when we'd known him, back when Zach Gaffaney had lived a few blocks away and been married to Marcia, half of a couple we bumped into regularly over the years. Privately, I'd suspected that Kathleen was right.

"I'm looking for the Zach Gaffaney that used to live in Sacramento?"

"Who is this?"

"This is Curtis Kaufman. We used to be part of that neighborhood beautification group, painting over graffiti, that kind of thing."

"Okay. I remember you." There was a long pause. "I don't live in Sacramento anymore, though. I'm not even married anymore. So I think—I'm probably not the guy you're looking for."

"No, don't hang up." I almost dropped the phone, my palm was so slick with sweat. "I remember how we used to have those talks about the government, about our rights—that kind of thing. You're the guy I'm looking for."

"How'd you get this number?" He seemed less suspicious than curious now. This was why I'd remembered Zach Gaffaney, why I'd thought of him almost immediately, when Bill

Meyers was still talking to me about how he'd rediscovered his own purpose. I'd stopped listening—all that was required of me was a sporadic nod—and instead remembered a morning I'd spent pulling weeds at a neighborhood park with Zach Gaffaney, who had gone on and on about his gun collection, how he was prepared for just about anything—not just the threat of home invasion or small scale self-defense, but the inevitable failure of a government that was basically controlled by special interests and our streets being overrun by criminals because the government couldn't afford to keep them locked up. I hadn't taken him seriously, but Kathleen had. "*She* seems like such a normal person. *He's* a walking time bomb," she'd said, mimicking some of his rants as soon as we were home.

Now I told him, "I heard you were living in Winnemucca, working in a casino." This was true—a few weeks ago, I'd bumped into Marcia at the grocery store, and we'd exchanged casual information about our exes. I'd told her about Kathleen going to Omaha, and she'd been sympathetic. "Oh, Zach?" She'd laughed. "That was all a million years ago. He's back in Nevada, working at a dumpy casino, living in some shit-hole trailer with only his guns for company." I didn't tell this to Zach, nor did I mention that just about anyone was traceable on the internet.

"Okay," he said again, guarded. "I'm listening."

"Well, I need something, and I figure you could maybe help me out with that."

"You need what, exactly?"

I'd rehearsed this, too, trying for the right balance of vagueness and specificity. Zach Gaffaney was probably the kind of guy who doubted everyone, who suspected the government had wiretapped his trailer.

So I told him: I was looking for some protection. I know I could find that through other means, but I'd become concerned about the way the government was prying into the lives of average citizens, people like Zach and me. What business was it of theirs how I spent my money, what I had in my home? Didn't a person have a right to protect himself and his family?

"I hear you," Zach said, relaxing. "You have an idea what you want?" He rattled off a short list of options, makes and models and prices, deciding I could be trusted. Truthfully, I wasn't worried about the government at all—I was worried about keeping my plans secret from a very paranoid sixteen-year-old and her mother. And I had no intention of letting Robert Saenz live for an extra ten days during the mandatory wait period.

Obviously I wouldn't be a natural with a gun, and I knew that I could very easily screw the whole thing up if I tried to go with something too advanced. But I'd spent the past two nights researching and was pretty clear on the basics. I told him I wanted a revolver, something snub-nosed—easy to conceal, easy to load and shoot, no serious kickback.

"It's never going to get back to you," I promised him.

Zach snorted. "It's not going to be traceable."

"Perfect," I said.

There was a honk behind me, bringing me back to my present reality in the drive-thru line. I'd let a couple car lengths lapse and lurched forward to make up the difference.

Zach gave me the details, told me not to call again until I was ready, and we hung up. I kept his number in my contacts but deleted it from my outgoing calls, in case Olivia looked.

And then it was my turn to order. A voice crackled from the intercom, and I replied, "Two cheeseburgers, two fries, two Cokes."

I was surprised how normal I sounded, and that the man staring back at me in the rearview mirror looked normal, too.

olivia

Dad talked to Mom before me—the first time they'd talked in months, I was pretty sure. Mostly, they used me as a middleman to relay only the most necessary information—reminders of property tax payments, my dental checkups—and left it up to me to decide what else was important. Mostly, I didn't find it necessary to tell either of them *anything*; they were adults, I figured, and they could start acting like it at any time.

Dad opened the door to his office, where he'd been talking in a low voice, and passed me the phone. "Your mom," he said.

I took the phone into the kitchen, where I'd been trying to figure out what food might spoil before we got back. Mom was more puzzled than enthusiastic. I didn't know what to say, especially with Dad pretending not to eavesdrop from the next room. How could I give her the news about Dad and the incident on the roof over the phone? She would freak out—summon a small army of Sacramento connections to pop in on us, maybe, or start driving from Omaha now and meet us somewhere in the middle.

It was easier to pretend to be hurt than to tell her the truth. "You don't want to see me?"

"No, of course I want to see you. Haven't I been begging you to fly out here for the summer? I just don't think that now, while you're still in school…" She didn't mention Dad, who would obviously be arriving on her doorstep, too. Not once, in all her pestering about how much I would love Omaha had she suggested, *Why don't you and Dad just hop in the car and drive out here?* His name hadn't come up in connection with the idea, period.

"Mom, come on. You know I can't get on a plane, right?"

"Liv, of course you can." Mom sighed, but let it go. "Look, you understand. I'm just worried. I mean, what about school? It's your junior year. Don't you have a million projects and things to finish?"

"Yeah, but it's okay. We're basically done, and I can finish the rest on independent study."

"Please, Liv," Mom said, her voice low. She probably didn't want any of her colleagues to overhear. "Tell me what's really going on."

But I didn't have a name for what was going on. I was worried in general, but until Kara had found me in the girls' bathroom, and until I'd seen Dad on the roof, looking vacant and dazed, I hadn't focused my worries on anything specific. My fears had been as random as *nuclear attacks* one minute and *power tools* the next, things I'd dutifully listed in my Fear Journal.

Mom wasn't stupid—even from a thousand miles away, she could probably sense the tightening in my throat, the strange breathing sounds that signaled I was about to start bawling uncontrollably. "Liv," she pleaded.

I snorted back my tears and forced myself to sound normal. "We'll be there soon, and then I'll tell you everything."

Now she was crying, or close to it. "I'm going to worry about you every second until you're here."

I was grateful for the chance to make her laugh, even if it

didn't do much to cheer me up. "You leave the worrying to me, Mom. That's my job."

Dad raised an eyebrow curiously when I returned his phone, but didn't ask any questions. I stood in the doorway of his office and wondered if I had made a big mistake, or if the big mistake was still to come. He'd been organizing his desk, and his trash can was overflowing with papers. I looked closer and saw lesson plans, handouts and student tests, as if he'd just swept the whole mess into the can.

"You owe me," I said.

"I know," he replied, not meeting my eyes.

In a few days the remaining Kaufmans were going to be together again, but I couldn't sort out exactly how I felt about that. When Mom visited every summer, it had been beyond strange to have her ring our doorbell and wait politely to be let in, like a guest, like a person who'd never lived in our house at all. Before she arrived, Dad and I spent some serious time cleaning. Without discussing it, we made sure to rearrange anything we'd moved while she was gone, so that it looked like the exact same house she'd left, the same stacks of magazines we didn't read on the coffee table, the uncomfortable throw pillows back on the couch. It was as if we'd been preserving the house in her honor, just like we'd done with Daniel's room, still intact behind his closed door. During her visit, Mom tiptoed around our lives, barely leaving a trace of her existence—no smear of toothpaste in the bathroom sink, no plate with crumbs on the kitchen counter. She and Dad had been polite with each other, like houseguests at a B and B. Dad slept on the couch while she was there, waking with strange fabric impressions on his skin and a sore back, but he cleared out during the day, always with an excuse that felt contrived, like he just *had* to go look for a new set of solar lights at that exact moment. After she left, no matter how good it had felt to just be with her, the whole house let out a sigh of relief. The couch inched its way closer to the TV, the mail stacked up and a pile of laundry grew in the middle of the upstairs hallway.

In Omaha, Dad and I would be the guests. It would be our turn to tiptoe around Mom's life, around her creations, her wood shavings and cans of paint and varnish. She was living in the house she'd grown up in, renovating it room by room in whatever spare time she had when she wasn't at the store. In Omaha, she would have the advantage; we would be the ones afraid to leave a mess lying around.

Or maybe it would be different. Maybe I could open up to her the way I hadn't done on her visits or in our dozens of phone conversations. I'd have to tell her what happened with Dad, but there were secrets of my own I'd been keeping, too.

The few people at school who knew about my mom leaving couldn't understand how I didn't absolutely hate her. *You mean you still talk to her? Even after she walked out of your life? That's messed up!*

No, I didn't hate her—but at the same time, I did. I'd never really been able to sort out my feelings for Mom. I'd been shocked when she actually left, and felt guilty as hell that I hadn't left with her. I really, honestly hoped she was happier where she was, but I was afraid of that, too—it proved that she didn't need Dad or me.

That whole weekend—one of the longest weekends of my life, it seemed—I packed and unpacked and repacked and watched Dad do the same. I scribbled frantically in my journal. I watched Dad as if he were a two-year-old playing with matches. When he ran out to pick up dinner, I sorted through the papers on his desk, not sure what I was looking for.

And I realized I couldn't wait for us all to be together—good, bad or ugly.

Four more days.

curtis

On Monday, I gave up the pretense of sleep at four, switched on the light, and took inventory. This would be the last time I was ever in this bed, the last time I walked past Daniel's bedroom door, stopping to peek inside in case…in case. My last shower in our quirky claw-footed tub with its complicated system of curtains; my last cup of coffee in the kitchen, sipped while staring out the window.

Olivia and I had each packed a single suitcase, but in the end we started tossing other things into the backseat. Pillows, winter coats, CDs, random snacks from the pantry.

"You want to check all the windows?" I asked. As soon as I heard Olivia's feet on the stairs, I took the box from the top of the mantel and carried it to the car. Daniel's *cremains*. It didn't feel right to shove the box into my suitcase, where it bulged like a rectangular tumor, but it didn't feel right to leave him behind, either.

Olivia was waiting on the porch, scribbling in her Fear Journal.

I could stop this right now, I thought. We could unpack the car and go back to our lives—a staycation in our own home. Or we could head south, find a sandy beach. Or north, to the sort of tall trees that made a person realize he was really noth-ing, just a speck in the world.

But I wouldn't stop it now. I couldn't. Robert Saenz was out there. He was a free man who didn't deserve his freedom, and it was my duty—my right—to take that away from him.

Olivia stood, tucking a pen into her journal. "Let's take a picture," she said, pulling out her cell phone. "You know, photographic evidence of our journey."

We leaned against the Explorer, and I rested my arm on Olivia's bony shoulders. She angled her phone and tapped the screen. "You blinked," she accused, snapping a second shot. I tried to smile, but I was remembering our other family pic-tures, back when there were four of us. Or the picture Daniel had been carrying in his wallet: *The Fam.*

It was hard to look at our house as we pulled out of the driveway. This was our life, I thought. *Was.*

Now I was eager to leave it behind.

Since the night Daniel died, it was as if I'd been in a fog, one of those thick Central Valley fogs that descended without warning, making it difficult to see the house across the street, or the stop sign on the corner. By the time we left the con-gestion of Sacramento, easing our way onto I-80, mountain-bound, I felt the fog lifting. I kept this thought to myself; Olivia loved to mock clichés, and surely she would have seen that statement as sentiment, as a maxim for something so con-ventional it might not even be true.

But that's what I felt, giving the Explorer a bit more gas. In the foothills, the road opened up, the trees became taller and more closely, naturally spaced. With the fog lifted, I was Curtis Kaufman again.

There had been mistakes, but I had a chance to set things right.

That night, after we checked into the hotel in Winnemucca,

I would be meeting Zach Gaffaney. In a few days, I would be leaving Olivia in Omaha. By next weekend, I would be in Oberlin.

And soon after that, Robert Saenz would be dead.

olivia

Once we were actually on the road, I could hardly sit still. I'd never looked so carefully at my own city before—the city I was born in and had lived in my entire life. I craned my neck as we passed through town, the skyline in the distance, the businesses and buildings and billboards and street signs, the leafy trees wavering in a slight breeze. When we passed homes, I wondered who lived there and what they were doing right at this very second. Probably they were at work or school, doing the normal things that normal people did. I dared myself not to close my eyes as we passed over one of the smaller tributaries of the Sacramento River.

Goodbye, river. Goodbye, city.

Dad asked, "You're not going to fidget around like that for two thousand miles, are you?"

"That's how far it is?"

"Sacramento to Omaha is one thousand, five hundred eighty-two miles."

"So, barely nothing."

Dad grinned, flipped the dial on the radio and found Aerosmith, a band that proved strangely generation-bending. "How are you doing so far? Everything's okay?"

I rolled my eyes. "Sure. What in the world do I have to be afraid of?"

Only everything.

But as the traffic thinned and I sat with my Fear Journal open on my lap, I found that I wasn't that afraid, after all. Sure, the road through the foothills was curvy, with long climbs and sudden descents, lined with the sort of trees that looked as if they could take out a small village when they finally went, and I couldn't see myself through to our destination—but somehow, what we were doing was liberating. Instead of sitting through the daily tedium of American History/Statistics/PE/Spanish/Chemistry/English, I was doing something brave and unexpected. I might have been a character in a movie, minus the expansive "open road" music that usually accompanied such scenes. Maybe my lack of fear was related to our spontaneous (poor) planning—if I didn't know what was ahead of us, I could only form very general fears: large stretches of uninhabited spaces, winding roads, mountains.

It wasn't so bad. Four days, and the hard part would be over—at least until our return trip.

And then, somewhere outside Auburn, I lost reception on my cell phone. I held it up to the window, toward the dash and against the roof of the car, trying to get more than a single bar.

Dad laughed. "You might not be able to rely on that the entire way."

"What do you mean?"

"Well...there's going to be some spotty service, plus if you drain your battery on the road, you'll have to wait to charge it until we get to the hotel."

I grimaced. "Like the pioneers, then."

Dad chuckled. One of the coolest things about my dad was

that he could be counted on to laugh, even if my joke wasn't in the realm of funny.

We lost one radio station after another as we entered the Sierra Nevadas, until the dial held nothing but a buzz of static. I played a few hollow-sounding songs through my phone and leaned against the window as the scenery became majestic— white-capped peaks, towering evergreens, stately redwoods. Our gray strip of I-80 was like a flimsy string threading over and in between and around the mountains, as if the path had been designed like one of those fun house mazes. I read each of the warning signs along the route to Dad, in case he missed them: *Landslides! Avalanches! Danger black ice! Deer crossing!* But it was a beautiful spring day, the air clear, the sky cloudless. The landslides, avalanches, black ice and deer must have been on some other road, interrupting someone else's drive.

I tried to take a few photos on my phone, but the results were indistinct blurs. "Why didn't we ever do anything like this before, like take a road trip?"

"Because we were so…" Dad's voice trailed off. Maybe he was regretting, like I was all of a sudden, the cloistered, practical life we'd lived the past few years, like fugitives in our own home, only venturing out for the necessities. "I don't know. We should have. I'm sorry, Liv. We absolutely should have."

His voice had this strange, almost weepy quality to it, and I blurted quickly, to change the subject, "Nah, forget it. Even if you'd suggested it, I would have been too scared. Like right now, these mountains are pretty terrifying."

"Because of their height?"

"No, because they're mountains."

Dad smiled. "Give me one good reason other than heights to be scared of mountains."

"I'll give you five," I said, counting them off on one hand. "Mountain goats, mountain lions, black bears, coyotes and…"

I did a drumroll with both hands against the dashboard. "The Donner Party."

Dad shook his head, laughing. "Ah, a history lesson that has stayed with you. No doubt because it involved tests of human strength—"

"And cannibalism."

"—an expansion of the Western frontier—"

"And cannibalism."

"—and an extraordinary rescue effort."

"Don't forget cannibalism." I shuddered, studying my arm. "Can you imagine a world where your best option includes a bite of someone's bicep?"

"So, to clarify—essentially, mountain equals cannibalism."

"Right."

Dad threw back his head to laugh, the first real laugh I'd heard from him in what felt like a million years, an actual belly laugh. "The Donner Party," he mused. "Now *that* was a road trip."

We stopped for gas and a bathroom break in Truckee, and that's where it all went to hell.

Actually, hell came at the exact moment when I realized my bladder was about to explode and my only option would be a public restroom. At school, I didn't drink anything and still ended up crouching over a toilet once a day, but that was nothing compared to the horror of a gas station bathroom. I did some quick mental math: if I used the bathroom twice a day while we were on the road, and we were on the road for four days, this meant eight encounters with public restrooms— and that was being optimistic

Inside the store, I glanced around, taking in the aisles of chips and candy, the nacho cheese dispenser, the hot dogs rotating slowly on a rotisserie. I tugged on Dad's sleeve like a two-year-old. "I don't see a bathroom."

The clerk behind the counter, with a Metallica shirt and greasy hair, held up a massive board with a single key attached. "It's around the side of the building, toward the back."

"Um," I said, still clutching Dad's shirtsleeve. "This is how every episode of *Criminal Minds* starts, with someone heading into a bathroom at a deserted gas station."

"Not every episode," Dad corrected. "Also, it's not deserted. I'm right here."

The clerk was staring at us as if we were both out of our minds. "You want the key or not?"

I squeezed Dad on the shoulder. "You're coming with me."

The clerk rolled his eyes.

Dad laughed. It worried me that he had such a hard time separating my jokes from my cries for help, but he bought a cup of coffee and followed me around the side of the building.

I hugged him at the door. "If I'm not out in exactly thirty seconds, please call 9-1-1."

Back in the car, I gave Dad the play-by-play: my boots had stuck to the floor; there was a puddle of mystery moisture next to an overflowing trash can; the mirror was cloudy; the toilet had so many rings it seemed to be measuring either age, like a tree, or despair; and instead of a hand dryer there was a crusty loop of fabric carrying at least twenty types of bacteria whose names we would probably never know.

Dad was unconcerned. "Yeah, but you still washed your hands, right?"

What I wanted was to wash my whole body, clothes included.

"Life's about the journey, not the destination," Dad reminded me. "Isn't there a famous quote about that?"

I rolled my eyes. "There are a thousand quotes about that. And each one is a cliché."

But Dad had gone quiet, retreating to that place inside himself where he'd been for the past week, thinking about things I didn't know and might not understand if I did. I figured we would be lucky if this trip was nothing more than a cliché, just a few days on the open road and a happy reunion waiting for us at the end.

But none of that, of course, was guaranteed.

curtis

It was one o'clock by the time we reached Reno, and between the two of us we had devoured a half-pound bag of gummy bears to stave off our growing hunger. I'd been to Reno a few times for conferences, the sort supported by California school districts but held in Nevada for the cheap casino stays and the obvious entertainment options. Still, we spent twenty minutes circling before we decided to take our chances on a $4.99 all-you-can-eat casino buffet.

"When was your food last rotated?" Olivia asked the cashier as I paid.

"It's always fresh!" the cashier replied, tossing a very full head of blond hair.

Olivia ended up picking skeptically at a salad. "Fast food might have been a better option," she said, frowning at my plate of chicken fingers and mac and cheese.

I shrugged. "Got to keep my strength up for the journey." Even if the possibilities for bacteria were high, I had to admit the food tasted good—or maybe I was just hungry for the first time in a long time. If life as I knew it was going to end in a week, I was going to eat all the junk that a middle-aged man with a definite belly shouldn't eat. On the other hand, this was probably the exact sort of food that was served in prison cafeterias, and therefore was awaiting me for the next twenty-five years, minimum.

Rather than eat, my ninety-eight-pound daughter tried not to stare openly at some of our fellow diners, like the man who was pushing eighty in a corner booth, wearing dark sunglasses and a frosty, much younger blonde on each arm, or the woman in a skintight leopard-print dress and matching five-inch leopard-print heels.

When I returned from the buffet with a towering bowl of soft-serve ice cream, Olivia grinned at me. "Do me a favor?"

"Maybe."

"Can you please go out into the casino for ten minutes and then come back sobbing, with your hair all disheveled and announce that you've lost the farm? *Please.* It could be an early birthday present for me. I'll film the whole thing."

"How about instead I give you a few bucks for a round of blackjack and see if they kick you out?"

"What makes you think they would kick me out? I could pass for twenty-one."

"Sure you could." I laughed and Olivia took an indignant bite of her salad.

I didn't press the point. Olivia was sixteen-and-a-half and looked fourteen. She basically wore the same skinny jeans and oversize combat boots every day, a combination that made her look comically childlike. Any curves she did have were hidden beneath her ubiquitous black hoodie, sized more appropriately for a linebacker. When she'd started hanging around with the Visigoths a few years ago, she'd begun wearing light face powder and dark eyeliner. I'm not sure what the desired effect was, but I thought it made her look like a kid dressing as a teenager for Halloween. Not that this was the sort of thing a single dad could mention to his daughter. When it was just the two of us at home, or when Kathleen visited during the summer, Olivia toned it down, as if only her family could be trusted to view her actual face—a face so small and lovely and so much like Kathleen's, at times I could hardly bear to see it.

"You want to walk around for a bit?" I offered, when Olivia couldn't be persuaded to eat another bite. "We have another half hour of parking."

"Okay."

We wandered a bit off the main drag, the weekday crowd thinning as we went. Olivia pointed at an old-fashioned costume shop, and I waved her in alone. She had inherited Kathleen's love of the antiquated and interesting. Kathleen couldn't pass a piece of furniture without running her hand over the grain, or pulling the piece away from the wall to get a better look at its construction. Daniel had once called her "The Chair Whisperer"—a name she'd pretended to hate. Watching Olivia pick her way through this secondhand store, fingering a fur coat, holding a tiny glass egg up to the light—it was déjà vu; throw out the all-black clothes, and I could have been looking at a young Kathleen.

My stomach clenched. What was I doing? The vision that had suddenly become clear to me last Friday, with the world as I knew it spread out before me like a road map, wavered. *I can't. I can't do this.*

I switched my attention from Olivia, who was now pawing through a collection of old postcards, to the man staring back at me from the hazy surface of the shop window—a mad artist's caricature of the person I used to be. A sad person, an angry man, a failed father who had let his son die and his wife leave and his daughter surrender to her fear of everything.

I knew the answer, but begged the question: Where did it all go? How did it all get away from me? How had we gone from four to three to two, reducing ourselves to insignifi-

cance? And how could I do what I was about to do, and reduce the number to one?

I can't.

Then Olivia was in front of me, tapping on the glass to get
my attention. She was wearing a top hat and carrying a cane,
and while I watched, she did a strange little tap dance in her
combat boots, ending with a two-arm flourish. I clapped,
not caring about the glances from a couple who passed me
on the sidewalk.

Olivia grinned and took a deep bow at the waist.

My throat almost squeezed closed, the love I felt for her
gathered into a solid lump. I didn't know if all parents felt
this way from time to time, but right then I didn't see just the
tap-dancing teenage Olivia, but all the versions of her melded
together: the chubby infant, the sturdy-limbed toddler, the
gymnastics tumbler, the thrower of noisy, sugar-fueled slumber
parties, the thin, quiet girl in her eighth grade graduation robe,
the skin-and-bones teenager hiding behind her Visigoth garb.

I have to do this, I thought, as if I could communicate the
thought to her telepathically, straight from my mind to hers.

It's because I love you that I'm going to do this.

olivia

Nevada, as it turned out, was a pretty desolate place. Once we'd left the lights of Reno—The Biggest Little City in the World, as about a thousand signs had reminded us—the road became flat, open, dusty and dry, the ground a bleached white. There seemed to be more cows than people, lone dots on the landscape, miles from anything. What would it be like to live out here, under a massive blue sky, your nearest neighbor the three cows in a sprawling fenced area, where you could see a car coming from miles away, kicking up a miniature dust swarm?

Dad broke through my reverie, saying, "See that? That's the first one."

"The first what?" I scanned the road and saw that he was pointing to little collections of black stones.

"Along the side of the road—see? They're names, messages, that kind of thing."

I stared, fascinated, as we passed dozens—hundreds—of these piles of black stones. They were like shrines, little monuments to the moment.

Johnny + Stacy.

Bill 2013.

I was here.

The messages seemed prehistoric, almost—as basic a form of written communication as a cave drawing, a million times more permanent than a text message. It was sort of beautiful, in a way that would make no sense if I tried to explain it.

"So," Dad was saying. "I figured we'd go for Winnemucca."

"What? You're talking gibberish. Do I need to feel your forehead?"

"Winnemucca. It's a city in Nevada. Look it up." Dad tapped the road atlas wedged between my seat and the console, and I sighed, obliging. It was funny the way I-80 snaked across Nevada, not in any kind of straight line, but jutting north and humping back south. There weren't many cities on I-80 in Nevada, period: Reno, Sparks, Fernley, Lovelock, Winnemucca, Battle Mountain, Elko, Wendover.

"We're using the term *city* pretty loosely," I commented. "According to this, Winnemucca has 7,000 residents."

Dad laughed. "And a somewhat inflated ego. But from what I remember, it has hotels, restaurants, everything we need tonight. Besides, the next decent place is another couple hours east."

I fiddled with my seat belt, loosening it so I could turn to face my father more directly. "Wait—what do you mean, from what you remember? You've done this before?"

"Your mom and I...when we were..." He stopped, changing tracks. "You're right, there might be more places along the way. What does it say in the atlas?"

"Sure. There are probably entire bustling metropolises that have sprouted along eastern Nevada. I'm sure I'll lose count of all the Starbucks and IKEAs we pass. But don't change the subject. You and Mom did this? You took a road trip?"

Dad smiled, shaking his head. "You crack me up, kiddo."

"I'm waiting."

"Liv, it's not the romantic odyssey you're imagining. It was twenty-some years ago, and we were driving in a little yellow Datsun packed to the gills with books and clothes and junk."

"Actually, that does sound like a romantic odyssey. When was this—when you moved to California?"

"Yeah. We were just married, and I had the job offer in Sacramento. We had about two hundred dollars in cash plus a credit card to last until my first paycheck."

"Why am I only hearing this now?" I demanded.

"I didn't think you'd find it interesting."

"Well, I do. It's part of my history, too."

"You weren't born yet. Daniel wasn't even born yet."

"But…*still,*" I huffed. Sometimes completely ordinary, everyday things blew me away. Like the fact that my parents had ever lived without me, or that they had done exotic things like drive across the United States in a yellow Datsun.

"How old were you guys? What were you like then? What was Mom like?"

Dad ran a hand slowly over his face and then returned it to the wheel.

"Never mind." I had asked the wrong questions. Out the window, Nevada kept zipping past. It wasn't even summer yet, but everything was *dry* dry, the earth cracked, each fissure opening up like a gaping, parched mouth. "You can tell me the rest of the story later."

"There's not a rest of the story," Dad insisted. "It's a very simple story, really. I think you have the gist of it."

"Like 'See Dick. See Dick and Jane. See Dick and Jane drive. See Dick and Jane arrive at destination.'"

"Almost," Dad said, his voice strangely distant again, miles ahead of me on the road. I had this weird feeling that if I knocked on his chest right then, I would only be able to hear the echoey sounds of my own knuckles.

I let it go and instead dug out my Fear Journal. There were plenty of things to be afraid about on the road right in front of me, but I wrote first: *All the things I'll never know about the past.* At that moment I wanted badly to fall into the past, even into one of our old family photo albums.

After Daniel had died, I'd gone through all those albums, trying to memorize every detail. When she was in college, Mom had driven an orange VW Rabbit and worn her hair long and feathered back from her face, like a Charlie's Angel. When Daniel was young, Dad had worn his shorts shorter than any straight man would dream of wearing them today. Daniel as a baby had been bald except for a single patch of hair on his crown; he had looked unfocused and dreamy, as if listening to a melody only he could hear. I saw Daniel in red-footed pajamas, playing a plastic xylophone, and Dad, Mom and Daniel on a green corduroy couch I didn't recognize. It had hurt me then, and it hurt now, remembering—my family had made all these memories without me, had lived in a different house, even. This—my parents' westbound road trip—was just one more thing I had missed.

"Hey," Dad said softly.

I sniffed. "Hmm?"

"Some things are hard to talk about. You know?"

I nodded.

"Look, do me a favor, will you? Get out that atlas and tell me how far we are from Imlay."

It turned out that we weren't far at all. "What's in Imlay?" I asked.

"Just wait," Dad said, and a few miles later, he slowed for an exit that read "Thunder Mountain."

"Another mountain?"

"Patience…" Dad said. "When we took our trip out here, along I-80, your mother had us stop at every single brown historical marker. You know, every place a president spent the night, every stop on the Pony Express."

I smiled. That was Mom. Give her a teachable moment, and she learned or taught or both. "So, what president spent the night in Imlay, Nevada?"

Dad shook his head. "Look."

And then in front of us, a strange mountain was rising on the horizon, a mountain made of stone and metal and wood, a giant man-made sculpture.

Dad told me the story: A man from Oklahoma had relocated to Imlay after fighting overseas in World War II, and he'd built the monument with scraps of found art as a tribute to Native American life. As we got closer, I spotted car hoods, a giant metal arch, a white staircase leading to an upper level. Dad and I circled the monument on foot, pointing things out.

"I bet Mom loved this," I said.

"She was fascinated, of course. We spent hours crawling all over this thing. The owner was alive then, and he gave us a guided tour in return for a small donation."

"Someone lived here?"

"Part art, part insanity, I figured," Dad said.

Back in the car, I was suddenly starving, my buffet salad long forgotten. I popped the top of a can of Pringles, fished out a handful, and passed them over to Dad. "Original flavor, the way you like them."

Dad must have been hungry, too; he downed the chips with little concern for chewing before swallowing. "The original is always better."

"You sound like a cheesy inspirational poster."

"That's me, a walking cheesy inspirational poster."

"All you need is a backdrop of snow-capped mountains or hot-air balloons."

"Or a rainbow."

I laughed. "Definitely a rainbow."

Dad was quiet a minute, crunching. Then he said, "I think I got pretty lucky with my road trip companion. Not everyone's as funny as you."

I pretended to glare at him. "You calling me funny?"

He grinned back. "I mean, not *funny*-funny, but cool."

"Dad, I got news for you. I'm definitely not cool."

"Sure you are, kiddo. In every way that could possibly matter."

It was almost too great of a compliment to take, and to deflect the awkwardness of a father-daughter-Disney-Channel moment, I had no choice but to reach in my backpack for my iPod and snug the earbuds gently into each ear.

curtis

The closer we got to our hotel in Winnemucca, the more jittery I felt, as if I were coming down from a major caffeine overdose. Even though reception had been spotty, I kept checking my phone obsessively for new messages. "In case Mom calls," I said, when Olivia noticed.

"Since when does Mom call you?" she asked.

"Like I said, just in case."

"Just in case what? That something goes wrong in Omaha and you have to change into your superhero costume and fly there at the speed of light?"

I stopped checking my phone, although it didn't stop me from being nervous. Sometimes Olivia could be a bit of a pain.

The hotel was decent, part of a budget chain that wasn't connected to a large casino, although there were two rows of slot machines in the lobby. A grizzled-looking woman was planted in front of one of the machines, pressing buttons repeatedly with her right hand and inhaling intermittently from a stubby cigar in her left. I caught Olivia's raised eyebrow and asked the front desk attendant for a nonsmoking room.

After Olivia pronounced our room—with its double queen beds and bolted-down television—"do-able," I stepped out with the ice bucket and took my time coming back from the lobby, wandering the perimeter of the property instead of cutting through the parking lot. In a few hours I would be meeting Zach Gaffaney; I would be buying a gun and crossing a boundary, and there would be no going back. I slowed further, wandering past the pool, a dinky rectangular hole with greenish water and a dozen SWIM AT YOUR OWN RISK, NO LIFEGUARD ON DUTY signs. The air was markedly cooler than it had been in Reno, and it definitely wasn't swimsuit weather. I glanced at the license plates in the parking lot: Nevada, Utah, Wyoming, Colorado, Arizona. Ours was the only California plate, which didn't surprise me. Most of the Californians I knew didn't venture beyond Disneyland or the San Diego Zoo or Las Vegas, unless they were on a plane. I figured this accounted for the weak grasp of geography among my students—they knew the states that bordered the Pacific Ocean, plus Texas, Florida and New York. If I had mentioned Nebraska, they would have had to Google it. No, Winnemucca, Nevada, was far off the radar of anyone I knew, save Zach Gaffaney.

"Dad?"

I whirled around, ice spilling out of the plastic bucket. Olivia was on the balcony above, barely visible since she was standing well back from the edge.

"What are you doing? You were just staring into space."

"Just thinking, I guess."

"Well, don't think so hard. You freaked me out. Plus, the ice is melting."

"We'll get more later. You hungry?"

"For real food, you mean? Not a bacteria-laden buffet? Not candy and cookies?"

I started up the stairs. "Real food. Tell you what, kiddo. We'll drive around and you'll pick."

"Breakfast for dinner?" This was Olivia's favorite meal—maybe because the fantastic weekend breakfasts Kathleen had made, bacon and eggs and sausage, sometimes pancakes or waffles, too, had disappeared along with Kathleen. Most mornings, we were lucky if there was enough milk to cover our stale cereal.

When I reached Olivia, I gave her a little squeeze and then removed my arm carefully. Could she tell I was shaking?

It wasn't hard to find a restaurant with a twenty-four-hour breakfast, probably because everything in Nevada seemed geared to a round-the-clock schedule. Olivia ordered the endless stack of pancakes, and I went for the French dip, taking only a few bites before setting the sandwich down.

"Must be all the sweets along the way," I said.

"I didn't know it was possible for your appetite to be ruined," Olivia commented. She had taken on Kathleen's role of monitoring what I ate, commenting when she found an empty container of ice cream in the trash can or a candy bar wrapper that had gone through the wash with my pants. "So, what is it? Are you nervous or something?"

I tried not to react. "About...?"

"Um, seeing Mom. Hello—your wife? My mother?"

I took a sip of water. "Aren't you?"

"Was that a 'yes'?"

"Sure, I suppose," I said. Over Olivia's head, I kept an eye on the clock, watching as the second hand raced around the digits. *Stop,* I thought, willing the universe to understand my wordless plea. *Just give me another minute to think.*

After dinner, I pulled into a parking space at our hotel. Liv unlocked her door manually and let herself out, then looked back at me, realizing that I hadn't turned off the engine. Her look lasted a long moment. "What." Her voice was flat, as if she couldn't bear to ask a question because I would have to answer, and the answer wouldn't be what she wanted to hear. Or, more likely, it would be what she wanted to hear, but it wouldn't be the truth.

It was hard to look at her. "I think I'm going to drive around for a few minutes, clear my head."

"We've been driving all day, clearing our heads," Olivia pointed out. She was standing in the gap of the open passenger door, probably considering whether she should hop back into the car. But I couldn't let her, of course.

"Twenty minutes," I told her. "Half an hour, tops."

She laughed. "Is this some kind of test?"

"Test?"

"You know, throw the girl who's afraid to swim into the middle of the deep end and see if she can make her way out?"

"Liv. No."

She folded her arms across her chest. "Dad, what's going on? Are you trying to ditch me here or something? I mean—" she spoke through my protests "—it would make a great headline and a nice chapter in my memoirs and all, but I'd just as soon not be the girl who has to make her own way in the world after being left at a second-rate hotel in Winnemucca, Nevada."

I put my hand over my heart, offended. "You think this hotel is second-rate?"

It was the best flippant comment I could come up with on short notice, but it must have worked. Liv shook her head at me and fumbled in her pocket for her room swipe-key. "All right, Mr. I Don't Want to Spend the Evening in the Company of my Eccentric Sixteen-Year-Old Daughter. If you're gone for more than half an hour, I'm alerting police and local authorities and Mom. We'll put out a—what do you call it?— elder alert."

"Deal." Even though my entire body was on edge, and the few bites of French dip were threatening to make a reappearance, I grinned at her. *Everything's fine. Why wouldn't it be?* "Hey, I'm going to make sure you get in okay. Why don't you get into the room, look around and wave to me from the balcony. And I'll have my phone on, just in case."

She nodded slowly, then shut the door and walked away, her hands balled into fists, her fists crammed in her pockets. I tracked her all the way up the outside staircase and watched her use the swipe-key at the door. The interior light flicked on. A few seconds later she stepped back into the doorway. Instead of a wave, she gave me a military-style salute, turned on her heel and closed the door behind her.

It wasn't too late to back out of this. The words played like a broken record, stuck on the needle of my conscience. I could dial Zach Gaffaney's number and feed him some excuse about government surveillance and wiretapping. It wasn't too late to slide the gearshift into Park and head upstairs with the doggy bag of French dip I was never going to finish. Olivia and I could settle into our beds and watch some mindless TV together, like a dancing competition or a celebrity cook-off, things that were high stakes for other people, but not for us.

I could try again to forget Robert Saenz.

I'd almost managed to do it before, during his short prison tenure. And maybe I would succeed again, at least for a while.

But I knew he would always be there, in the wrinkles of my brain, waiting. As long as he was alive, I would think of him, the man responsible for the death of my son and the wide swath of destruction in its wake.

So long as he was alive.

What's your purpose in life? Bill Meyers had asked. And in my mind I'd answered, *To make things right. To kill Robert Saenz.*

I pulled over a block from the hotel and dialed Zach's number. The phone rang once, twice. Maybe he wouldn't be home, and I would have to call it off.

"Yeah?" It was the same suspicious voice, wary. What had happened to Zach Gaffaney that living in a trailer with all his guns was the life that made the most sense? Was he wondering what had gone wrong with me, for me to be making this call?

"It's...Curtis."

"You got the money?"

"Yes." My right hand went to my wallet, instinctively. It was fatter than normal, stuffed with twenties.

"Cash?"

"Yes."

"And you're alone?"

"I'm alone," I confirmed.

He gave me directions to his place on the outskirts of town, and as I drove, I wiped my clammy palms on my jeans. The night was clear, every branch and mailbox standing out in relief under a garish moon. The whole world was trying to get my attention: *This is real, this is no joke.* I glanced in my mirrors, half expecting lights behind me. Or maybe judgment would come from above—a single bolt of lightning out of a clear sky.

Zach was waiting for me, peeking out of his trailer to make sure I was alone. He took a half step onto a metal fold-down stair, looking twitchy and restless. I might not have recognized him—when he'd been with Marcia he had been more or less clean-shaven, even if he had preferred concert T-shirts and jeans with ragged hems. Now he wore camouflage pants and a stained wife beater, and his hair hung long down his back.

He held out a hand, palm up, and I passed him the wad from my pocket. He counted it slowly out loud.

I glanced around, but the nearest residence, another trailer, was at least a quarter mile down the road. I had been prepared to say no if asked inside, but Zach seemed as uneasy about having me there as I was uneasy to be there. For all I knew, his entire property was rigged with homemade explosives, ready to be detonated at the first sign of trouble.

He reached back through the open door into the trailer and came out with a revolver—a Colt .38 special, as we'd agreed. "It's loaded," he said, and I took the gun carefully, remembering the golden rule I'd learned in my research: keep your finger off the trigger and the gun is completely harmless. Again, I felt the shakiness in my hands and tried to hide it by stowing the gun in my waistband.

When I looked up, Zach was studying me, more relaxed now that the money was wedged deep in his pocket. "So, you're just passing through or what?"

"Yeah, passing through," I confirmed.

He seemed to consider me, more focused now. I wasn't sure if he remembered me from all those years before; he wasn't the only one who had changed. "Well, you take care," he said finally, and with a last look around, he vanished inside the trailer, the door slapping shut. He must have pressed a switch, because a second later the light outside his trailer was extinguished, and I had to stumble my way, half running, back to the Explorer.

It wasn't until I was back in the hotel parking lot that I gave into my fear, realizing how wrong things could have gone. I might have walked into some kind of sting, for example, with an entire SWAT team waiting for me at the other end. Zach might have been waiting to rob me, the unsuspecting moron who had shown up at a secluded location with hundreds of dollars in cash. Any number of things could have happened, and then Olivia would have been left in our hotel room, waiting, her anxiety escalating to full-blown panic.

But somehow, it had worked. I almost felt like laughing— this was exactly the sort of nightmare that gun control advocates worried about, if even an idiot like me could get his hands on a weapon.

Now I just had to get to Omaha, drop Olivia off safely and finally, be on my way.

olivia

In the morning Dad was awake before I was, showered and dressed and sipping coffee from a paper cup by the time I opened my eyes.

"Ready for some fun?"

"Um, no," I groaned, looking at the digital alarm clock on the nightstand. "It's only 7:45."

"Usually we're at school by now," he pointed out.

"But this is vacation. This is our grand *voyage*."

Dad rolled his eyes. "Still. Bus leaves in half an hour."

I struggled to a sitting position. "What bus?"

"It's an expression."

"I don't think that's an expression."

He sighed. "Just hurry up, Liv. I've got a surprise for you."

Grumbling, I dragged myself out of bed and began digging around in my suitcase, sorting my clothes into piles. I'd been living out of a suitcase for exactly one day, and already my whole world felt disorganized.

We were on the road by eight-thirty, an undigested, doughy cinnamon roll from the sorry-looking continental breakfast lodged awkwardly in my stomach. I dug in my backpack and came up with my Fear Journal, just so I could have it at the ready. I'd filled several pages last night, while Dad was "clearing his head," but he'd been back within a half hour, as promised, bearing his and hers giant blue slushies. We'd fallen asleep in front of an episode of *Law and Order: SVU* and I'd woken with an electric-blue tongue.

And now this, whatever *this* was. We passed Battle Mountain and Elko, the towns resting flat on the horizon, their buildings as small as doll furniture. I squinted into the distance, trying to figure it out. *Surprise! I'm leaving you in the middle of Nevada.* Or *Surprise! We're not going to Omaha at all. We're going to drive all the way to the East Coast to get some really great lobster.* Whatever he was thinking, Dad seemed more relaxed than he had yesterday, but more focused, too—like a ship captain following the route that had been charted for him.

Eventually, we took an exit marked by a small sign: Bonneville Salt Flats. I took off my headphones and sat up straight, paying attention as we drove north, the freeway behind us.

"Where are we going?"

"You'll see."

We went miles without passing another car. I looked at my cell phone: one single bar for reception. A mountain range was ahead of us; to the right was a vast, empty space that I realized must be the salt flats. The experience was freaky in an end-of-time sort of way, as if we were driving into a *Twilight Zone* version of our own world after it had been decimated by an asteroid or whatever it was that decimated entire worlds.

And then we turned right, down a skinny road that led to nowhere. The pavement stopped abruptly and all around us, as far as I could see, was a shimmering white sea of salt. Above us, the sky was so blue it made my eyes ache.

"What is this?"

Dad explained it to me: we were looking at the remnants of a massive salt lake, now a forty-mile stretch of land so desolate that it was used for setting land speed records. "That's later in the year, though—August, mainly. Right now we've pretty much got the place to ourselves. What do you think?"

"It's cool." It was a bit of an understatement for how vast the space was, how shiny and strange.

Dad slid the Explorer into Park and took the keys out of the ignition.

"What are you doing? We're getting out?"

He unbuckled his seat belt. "We're switching places. You're going to drive."

"Um, no. I'm not."

"Yeah, you are. Think about it, Olivia. There are no other cars out here, so you can't possibly bump into anyone. There's nothing for miles that you could crash into. You can go as slow or fast as you want. There are no lanes, no crappy drivers who don't use their blinkers. It's perfect."

I could see that these were excellent points, but I was shaking too hard to concede. "I don't know. I think I'm a better passenger than a driver."

"Well, let's find out." He used the lever on the bottom of his seat carefully, inching the seat forward to accommodate my height.

"But I don't have any training or anything."

Dad walked around the Explorer and tugged the passenger door open. "Let's go, Liv. The world is your salt flat."

I bit my lip. "Is that supposed to be funny?"

"Definitely not." He gestured over his shoulder to miles of glistening, empty white. "What could go wrong?"

"That's the last question to ask *me*," I said. "I'm the chief cataloguer of what can go wrong."

Dad waited.

"It is pretty," I conceded, stepping out of the car. Pea-sized pebbles of salt crunched beneath my feet like clumps of snow.

I took a few steps, digging the toes of my combat boots into the salt, and then picked up speed, breaking into an almost-run, sending salt flying like gravel. "Dad!" I called over my shoulder, the words reverberating off the flats.

For just a moment, I felt like a kid—a happy kid, the one I'd almost forgotten about, who had lived in my body before Daniel died.

"Liv! Catch!" Dad called suddenly, and I turned in time to see his key ring hurtling through the air in my general direction. I sighed, snagging the keys before they hit the ground.

We climbed back in the Explorer, and Dad talked me through it—foot on the brake, shift to Drive, ease onto the gas. We left the paved road and glided onto the flats, the tires slipping at first, skidding slightly before finding their traction.

It was the coolest and the scariest thing I'd ever done.

"Okay," Dad said, settling back for the ride. "Now don't be afraid to go more than ten miles an hour."

I felt his smile rather than saw it, since I didn't dare to look anywhere other than straight ahead. The Explorer was parallel to the freeway, which was just a tiny gray line in the distance. I took a deep breath, pressed down on the gas and just *drove*. The sun glinted off the salt, the whole valley a vast mirage of diamonds. Dad rolled down the windows and the air hit us, briny and sharp, the way wet beach towels smelled on the drive back from the ocean. My skin felt tingly and alive. I was having way too much fun to remember how terrified I was.

"Let her loose," Dad instructed, and I pushed down harder on the gas, squealing as the Explorer lost its footing and found it, digging eagerly into grooves of salt left by other drivers, releasing a reservoir of pent-up energy.

Tears gathered in the corner of my eyes, but I was laughing, too. I brought the speedometer up to eighty before I eased up on the gas and spun the car around in a wide, arcing turn. We lurched forward as the car came to a complete stop, but Dad was right—it didn't matter. There was just about nothing I could screw up here. There was no speed limit to break and, as long as I stayed clear of the mountains, nothing to brake for, either. There wasn't one single thing like a tree or a street sign that I could hit, not a single pedestrian in danger. And even though I was in the middle of nowhere, somehow it wasn't lonely at all. It was almost as if the whole universe had taken me into its arms and given me a big, gentle squeeze.

Let it go, Olivia. Let it go.

curtis

After her drive on the salt flats, Olivia was giddy, putting her feet up on the dashboard, even removing her seat belt for the quickest of moments to struggle out of the cocoon of her sweatshirt. One fear down. How many millions to go?

When we stopped for lunch and gassed the Explorer, she went inside the Quik Mart by herself and came out lugging a twenty-pound bag of charcoal, grinning. We stopped not far from the Metaphor Tree sculpture and made our own monument on the flat canvas of salt, while cars and tanker trucks whizzed by on I-80. First we wrote THE KAUFMANS, and then I stepped back to take some pictures while Olivia continued, adding each new piece of charcoal with studied precision. HERE IN SPIRIT, it said—"for Mom and Daniel," she explained.

I turned away, tears smarting in my eyes. *Remember this,* I wanted to tell her. Remember the way the lake reflects the mountains, a perfect doubling of the world. Remember everything good, so you can balance out the bad.

We spent the afternoon wandering around Salt Lake City and the evening in front of the TV with a cheese and extra pepperoni pizza. Olivia fell into a fully zonked-out, open-mouthed sleep, but I stayed awake for a long time, thinking of the gun and Robert Saenz.

In the morning we drove on, Salt Lake City disappearing in the rearview mirror. Olivia pronounced the barren landscape "vastly less interesting than yesterday" and retreated into the world of her black hoodie. As we crested a hill, the engine on the Explorer revved suddenly, the needle on the rpms shooting from 2 to 5 and sinking down again.

"Whoa," Olivia said, shucking off her headphones. "Is that supposed to happen?"

"I don't think so." I considered pulling over, but the Explorer kept right on churning along, ribbons of highway vanishing beneath our wheels and disappearing in the rearview mirror. I shrugged. "Seems to be fine."

Olivia fished between the seats and pulled out the atlas. "Where are we stopping tonight?"

"Cheyenne."

I watched as she creased the pages open at Wyoming and traced her finger along the red line of the interstate. "So, we're only two away right now, and tomorrow we'll only be one away."

"Days, you mean?"

"I mean states. We're two away."

"By that logic, we're only three away from Canada, and seven or eight away from the East Coast."

"Why don't we go there afterward?" Olivia asked. "We could stop in Omaha for a while, and then keep going to somewhere, like, I don't know, Atlantic City. Or one of those tiny little islands off the coast of Maine."

"Right," I said, anything more frozen in my throat. When we reached Omaha, I would be leaving without her, sneaking off late after she and Kathleen had settled in or early, while they were still asleep, when Kathleen's breath was coming out in her soft, sighing snore, when Olivia's face was buried between two pillows. When they woke, I would be gone.

We were only two away from Kathleen now, which meant that I was only four or five, at the most, away from Robert Saenz. The mile markers along I-80 had been slowly ticking off our progress, one tiny green rectangle after another. Two more nights in hotels, maybe six more stops for gas and bathroom and prepackaged convenience fare: packets of chili-lime peanuts, giant cinnamon-sugar-covered muffins, sodas in Styrofoam cups. Two more continental breakfasts, two more fast-food lunches, two more dinners at diners, unless we made good time to Omaha and ate that last meal at Kathleen's.

It was going too slow and going incredibly fast, both at once.

And then, like a practical application of Murphy's Law, the Explorer did this weird chugging kind of thing and lurched forward, then choked, then lurched again.

Olivia said, "Um…"

We were going up a hill, if you could call it that. It was more like a gentle rise, not a serious climb like the one just outside Salt Lake City, but for some reason the Explorer staggered forward, as if out of gas, or maybe out of breath. I steered to the side of the road and came to a stop. The car was still running, but nothing happened when I put my foot on the gas. After a moment, I turned off the ignition.

We were quiet for a stunned moment, and then Olivia chirped, "Now we just have to wait for that nice gentleman from the Motor Club to show up."

I raised an eyebrow.

"*Groundhog Day,* remember? We must have watched that a dozen times together."

I chuckled, and then, letting the absurdity of the situation sink in, I threw back my head and laughed.

We were in the middle of nowhere. Traffic whizzed past on the freeway, going far too fast to stop. Mostly these were trucks, speeding onward, needing to make good time on the road. When people talked about population explosions and a lack of available land, etc., they were clearly discounting eastern Utah and western Wyoming. It was miles of nothing, as far as the eye could see.

"Okay," I announced. "I'm just letting the engine relax for a minute, and then I'll start her up again."

"Is that a proven mechanic's technique, letting the engine 'relax'?"

"I know very little about proven mechanic techniques." In fact, there were exactly four things I knew how to do to a car: replace the battery, fix a flat, jump-start an engine and change the oil. Somehow, I suspected this was a more complicated problem.

Olivia nodded gravely. "Sounds like a good enough technique to me, though."

"Here goes. One, two..." On three, I turned the key in the ignition, the engine started, and I turned to grin at Olivia. "See? It just needed to relax." I grasped the gearshift, shifting from Park to Drive, and gave the car a little gas. Nothing. I tried again. Nothing.

"I can't help but notice that we're not moving," Olivia commented.

I turned off the engine, turned it on, went nowhere and repeated the process once again. "Well, kiddo," I said. "Time for Plan B."

Olivia reached into her backpack, rustled around and came up with her Fear Journal.

"What are you going to write? 'Breaking down in the middle of nowhere'?"

She didn't look up. "That and getting picked up by a seemingly normal rancher who turns out to be a psychotic killer who hangs his victims upside down in his basement until the blood drains completely out of their bodies."

I wanted to say something funny like *That's exactly what I'm afraid of,* but Olivia was actually writing this down, her brows narrowing with focus. "Geez, Liv," I said and, releasing my seat belt, stepped out of the car. It was sunny, but the air was crisp. I pulled out my cell phone. No bars. Twenty paces ahead, at the crest of the hill, I finally got some reception. After some consideration, I dialed 9-1-1. It didn't seem like an emergency, exactly, but I wasn't sure what else to do. If Kathleen were here, she would have located our AAA card by now. Of course, Kathleen would also have renewed the membership when it expired, and I hadn't bothered.

"Dad?" Olivia was standing behind me, her arms tucked into the body of her sweatshirt, the sleeves flapping loose. I held up a finger to quiet her while I talked to the dispatcher.

When I finished, I slipped my phone back into my pocket and repeated the news. "Someone's coming to tow us to Lyman," I said.

"What's Lyman?"

"Nearest town, I guess."

Olivia frowned. "I haven't seen any signs for Lyman."

"That's because psychotic killers who hang their victims upside down prefer to keep their locations anonymous."

"Dad!"

We waited on the side of the road for about forty-five minutes, me pacing in front of the car and Olivia sitting inside it, probably thinking of more ways this could turn out badly. She didn't even know the worst of it, that there was a revolver wrapped in one of my T-shirts and wedged tightly into the spare tire compartment, where I had been planning to keep it until Oberlin. This problem with the Explorer, whatever it was, threw a wrench into my plan. I didn't have a holster; I hadn't exactly been planning to walk around with a revolver tucked into my waistband. Could I leave the gun in the car, and leave the car in someone else's hands?

"How long has it been?" Olivia called. "Maybe they've forgotten about us."

Just then a car passed us slowly and pulled over to offer help. It was an older couple; whatever they could offer probably wasn't going to get the Explorer back on the road. I urged them on with a friendly wave.

"You were our last hope!" Olivia yelled after them mournfully through the open window.

"You know," I told her, "It could be worse."

"Of course it could. We could be in the middle of the Mojave when it was a hundred-and-thirty degrees."

"Or a massive snowstorm."

"Tornado."

"Wildfire."

"And I could have finished my Big Gulp already."

"And the gas station could have been out of apple-cinnamon muffins," I added.

"And no cell service. That was the problem with the Donner Party right there, wasn't it? They took their trip about a hundred and fifty years too early."

"If only they could have held out for a bit longer," I said, and Olivia doubled over in her seat, cracking up.

I laughed, too, in tight little barks. The more we waited, the more nervous I became. What was I going to do with the gun? If the car was towed away, someone else might find it, steal it, use it. One phone call to law enforcement and my plan to arrive in Oberlin would be an unequivocal failure. I walked around to the back of the Explorer, popping the latch and staring into our mess. Only two days on the road, and somehow the zipper tab on my suitcase had disappeared. Yesterday's clothes were now balled-up in a mesh laundry bag. My lone tennis shoe, its mate out of sight, probably accounted for the tumbling sound I heard whenever we took a corner. Olivia's textbooks, all untouched, littered the floor.

"You think you can fix it from back there?" Liv called over her shoulder.

"Very funny. Just trying to straighten up a bit." When I was sure she was looking the other way, I pulled up the floorboard and peeked into the spare tire well. Zach Gaffaney had handed the gun to me, loaded; I'd removed the cartridges, figuring if I was found with an unloaded weapon it would be better than being found with a loaded weapon. I'd stowed the cartridges carefully, out of Olivia's sight, and promised myself not to touch the gun until I was in Oberlin. Even unloaded and wrapped in my T-shirt, the gun managed to terrify me— it was unregistered, illegal, recently transported across state lines. But could I leave my unregistered, illegal handgun in the hands of a mechanic, even if there was no need to poke around in my spare tire well? Desperate, I entertained the idea of ditching the gun along the side of the road now and somehow doubling back to get it later.

"Dad?"

I stood up too quickly, cracking the top of my head against the roof of the car and followed her trembling, pointed finger. A tow truck had passed us, was slowly backing up on the side of the road. Leave it to Liv to be terrified of the one person who could actually rescue us. "Get your stuff ready," I called to her, unwrapping the Colt and wedging it inexpertly in my waistband, where I hoped it was hidden by the untucked hem of my shirt.

The tow truck driver was huge—six-five easily, with a stomach that hung over his belt. "Raymond Ellis," he boomed, stepping out of the truck. "What have we got here?"

"I'm Curtis Kaufman," I said, coming around from the back of the car. I'd figured the Colt would be small enough to conceal, but now I wondered if I'd only been kidding myself. Was it obvious I was carrying a weapon? Did it stick out like a sore thumb? I cleared my throat. "Well, the engine starts up fine, but then that's it."

"Could be a lot of things. Radiator, transmission…"

I described our sudden acceleration just outside of Salt Lake City, more than an hour ago now.

Raymond whistled. It wasn't warm, but he was sweating, the way big guys did. "Could be the transmission, then. Anyway, looks like you'll be needing a tow. Someone's going to have to look at her."

Olivia had come up behind me, silent as a thief. I felt, rather than heard or saw, her presence. She was probably assessing Raymond Ellis's height and weight, trying to figure out the level of threat he posed, or how the two of us might be able to overpower him, if needed.

"What are my options?" I asked. I was doing some calculations of my own—"transmission" had a frighteningly expensive ring to it.

Raymond shook his head a bit. "Well, back to Salt Lake City might be best. Course, that's a ways in the other direction. You've got Cheyenne about three, four hours east. Closest option would be Lyman, maybe ten minutes down the road."

"There's a mechanic in Lyman? And services? Because we would probably have to spend the night."

Raymond considered. "Sure—it's got all the services you

would need. Motel, restaurant, the works. Best mechanic in all of Wyoming is in Lyman."

I raised an eyebrow. "Is that right?"

Raymond grinned. "Well, I oughta know. He's my brother."

A few minutes later, Raymond had the front end of the Explorer off the ground, and Olivia and I were wedged into the front seat of the tow truck, with Olivia's knees angled sharply toward mine and away from the driver's seat.

"This is the time for you to say I told you so," I prompted, but Olivia only shook her head. She wasn't one to gloat, especially in the worst of circumstances. In fact, she looked more than slightly miserable, her face tucked deep into the recesses of her black hoodie.

Raymond, finished with whatever SUV-wrangling needed to be done, hopped back into the cab and fastened his seat belt. "Next stop Lyman, Wyoming," he announced, and the truck lurched forward.

olivia

Lyman, Wyoming, might be the last place on earth that anyone would want to get stranded. At least that's what I was thinking—but as we passed the trailers on the outskirts of town and houses and businesses along the main drag, I realized that some people had chosen to be stranded here, and I ordered myself not to be such a snob.

Dad had assumed a false, nervous cheerfulness, as if he were thrilled by this *new experience*. It was the same sort of fake cheerfulness I'd received from the school secretary when I started my period in the sixth grade, right in the middle of a math test. She'd been absurdly excited for me, producing an alarming array of feminine products from her bottom desk drawer, as if the arrival of my period were the *best thing ever*. Anyway, that's how Dad was talking about Lyman, as if we'd stumbled on one of America's best-kept secrets: the small town in the middle of nowhere.

"Look, they've even got a bank," Dad said, pointing out the window at a tiny storefront.

"Last bank until you hit Green River," Raymond acknowledged proudly.

"And I've seen at least two restaurants," Dad said.

I'd seen them, too. A pizza parlor and a Taco Time, as well as a few other places boasting "Restaurant" and "Saloon" and "Diner"—no other explanation needed. We passed the fire department, the Church of Jesus Christ of Latter Day Saints, the Uinta County Library.

"Up ahead a bit's another diner," Raymond said. "Closed Sundays, though."

"Is today Sunday?" I asked, incredulous. Our trip had a timeless quality to it, as if we were driving and time was passing, but everything around us was standing still. Or maybe it was the opposite—we were standing still, but everything else was advancing into the future. Either way, the sync was definitely off.

But then Dad said, "It's Wednesday," and I felt relieved.

"There's the hotel," Raymond gestured, slowing for a turn.

I blinked. He must have meant *motel*—The Drift Inn was a single-story structure, with its few rooms laid out in a short row. There were only three cars in the parking lot. It looked cheerful enough, with bright blue trim and white siding, but I had to fight down the urge to grab for my Fear Journal and scribble down *Bates Motel knockoff*. If I had gone insane and was going to store my dead mother somewhere indefinitely, this might be just the place. Our brightly lit, national chain lodgings in Winnemucca and Salt Lake City seemed like a distant dream.

"I'm sure that will be fine," Dad said, rather optimistically, I thought. It was as if he'd lost the use of advanced vocabulary and could no longer summon appropriate adjectives. Not *fine*, I thought. Not even adequate or sufficient or acceptable.

We pulled into a gravel lot that faced a building with a faded sign: J & E Automotive. There were a few other cars in the lot, rusted-out and in various stages of disrepair. It was like car purgatory—where cars that had been less than perfect during their lives went when they died.

Dad hopped out of the truck, and I slid out, and then Raymond Ellis maneuvered our Explorer into one of three empty garage bays. *Stop being scared,* I ordered myself, even though this was a strategy that never worked. *It doesn't matter that you're in the literal middle of nowhere without any transportation—you're going to be fine.*

Dad disappeared into the tiny front office of J & E Automotive, the glass door swinging shut behind him.

"Fine! I'll wait outside!" I called, to the listening ears of no one.

The auto shop was just off Lyman's main street, but I saw few signs of life. In one direction was a neat row of homes, each with a massive satellite dish in the front yard, or peeking out from the backyard, or mounted to the roof. Lyman took its TV-watching very seriously. It wasn't even noon, but the whole place was *Twilight-Zone* quiet. I half expected a tumbleweed to come rolling down the road in a cloud of dust. Instead, a compact car drove by, slowing while its single occupant stared at me, and speeding up again to head out of town.

"Hey," someone called, the voice too nearby for comfort.

I whirled around, trying to remember my self-defense training—the single useful thing that came out of my two botched attempts at P.E. *SING—Solar plexus, Instep, Nose, Groin.* It was a very useful acronym, although I'd forgotten how to put it into practice. What was a solar plexus again?

"Sorry, didn't mean to scare you." The guy who was suddenly standing next to me was about my height—which is to say, sort of short for a guy—with shaggy blond hair that covered most of his face. He was wearing an oversize black T-shirt with a picture of a bone and the words "I Found This Humerus."

"Where did you come from?" I demanded. I looked toward the office of J & E Automotive, wondering if my dad was watching me. *He should be,* I thought. He should be watching right now, ready to charge toward me if this guy made so much as a single move. But of course, he wouldn't be. He would be facing the other direction entirely, talking to someone behind a counter or signing a form in triplicate. It was amazing how oblivious he was to obvious dangers.

"Over there," the guy said, pointing. Just beyond the parking lot, I spotted a tiny roadside stand, which was basically a couple of folding tables and a metal chair beneath a faded beach umbrella.

"Oh," I said, glancing back to the office of J & E Automotive.

He tossed his hair away from his face. "You want to see what I'm selling?"

I looked at him just long enough to notice that his eyes were a greenish-blue, like seawater. "Sorry, I don't have any money." That was a lie, though—I had the change from our last convenience-store purchase in my jeans pocket, and it burned there like a shameful secret.

"You don't have to buy anything. I just wanted to show you."

"Well, thanks," I said, "but I'm waiting for my dad. He's probably going to come out any second now."

"I doubt that." He laughed. "That's my stepdad's shop. He likes to get all the facts about the cars he works on, kind of like a medical history."

I hesitated.

"It's like, literally, fifty feet away," he said.

"Um…" I felt like telling him that I hate it when people say *literally.* They never actually mean literally. In this case, it was at least a hundred feet away, so literally *not* fifty feet away, and out of view of the office entirely.

"I don't bite," he said, sounding hurt.

I gave a last glance in the direction of my absentee father and surrendered with a shrug. We walked side by side, falling into the same pace, the way you can with someone who is exactly your height.

"So you're from California," he said, and I looked up, alarmed.

"How do you know that?"

"It's on your license plate. Shit. Are you always so jumpy?"

"Yes," I admitted.

"What do you think I'm going to do to you?"

I had a thousand smart-ass answers running through my mind, the vocabulary of someone who knows that bad things can happen at any moment, at any time, to any person. *Thank you, Daniel, for this, the most important lesson of my childhood.* "I don't know. I don't know anything about you," I said finally.

"Well, I'm Sam, for starters. Sam Ellis." He was grinning, and I let myself relax a bit. It seemed unlikely that his grin—part sheepish, part amused—was going to precede any overt violence.

"So, what are you selling?" I asked, even though we were standing right in front of the folding tables at this point, and the answer should have been obvious. One table was strewn with a hodgepodge of secondhand objects, your typical garage-sale fare: paperbacks with cracked spines, mismatched glassware, a VHS copy of *The Breakfast Club,* a sparkly evening clutch that was missing a number of beads. I picked up one of the books—*The Jungle* by Upton Sinclair—flipped through a few pages, and set it down, feeling very glad that I'd lied about having any money.

"Oh, this and that. These are just things I've found," he said, proudly emphasizing the word. "Things that still have some use in them, but people have just thrown out. It's amazing the things people throw out. You wouldn't believe."

I ran a finger over the beaded evening clutch. I could imagine someone throwing it out, actually, since it seemed beyond repair. Worse, it was too brittle—another bead rolled away when it came in contact with my finger. The next table held a dozen or so snow globes, the kind that usually made an appearance in department stores around Christmas, with happy little scenes of European villages or little towns in Vermont under a gentle snowfall. I leaned down for a closer look. "What are these?"

He beamed. "That's what I wanted you to see. This is what I do. This is my art."

I bent down, getting a closer look. "You made these?"

"Yep. I'm working on another one right now. Well, the idea for it, I mean. That's half the trouble, getting the concept right."

My nose about level with the table, I could see that each of the snow globes held delicate figures, tiny people and buildings and plant life, each intricately assembled out of minuscule scraps of wood, fabric and leaves. I picked one up, holding it closer to my eye.

He toggled back and forth from one foot to another, like a nervous toddler. "Can you guess what that one is?"

"What do you mean, what it is?"

"Well, what do you see?"

I looked closely. Tiny blue-clad figures, about a quarter of an inch tall, were facing a large rock castle. A red flag waved from the battlement. "I'm not sure."

He looked disappointed. "It's the storming of the Bastille. You know, the French Revolution?"

"Oh, sure. Now that you say it..." I tilted the snow globe,

letting a few flakes tumble, then tipped it all the way over, so that a light, glittery dusting of snow fell over the French Revolution. It was strangely beautiful. "This is really great," I told him, honestly. "I've never seen anything like this."

He pointed down the row of snow globes, identifying them for me. "These are the historical ones—I have the bombing of Hiroshima, the Valentine's Day Massacre, the Christmas Day tsunami…"

I shivered. His designs were beautiful, but awful, too, full of the kinds of things I saw on the History Channel and then wrote down in my Fear Journal, things that were almost too horrible to name, let alone visualize. I squinted at another globe, which had some tiny figures lying on the ground next to empty half-bushels. "What's this?"

"Forced famine in Ukraine."

"Oh." I felt a bit sick. "Do you sell a lot of these?"

"Well, I've only sold one so far, although I've had a few people interested. The trouble is, sometimes people want to buy one, and all of a sudden I realize that I can't possibly sell it. I start to worry that, like, it won't go to a good home, to someone who would really appreciate it. You know?"

"Sure." Even considering the limited population that could appreciate a miniature tableau of an unspeakable tragedy, the purchase would be problematic. Where exactly could it be displayed—on a mantel or a nightstand, on top of a media console, next to the flat-screen TV? "Maybe they're more like museum pieces," I offered. "I mean, isn't *Guernica* one of the most famous paintings in the world? But not many people would want it in their homes."

"I see your point. I do see your point." Sam was nodding seriously, as if my opinion held incredible value. Then he brightened. "But if there was something you wanted, something not so bleak maybe, I could make it for you. I could do that on a special request."

I smiled, trying to diffuse his eagerness gently. "I don't think I'm going to be here very long, though."

As if on cue, I heard my dad holler, "Olivia!"

"That's my dad." I gestured back toward the storefront. "I'd better go. Um, thanks for showing me…"

"That's your name? Olivia?"

"Yeah."

He smiled, hair flopping again in front of his eyes. "Olivia. I like that."

I turned away, but I could feel him watching me. It was an uncomfortable feeling, but not necessarily uncomfortable in a bad way.

"And I'm Sam," he called after me. "In case you forgot. I'm Sam Ellis."

curtis

"So?" Olivia asked, coming toward me.

I nodded at the boy beneath the beach umbrella who was openly staring at us. "I see you made a friend."

"I'm fine, by the way," Olivia snapped, ignoring my comment. "No one managed to snatch me off the side of the road while you were gone."

I looked down the road, which showed few signs of life. "Liv, of course you're fine."

"What's going on with the car?"

I repeated what Jerrod Ellis, brother of Raymond and sole proprietor of J & E Automotive, had told me, with all the gravity of a surgeon notifying the family. "It's the transmission."

Olivia said, "That's bad, right? The transmission?"

I nodded.

"I mean, expensive," she clarified.

"It's not your job to worry about that."

"I worry about everything, remember?"

"Not this," I told her. "This one is solely my territory."

A new transmission, Jerrod Ellis had informed me, wiping his hands against his work pants, would cost a thousand at the least. A rebuilt transmission was cheaper, but would take longer—it would be a day before he could get the parts from Rawlins. It was our only real option, save for abandoning the trip entirely and settling down in Lyman—which may have been the fate of the drivers of the rusted-out cars at the front of the property. When I leaned against the counter to sign the triplicate form, the handle of the Colt had dug into my paunch. If it wasn't for Olivia, I would have been on the next bus out of Lyman, Oberlin in my sights.

"So." Olivia dug in the dirt with the toe of her combat boot. "Now what?"

"Now we settle in. We're going to be here for a couple days, at least."

"Days?" Olivia echoed doubtfully, casting a glance down the street. I could see what she was thinking—a couple of days *here?*

"It's okay. We're not in any hurry." Saying this, I almost convinced myself. What were a few more days, after I'd been waiting four years? Robert Saenz had a few more days of life, liberty, and the pursuit of whatever happiness he could find at the bottom of a pill bottle.

"I guess." She looked down at the small mountain of dirt she had displaced. It was kind of her not to point out that our options were extremely limited.

While Olivia unloaded her belongings from the trunk, I sat in the driver's seat, pretending to gather a few bits of trash. I ran a hand beneath the seat to where I'd stashed the six bullets, and one came loose, dropping into the palm of my hand. I froze.

"We'll need the laundry bag, right?" Olivia called.

"Right."

There was no time to retape the cartridge, so I slid it into the pocket of my jeans, where it made a small clink against my loose change. I looked up to see Olivia balancing her pillow

on top of her suitcase. The boy she had been talking to earlier was still staring at us from his seat behind a rickety folding table. I nodded to him.

"You need a ride?" he called. "I could take you to the motel.
That's my truck."

Olivia looked at me.

"We'd appreciate it," I called, and he ambled over to help
us with our bags.

"I'm Sam Ellis," he said, shaking my hand. "That's my dad
you were talking to, Jerrod. Well, stepdad." Even if there
wasn't a biological connection, Sam had the same confident
handshake. He loaded our bags into the back of his pickup in
two fluid movements. Since he barely came up to my shoulder, I realized I'd probably mistaken him for being younger
than he actually was. Up close, he looked more like twenty
than Olivia's age.

"You're just going to leave everything out there?" Olivia
asked, indicating the card tables.

Sam shrugged. "Not a lot of theft around here. And not
too many suspects, either."

Olivia pressed up against me as she had in the tow truck, her
knees angled to avoid the gearshift and, I suspected, Sam Ellis.
She braced herself against me as we made the few turns and I
flinched, hoping she hadn't noticed the hard body of the Colt.

What the hell was I doing, riding around with my daughter,
a young man and a gun in the middle of nowhere? With every
moment that passed, what I had long suspected was becoming
incontrovertibly true: there were two kinds of people in the
world, and I was the kind that didn't like guns. I was no Zach
Gaffaney, comfortably at home amid dozens of loaded weap-
ons. With Olivia's body bumping up against mine, the gun
felt like a huge mistake. Only a giant red Bozo wig or one of
those flowing black capes worn by some of Olivia's friends, the

Visigoths, would have made me feel more conspicuous right then. Yes, I'd determined that in order to do what I was going to do, I needed a gun—but actually having one made me feel less, not more, safe. I might as well have had sticks of dynamite strapped to my chest.

"So, you're going to be in town for a few days, then?" Sam asked, startling us out of our silence. I'd been staring out the window, noticing again the restaurants I'd spotted earlier, a small convenience store, window displays in need of some updating. The question, I knew, wasn't directed toward me.

"I think so," Olivia said, looking down at her lap. She was rolling the hem of her sweatshirt back and forth between two fingers.

"Maybe, um…" Sam began, and then stopped. I glanced at him; his entire neck and face were flushed as red as a sunburn. "I mean if…maybe…"

His voice trailed off, and the pickup slowed for a turn into the parking lot of The Drift Inn. I counted eight rooms in a single row, backing up against a field of scrub brush that would soon break away into tumbleweeds. I tried to pretend that this field was very interesting, that it required my attention and concentration. The truck was in Park now, the engine idling, but still Sam hadn't found a way to finish his sentence.

I expected Olivia to have some excuse at the ready, since she could surely see where this conversation was leading. But then I realized she was looking up at me, expecting me to say something. I cleared my throat, choosing my words. He seemed like a nice enough kid, and I didn't want to crush him too flat.

But Olivia surprised me. Quietly, so that I almost couldn't hear, she said, "I would love to."

olivia

When Sam knocked on our motel door at seven-thirty, he was wearing the same shirt with the "humerus" joke under an oversize flannel jacket. "What's in there?" he asked, spotting the backpack on my shoulder.

"Nothing, just stuff." Actually, it held my phone, which Dad had programmed with local emergency numbers for Lyman and the surrounding county; an extra sweatshirt in case my giant hoodie wasn't enough; a chocolate bar that I could break into pieces and ration in case I got stranded alone in the wilderness for days; my Fear Journal and a couple of pens. In case Sam turned out to be someone horrible and dangerous, I could stab him with the pen, call the authorities and be warm and reasonably well-fed when they arrived.

Sam was smiling at me and I smiled back at him sheepishly. It wasn't exactly the premise for a lovely first date.

Dad asked Sam, "Where are you taking her?" as if this were the most ordinary thing in the world, that a boy I'd met only a few hours earlier, who I knew next to nothing about except that he made snow globe art of the great human tragedies, was going to take me on a date. I was surprised both that I'd said yes and that Dad hadn't said no—not that I'd absolutely wanted him to.

"Just…dinner, and a drive around town," Sam told him, and then to me, "If you're only going to be in Lyman for a short while, there are some things you definitely have to see while you're here."

This made me think of the *New York Times* travel section, back when Mom was home and her favorite thing in the whole world was to drink her way through a pot of coffee while reading the Sunday paper. No matter that we didn't live anywhere near New York, or that she'd only been there one time in her life. She particularly loved the travel section, with its practical articles informing people how to spend three days in Cozumel, or eighteen hours in Bangkok, places where she would probably never find herself. Maybe I could pitch this idea to the travel editor of the *Times:* Three Days in Lyman, Wyoming. Agenda for Day One: Break down on I-80. Get towed into town for expensive repair. Meet strange boy who makes even stranger art. Dinner with said boy. Take in the sights.

Dad said, "She needs to be back by ten sharp. Not ten-oh-two, not ten-oh-one. Ten o'clock. Got it?"

Sam nodded seriously. He didn't seem nervous at all, but why should he be? There was nothing particularly threatening about either me or Dad, who was fiddling with the remote. He'd already dismissed us. He was probably going to spend the night in front of the TV in his sweatpants, glad for the time without me.

"We're synchronizing watches right now," I said, amazed at how glib I sounded when my whole body was a quaking mess of nerves. Was I actually going on a date? With a person I had known for about five whole minutes?

Sam opened the passenger door of his pickup for me, and I scrambled up into the seat, hoping my jerky movements somehow looked cool. As I was fastening my seat belt, I saw Dad's face at the window, a pale oval. I gave him the A-OK sign with my thumb and forefinger, but he didn't react. I had the unsettling feeling that what he was seeing wasn't what was actually in front of him. Maybe the danger wasn't me going on a date, but leaving Dad by himself.

"Where are we going, exactly?" I asked as Sam turned left onto the main road, heading away from town. I wondered if I'd made some massive miscalculation. I suddenly remembered an episode of *Criminal Minds* where the serial killer had a clear advantage since he knew the terrain like the back of his hand, and the Behavioral Analysis Unit was left to try to triangulate his movements through a complicated series of computer commands. How long would it take the BAU, working with local law enforcement, to locate one tiny me in the vastness of the Wyoming landscape?

I flinched when Sam spoke. "What?"

"I said it was going to be a surprise. What are you so afraid of, anyway?"

I shrugged, my code for a question too complicated to answer.

"Well, don't worry. You're completely safe. I packed us a dinner—" he indicated a cooler tethered to the trunk of his pickup, something I'd failed to notice until that point "—and I'm going to take you to one of my favorite places."

"We're going on a picnic?" I asked. It was barely fifty degrees. Thank goodness I'd brought the extra sweatshirt.

"It's going to be great. So, Olivia. Where in California are you from?"

I relaxed a bit, telling him our story—or an edited version, at least. I left out the complicated facts of a dead brother and a father who may or may not have been planning to jump from the roof of the school cafeteria, but mentioned that we were going to see my mother in Omaha. Sam was a steady driver, shifting gears smoothly, keeping his eyes on the road—except for when he was glancing at me. I was glad for the dark, since my face felt warm.

Soon Lyman was behind us, and we were on a single-lane road, paved but only barely, like some kind of Depression-era WPA project that had been neglected ever since. Sam had slowed down, and we were barely crawling through the sparse landscape. The headlights illuminated only the area immediately in front of us, so rocks and shrubs appeared in brief flashes and disappeared into the darkness.

"What about you?" I asked, my voice spilling into the silence.

"Well, my parents are divorced, too," he began.

I didn't correct him. Most people I knew thought that my parents were divorced. It seemed kind of lame to protest, "Just because they live thousands of miles apart and refuse to talk to each other, doesn't mean they're not still married." They might as well have been divorced, even if it wasn't written on any official document.

Sam, it turned out, had just turned nineteen, although he'd finished with high school two years earlier, dropping out and doing what he called a "GED-type thing." He was taking classes right now online, and maybe in a year or two he would go to Laramie, to the University of Wyoming. Or maybe not, because he wasn't sure exactly what he wanted to study, and besides, he said, he wanted to give his art a chance to really take off. He lived with his stepdad, did oil changes at the shop. His mom lived in Cheyenne with his ten-year-old brother, who he only saw a few times a year, a side effect of what had been an ugly divorce.

"Do you miss him a lot—your brother?"

Sam was wistful. "I've been thinking about him lately. Like, maybe I should just drive over there once in a while and hang out with him."

"You should," I told him. "You absolutely should." I started to say "My brother..." but my throat constricted, and whatever I was going to say came out like a little squeak instead. I gave a weak cough to cover it.

We slowed further, and I realized we weren't even on a road anymore. My heart started hammering again, and I wished I had packed one of those when-all-hell-breaks-loose survival handbooks. Dad had bought me one for Christmas because I'd pestered him endlessly. We'd taken turns reading from the book over our holiday break. Dad had found the advice to be hysterical, but it had all seemed incredibly practical to me.

"Just a little farther," Sam said.

The ground had been basically flat for the most part, but when we turned to the right, I saw we were heading toward a raised outcropping of rock. Sam pulled up as close as he could and gestured with his head. "Here we are."

I looked at him doubtfully. "We're going up there?"

"Yep." He hopped out of the truck and began to maneuver the cooler out of the back. "Grab those blankets, okay?"

"Sure." The *blankets*. I found a stack of old quilts, battered but soft. Sam was already ahead of me, starting toward the rock. "I have a great fear of climbing rocks," I said, but quietly enough so that he wouldn't hear me. It wasn't really a climb, though; it was more of a steep walk. Sam reached out a hand to help me steady myself, and I thought: *I'm holding hands, sort of, with a person who doesn't know the first thing about me.* Okay—the first things, maybe, but that was it. Sam's hand felt like the exact right size for a hand to be.

When we made it to the top, Sam dropped my hand and gestured around. "Top of the world," he said, grinning.

We were only about ten feet off the ground—high enough

so that a person with a mildish fear of heights would take notice—on a smooth, level surface of reddish rock. It occurred to me then, as Sam spread out a blanket, that we were miles from any kind of civilization or streetlight, and yet it wasn't completely dark. I looked up and saw stars that were intensely, almost cartoonishly, bright.

"Whoa," I breathed, craning my neck backward.

"It's cool, huh?"

"Very cool." I settled onto the blanket and leaned back, propping myself up by my elbows. "I don't ever think I've seen the sky like this. Or maybe I just haven't noticed it."

"Too many lights around, maybe," Sam said, easing himself down next to me. I wasn't looking at him, but I could feel his nearness, his thigh practically touching mine. "Even in Lyman, small as it is, there are too many streetlights. It makes the sky seem kind of hazy."

"I don't really know what I'm looking at," I confessed. "I mean, the moon, sure. And three stars in a row—that's Orion's Belt."

He leaned closer, pointing so that his arm reached across my body. "Over there, you'll see Sirius—the Dog Star, brightest star in the sky. That's what people used to navigate with by night in the ancient world, when they were on the sea or in the desert and didn't have other landmarks to go by."

"Or GPS," I breathed, my entire body on alert. "I gotta figure the ancients would have killed for GPS." I giggled nervously at my own joke, but Sam continued, extremely serious.

"And, yeah, over there, of course, you see the handle of the Big Dipper."

I followed his gesture. "Like a giant measuring cup in the sky."

"You're funny," he said, but he wasn't laughing, or even cracking a smile. I know this, because his face suddenly seemed very close to mine, and I thought if I concentrated hard enough, I might hear his heart beating alongside mine. It was cold, and in a few minutes I would probably need to put on the other sweatshirt, but right then my whole body felt embarrassingly hot. If I leaned even slightly to the side, our faces would be right next to each other.

"I'm not going to kiss you," I said suddenly, my heart thumping.

He was quiet for a moment, and I knew that I'd blown it. What an idiot I was, how ungrateful and inconsiderate. He'd shown me his art, he'd given Dad and me a ride to our motel, he'd brought me to one of the most amazing places on earth, he'd shown no signs of being a creepy serial killer, and besides, I realized as soon as I said that, I *did* want to kiss him—I was just more or less terrified of it. My experience with kissing was embarrassingly slim.

"Oh," Sam said, sounding wounded. "You mean ever, or just right now?"

"Fair question." I laughed. "Right now, I guess."

"That's cool," he said, and we leaned back to look at the stars.

curtis

Alone in the motel room, with the door locked and the shades pulled, I went right for the gun. I was going to confront Robert Saenz in a few days, so I needed to be ready. This was my first free moment without Olivia since buying the gun.

I'd watched a few how-to videos, although on the three-inch screen of my cell phone most of the details were too small to fully appreciate. Along with the lineup of prime time police dramas, this was the extent of my experience with guns. We'd never been gun people. Mention the NRA at a cocktail party, and Kathleen practically had to be restrained; it went without saying that there wasn't a gun in our house.

Until that night at Zach Gaffaney's trailer, the last time I'd touched a gun had been close to forty years ago, a one-time hunting excursion with my dad and a buddy of his, somewhere northwest of Chicago, and that had been a shotgun, of course. Dad had shown me how to hold it, how to sight along the barrel, but he'd been the one who fired. The rabbit had been bounding along, but then it stopped, ears alert, and a second later it was nothing more than a smear of blood

and fur against the snow. Forty years later and the memory
still made me sick.

But that rabbit had been innocent, and Robert Saenz was
not.

My hands were shaking as I took the single bullet from my
pocket. The Colt wasn't a complicated piece of equipment,
but I fumbled pulling back the latch and pushing the cylinder to the side, and my hands sweated as I inserted the bullet into the chamber and then popped the cylinder back into
place. How did criminals do this? How were they so sure of
their movements, their aim? I reversed the motions, tipping
the bullet into my palm, then reloaded, unloaded.

I didn't have a human silhouette as a target, but I picked a
nail hole on the wall and dry fired, imagining Robert Saenz's
face as I'd seen it in his mug shot—the jowls, the bloodshot
eyes looking at nothing. I moved closer, fired at what I figured would be his chest. It would be at close range. Robert
Saenz would see me, would know who I was and what I was
going to do. I could only fire six rounds with the Colt, but
this wasn't real yet, and in the silence of the motel room, I
could take all the shots I wanted. Saenz wasn't going to survive it. He didn't deserve that chance.

When my arms began to ache, I wrapped the Colt in two
shirts and tucked it into my suitcase, slipping the unloaded
bullet back into my pocket. It couldn't have been more than
sixty-five degrees in our motel room, but I was sweating. At
the sink, I splashed water on my face, refusing to meet my
own eyes.

The digital alarm clocked read 8:17 p.m. in red block letters. Unless things went horribly wrong, Olivia wouldn't be
back for quite a while. It was maddening to be stuck in a motel
room, waiting, while five states to the east Robert Saenz went
calmly about his life.

Restless, I stepped outside into the parking lot of The Drift Inn. There was only one car in the lot, which probably belonged to the owner. "Betha Caldwell," she'd introduced herself, with the sort of bone-crushing handshake that seemed appropriate in a Wild-West sort of way. A light was on in the office, and I could make out her silhouette in the ambient glow of a television screen. I imagined a laugh track unspooling, housewives who weren't really housewives screaming at each other.

Close by, an engine accelerated and I startled, thinking of Olivia with Sam Ellis. But this truck was loaded down with rangy-looking teenagers, none of whom had been visible in Lyman during the day. I relaxed; they were just kids, doing the stuff kids did. Normal kids—not like Olivia, who had spent far too long not being a kid at all.

I hoped, fiercely, that she was having a good time with Sam Ellis, the best time in the world. Maybe this would be the start of something for her—not a relationship, necessarily, but a new phase of confidence. The Olivia Kaufman who had squealed with delight, not terror, on the Bonneville Salt Flats would do just fine in the world, would grow into a quirky, funny, intelligent woman, not held back by thousands of fears.

Robert Saenz's death would set her free, too—I believed that with everything in me.

If nothing else, she would see that I was a father who took action, who loved his kids so much he would do anything for them. I owed this to her, and I owed it to Daniel. I owed it to Kathleen, even though she might never understand. I owed it to myself as a father, as the man who'd been there in the delivery room, watching their bodies pink with breath. I'd promised to protect them, although I hadn't known this promise might mean *to the death*.

But if a promise had contingencies—if it had caveats and

stipulations, if it was only applicable under a certain set of circumstances, like a complicated math problem where the variable applied *if and only if*—then what good was the promise? What good was it to only do the easy things, the tasks that required no effort at all? Love wasn't easy; it was, to paraphrase a Bible verse Kathleen's mother had cross-stitched and framed for us, tenacious and assertive and protective, and it never failed.

I wasn't going to fail them again.

olivia

Sam Ellis and I stayed that way for a long time, side by side, listening to the quiet. I was trying to remember if there had ever been a time in my life when I hadn't been able to hear cars on a road, or any kind of human-related noise. If I concentrated really hard, I could hear only my breath and Sam's.

"Why did you bring a notebook?" he asked suddenly.

"Oh." I was caught off guard. It was too late to say *What notebook?* because he must have seen it when I took the sweatshirt out of my backpack. "It's just for things I'm thinking about."

"Like a diary, you mean?"

"Sort of."

"What did you write in it today?"

I thought back to all the things I'd written about being kidnapped on I-80 and killed in some horrible way and left to rot in the Wyoming wilderness. And then before Sam had picked me up at the motel, I'd added all the ways our evening could go wrong or he could turn out to be psychotic. "Just…things."

"Could you read something to me?"

I was glad it was dark so he couldn't see my face. I remembered reading somewhere the writer's prayer: *If I should die before I wake, please throw my journal in the lake.* "It's not really happy stuff," I confessed to him finally. "I mean, I write about things that are worrying me. You know, things that can go wrong."

"That's cool," he said. "I get it. I totally get it. That's what I do with my art. I mean, the world has enough pictures of rainbows and kittens, you know?"

I did know. I knew exactly. But still, sometimes I wished all the other stuff could go away, so there would be no need for anything except rainbows and kittens.

He continued, "I mean, when I'm getting an idea for a new design, I'm thinking of things that already exist but shouldn't necessarily exist. The things our world doesn't think about, because we're too busy thinking about everything else."

"Yeah," I said. "Makes sense." I remembered the tiny, horrific detail of his snow globes, the figures fallen on the ground—the forced famine in Ukraine.

"The truth is," he said, "the world is full of horrible things. I mean, everywhere you look, it's horrible. The worst things you can imagine are happening somewhere, right now."

"I know," I said sincerely, propping myself up on my elbows. Even when I started to think, *Everything's going to be okay now,* I would see something on the news, about an earthquake that had buried a village or a school shooting or a homeless person whose body had been discovered beneath a bridge, and I would realize there were still horrible things I hadn't even bothered to consider.

"You want to know my worst horrible thing?"

I shifted nervously. "Um…okay." This didn't seem like the typical information that was shared on a first date—not that there was anything typical about Sam Ellis, or about me, either.

He settled in a little closer to me, so that our shoulders and our arms were touching, and he said, "This is the story of my real dad."

"Not the guy I met earlier?"

"Right. Jerrod Ellis is not my real dad, biologically speaking. He happens to be my stepfather, but in every way that counts, he's my real father," Sam explained patiently. "My real dad was this pawnbroker…"

He was right: it was the worst horrible thing. His real dad had suffered from mental illness when Sam and his brother were younger, and one day before opening the store, he'd taken everything that was breakable out of the display cases, and he'd smashed the items against the wall in the back of the store. Sam didn't know why he'd done it, exactly, but he remembered being there that day, trying to calm his brother and dodge flying shards of glass and pottery and even jewelry. And then his father had picked up a sharp chunk of broken metal and carved a huge gash down his own face. Sam had grabbed his brother, and they'd waited in a locked office for the police to come. All the while, his dad had been hammering at the office door with his fists, and Sam had been so scared that he'd wet himself while he was waiting.

"When I think about it now, that was the worst part, that I stunk like piss when the police finally got to us." He said this calmly, as if it had been so long ago that it wasn't a part of him anymore. As if it were a small thing that could be put in a box, and the box could be packed away, and it never had to be opened again.

In the quiet after he finished, I leaned my head against his shoulder. "That is a really awful thing."

"Thank you."

"What happened to your father?"

"He killed himself. Hung himself by his sheets in the hospital."

"Oh, my God." I swiveled around to look at him, amazed by the truly awful things a person could carry around inside himself and still go on living and breathing—and more than that, creating things and appreciating the simple beauty of a night sky.

"It's better now, though," Sam said. "If that hadn't happened, my mom never would have met my stepdad. You see?"

"I guess." Sam's story made at least three-quarters of the things I'd written in my Fear Journal seem petty—all the more so because most of them were invented, could-happen things, and Sam's terrible thing had actually happened.

"Is it weird that I told you that?" His voice was close to my ear. "Sometimes, I just feel like I need to put the worst thing out there, to get it all out in the open."

"No, I understand." I meant it. In a way, that's what my Fear Journal was all about. If I wrote it down, it wasn't some mysterious, nebulous concern floating around in the universe, but something I could own, something I could record and then release from my mind.

"I have a worst thing, too," I whispered, surprising myself. If Dad or Mom had guessed, they would have expected me to say that the most awful thing that happened to me was Daniel dying. Of course, that was a horrible thing, and maybe even the actual worst thing, but instead, I took a deep breath and told Sam Ellis about something that *I* had done. Even though there were only a few insects around to hear, I told him the entire story, beginning to end, in a whisper.

Just a few days before I started high school, there was a party at the home of this junior boy named Shawn, whose parents were in Hawaii. A couple of other incoming freshmen were invited, too, including my friend Kendra, one of the few girls from my middle school who was going on to Rio with me. Although we had begun to drift apart after Daniel had died, we still saw each other every day, saved each other seats at lunch and partnered up on group projects. She knew everything that had happened with Daniel, and about some of the weirdness between my parents—although Mom's leaving was so fresh, I hadn't yet told Kendra it was a permanent thing. I'd made it seem like no big deal, as though Mom took trips by herself all the time and Dad and I were completely used to fending for ourselves.

The night of the party, I told Dad I would be at Kendra's house, and Kendra told her parents she would be at mine, and as far as I knew, no parent was ever the wiser. We'd dressed up too fancy, the way freshman girls did at parties: black skirts made shorter by rolling over the waistbands, heels higher than we could comfortably walk in, so much perfume that we could smell each other even as we walked through the streets from Kendra's house. We giggled, drunk on our newfound freedom. My laughter had been forced at first, like a parody of what real laughter should sound like. I was rusty, not having laughed in so long. As we walked, though, I was determined to put it all behind me. Daniel, the dead brother. Mom, the absent parent. Dad, the parent who was always there, although he seemed miles away, too. I was just going to be a regular girl, fun and silly and sociable. Before we went inside, Kendra snapped a photo of us with her phone.

Shawn's house turned out to be one of those cookie-cutter mini-mansions plopped down next to a few dozen other mini-mansions on what used to be an almond ranch. It was the kind of house Mom would have hated. Everything was tastefully neutral, beige on blah. The house was packed, mostly with upperclassmen I didn't know. Kendra recognized a group of girls in the kitchen, standing around the island with red plastic cups in their hands. "They're all in the leadership class," Kendra said, and I saw in them the same kind of crazy confidence Daniel had always had, a buoyancy that kept them floating above the rest of us mere mortals.

"Let's see what's going on outside," I murmured to Kendra. Through the window I could see boys in trunks cannonballing into a pool. It was one of those fancy pools with a disappearing edge, so that it looked like all the water was going to spill right out and cascade down in a waterfall on the other side.

But Kendra shot me a look and dove right into the conversation. She'd been elected incoming freshman class secretary at the end of eighth grade, and I realized that these were her people, and I was just someone she knew, a friend from her past who would be shucked off like a pair of woolly boots at the beginning of spring. I tried not to be hurt, but as a few more girls crowded in, I found myself edged out of the circle, standing behind Kendra like a toddler afraid to leave her mother's side. One of the girls was retelling a story loudly, the sort of story that was only funny if you were an insider. Kendra laughed too enthusiastically, as if she had never heard anything so funny. She might as well have announced that she was available as a loyal, adoring sidekick.

Not like me—the no-fun friend.

Suddenly, one of the seniors announced that she had gotten a tattoo for her birthday, and the entire group charged from the kitchen en masse, through the dining room and up the back staircase. I followed a few feet behind, taking the steps slowly in my wobbly heels. I was sick of them already, but most of all I was sick of myself, for being the way I was. It could not possibly be normal that I was an almost-fourteen-year-old girl who wanted nothing more than to go home, throw on a three-sizes-too-big T-shirt and watch a classic movie with my dad, something like *Platoon* or *Escape from Alcatraz,* for the twentieth time.

At the top of the stairs, the girls pushed into a bedroom,

locking the door behind them. It was a private tattoo-viewing party, and I had fallen too far behind or else been deliberately excluded. It didn't really matter—I would have felt shitty either way. Kendra was on the inside, and I was out in the hall, holding a cup of warm beer that I had no intention of drinking. I wanted to head right back down the stairs and walk home, although I knew I'd have to stop somewhere to change into the shorts and T-shirt in my backpack.

"I almost did it, too," I told Sam, still whispering, as if whispering could make it less real and less horrible. "I was *this* close to walking away."

"But you didn't," Sam said, squeezing my hand.

But I didn't.

I was just standing there in the middle of a hallway, looking at a series of framed studio portraits of Shawn's family, when someone stumbled up the stairs, tripped over the top step and fell down at my feet, cursing. He was older; I didn't know his name. I set my cup down on the ledge of one of the portraits, and with an entire photogenic family of strangers staring at us, I let him plant a big, beery kiss on my mouth.

I can't say it was pleasant—his tongue was a little too meaty and rough—but it wasn't completely unpleasant, either. It was my first real, non-parent and non-relative kiss, although he was probably too drunk to notice my inexperience. The best part of it was that I instantly felt better for not being included in the tattoo-viewing that was happening behind the locked door down the hall. *I don't need to be with those stupid girls,* I told myself, and I kissed him harder.

Here's how I envisioned having sex would be: on a blanket in a field of wildflowers, under a blue sky. Or in a big, beautiful bed with crisp white sheets, with candlelight and roses and music. I didn't have a clear vision of *him,* exactly—only that he was someone handsome, someone funny, someone who loved me. Also, I pictured myself older, with a body that didn't resemble a twelve-year-old boy's no matter how much I dressed it up—at a distant point in my life where I appreciated things like manicured fingernails and waxed eyebrows.

But I guess no one thinks: I'm going to have sex on a bathroom floor with someone I met three minutes before, with one of my knees knocking against the vanity and my head butted up against the toilet. No one envisions: I'll still be mostly clothed, with my short skirt pushed up around my stomach and my completely uncool underwear pushed down, hanging off one ankle. No one wishes for the stab of pain, for the smear of blood. Maybe the worst of it was that he was drunk and wouldn't remember a bit of it, and I was sober and would remember every second. Or maybe the worst of it was that when he'd said, "Wanna do it? Wanna go somewhere private?" in my ear, it hadn't taken me long to consider. Why not? My life absolutely sucked in every way. Mom wasn't around to find out, and Dad wouldn't notice, anyway. At least for a few minutes, I could feel special.

Kendra found out what happened—one of the other girls had seen me coming out of the bathroom after him, my skirt twisted—and wrote me a long message on Facebook in which she said I was a "slut" and "desperate to be liked" and even "a bad influence" and not the kind of person she wanted to be associated with. And then she unfriended me—there and in real life. When we started school, she completely avoided me. In the one class we had together, Honors English, she never even looked in my direction. She got her wish and became one of those cool leadership girls, and her life was all Homecoming and rallies and making posters after school and delivering the daily announcements—a fear that popped up regularly in my journal.

But I couldn't blame Kendra, not at all. I agreed with everything she said; I *was* disgusting. When I remembered that night, and how I'd gone from standing in the hallway one minute to lying down next to a bathroom vanity the next, it was like it had happened to someone who wasn't even me but some weak, stupid girl who didn't have any self-respect or dignity or hope for whatever might come next in her life.

At my annual checkup about a month after the party, while Dad waited in the lobby, I received a pelvic exam, a blood test and a stern lecture. My primary care doctor, who was sworn to the silence of her profession, was stiff-lipped when she pushed a sample pack of birth control pills into my hand. I hid them in my backpack and later threw the pack into the trash can of a neighbor down the block. The sex certainly hadn't been spectacular; it wasn't like I was planning to do it again.

That year, I started hanging out with the Visigoths, the kids who wore all black and regularly professed that they didn't care about *anything*—which was perfect for me. I did my work and got As and Bs in everything except P.E., but I basically stopped participating. I became the kid teachers hate, the one who has the answers but refuses to raise her hand or join a group or speak at all, unless absolutely necessary. I saved all my talk for home, where I could impress Dad with my opinions about Ho Hos over Ding Dongs because of the creme-to-cake ratio; I could explain perfectly to Dad why I preferred *The Grapes of Wrath* to any other Steinbeck; I could play Mom and Dad's old '80s version of Trivial Pursuit and rattle off things about Boris Becker or Margaret Thatcher or apartheid—things that none of my fellow students at Rio knew, I was fairly certain.

Maybe the worst part about what I'd done at that party— the absolute worst in an episode of worsts—was that I'd kept it all inside me. "You're the first person I've told," I said to Sam, who was still holding my hand. I had the feeling I could have told him I was secretly an ax murderer and he would have withheld all judgment. Even if I lived to be a hundred years old—which would make Dad a very unlikely one-hundred thirty-three—I would never breathe a bit of it to him. I probably couldn't conceive of all the ways he would be hurt, but for starters there was the fact that I had lied to him. Plus, he would have felt responsible for what had happened, the way he somehow did for Daniel's death—as if he could have protected either of us from all the dangers of the world. In a way, I was protecting Dad, because he would have killed Mike Russi if he knew—maybe even literally. That was his name, Mike— which I only learned later, when I saw him at school. He was a senior who played baseball and didn't seem particularly intelligent. It was a ridiculous relief that he never recognized me—I was just one girl, one party, one time.

And of course, I hadn't told Mom, either. The pain of her leaving was still too fresh, and she would have blamed herself for not being there for me, and felt justified in believing that Dad was a bad parent, and that I was going to grow up all kinds of wrong for being in Sacramento with him instead of in Omaha with her. She might have flown back to Sacramento, packed my bags and forced me, kicking and screaming and hyperventilating, onto a plane. It would have been the lecture from my doctor times a thousand, plus the broken trust, the sad-eyed looks, the awkward conversations. Besides, even if I could have trusted her to respond in a rational way, how could such a thing be revealed *over the phone?* How would that conversation go, exactly? "Mom, I had sex at a party"? Or maybe I'd open with, "I thought you should know that I lost my virginity"?

The really crazy thing was that I told this all to Sam Ellis, but somehow I'd known he would understand. Maybe it was because he was able to take major tragedies and reduce them to a small scale, or maybe it was the whole under-the-stars thing: even the biggest, stupidest things I had done felt pretty insignificant with the universe bearing down on us.

And Sam didn't judge. After a while, he sat up and reached into the cooler, handing me a bologna sandwich in a Ziploc bag. I ate it, even though I don't think I'd had a bologna sandwich since I was a kid, and the ingredients of bologna, not to mention the bologna-making process, were enough to give even a very rational person pause. Then he opened a lukewarm two-liter of Coke and we passed the bottle back and forth between us, taking swigs.

When we'd finished the sandwiches, Sam and I lay down, side by side, not saying a thing. I wrapped one of the extra blankets around us, and after a while, Sam reached over into the space between us, curling one of his pinky fingers around my own.

It was the best night ever.

curtis

I nudged Olivia awake at nine o'clock.

"It is not nine o'clock," she answered from beneath the covers.

"Yeah, it is. And breakfast is only available until ten."

"Really?" Olivia heaved herself to a sitting position. Her hair was matted flat on one side of her head and sticking straight up on the other. "How can it be that late? I told Sam I'd meet him by ten." She hopped out of bed and grabbed a few things from her suitcase, which was sprawled open on top of the room's only table.

"You…what?"

"It's not like you and I have any plans for the day." She turned, studying me. "Do we?"

"I don't think—"

"So, what should I do? Hang around the motel all day? I figured I might as well head into town and help him out at his booth."

"Liv," I began, worried. She gave me a kiss that reeked of stale breath and dashed past me into the bathroom. Kathleen would be handling this better, I knew. She would be able to point out in a friendly, helpful way that there was really no point in Olivia getting close to someone she might never see again. Kathleen would have pried until Olivia told her everything about her date last night, while I'd gotten only a happy sort of shrug and one-word responses like "picnic" and "sandwiches." Of course, Kathleen wouldn't have let her sixteen-year-old daughter go on a date with a complete stranger in the first place.

"Dad," Olivia called through the bathroom door. "You don't need to worry. He's totally normal. Not even a little bit psycho." The shower started, water smacking hard against the plastic curtain.

When I was sure Olivia wasn't going to dash out, I went to my suitcase, unwrapped the Colt from its layers of T-shirts and tucked it into my waistband. I studied the effect in the mirror over the dresser. I didn't look as if I were packing a revolver; if anything, the bulk of my warmest—and largest—sweatshirt hanging down to the low hip area made me look as if I were packing a watermelon. Or not a watermelon, but one of those padded pregnancy simulators that strapped over the shoulders and clasped at the waist, like I'd worn in a Lamaze classes during Kathleen's pregnancy with Daniel. The pants I'd worn yesterday were draped over a chair back, and I fished in the pockets for my loose change and the room key, transferring them to my jeans. The bullet from last night was there, too; in this context, it looked completely harmless, like one of the odds and ends from a junk drawer. Still, I should get rid of it, toss it into a trash can somewhere in Lyman. The last thing I needed was to freak Olivia out.

It didn't take long for us to walk from the Drift Inn to J & E Automotive, to where Sam Ellis was waiting, his strange wares already set up for the day. What did he do during the winter, I wondered, when the town was all but closed by snow?

"I thought maybe you wouldn't come," Sam said as we approached.

Olivia shrugged. Was she blushing? "Well, here I am."

I lifted a snow globe off the folding table and studied it. The scene inside was grim, all browns and grays, buildings with flat roofs surrounded by a tiny fence.

"Do you like that one, Mr. Kaufman? It's a POW camp. Well, it's not any camp in particular, so maybe I'll just say it's representative of all forced internment centers."

Olivia beamed proudly. I gave the snow globe a little shake, and tiny flakes of silver and white glitter rose, then settled again, burying the compound until it looked peaceful, almost like one of those New England scenes on the old Currier and Ives tins.

"It's impressive," I told Sam, which wasn't the right word. Strange, maybe, but interesting, too.

"So, do you, um...want me to get a chair for you, too?" Sam asked politely, and I set the snow globe down.

"No, that's okay. I'm just going to..." I gestured around aimlessly. What would I do with myself all day?

Olivia pointed at my head, grinning. "I think you should get a haircut, Dad."

Look who's talking, I almost said. Olivia's riot of hair was a constant surprise, with strange curls springing out of the confines of her hoodie and big flyaway waves half shielding her face. Then I noticed that Olivia's hair wasn't hidden at all. Still damp, it was tousled and sprayed, and for just a moment, until she rolled her eyes at me, she looked again like a younger version of Kathleen—like Kathleen had looked when I first knew her.

Sam was giving me enthusiastic directions to a barbershop, ending with "...one of those stripy poles in the front and the whole bit."

I thanked him and wandered inside J & E Automotive, where Jerrod Ellis sat reading a newspaper with his work boots propped up on the front counter. "Waiting for that part," he said in greeting.

"But today, do you think?"

"Part should be in this afternoon. But with labor...better figure on tomorrow morning."

I considered joining him there, in the lone padded chair that constituted the waiting area, maybe borrowing the sections of the paper he had discarded. According to the clock on the wall, an antique that read Drink Coca-Cola beneath a half inch of dust, it wasn't ten-thirty. The day stretched long in front of me, lacking purpose. I wished I were in Oberlin already, driving past the towering campus structures and the stately older homes, finding my way to Robert Saenz. Leaving the J&E office, I brushed a hand against the Colt at my waistband for reassurance. It was still going to happen—just a day or two behind schedule. When I passed Olivia and Sam, they had their heads bent close together, and neither looked up.

I was overdue for a haircut, but really, it seemed like the least of my worries. What did a haircut matter in the grand scheme of things, which involved traveling cross-country to reunite my dear, funny, wise daughter with her mother and then proceed to hunt down the man who had killed my son? A little bit of shaggy hair didn't matter at all—not that it had mattered much in my teaching life, either. One of the perks of being a science teacher with a life-sized Einstein poster on his wall was that an eccentricity such as perennially bad hair was not only accepted, but expected.

It wasn't hard to locate the barbershop, which I'd seen yesterday on our way into town. The barber, a Hispanic man with a fantastic curling mustache, looked me up and down as I entered. He wore a white smock with the name "Eddie" embroidered in cursive letters on the pocket. "Haircut and shave?"

"Why not?" I replied. I'd had exactly one actual barbershop shave in my life, with Kathleen's father, brother and male cousins on the morning of our wedding day. It was the closest I'd come to a bachelor party.

Eddie ushered me into a chair. "Would you like to take off your sweatshirt?"

"No," I said quickly, and then felt the absurdity of the situation. Eddie probably had a gun stashed in his shop; I'd seen enough gun racks mounted to the backs of pickups with Wyoming plates to stop being shocked by them. The difference was that these gun owners probably weren't criminals, and I was—or would be, soon.

Eddie tucked a smock into the neck of my sweatshirt and wetted down my hair.

"Not too much off the top," I said, meaning it as a joke, since there wasn't much left on the top to begin with.

The bell over the door tinkled lightly, and a girl who looked about Olivia's age entered, coddling a fat baby in her arms. "You busy, Eddie? I can come back."

"Half an hour," he called, not looking away from my head. His scissors moved deftly, and small clumps of hair fell to the floor. Olivia had given me my past few haircuts, since I hadn't seen the need to bother with a professional. But she'd been tentative, taking only the smallest of snips, then backing up five feet to examine me from the long view.

Eddie whisked the hair off my neck, and I caught a glimpse of myself in the mirror, more spruced up than I'd been in a long time. *At least I'll look good for my mug shot,* I thought darkly and almost laughed out loud. I had the brief thought of sharing the joke with Olivia, who would have found it funny if it hadn't been about me.

Then I relaxed as my chair was angled backward and my face was covered with a steaming towel.

"First, we let the pores open," Eddie explained, the same as he probably did for every person who walked through the door, for generations of Lymanians.

I kept my eyes closed beneath the dark tent of the towel, flinching as it was removed and a cool lotion was slapped onto my skin. It felt like a gift to have someone else in control, even a stranger. Why hadn't I ever done this with Daniel? Just two men out on the town, hitting a barbershop.

Next was the hot lather, the scraping movements of the straight razor up my throat. If Olivia were here, she would have known offhand the number of people who were killed each year by straight razors. It was the sort of odd fact she collected and catalogued, no matter that the chances of her receiving a barbershop shave were nonexistent.

"Hold still, now," Eddie ordered, and I relaxed, compliant. If I could have stilled my mind, I would have fallen into an immediate sleep. Instead, I thought of Olivia, wondering if I should have let her out of my sight. There was something strange about Sam Ellis, even if it might turn out to be a good strange. On the other hand, it was a thrill to see Olivia *happy*. I remembered what Bill Meyers had told me, while I had sat on my own couch, completely oblivious to my own life. Olivia doesn't have any friends, he'd said. She eats her lunch alone in the library. Even if it was only for a single day, didn't Olivia deserve this little bit of happiness?

Distantly, I heard Eddie say "Now we prepare to go against the grain" and again my face was buried with a steaming towel. Heaven was like this, I thought—quiet and warm.

Tomorrow night, with any luck, we'd be in Omaha. This part of my plan had been vaguely formed. Of course, I couldn't just drop Olivia off, tossing her belongings onto the curb. I would have to have a real talk with Kathleen—something I'd managed to avoid for years. She'd never understood my anger at Robert Saenz, or how I felt I'd failed Daniel by not managing to do the one thing a father should do for his child—see him through to a happy, long life. And I'd be confronted with the physical evidence of how she'd moved on—the house she was renovating, the home furnishing shop where she served as part-owner and creative visionary. But that was fine. She could have that. She deserved that much and more. Hadn't I always wanted that for her, the best things she could wish for herself?

I was hit by a sudden, dizzying barrage of memories, a funnel cloud full of the debris of my own life. And the clearest memory was of Kathleen herself.

Kathleen at Northwestern—the girl with that spectacular laugh, so big and open and genuine that I told myself I would go anywhere, do anything, just to be with her. How often had I followed that blue-black head of hair, the springy curls she hadn't been able to tame with a ponytail or a braid without wild wisps escaping? That hair had made her instantly recognizable in any crowd, coming down the bleacher steps at Liv's soccer games, wandering through the various church fellowship halls and concert venues of Daniel's piano recitals, pushing a cart in Costco a half acre away.

Kathleen at work—curls tied back in a complicated knot with a scarf, her forehead creased with deep concentration, her hands—the fingertips rough, like coarse-grade sandpaper— moving deftly, surely, lovingly across a wooden surface. She had *loved* her work in a way that made me jealous; she had cared for each piece of furniture in her studio, she had known each piece down to its smallest detail, the grooves and hinges, the dents and scratches. She had made everything beautiful— things and people, too.

It was all so long ago.

But of course, everything I'd loved about Kathleen then was still there now, although I'd packed it away on a high shelf in my mind, out of reach. All those months after Daniel had died, I couldn't bear to be in the same room with her. That was *our* son—that perfect union of the two of us, that perfect representation of our love, and he was gone. He'd had Kathleen's pale skin that pinked up so quickly on a single summer afternoon; he'd even had a mole along his jawline like Kathleen had, a mole I had loved to bend down to kiss while she prepared dinner, while she brushed her hair.

I heard someone moan nearby and was aware, suddenly, that it was me. The towel on my face was cool now, and my cheeks stung with a minty aftershave lotion. "I'm so sorry," I said, getting to my feet, reaching carefully into my back pocket for the wallet, the handle of the Colt surprising me again. "I think I must have dozed off there."

"It happens," Eddie said, giving my face a final pat down with the towel. "Sometimes the whole body just needs to breathe, you know?"

I did know.

olivia

It was amazing how easy it was to sit next to Sam and say absolutely *nothing*. I was so used to my own mind going at a reckless, autobahn speed—this worry, that fear—that I was amazed a person could be so absolutely *still*. We spent the morning manning his sales tables outside J & E Automotive. If I strained a bit to peek around the corner, I could see our Explorer in an open garage bay, waiting. Another driver pulled in for service and then left on foot for the diner across the road, the one that said only DINER in huge red letters, as if it were the only such place in the world. No one seemed interested in purchasing a snow globe re-creation of one of humanity's great tragedies, although a surprising number of cars with out-of-state plates rumbled past. Maybe Lyman, Wyoming, had a strange electromagnetic force that was compelling them off the interstate.

I repeated this thought to Sam, who said simply, "Huh."

"Like something that might have been on *The Twilight Zone*."

He nodded, then added a minute or so later, "I've never seen it."

This made me feel very sorry for Sam Ellis. It also made

me remember the giant satellite dishes affixed to every house we'd passed in Lyman, and made me wonder how that could be true. Find the one house without a satellite dish, and that must be where he lived. I was thinking about reaching for his hand under the table, remembering how his skin had felt last night, so warm next to mine.

But then he asked, "What's up with your dad?"

"Excuse me?"

"I just mean, what's his deal?"

"What's his deal?" I echoed. "I don't know what you're asking."

He held up both hands, palms out in surrender. "Okay. It was just a question."

We were quiet for a long time, watching people go in and trickle out of DINER, and a woman push a baby stroller with twins past us and then, completing a loop, back again. The twins were screaming, but the woman had on headphones and didn't seem bothered by their noise. I was annoyed, both by the crying twins and Sam's question; after our heart-to-heart last night, it didn't seem that I should have to put this into words, too. If only there was some sort of electrode I could plug in to each of our brains, so we could know everything without having to ruin it with more talking.

"Fine," I announced so abruptly that Sam jumped, banging his knee against a table leg. "Fine. It's none of your business, but I'll tell you what's up with my dad. What's up is that my older brother, who was this musical genius and a way better kid than me, died four years ago. What's up is that my dad and mom couldn't handle being together, so my mom left. What's up is that my dad had some kind of psychotic break at work and he was, like, *this* close to jumping off a roof." I held up my thumb and forefinger a centimeter apart for emphasis. "So that's *what's up* with him, if you must know." I stood, wanting to make some kind of dramatic exit, and then, considering that I really had nowhere to go, plopped dramatically back into my chair.

Sam contemplated this for a long time. At least, that's what I figured he was doing. With anyone else, there would have been an instant apology or a hug or a spilled tale of similar woe, but Sam really seemed to be pondering everything I'd said. When he finally spoke, it was to say "That can't be true, though."

"Excuse me?"

"I mean, he can't have been a better kid than you. I hope you know that."

I stared at him.

"But you're right, it isn't any of my business."

"Thanks," I whispered. Tears smarted in my eyes, and I half turned on my folding chair so that I was facing away from him and toward the parking lot with the rusting car skeletons.

Sam was quiet again, although I could tell he had something more to say. This was Lyman time: nice and slow, no need to get in a rush and mess things up. He cleared his throat and swallowed. "I just—thought I should tell you. I would want to know if it involved me."

I whirled around. "Want to know what?"

"It's just that I might know something about your dad that you don't know."

The little hairs on the back of my neck were standing up. Where the hell was my Fear Journal when I needed it? I had this sudden *Star Wars*-inspired flash of Sam Ellis telling me that my dad was also his father, relic from a long-ago trip across I-80. Or else that the barber down the road was part of a cult that practiced human sacrifice, and right now my father was bound and gagged and wrapped in someone's throw rug, mummy-style, ready to be placed on an altar. But for once those fears seemed ridiculous. The panicky feeling in my chest wasn't new; it had only been lying dormant. There *was* something wrong with Dad, and I had known it since the moment I saw him on the roof. I'd been beating back that fear all week, pretending this trip was some kind of normal father-daughter bonding ritual.

"You'd better tell me," I ordered, breathless, "or I'm going to hyperventilate, and it's going to be ugly for both of us."

But instead of telling me—really, this boy was too infuriating for words—Sam reached into the pocket of his jeans with cinematic slowness and pulled out something, which he held out for me in the palm of his hand.

"What is that?" I asked, and then, understanding and not understanding all at once, I demanded, "Where did you get it?"

"It's a bullet. A cartridge, whatever you want to call it," he said. "It was in your car."

"It was not." My face was hot. "That was not in our car. We don't have a gun. My dad doesn't have a gun. So why would we have a bullet in our car? And what were you doing in our car, anyway?"

He closed his palm around the bullet, and it disappeared, like a twisted magic trick. I felt sick to my stomach all of a sudden, like I had a bad case of cramps, or the bowl of out-of-season fruit from breakfast was catching up with me. Slowly, Sam explained, "When I got here this morning, my stepdad asked me to check for any warning lights in your car, and I moved the driver's seat forward a bit. Your dad's a lot taller than me. So I reached under the seat—"

"And there was just a bullet lying there, under the driver's seat?" Two pink spots rose like balloons on my cheeks. I didn't wait for him, but answered my own question. "You're wrong. Believe me, I would have noticed if there was a bullet rolling around down there." I wasn't absolutely sure this was true, given the amount of snack wrappers and pens and other things that tended to accumulate on the floor of our car—but still.

Sam opened his hand again, rotating the bullet back and forth along his palm. It was funny how small and innocent it looked, like something that couldn't possibly hurt anyone. *Guns don't kill people,* I thought, stupidly. *Bullets do.* "When I was reaching down there, my hand rubbed against the top of the underside of the seat, you know?"

I stared at him.

"And I felt something kind of funny, so I got out of the car and I bent over to check it out. They were taped to the bottom of the seat with a bunch of duct tape."

"They?" I was going to throw up. I leaned over my knees, breathing hard, but still I heard Sam say "Yeah. Five bullets, all taped up there."

I concentrated on breathing in and out, my eyes pinched closed. *In and out, in and out.* Where was Mom, to come to the rescue with a paper bag?

"Maybe it was for—I don't know, some kind of protection for your trip," Sam offered.

"But he doesn't have a gun," I huffed. "I would know, believe me. He doesn't even go hunting or anything. He's not a gun guy."

"These bullets aren't for hunting," Sam pointed out. "I've been hunting, and I would know. These are for a handgun."

"No way, there's no way," I whimpered, pulling my hoodie over my head so that it shielded most of my face, and Sam Ellis wouldn't be able to see me cry.

Sam tried again, probably alarmed by my display. "You know, there are a lot of reasons why—"

I cut him off, blubbering. "No, there aren't. There are no reasons." I couldn't think. Why in the world did my dad need a gun? Was he involved in—something? I couldn't even imagine. He was my dad, for goodness' sake. What was he hiding from me? I sniffed, trying to hold back an impending tidal wave of mucous. And then I felt it, hesitant at first, and then firm as anything: Sam's hand on my back, rubbing a slow, comforting circle.

"I'll help you," he promised. "Okay? We'll figure it out."

curtis

I emerged from the barbershop in a daze. Catching my reflection in a storefront along the main drag, I saw a middle-aged man with a new haircut and a shiny face, but I had to stop to make sure it was really me. In my post-dream haze, I half expected to see a younger version of myself, the young man who had escaped an abusive childhood to luck into the good life with Kathleen Eberle.

I popped into a convenience store and emerged a few minutes later with a two-pack of pens and a pad of writing paper, the words already forming in my mind. When I rounded the corner, Olivia and Sam were still sitting at the folding tables, the display of snow globes arranged before them. Olivia had her hoodie up, and Sam had his arm on her back. I restrained myself from crossing the street and instead entered the diner with its blazing red sign. She's being a teenager, I reminded myself. I'd spent most of my life around teenagers, but couldn't pretend to fully understand them—because even though I'd lived through those years, I hadn't been one myself. She's having a little flirtation, and good for her. Why should she be miserable? Why should she carry the weight of the past, when I could do it for her?

It was just after eleven, and only a few tables in the diner were occupied. I was seated in the back, although if I strained I could make out Olivia and Sam, who seemed to be having an intense conversation.

A waitress approached, handing me a laminated menu. "You're a little late for breakfast, but if you want, we could probably rustle something up."

"Oh, no—just some coffee, black."

"You got it," she said, and I set the pad of paper and a pen on the table in front of me. My palms were sweaty; holding the pen, my hand shook. The first words came out more like a child's scrawl, I was fairly rusty at this, one of the most basic forms of communication. When had I written anything besides a grocery list, a lesson plan? Every few weeks I'd bundled up mail that came to Kathleen and forwarded it on to her in a padded envelope, writing nothing more than her name and Omaha address across the front.

It took several tries to get it right. First I wrote, "The Last Will and Testament of Curtis Kaufman." Too formal—like a character on an old episode of *Murder, She Wrote,* with a room full of weeping relatives who had gathered to hear how my wealth was going to be distributed. There wouldn't be much wealth at all, when it came down to it. The house in Sacramento was paid off, and that could be sold—but the housing market was in a slump. I'd managed to stay debt-free by driving an old car, by planning our purchases in advance—but Visa would be paying for a rebuilt transmission, and after the hotels and gas and food for this trip, there wouldn't be much left in savings.

Besides, it wasn't absolutely certain what would happen to me. That was the great unknown, the variable I wouldn't be able to control. Robert Saenz could easily fight back, wrestle the gun from me, return fire for fire. If everything went according to my plan—but why would it?—I'd be arrested by the Oberlin police, booked and put on trial. I would request only a public defender—no heroics. I wasn't planning to deny anything. I imagined A.D.A. Derick Jones handling my case for the prosecution, laying bare the facts: a man who hadn't come to terms with his son's death, a man who was so consumed by his desire for revenge that he allowed his family to fall apart, a man who had executed his crime with malice aforethought—traveling thousands of miles and purchasing a handgun illegally along the way, all to hunt down his son's killer. I would plead guilty, not denying anything. Best case scenario, I'd only be locked away for half of my remaining years.

The coffee came, and I angled myself in the booth so that my writing wouldn't be visible to anyone walking by. I tried again: "To Whom it May Concern"—but that was ridiculous. There were only two people on earth who this would concern, and they deserved to be named.

I began on a third page, "Dear Kathleen and Olivia." For a long time, letting the coffee grow cold, I stared at the paper. A few people trickled in and out of the diner; a man at the counter spoke loudly about the construction on Highway 189, leading north. I imagined Kathleen finding the letter, long afterward, opening the sealed envelope with trembling hands. I pictured Olivia reading it, encountering for her what must have been the sum of all her fears. Even after the fact, I didn't want them to feel responsible, to carry secret knowledge, to be hounded by a relentless D.A. in search of the truth. I needed to be vague, to speak in generalities. I wouldn't allow myself to hope that Kathleen or Olivia would visit me in prison, that they would send letters, that they would be waiting for me on the other side.

And so I wrote:

Dear Kathleen and Olivia,

You will want an explanation, and you deserve that, and so much more.

I could say that I did it because I was hopeless and desperate, but that wouldn't be true. With both of you, how could I have been?

It may be said that I was full of rage, but that isn't true, either. At least, I am equally full of love for both of you, for Daniel, for the life we had, all four of us together. All my rage was focused in one direction, but I wouldn't say I was blinded by it.

Years ago, I made two promises. One was to myself, that I would rise above my circumstances and be a better person. Another was to you, Kathleen, and I kept that promise as best I could. I'm still remembering it now, even as I write this, even when I find it's too late to convince myself of any other alternative but what I'm about to do.

If you had known what I was planning, you would have talked me out of it—and that's exactly why I couldn't tell you. I knew I couldn't be stopped, and I didn't want either of you to get hurt in the process.

This letter is a goodbye, because I don't know when or if I will see either of you again. It would be bliss for me to believe that you have moved on. I can only be sorry, Kathleen, now and always. Remember your drive, Olivia? The way the sun glittered off the salt, and the world was peaceful and quiet and endlessly good? That's what I'll remember, too.

I thought for a long time, and signed the letter simply,

Curtis (Dad)

I bunched the other pages with my sloppy beginnings into little balls, and tossed them into the trash basket next to the counter. Somehow, without my notice, most of the booths were full. The diner smelled pleasantly of grease.

"I should hardly charge you for that," the waitress commented, ringing me up for a $1.19. "You barely drank a sip." Her tone was faintly accusatory, fishing for an explanation.

"Thank you," I said simply, handing over two dollars.

Outside, the day had gone cloudy, and Lyman looked faintly gray, as if it were buried beneath a layer of dead skin cells waiting to be sloughed off. I was suddenly hungry, the overload of carbohydrates at breakfast long forgotten. Maybe Olivia was ready for some lunch, too. I'd get her and Sam, too, and come right back to the diner.

When I looked across the street, the tables were still there, light glinting faintly off the snow globes—but Olivia and Sam were gone.

olivia

As I saw it, once I stopped hyperventilating with my head between my knees, there was only one reason why my father might have bullets taped to the underside of his driver's seat: he was planning to kill himself.

Wasn't that what I'd been worried about all along—the real reason I'd stayed with him in California rather than gone with Mom to Nebraska? It hadn't been about my fears for myself, but my fears for *him*. Hadn't I watched him carefully these past few years, playing straight man to his jokes, finding excuse after excuse for why I couldn't hang out with the Visigoths after school at the skate park, subconsciously devising some of my more elaborate fears as a way of keeping myself close to him, and keeping him close to me? I gulped in air greedily, remembering Dad on the roof. My airway felt no larger than a pinprick. Of course, *of course,* he'd been about to jump.

Sam was trying to calm me down, his knuckles zigzagging back and forth across my back. It was helping, because I could feel my lungs expanding, the frenzied pace of my breath slowing. "I'm probably wrong about the whole thing," he said. "What do I know? Maybe the bullets weren't even his."

I couldn't answer. They weren't mine, that was for sure, and there was no way in the world they belonged to Mom, who hated guns. And before that, the only other person I could remember being in the Explorer was Daniel, who wouldn't have had any need for bullets or guns, who would have looked at the bullet in Sam's outstretched hand and been just as confused as I was.

Sam tried again. "Maybe they've been there for a long time, and your dad has forgotten all about them. See? It's probably nothing."

Gathering my breath, I told Sam, "My dad is a Democrat," hoping that this would explain everything. He raised an eyebrow curiously, as if I'd named a rare type of parakeet. "My whole family—we're Democrats. We don't believe in guns. I'm serious. My parents would never in a million years have had a gun in our house. My mom, especially. She would have flipped out if..."

Sam glanced at me sideways, afraid to suggest it.

"No," I said firmly. "That is *not* why she left. She wouldn't have let me stay if she thought he had anything to do with a gun."

He nodded slowly, probably thinking I was the biggest nutcase in the world, and probably relieved that he hadn't actually kissed someone with such a screwed-up family. "Okay, then. Maybe the bullets came with the car?"

"You mean an added feature, like heated seats or a moonroof?"

Sam didn't register the sarcasm in my voice. "Was it a used car?"

I thought back, remembered the four of us at the dealership, piling into the Explorer for a test drive, years and years ago now. "No. We bought it new."

Sam considered, then held up his hands, as if to ward off an attack. "I'm just going to say this, because sometimes you never know. Is there a way your father is involved in something illegal, like a burglary ring?"

My laugh turned into a wheezing cough. "You mean, has he been robbing gas stations along I-80 to finance this glamorous trip?"

"Well. You've been together this whole time?"

"Yes, the entire time." And then I remembered. "Except three nights ago."

"What happened three nights ago?"

"He dropped me off at the hotel and went for a drive. That was in Winnemucca."

Sam nodded soberly, considering the possibilities. "What was he like when he came back?"

"I don't know. Fine. Normal. He brought me a slushie. We watched TV."

Sam looked at me knowingly. "And where do slushies originate from?"

"Really? You think he filled up my giant slushie cup before or after he robbed the convenience store?"

"Okay," Sam agreed. "That doesn't make much sense."

"Forget it. My dad couldn't rob anything. He *wouldn't* rob anything. He's not some criminal, he's my dad. He's Mr. K. He's a freaking teacher."

"What kind of teacher?"

I glared at him, not answering. Even though I wasn't hyperventilating anymore, I put my head back in my hands. Dad wasn't a drug manufacturer, or an armed robber, or some kind of negligent chump who was unaware that five bullets had been taped to the underside of his driver's seat. Those possibilities were each worth their own panic attack, but the possibility of Dad wanting to kill himself was infinitely worse.

"Well," Sam said finally. "I think we should go to your motel room while we can."

I raised my head slowly, giving him a sharp look. My world was crumbling around me, and he thought there was the possibility of sex in his future?

He sighed, reading my mind. "I'm only thinking that if there's a gun, we should find it."

Oh. *Right.*

The Drift Inn was completely deserted, a closed sign flipped in the office window. "Tell the truth," I whispered to Sam as we left his truck and crossed the empty parking lot. "Doesn't this place remind you of Bates Motel?"

"You watch a lot of television," Sam commented, and I bit back the urge to say that actually I was referring to a *movie,* a classic, spawn of many a late-night fear. For an intense moment, I wanted to be back in my life in Sacramento, even sitting in the far stall of the D-wing girls' bathroom, where there were no bullets beneath car seats and no strange boy accompanying me into a desolate motel room. When I pulled the key from my back pocket, I was surprised to find that my hand was shaking.

"We have to be fast," I said, pushing open the door. The room had been cleaned, and a fresh set of towels was sitting on the end of each bed. My suitcase was still heaped on top of the table, contents spilling out. Dad's bag was on the floor next to the vanity, neatly zipped. Nothing was wrong, exactly, but I felt wheezy and light-headed, anyway.

"Are you okay?" Sam asked, and I shook my head.

Sam nodded sympathetically. It occurred to me that he was the best possible person to be around in a crisis. He didn't get upset—or show emotion at all, really—didn't yell, didn't panic, didn't judge. Instead, he began to tackle the task in front of him, which involved systematically lifting each corner of Dad's mattress and neatly retucking the sheets.

"Nothing?" I asked.

Sam shrugged. Flat on his back, he poked his head into the narrow space between the bed and the wall and came up a few seconds later, coughing. He checked behind my bed the same way, while I felt around beneath the pillows and blankets. We worked our way silently around the room, moving and replacing the items in the center nightstand, then turning our attention to the dresser. Sam pulled out the bottom drawers, running his hand into the dark space at the bottom of the dresser. He yanked his hand out, grimacing, and wiped a dusty smear across his jeans. Apparently deep cleaning was not a high priority at the Drift Inn.

I entered the bathroom in a state of dread, considering how many *Godfather* marathons Dad and I had watched together. But there weren't too many hiding places, and each was empty—the cabinet beneath the sink, the single drawer on the vanity, and the inside of the toilet tank. I scrubbed my hands fiercely after repositioning the lid, and when I came out of the bathroom, Sam had unzipped my dad's suitcase.

"Um," I said.

"What?"

"It's just that…I mean, those are private things."

Sam looked offended. "Do you want my help or not?" He didn't wait for an answer, but kept patting his way through the suitcase—Dad's boxers, a few pairs of jeans and khakis, T-shirts. He held up a roll of gray duct tape, raising his eyebrows significantly.

"Doesn't prove anything," I said, although my heart was clamoring around in my chest loud enough to be heard. "My dad likes to be prepared for things. Once he fixed a hole in his shoes with duct tape."

"But still. It's the same color."

"I mean, what are you going to do, some kind of forensic

fiber analysis to see if the threads from that duct tape match the threads of the duct tape you found in our car?"

Sam frowned at me. "It's called putting two-and-two to-gether."

"And getting five," I muttered. "A lot of people have duct tape, and it doesn't mean anything." I suddenly wanted to be done with the whole mess. We were being ridiculous. Dad didn't have a gun. Or Dad did have a gun, and there was noth-ing we could do about it.

"Fair enough," Sam said evenly, although he sounded un-convinced. Moving Dad's jacket, he uncovered a small card-board box, and my mouth went dry. It was a good thing I was sitting down, because I felt a bit dizzy with déjà vu.

"Heavy," he commented.

I held out a hand, not able to speak. Sam handed me the box, and I sat on my bed, feeling the weight of it in my lap. I didn't need to pull back the flaps to know what was inside. Over the years, I'd looked a few times, curious at first, and then wanting to reassure myself that Daniel's ashes were still there—that Mom hadn't taken them to Omaha, that Dad hadn't scattered them somewhere without telling me.

"Aren't you going to open that?"

I shook my head. "I know what this is. It's not a gun."

Sam considered this for a moment but didn't protest. He knelt again in front of Dad's suitcase. "What's this?" He held up a bulging zippered case.

"I don't know. His shaving kit, maybe?"

Sam pointed to the dresser, where Dad's shaving kit was open, a travel-sized bottle of mouthwash poking out.

Sam handed me the case. It seemed too flat to hold a gun. "You open it," he said.

Carefully, I set the box with Daniel's ashes to the side and worked the zipper, tipping the contents onto the bedspread.

"Whoa," Sam said, as if we'd found a hidden stash of drugs.

I got that woozy feeling again, because I knew what I was looking at instantly. My dad's stash, his most private possessions, didn't include cocaine or bottles of prescription pills. What spilled out of the bag was the entire existence of my family, a collection of all things Kaufman.

The heaviest object was a three-by-five frame, holding a picture taken about eight years ago, during my frizzy ponytails phase. Dad looked younger, too—his hair fuller, darker where it was now peppered with gray. He had one arm around me and the other around Mom, and Mom was beaming, happy in a way that brought back a rush of long-ago memories. Daniel was on the far right, this big goofy smile on his face. It must have been just after he got his braces off, because his teeth were almost startlingly white.

Sam took the frame from me, holding it only inches from his face, studying each of us as if he might be required to pick us out of a lineup.

The rest of the stuff was mostly paper. I undid the rubber band on a bundle of wallet-sized photos—Daniel through the ages, kindergarten all the way up through high school, with his senior picture on the bottom of the stack. There were a few other snapshots of our family, including one I remembered from a trip to Yosemite. Dad had taken the photo, and Mom had an arm around both Daniel and me.

Sam felt in the bottom of the bag and pulled out a neat stack of newspaper clippings. As he spread them out on the bed, I saw that each one mentioned Daniel in some way—his piano recitals, chamber orchestra concerts, awards from musical competitions, scholarship announcements. Local-boy-makes-good kind of stories.

"Whoa," Sam said again, reverently. "This is your brother?"

I didn't correct him with the past tense. I was finding it

difficult to speak, since Daniel's face was looking up at me from just about every clipping. In some he was the smiling boy in the black tuxedo jacket; others were action shots with Daniel leaning over the keyboard, his fingers making magic.

"Oh," Sam said, unfolding a page ripped from *The Sacramento Bee,* dated Friday, October 30, 2008. The headline read: Area music prodigy killed in Ohio car accident.

"Yeah," I said, gulping in that funny way I did every time it came back to me. The 2:00 a.m. phone call, the end of everything.

The other clippings included Daniel's obituary, an article from an Oberlin College publication and a blurb about a plea deal copped by the driver who'd killed Daniel. I sifted through the articles carefully, smoothing out the wrinkles, and returned them to the bottom of the zippered pouch.

Sam watched me quietly, and I was grateful for the way he didn't need to say anything. There was no need to put an arm around me or ask how I was feeling, and no need to offer a shoulder to cry on if I wanted to spill the whole sad story of my life for the past four years.

Together, we repacked the photos and returned the case to the bottom of my dad's suitcase. I replaced the box with Daniel's remains beneath Dad's jacket and carefully zipped the entire suitcase, so he would find it exactly as he had left it.

Sam sat next to me on the bed. "Well, we didn't see any sign of a gun."

That was true, but somehow it didn't make me feel any better.

curtis

I dialed Olivia's phone twice, getting her voice mail. "Olivia, I need you to call me back right away," I barked. I tossed the pad of paper into a trash can and then, with the letter to Kathleen and Olivia folded in my back pocket, I took off in the direction of the motel at a breathless, clumsy run, one hand in the pocket of my sweatshirt to grip the Colt. What the hell had I been thinking? I didn't need Kathleen here to tell me that I had managed to fuck this up, that my daughter and a near-stranger had gone completely off the grid.

"You're in a hurry," someone called, and I looked up to see Betha Caldwell grinning at me from beneath red, penciled-in eyebrows. She had pulled her truck to the curb and was inching along to keep pace with me.

"I'm trying to find Olivia. She's with that Ellis boy—Sam."

One fake eyebrow rose higher than the other. "I see."

I leaned into the open window. "Could you— Are you going in the direction of the motel?"

"The motel is exactly where I'm going. Hop in."

Betha waited until I fastened my seat belt, an episode made all the more difficult by my shaking hands. "She's fine," Betha pronounced, chuckling. "Are you always this protective?"

"She's sixteen." Didn't this say everything?

Betha gave the truck a little gas, and we rolled along the main drag at an infuriatingly slow pace. I had the feeling that I could have done better on the outside, jogging along one-handedly. She reached over to pat me on the leg. "Around here, sixteen is a full-fledged adult. Hell, I was married by the time I was seventeen, had my oldest only a year later."

"I don't mean to sound rude, but that is exactly what I'm worried about," I told her. "Plus, Sam is nineteen."

Betha threw back her head and laughed. "That boy is not exactly what I'd call sophisticated."

I didn't wait for her truck to come to a complete stop before I started running toward our motel room. Betha parked and followed behind me, curious, as I fumbled with the room key. The door swung inward, and I saw Olivia and Sam on her bed, sitting side by side, not touching.

"Liv?" I demanded. "What's going on?"

"Nothing." Her voice was too defensive. Something was going on, even if it wasn't the something I'd feared. She was still dressed in her black jeans, black boots and black hoodie—the Olivia uniform—and Sam was fully dressed, as well. But both of them looked guilty as hell.

I came closer. "Nothing?"

"Nothing, *sir*," Sam added helpfully.

I glared at him, the hand in my pocket bumping up against the now-familiar bulge of the handgun at my waist. Thank God I hadn't left it in the room, where one or the other of them could have stumbled across it. If not sex, what were they doing in the motel room? Drugs? I stared at Olivia, my crazy-smart, scared-of-everything, too-old-for-her-age daughter, and we both spoke at the same time.

"Olivia, I think we need—"

"Dad, I just wanted to—"

I took a deep breath. "You first."

"I wasn't feeling good," Olivia said. "I thought I was going to throw up, and I wanted to come back here. Sam didn't want to leave me alone until you got back."

I considered this, anger seeping out of me. "You could have called, though. You should have. In fact, I called you twice, and you didn't answer."

"I forgot to charge my phone last night."

I stared at her for a long moment until she blinked, looking away.

Sam cleared his throat and stood, patting Olivia on the shoulder like a younger sister. "Guess I'll get back to it, then," he said. He nodded at me sheepishly, and a minute later we heard the clunk-whirr of the transmission as he reversed, then accelerated out of the parking lot.

Betha Caldwell, listening from the door, asked if Olivia wanted some chicken soup.

Olivia smiled weakly. "Maybe just a few crackers?"

"A few crackers it is. Be right back," Betha called cheerfully.

I closed the door and walked over to my bed, plopping down on it. Olivia half turned and we stared at each other again.

"I was worried," I told her. "You said you would be right there."

"I know. But I told you what happened."

"Liv—"

"Your hair looks nice," she said, giving me a little smile.

I ran a hand over the top of my head distractedly. "So, what do we do now?"

Olivia shrugged. "Maybe we can watch some crap TV for a bit, just the two of us."

"Sounds good." I leaned over to give her a kiss on the forehead, and she tried to wrap me in a hug that I sidestepped at the last moment. Having the Colt in my waistband was like walking around with a ticking bomb strapped to my chest. I dreaded Olivia bumping against the handle, asking, *What's that?*

"I don't need whatever bug you've got," I explained, settling back onto my bed. Olivia was watching me from beneath her hoodie, her expression unreadable.

We spent the afternoon in our side-by-side beds, the top sheets tucked in too tightly, the pillows slightly too hard. Betha knocked, bringing a sleeve of Saltine crackers and a plate of breakfast leftovers: muffins, scones, little butter and jelly packets.

Olivia ran through a dismal channel selection before settling on reruns of *The Fresh Prince of Bel-Air.*

"I can't believe this show is still rerunning," I commented, two episodes in, brushing crumbs off my sheets. "Your brother used to watch this every morning during the summer, but that was years ago now."

Olivia shifted in bed, a complicated undertaking, considered that she was buried beneath several layers. "He did? Daniel used to watch this?"

I started, hearing his name. How long since we had mentioned him so casually, this ghost who flitted around our lives? "Sure," I told her. "You don't remember?"

On the screen, Will Smith was trying to impress a cashier with his over-the-top cockiness. The laugh track cackled. Everyone thought he was funny except for the cashier.

"No," she said. "I barely remember anything."

"That's not true," I said reflexively, although of course it might have been. I felt defensive on her behalf. Didn't she remember? All our day trips around California, our family dinners, Daniel's endless piano practicing, our lazy Saturday mornings... Was this another thing Robert Saenz had taken from us, our ability to remember happiness?

Then Olivia blurted, as if she'd been holding it all in for a long time, and the only way to let it out was in a fast gush, "I wish I knew more about Daniel. He had all these years of life when I wasn't around, or when I was around, but too young to remember. Or when I was old enough to remember, but too self-absorbed to think it was anything important that I should pay attention to."

"Oh, Liv."

"I would have paid attention," she said. "If I had known what was going to happen, I would have memorized everything, or written it down, or shot a vid—"

She stopped abruptly, and when I glanced over, she was crying. I reached for the remote and muted the television. Will Smith was still there—in his uncle's home now, in the mansion in Bel-Air, talking to the family butler. Minus the sound, everything seemed like elaborate pantomime, the gestures too big, the facial expressions too exaggerated. Olivia's sobs, hidden against her pillow, were tiny and pitiful as a kitten's.

"Do you want to talk about it? We should." I took a deep breath. "We should talk about Daniel."

"There's too much to say."

"We've got time."

Olivia wasn't looking at me anymore; she was squinting at the screen, trying to puzzle out the words we couldn't hear.

"The thing is—" I stopped, forcing down the hatred I felt right that moment, sharp and strong as a paring knife, for Robert Saenz. It was amazing how he could be free as a bird in Ohio and be here, too—a vision in my mind, sharp as a make-believe target on the wall of our motel room. But Olivia didn't need to share these feelings; she needed something else—a long overdue apology. "I know we didn't handle it well. Me, especially. I guess when you become a parent, you worry about all these little things—a cough, a skinned knee—but you never actually expect that any harm will come to your own child. There are parenting manuals that cover every happy moment, like first words and first steps, but there's no manual that tells you how to handle the awful things, too."

"No one would buy that manual," Olivia protested, sniffling. "That would be the worst baby shower present ever."

I chuckled despite myself.

Olivia, her voice so soft that it might have been coming from the parking lot, said, "If I were you, I would think to myself, why did it happen to the super-talented kid? Why did I get left with this one?"

"You don't believe that, do you? I've never thought that for a second." My voice came out thick with grief.

"Mom, maybe."

I felt a rush of vehemence on Kathleen's behalf. "Not at all, not ever."

"Not even a little bit?"

"Liv, so many things went through my mind when Daniel died. How I should have been there, how I should have insisted that he go somewhere close, like UC Davis or Sac State, where I could keep an eye on him. How I should have gone to more of his concerts—every single one, instead of begging off to finish grading—how I should have set aside my schoolwork to just spend more time with him on weeknights, how I never ever should have asked him to stop practicing when I had a headache or just needed a moment to myself. That and a million other things, all the ways I'd failed him as a father over the years. But I never, ever felt that it should have been you. And your mom felt the same." I let the tears balance in the corners of my eyes, not wanting Olivia to see them.

She clicked the mute button again so that sound—a commercial for a shampoo that would *revolutionize* hair care—came flooding back into the room again, and I realized that she was crying, too, hiding her sobs underneath the announcer's voice.

"It's all going to be okay, Olivia," I promised, and I could only believe it myself because I was looking past now, past the near future, past the horrible news that would come to her one way or another, to a world where Daniel's life had meant something. "Not today, and probably not tomorrow, and maybe not for months and months, but I promise you that one day, it will be okay."

She sniffled wetly, her nostrils clogged with gunk, and propped herself onto one elbow to look directly at me. "Dad, if anything happened to you or Mom, to either of you or both of you—I couldn't handle it. You have to know that."

"I know."

Olivia turned back to the television, surrendering to the glow and comfort of a situational comedy—the canned laughter, the lessons learned, the happy resolution at the end of each half hour. She blew her nose into a napkin, then crunched a few more Saltines. When her breath became regular, I turned off the television and stared into the semidarkness of the room, lit only by weak shafts of light through the vertical blinds.

It was hard not to think that I was the worst person in the world, maybe even worse than Robert Saenz himself.

olivia

For the first few minutes the next morning, I felt a hundred pounds lighter than the day before, as if I'd shucked off my whole worrisome self. I woke to the sound of Dad showering, the water rushing powerfully through the pipes, and stretched happily.

And then I remembered: the bullets, but no gun. Daniel's ashes, which should have been waiting on our mantel in Sacramento, along on this crazy road trip with us. Not to mention Dad's portable memorial to Daniel, the dead son he never mentioned.

I tiptoed to the bathroom door and tried the knob, which was locked. Did Dad always lock the door when he showered? The four of us had shared a single bathroom in Sacramento, and occasionally Mom and Dad had popped in on each other, or Dad and Daniel, or Mom and me, but the opposite-gender parent-child privacy had been fully respected. For all I knew, Dad had always locked the bathroom door ever since it was just the two of us. But maybe the door was locked now for a different reason.

Acting quickly, I repeated the search Sam and I had conducted yesterday: in Dad's suitcase, under the mattress, making sure everything was undisturbed by the time I heard the water stop.

"Liv? Are you up?" Dad called through the door.

"Yeah."

"Feeling better this morning?"

"Fine," I said, and sat on the bed to think.

If Dad had a gun, it was in the bathroom with him now, and he would be carrying it underneath his clothes when he came out. If Dad didn't have a gun, I was an idiot. It wasn't hard to believe in my own stupidity, and I wanted to, more than anything, but somehow, our conversation yesterday hadn't completely reassured me. Dad had done it again—looked straight at me without seeing me at all; said one thing while his mind seemed to be moving in a completely different direction.

Since Sam had held out his hand yesterday afternoon and I'd seen the bullet, my mind had been whirling. I wasn't any kind of mental health expert, and a few sessions with a family therapist didn't qualify me to be a crisis counselor, either. After our search of the motel room, Sam suggested I come right out and ask Dad about the bullets. I'd turned the question over in my mind that afternoon as Dad and I watched TV, but couldn't bring myself to ask. I was fairly sure he would lie, feigning surprise, becoming defensive. And where would that get me? On the other hand, I wasn't sure I could face the truth.

But I knew what I had to do, had known it since the second I rounded the corner of the administration wing at Rio and saw my father on the cafeteria roof. I had to come clean to Mom. I had to tell her the whole sorry mess. I should have told her on the phone, when I'd announced we were coming to see her in Omaha, or during any of our quick conversations since, when I'd done nothing more than update her about the weather and mileage and things I'd seen along the road, like circling vultures and shredded remains of tires from eighteen-wheelers. It had seemed unfair, an awful thing to dump Dad's craziness on her when she was too far away to do anything about it. One more day, I promised myself. I would spill it all to her the second we pulled into her driveway in Omaha.

Just then, Dad emerged from the bathroom, looking fully rested and relentlessly chipper. "Let's get this show on the road," he said, slapping his hands together. The sound felt too loud for our little motel room, as if he'd miscalculated the volume. I noticed that he was wearing the same hooded sweatshirt as yesterday, its hem hanging low over his pants.

At breakfast, Betha Caldwell pressed her palm against my forehead, checking for fever, and I missed my own mother all over again with an intense, almost physical ache. *Soon.*

Because Dad was hoping to get on the road as soon as possible, Betha gave us a ride to J & E Automotive, and by nine-thirty, our suitcases and backpacks and extra shoes and books were heaped haphazardly on the sidewalk in front of the shop, waiting to be stowed in the Explorer. While Dad went inside to check on the progress, I plopped myself down on the cement next to our belongings, aware that to any passerby our junk probably looked like a homeless camp, missing only the shelter of a giant cardboard box.

Surprisingly, Sam wasn't sitting outside the store, and his roadside stand wasn't there, either. The folding tables were leaning upright against a fence on the side of the J & E Automotive property, and the chairs were there, too—but there was no sign of his snow globes depicting their miniaturized scenes of horror. Had he come back here yesterday afternoon, after our failed search of the motel room, and packed up for good? Or was he waiting until I was on the road again, out of his sight and mind, before he resumed business as usual?

It had only been two days, but I was already taking Sam's presence for granted. This was where he always was, and this was what he always did. At any minute, Sam's stepdad was going to announce that the Explorer was good to go, and that would be the end of Sam Ellis and me, if there had been a Sam Ellis and me to begin with.

I hadn't even thanked him, I realized—not for taking me out to see the stars or exchanging stories of our worst things. I hadn't thanked him for standing on top of my bed in his socks, unscrewing the overhead vent with a handy little tool on his Swiss army knife. I'd protested that my father really wasn't that savvy—I was pretty sure he didn't have his own multi-tool, anyway—but I'd felt relieved when Sam's searching had produced nothing except a small shower of dust bunnies. I hadn't even said a decent goodbye after Dad had barged wild-eyed into the motel room, looking as if he might strangle Sam, and me, too. At least Sam's shoes had been back on his feet by then, so Dad hadn't been able to collect evidence to support his wrong conclusion.

The office door swung open, and Dad came out.

I tried not to sound as if our car being fixed would be the end of the world. "The Explorer's ready?"

"Not yet. Within the hour, they said. I'm going to grab some coffee. You in?"

I shook my head. If Sam Ellis came by, I wanted him to see me here, waiting for him. "I'm saving room for forty-four ounces of sugar and cancer-causing additives once we're on the road."

Dad patted the top of my hoodie affectionately as if I were a small dog and crossed the street. I was leaning back against my suitcase, staring after him when Sam said softly, "Hey."

I whirled around to find him a foot from me. "Sneak up on me, why don't you?"

Instead of saying anything, Sam crouched down beside me and grabbed my hands. Actually, he grabbed at the outline of my hands, which were tucked up into my sleeves. Even though our actual skin was separated by a thick layer of fabric, I swear I could still feel the warmth of him coming through.

"Where did you come from?" I demanded.

He jerked his head in the direction of the shop. "Inside. I've been helping out with your car."

"I tried to ask him, but I couldn't," I whispered. "What am I going to do?"

He smiled shyly, as if we'd just met. Except when we'd met, he hadn't actually been shy at all. "I figured you weren't going to say anything, so this morning I took care of it for you."

"What do you mean? You took care of what?"

He sank down next to me, reached into the pocket of his jeans, and held out five bullets in his cupped palm.

I leaned away from him, feeling sick at the sight. "You just took them out?"

"Yep. All of them."

Panic was rising in me again, like water in a backed-up sink. "But what if he notices? What if we get on the road and he feels around under his seat and they aren't there? What am I supposed to say then?"

Sam smiled his smile that wasn't all the way even, but a little crooked, so that his lips met in two not exactly parallel lines. "Well, I replaced them with something else. So if he just feels around down there…"

"He'll think the bullets are still there."

"Right."

"What did you replace them with?"

"Some AAA batteries."

I let out a snort of laughter. "Oh, wow. That shouldn't be funny. But it is."

"They're about the same size, and it might work."

"Yeah." Relief had flooded through me, and something

else—gratitude. A warm, happy flush snuck up my face. "It might."

"But you're going to tell your mom everything, right?"

"Tomorrow."

"And you're sure you're going to be okay until then, between here and Omaha?"

I slid my hands out of my sleeves and locked fingers with Sam. His hands reminded me a bit of my mom's, gently calloused, hands that knew how to make intricate pieces of art, or take the cover off a heating vent, or help with an oil change. "My dad isn't going to hurt me. He wouldn't ever."

He gave me that crooked smile again, and I leaned close to him, so close that I was pretty sure the heart I heard beating wasn't my own. "Sam Ellis. Do you know what I'm going to do right now?"

"You're going to kiss me," he said.

And he was right.

curtis

An hour later, I had almost used up the credit on my Visa, and the Explorer was ready to go. Jerrod Ellis backed it to the curb, and I loaded up the trunk. With Olivia conveniently distracted—I tried not to flinch too hard when I saw her *kissing* Sam—I eased the revolver from my waistband, wadded it in a T-shirt and tucked it back into the spare tire well. I felt an immediate, almost physical relief. We were back in business. Olivia and Sam moved slowly toward the car, their arms wrapped around each other's waists. It struck me that they were exactly the same size, like matching chess pieces.

I cleared my throat pointedly. "Ready?"

Sam held out the hand that wasn't hugging Olivia and said, "It was very nice meeting you, sir." The same grin was mirrored on Olivia's face. They were *happy*. I felt a little rush inside my head. How strange—I had completely discounted the possibility of happiness.

"Likewise," I said, returning Sam's firm grasp.

Olivia was beaming, her cheeks burning red through a fine layer of pale powder. "We're going to see Sam again in what, a week? Two?"

I stared at her, not understanding.

"On our way back home, right? We could swing through Lyman, couldn't we?"

Oh, shit. Not only was I going to break Olivia's heart, but I was going to crush poor Sam Ellis, too. Add that to my list of wrongs in the universe—not protecting my family from tragedy, not being there for Daniel when he lay on the sidewalk, his heart beating for the last time, not being the husband Kathleen needed and, of course, *deserved*. And now this. I was simply dragging my misery eastward, scattering bits of it along the interstate.

"Dad?" Olivia's smile had faded. "We'll be coming home this way, won't we?"

I needed to get to Oberlin fast, like yesterday. I needed to be out of Olivia's life before I could hurt her any more. "Of course," I said, with a little shrug. "But maybe you should exchange addresses just to be safe."

Olivia rolled her eyes. "Maybe we could send each other telegrams while we're at it."

Sam leaned his head against Olivia's. "I'm making her something. It's a surprise."

Olivia smiled. "You are?"

"Yeah. It might take a while, though. I'll have to send it to you when you get home."

Home, I thought.

Olivia's nose brushed Sam's, reminding me of the penguin kisses she used to give each night after her bath, when her hair was still tangled and she was wrapped only in a towel. *Daddy!* she would shriek. *I'm all wet!* But the Olivia standing in front of me was a woman—a girl who could soon be independent, who was in the process of becoming the person she was.

"Okay, then," I boomed, clapping Sam on the shoulder. I rounded the Explorer and climbed inside. Sam and Olivia separated like taffy pulling apart. My legs felt cramped, and I reached down, adjusting the driver's seat. With a quick glance to make sure they weren't watching, I ran my hand along the underside of the seat. Everything was intact—the duct tape, the bullets—and I withdrew my hand quickly.

Olivia buckled herself in and rolled down the window for a last goodbye.

"Remember your promise," Sam said, and Olivia nodded.

Promise? We needed to leave before Olivia and Sam became engaged. I adjusted the visor, squinting into a hearty sunlight. The day was getting away from us. When I backed out of the parking lot—the Explorer revving harder than I'd intended—Olivia waved her hand out the window. In the rearview mirror I saw Sam raise a single hand and hold it over his head in a solemn goodbye.

And we were on the road. The Explorer moved along smoothly, rejuvenated—no odd starts, no sudden acceleration. I gave it more gas, pushing the speedometer to eighty, thinking of lost time, the long, open stretch of road in front of us. Olivia didn't comment on the speed, which meant she hadn't noticed. Her face was averted from me, but I could see her reflection in the dusty window. If I hadn't known it was Olivia in the passenger seat, I wouldn't have believed it. That girl wasn't my moody, brooding, darkly funny daughter. That girl was smiling. That girl was grinning like a fool.

"So," I said, breaking a twenty-mile silence. "If we push through, we could be in Omaha late tonight."

"Really?"

"About eleven hours, give or take stopping time. What do you say?"

She was still smiling, her face open and happy. "I say drive, Kemosabe."

I chuckled, enjoying the small release from the tension well-ing inside me. Robert Saenz was back in my sights, and my whole body felt sharp and alert as a nerve ending.

"So," Olivia said. "Lyman, Wyoming. Who knew?"

"Not me."

I could hear the smile in Olivia's voice as she said, "Love."

I turned to her sharply. "What?"

"Love," she repeated.

It took me a long moment, during which my mind probed for the kinds of words used by therapists on TV talk shows: *get to know a person before you commit...don't jump into things too quickly...*

Olivia was looking at me, an eyebrow raised significantly.

"Oh! Um...electrostatic."

"Canyon," she countered.

"Necrosis."

She pulled a face. "Scrambling."

"Ghoul."

"Labyrinthine."

I gave her a small salute. "Not bad. Been reading a dictionary again, have you?"

She laughed, turning again to look out the window.

The sky was an endless blue, so large overhead that even the distant rocks and ridges, enormous up close, looked inconsequential as anthills.

This, I thought. Even at the end of it all, we'll have this one happy moment.

olivia

It was ridiculous how happy I felt. Twenty-four hours ago I'd been in a panic because I thought my dad might have stashed a gun in our motel room, but right now, I was riding along like everything could be okay. It was possible—maybe even probable—that we would make it to Omaha, and things would be good. At the least, we could have a few happy days together. I was too cynical to believe in some kind of *Parent Trap* reunion, as if Mom and Dad had secretly been in love with each other this whole time, and in a week Mom's belongings would be packed in a U-Haul trailer being pulled behind our Explorer westbound on I-80 on our way to happily ever after. But at least, maybe, things would be *okay*.

I smiled at the Olivia whose face was reflected in the window. It was a different face than this morning, before I'd kissed Sam, and he'd kissed me right back. Could everyone in the world tell that I was a girl who'd been kissed? Would Mom be able to tell instantly, as quickly as she could spot Dad's new haircut?

My stomach rumbled, and Dad said we could stop in Green River, just down the road.

"Green River," I said. "That sounds pretty."

"It is," Dad told me. "I mean—it was, at least. Your mom and I stopped there overnight."

"On the mythical expedition across America?"

He laughed. "Right—it was really mythical. The Datsun overheated about five times, if I remember."

"What did you do in Green River?"

"We spent the night, wandered around. There was this trainyard…" He cleared his throat, his words coming out thick. "I remember we stood on this bridge for a long time, watching the trains come and go beneath us. It was—" He stopped.

"Beautiful? Amazing? Lovely? The ultimate Wyoming experience?" I prodded.

"All of the above," he said, and went quiet. This time I thought his faraway look wasn't directed to the future, with all the possibly frightening things I couldn't imagine, but into the past. Both were places where I hadn't been granted access.

We stopped at a McDonald's off the freeway. A long drive-thru line snaked through the parking lot, but only one other car was actually parked.

"Whoa," I said as we entered. "It's the McDonald's that time forgot."

"I was thinking Reagan-era," Dad agreed.

The seats were yellow plastic, attached via metal arms to the central tables, which were topped with a dull wood veneer. Standing in line, I was dwarfed by a towering cardboard Ronald McDonald in massive red shoes. Strange, I thought, that plenty of people, including me, were scared of clowns but not necessarily scared of Ronald McDonald.

The only other customers in the restaurant were a frazzled-looking blonde woman and two young boys with matching wispy ponytails. Dad and I watched the boys chase each other through the play area, wiggling their way through a plastic tunnel, climbing the rope ladder and skidding down a red slide with a dingy gray streak in the middle where the paint had worn off.

"Every McDonald's should have a play area," I mused, slurping my too-sweet orange soda.

Dad nodded absently, taking a bite of his sandwich.

I watched as the taller boy reached the top of the play structure and pounded on his small chest, Tarzan-style. "And not just every McDonald's," I continued, dunking a French fry in a tiny paper bucket of ketchup. "Every restaurant. Every building, period. Can you imagine what it would be like if you went to, like, the DMV and while you were waiting for your turn at the counter, you could flop around in a giant bin of balls?"

Dad considered this. "Would you have to take your shoes off?"

I pretended to be offended. "Of course you would have to take your shoes off. Those are the rules. We're living in a society, after all. There are some rules that just have to be obeyed in order for society to function."

"Would the equipment be sanitized on a regular basis?" Dad teased.

I frowned. "That's a given."

The woman called to her children, and we watched as they struggled back into their tennies and sweatshirts, then raced each other to a minivan in the parking lot.

I glanced around and saw that we were alone. A few employees were rushing around, filling red-and-white bags for the drive-thru. My heart felt full. "Do you think anyone would mind if I'm slightly over the height regulation?"

"Seriously? You do realize that daily sanitization is pure fiction?"

I began unlacing my boots. "This is a new Olivia," I told

him. "And the new Olivia can handle a few million germs." Still, I hesitated outside the ball bin, pushing away my fears about how often—probably never—each individual ball had been sanitized and how often—probably frequently—the balls ended up in someone's mouth. "Wish me luck," I told Dad bravely, and then I climbed the steps, crouched and executed a perfect swan dive off my knees.

"Hey," Dad said when I rose triumphantly, arms out-stretched. "You're spilling everywhere."

"Come on in," I called to him. "The water's warm."

Dad grinned. "I forgot my bathing cap."

I tossed a ball at his head. "Then, how ever will we prac-tice our synchronized swimming?"

Dad fiddled around with his phone and held it up to eye level.

"What's this? Photographic evidence of my immaturity?"

"Something like that," Dad said, tapping the screen to take one photo, then another. A thousand miles of scenery, in-cluding the salt flats and the Rocky Mountains, and all we would have to show for our trip were a few shots of me in a McDonald's play area.

I could feel someone watching us from inside the main res-taurant area—a McDonald's manager, red-and-white striped shirt, black bolero tie, black polyester pants. No doubt I was violating some kind of cardinal law for play areas. Feeling bold, I tossed a handful of plastic balls into the air and let them hit my stomach with soft thumping sounds.

"Um, okay, Liv, get up now." Dad was backing away, tuck-ing his phone into his back pocket.

I tossed another ball at him. He caught it and returned it, firmly, to the bin.

"That's enough. Come on, please." He was almost begging.

"What's wrong?"

"I just got an idea of what this must look like."

"What do you mean?"

Dad nodded over his shoulder in the direction of the store employees. A small clump of them had gathered behind the counter and were staring in our direction. "Old man, young girl, camera..."

I laughed. "Okay, that's kind of funny."

"No," Dad said, "not at all funny. Come on, get out of there now. We've got to get back on the road...."

I laughed again. Dad looked so nervous, and he had switched into this overprotective father mode, which I barely recognized. He had hardly ever needed to protect me, since I was so intent on protecting myself. I stood up in the middle of the bin, displacing more balls. They tipped over the plastic pen, hitting the tile in rapid succession with the sharp explosion of kernels popping in a microwave. "Hey!" I called, waving my hands over my head, until I had the attention of every single employee in the store.

"Liv, *no*—" Dad said, reaching for me.

It was a strange feeling, exhilarating, a full-on adrenaline rush. Everyone was staring—but they were strangers, people I would probably never see again. I would be a little footnote to their dinner conversations tonight: "And then this weird girl wouldn't get out of the ball bin...." Maybe the girl-in-the-ball-bin incident would prompt a series of training exercises for McDonald's employees: How to Handle Unruly Customers.

I pulled away from Dad's reach, shrieking with laughter. I wish Sam could be here, I thought, and Mom and Daniel, too. "Hey! Hello!" I called again. "Do you see this man? He's my *father,* you creeps. So, get your minds out of the gutter for a change. And you know what? He's a damn good father, too!"

I was still laughing when we were back in the car. Dad had hustled me out in my socks, and it took me a while to wriggle my feet back into my combat boots while I was doubled over, wheezing. "Did you see—the looks—on their faces?" I gasped.

Dad was chuckling, too, but it was the silent, hard kind of laughter where tears come out, instead of sound. Even a few minutes later, when my boots were on and my breathing had settled and I was sitting quietly myself, in full awe of what I'd just done, I saw that Dad was still wiping tears out of his eyes.

But the weird thing was, he didn't seem to be laughing at all.

curtis

Olivia called Kathleen to report on our progress while I listened like a guilty eavesdropper, a third wheel to their conversation. I was already on my way out, already seeing Olivia and Kathleen as their own unit, a mother-daughter twosome that didn't include me and couldn't, shouldn't.

They will be fine, I promised myself. Olivia will be fine. It was easy to believe that, listening to her narration of our McDonald's adventure, her voice happy and light. A week ago, Olivia had been a girl who ate lunch alone and skipped P.E., who recorded her fears in her tiny, cribbed handwriting. Now she had driven a car, kissed a boy and had a public display of—whatever that had been—in a roomful of strangers. Now I was the one who was afraid.

"Mom wants us to call when we get closer," she said, dropping the phone into her lap.

"Okay."

"I think you should be the one to call her, though."

I glanced at her and back at the road. "Why? Is something wrong?"

"Not with *me*. With you two. You're going to be seeing

her tonight. We're all going to be staying in the same house together. It would be nice if you could figure out a way to actually talk without using me as a middleman."

"We have talked," I pointed out, although of course, we hadn't, really. Our conversations had been rare, delivered in a just-the-facts-ma'am way, business transactions rather than heart-to-hearts. "And we have seen each other. We were all together last summer, remember?"

Olivia shot me a look. "For two weeks, and the whole time you kept finding excuses to not be in the same room. Anyway, I'm just letting you know I'm not going to do it anymore. And you should know, I've been a pretty shitty middleman."

"Olivia," I said seriously, "you're shitty at nothing."

"Ha! Only a thousand things."

"But you're right. We will talk, your mom and me, and we won't use you as a middleman."

"You mean it?"

"What part?" I asked. She gave me a light punch on the shoulder. "Yes, I mean it." Kathleen and I would talk; we had to. There were things to be settled.

Olivia seemed satisfied with my answer. She looked out the window again, tapping her finger against the glass, drawing little heart shapes in the film of dust that coated the interior. "Dad," she said finally, earnestly, as if she'd been thinking about it for a long time, "tell me when you and Mom fell in love."

I groaned. "Liv, do we have to?"

"Yes," she said. "We absolutely have to."

"In college. You've heard everything already. Freshman year at Northwestern. We were in the same philosophy class together, blah blah blah."

"What do you mean, blah blah blah? It's not obvious that one thing follows from the other. 'We were in the same philosophy class, so we fell in love.' For one thing, there were probably a few dozen other people in that class, and presumably you didn't fall in love with any or all of them, and neither did she. And—" Olivia was working herself into a verbal deluge "—did you fall in love in class? Was philosophy the basis of your love? Were you reading Kierkegaard and then suddenly, *bam!*"

I sighed. "Okay, let me try again. We were in the same philosophy class. I missed a class and borrowed her notes. And then later that semester, we just kept bumping into each other, in the cafeteria and that sort of thing, and we started talking."

"So you fell in love over a plate of hamburger casserole."

"It's not like there's one moment, Olivia. It's just something that happens over a period of time. You know, you spend time together, your lives become more or less intertwined, and then I think you just realize you're in love." I was talking too generally; it hadn't been that way at all with Kathleen and me. It was simply a version of our life that felt less painful to relate, rather than the small details of her laugh, her wild head of hair, the touch of her hand on my arm, my hand on the small of her back. I was grateful that Kathleen wasn't here to contradict this version of events. If Olivia asked her the same question, would she point to a specific moment in time, one certain glance, one walk across campus?

"Like Sam and me, then," Olivia said.

"Excuse me?"

"A joke, Dad. A joke." She was quiet again, staring out the window. The sun was slipping lower in the sky, an orange ball about to bump into the distant horizon. We were approaching Cheyenne and Nebraska soon after, but it was a long haul across the state to Omaha.

Still facing away from me, Olivia asked, "Was it like that when you fell out of love, then? Was it so gradual that you didn't notice it happening, rather than all of a sudden, because you'd dropped one of the kitchen plates and she'd forgotten to thaw the chicken for dinner, or because one day you just looked at her and thought, not *this* person again—"

I hit the brakes on the Explorer suddenly, the car jerking, swerving, straightening out. Our suitcases in the trunk slid forward, smacked against the row of seats and shifted backward just as abruptly. I eased up on the brake, and we drifted to the side of the road before coming to a complete stop. I jerked the gearshift into Park a little too forcefully.

Olivia was bracing herself with an arm on the door ledge and a foot against the central divider, her eyes wide. "What the heck, Dad?"

"Listen to me. It wasn't anything like that, and not for any dumb reason like you're suggesting. Maybe you have a right to be angry with us, but we don't deserve to be talked about that way. Especially your mom. She *tried,* over and over." It was *me.* I deserved it, and more. Kathleen had left physically, but I hadn't given her much of a choice.

"All right," Liv said evenly. "But you owe it to me to tell me what happened."

"Olivia." I felt about ready to snap, from the exhaustion of it, the stress of being two people. The Caring Dad. The Vengeful Man. A normal guy. The man with the gun. Cars passed us on I-80, approaching quickly in the side view, whizzing past, and leaving us behind. A double-load truck thundered close by, shaking the Explorer in a private earthquake. Olivia flinched as if we'd been hit. "Look, I'm not going to tell you that it's none of your business, because that's not exactly true. But I will say that some things are so private they really shouldn't be shared."

Olivia folded her arms across her chest, her chin set, fuming hard through her nose.

"You should be glad, actually, that I'm not telling you all the details. You should be glad your mom hasn't told you. Believe me, plenty of divorced—or separated, or whatever—parents do that to their kids. One parent blabs all this bad junk about the other, and vice versa, and the poor kid doesn't know who or what to believe and ends up resenting or even hating them, and nobody wins there. No one." I stared ahead as I said this. It was true in a general way—as a teacher, I'd more than once stumbled into the middle of a custody arrangement gone bad, parents who refused to talk to each other, a text-book left at one parent's house that couldn't be retrieved until the following weekend.

Olivia bent suddenly, fiddling in her backpack, and then sat up, an oversize pair of white-framed sunglasses jammed onto her face to hide her tears.

I pressed on, more gently. "We tried to be adults about it, and that was the best we could do. We just—after Daniel died—we couldn't make it work, but we tried to keep you from the worst of it. I mean I hate to say it, but it's something you couldn't possibly understand at this point in your life."

She swiveled to face me, shoulders squared. "Here's the part in the script where you tell me I'm too young to grasp the big picture, right? Or that I'll never understand because I'm not a man, not a husband and a father, right? Because I never lost a child, and I should come back to you when I do, and then you can tell me, I told you so?" Tears leaked out the bottom of her sunglasses, leaving a shiny trail down her cheeks. With her hoodie pulled up on her head again, she looked like some tiny, tragic Hollywood star, going incognito on her way home from rehab or her latest police stint. I thought this—then im-mediately rebuked myself. What an awful thing to think. Olivia was worth a million times that.

"It's a stupid script," I acknowledged, reaching over to wipe away her tears with my thumb. "But it's the only one I've got."

Her face half-hidden by the sunglasses, Olivia slept her way across most of Nebraska, which was four hundred fifty-five miles wide along I-80, long enough for me to consume one Big Gulp and two extra-large Styrofoam cups of coffee, long enough to listen to the same CD eight times and long enough to have serious doubts about everything that had, for a while, seemed completely clear to me.

Only hours away now—six, five, four, the mile markers decreasing slowly, steadily—Kathleen was waiting for us, walking from one room to another in her parents' house, tidying furniture, setting out stacks of guest towels. I could see her doing this—I could picture her small frame, her hair tied back, the radio on, humming under her breath in her determinedly cheerful way. She would be preparing for the best but expecting the worst, the same way she had approached each day after Daniel died—planning things, making arrangements, trying to pull us out of our gloom, but knowing she was already defeated, that the plans and arrangements would come to nothing and we would have the same miserable day all over again.

I hadn't been able to see it clearly, not until that day on the roof when the world was spread out before me, a giant's playground, and my own place in it had felt so devastatingly small. But I would admit to Kathleen that I hadn't tried, hadn't even begun to make the necessary effort. I'd been content to run circles around my grief, like a hamster on a giant wheel. I would talk to her, like I'd promised Olivia—*really* talk, something I hadn't done since before Daniel died. We'd known each other for thirty-two years and been married for twenty-nine, but a three-year separation had somehow erased much of that time, leaving behind only smudges and smears, no clear impressions.

When Kathleen had left for Omaha, I'd expected her to mention divorce, to send a thick packet of papers in the mail, awaiting only my signature to put an end to things. I know others—people we knew in Sacramento and Omaha—must have speculated, but there hadn't been anyone else in the middle of our marriage. No fetching neighbors, no enticing coworkers, no alluring stranger at a bar—no one. What went wrong with our marriage had been me, and Kathleen deserved to hear me admit it. I would tell her she had made the right decision, returning to Omaha. I would have left myself behind, too, if it were possible.

This would most likely be the last time I saw Kathleen— my constant, my rock, even when she was thousands of miles away. She was the link between who I had been and who I became, the one person in my life who knew where Curtis Kaufman had come from, and the only person who could possibly understand, someday, where he had gone.

While Olivia slept and I drove on, the sky grew dark, the night split by twin beams of headlights. Memories of Kathleen flooded back to me, almost tangible—as if she were floating out in the darkness, just out of reach. Suddenly, I was filled with a desperate longing to go back to the last normal day of our lives, the day before Daniel died.

Kathleen's alarm had gone off at six, and I'd listened, half-awake, as she pulled on her sweats and tennis shoes. Cracking open one eye, I had peeked at her as she dressed. Even without makeup, even with her hair in a messy ponytail, Kathleen was striking. If I could go back, I would drink it all in, give her my full, waking attention. I should have—and would have, if I'd known what was to come—rolled out of bed and joined her. But I'd only smiled, closing my eyes, listening to her footsteps recede as she walked down the hall. Heidi had shaken herself awake and followed Kathleen, her toenails clicking on the hardwood. I'd listened as Kathleen leashed Heidi by the front door, which was no small task. Oh, the excitement! The frantic circling! The panting! The amused reassurances! Then the door clicked closed behind them, and the house was silent.

Less than twenty-four hours later, the world would come to an end.

If I could do it again, I would say "Don't go yet," pulling Kathleen back into bed with me, so that we could spend that last normal morning making love, sweet and slow, the world at bay.

It was just past midnight, and Olivia was awake again when we exited the freeway, the sunglasses tucked into her backpack. Even with the moon blocked by clouds, I knew exactly where to go. I'd spent three college summers in Omaha, sleeping on a basement pull-out couch, and several holidays here with Kathleen and the kids, so the city had that familiar-but-different feel, as if it had given up waiting for me to return and had begun, ever so slightly, to change. Straining, I looked for the all-you-can-eat pizza buffet where Kathleen and I had gone on summer weekends, staying too long in our cushioned booth, holding hands across the table.

Even though I had talked to Kathleen at our last stop for gas, Olivia called her again as we approached through darkened streets, giving her the play-by-play: "We're on 99th Street… we're passing a giant Walmart sign…we're turning right…"

I slowed for a turn, noticing that the pizza parlor was now a Payless Shoes, with towering rows of sandals and loafers disappearing out of sight. Someone honked behind me, and Olivia said, "Dad!" to me, and then to Kathleen, "Oh, nothing. Dad's just spazzing out again."

A few more turns and we were out of downtown, heading toward a residential area. If western Nebraska was mainly flat, the interstate a long trench splitting distant bluffs and

rock formations, Omaha was its opposite, a city built on rolling hills, with winding—*labyrinthine*—streets and towering
trees. The homes were comfortable, spaced far apart in a way
that didn't happen in Sacramento, unless you lived in one
of the wealthiest neighborhoods, locked behind a gate that
could only be opened by a security code. Less had changed
here, in an area of hundred-year-old homes; there was still
the brickwork, the white siding, the front porches, the lamp-
posts in front yards.

I made the final turn, slowing to ten miles an hour. Olivia
read the numbers off the mailboxes, like the countdown to a
grand reveal. "Eleven-oh-four, eleven-oh-eight…"

Here goes everything, I thought, as we crested a slight rise
and came downward.

"Eleven-twenty… Oh, my goodness! I see you!" Olivia
shrieked into her phone. She was fumbling with her seat belt
and out the door even before I came to a stop.

Kathleen was standing in the driveway, a shawl pulled over
her shoulders. She beamed, throwing open her arms and wrapping Olivia in a hug. Behind her was the house, a two-story
white Colonial with black shutters and a red, inviting front
door. At the north end of the property, a row of birch trees
glowed, ghostlike.

I cut the lights but stayed in the car for a long moment. Over
Olivia's shoulders, Kathleen and I locked eyes. Although she
was smiling, a line of worry split her forehead.

See, it's the right thing, I told myself. *Olivia belongs here.* She
deserved her mother, a big lawn, a clear change of seasons, a
place where things like gangs and drive-by shootings probably didn't even exist.

Kathleen stepped back, tugging off Olivia's hood to get
a better look, to really see our daughter. She smoothed her
fingers over Olivia's hair and smiled. I knew she was close

to tears, the way she'd been during those brief summer visits, when she'd been gone too long, and the time remaining
was too short.

"Dad!" Olivia called impatiently, waving me over.

I took a deep breath, bracing myself, and then I stepped out
of the car to join them.

olivia

D ad called that he would bring some things from the car, so Mom led me into the house, her right arm wrapped around my shoulders. "You'll be upstairs in my old room," she said, her squeeze tight and strange. My left arm hung awkwardly at her waist, not sure where to go.

"Where will you sleep?" I asked.

"I've been sleeping in your grandparents' room, which I've finally got looking somewhat decent. You can use that bathroom in the morning—it's got one of those rain forest shower heads." Mom smiled at me, and I realized that she was nervous, maybe even as nervous as I was.

Dad came through the door behind us, a suitcase in each hand.

"What about Dad? Where's he going to sleep?"

Mom looked apologetically at Dad. "I've been using the guest room as a workshop, and I didn't have time to clear out Jeff's room. Somehow he hasn't managed to reclaim any of his five dozen basketball trophies, even though I've asked him a hundred times. So I guess the best place would be…"

"The basement," Dad finished. "Wouldn't have it any other way."

I followed the glance that went between them, the hesitant smile. They hadn't hugged or kissed a hello; there hadn't been so much as a handshake. I remembered the basement, where Daniel and I had snuck away to mess around with piles of old furniture and boxes of yellowed papers. It was a step or two above a dog crate in the garage, but that was it.

"Let me grab a few more things," Dad said, heading back outside.

Mom turned to me again, smiling brightly. "Well! I know you must be tired, but I made a pizza earlier and popped it into the oven when you called...."

"Great, I'm starving," I said.

Dad came back with the stack of textbooks I'd packed nearly a week ago and promptly forgotten about.

"It's not like I'm going to need those tonight," I protested.

"Well, I don't know what you're going to need when. I'm just grabbing everything while I'm at it."

"In that case, don't forget the box of tampons in the glove box."

Dad and Mom rolled their eyes simultaneously, and Mom laughed. It was a nice moment, our puppet strings relaxed just for a second, to give us a little room to improvise.

It was nearly one-thirty by the time I slid beneath the covers in Mom's old room, exhausted even though I'd slept through most of our long drive. It was a relief to have our clumsy re-union out of the way. Mom had tried to kiss me good-night, which would have been fine, but it took me so completely off guard that she ended up brushing my shoulder with her lips instead. She'd mentioned school a few times, too, and Dad and I, by mutual consent, had changed the subject. Mom could find out about my failing P.E. grade later—or, hopefully, never.

Her room was the same as I remembered it from our previous visits, and probably the same as it had been when she was a girl. It was a relief to turn out the overhead light, blocking out the explosion of pale yellow and white, the curtains with eyelet trim, the ruffled bed skirt, the vanity with the attached curved mirror and a fancy three-piece comb set, better suited to girls in fairy tales who wanted to know who was the fairest of them all. "Ignore all that junk," Mom had said, indicating a stack of boxes along one wall, each labeled in her block handwriting: BOOKS, DOLLS, GAMES, CLOTHES.

I leaned against the headboard, the bedside lamp on, my journal open in my lap. We'd made it, we'd somehow survived the whole crazy trip despite approximately seven million things that could have gone wrong, and here we were. Why did it feel so anticlimactic? Had I expected my parents to take one look at each other and fall into each other's arms with declarations of love? Did I think the romance would be instantly rekindled when they had spent the past three years not even speaking to each other? No—I hadn't expected it, but I'd allowed myself to hope. Stupid, stupid girl. They had been about as passionate as two acquaintances bumping into each other at a Costco. *Oh, hello. Didn't we used to know each other?*

And then Dad, lugging in every single thing from the Explorer as if he couldn't sleep easy with my empty Sprite can in the console. While I devoured half the pizza and listened to Mom ramble on about all the changes she'd made to the house—the old wallpaper steamed off, the new chair rail in the dining room, the repainted cabinets, the butcher block countertops—Dad had wandered back and forth, carting my suitcase upstairs and his downstairs. *Sit down! Talk to us!* I wanted to command him, but he seemed restless, like he couldn't find a comfortable place to relax. After the twelve hours of driving he'd done that day, I felt a little guilty relegating him to the basement on that ancient pull-out couch with the flimsy mattress.

I'd left them sitting at the kitchen table with the few remaining slices of pizza. With any luck, Dad would come clean all on his own about his rooftop crack-up, and I'd be spared the task of telling anything to Mom.

If not, I'd have to get her alone tomorrow for a serious talk, the one I'd refused to have over the phone. I had to tell her about Dad on the roof of the Rio cafeteria, and how I'd seen my whole life flash before my eyes—or if not my life, then his. I would tell her how scared I'd been, how scared I still was, and how she needed to fix things, because it was completely out of my control, and I was sick of doing the worrying for all of us.

And of course, I'd have to tell her about the bullets, too.

Tomorrow, I promised myself. Tomorrow everything would get figured out.

curtis

Kathleen had done some work on the basement, but otherwise, it was exactly the room I remembered. The steps to the basement had been recarpeted, and the handrail, always a rickety metal affair, had been replaced with mahogany so polished and smooth it was almost slippery. At some point, she must have lugged away the foosball table, which through one enthusiastic tournament or another had accumulated a number of players on the injured list. But the couch was still there, covered in the type of scratchy plaid upholstery that made it unpleasant to sit on with any bare limbs. I recognized the end table and the antique lamp that worked by inserting a small key into a hole on its thick trunk.

Kathleen had left a set of sheets on the couch, and I set about the task of piling up the cushions on one end of the room, pulling out the hideaway and making up the bed. I was almost faint with déjà vu, the scene both natural and bizarre at once.

That first summer when Kathleen had brought me home from Northwestern, we'd given her parents only a day's notice. Better to surprise them, Kathleen had said; Owen and Barbara Eberle were the sort of people who handled unexpected visitors well. They had been immediately welcoming, making the subtle rearrangements to their lives that were required for the accommodation of an entirely new person for an extended period of time. Barbara offered to reorganize her guest room, which had doubled as a sewing and hobby room, but I'd insisted that the basement was fine. I could almost hear the sigh of relief—it would be much easier to keep an eye on me if I were sleeping two floors below Kathleen.

We'd kept this same arrangement three summers in a row. Kathleen's brother, Jeff, recently graduated from college, was working for Owen, and we'd developed an easy friendship. If the family had been initially wary of me—the boy from Chicago with parents neither they nor Kathleen had ever met and whom I never referred to—this was forgotten soon enough. I was Kathleen's boyfriend, sure, but they treated me almost like a prodigal son, as if I had been away for far too long between visits. Owen took me to the lake in his boat on Saturdays, and we caught next to nothing, smoked too many cigars—which I can only remember guiltily in retrospect, since it was lung cancer that would kill him—and returned home sunburned and sated. Jeff had gotten me the roofing job, and most weekdays I woke to the alarm at four-thirty, rolling off the hideaway bed, climbing the stairs quietly to shower on the main floor without disturbing anyone. By the time I was dressed, though, Barbara had breakfast going; when my ride pulled up curbside, she handed me a mug of coffee, a Coleman jug filled to the brim with ice water and a paper sack packed for my lunch. It was easy to think of them as my parents, too— the long-lost parents I never had, the type of parents I would have wished for as a child, if I could have believed they existed.

Over the years, Kathleen and I hadn't been back as often as we'd promised that day we'd pulled our packed-to-the-gills Datsun out of the driveway and left for California. I remembered the way they'd stood on the porch, waving goodbyes—

Owen puffing away on his signature cigar, Barbara wiping tears on the sleeve of her sweater. Each time we'd returned, it was to signs of their gradual decline. Owen's breathing grew wheezy first, then was aided by a pull-along oxygen machine. He'd refused chemotherapy and radiation, insisting that he would go how he wanted to go—which was only six weeks from the date of his diagnosis. Barbara's quaint forgetfulness rapidly became more than absentmindedness, and she died a year later in an Alzheimer's ward. So young, both of them, so seemingly healthy and vibrant and productive. Their deaths had been devastating for both of us, but I was, in a way, relieved that they hadn't outlived Daniel, hadn't lived to see what a mess we'd made of things.

I was sitting on the bed, remembering this, when Kathleen came down the stairs. "I moved some of the old things into the garage," she explained, as if we'd been in the middle of a conversation. "I'd like to save as many things as I can, refinish them one by one, but between that and all the work at the store…"

"You want to sit?" I asked, gesturing to the end of the bed. I'd heaped my suitcase on the old armchair with the matching scratchy fabric.

She shook her head, leaning back against the wall. Had it been strange for her to come back here, to live in her childhood home? She'd exchanged one house of ghosts for another. But she'd thrown herself enthusiastically into the renovations, a seemingly never-ending project.

She continued, talking fast to fill the silence. "I'm thinking of renovating the whole basement, maybe making it a separate apartment for some income. But I'd have to figure out the access. There's that old door off the laundry room, obviously, but it's just about impossible to reach from the driveway, so not such a grand entrance. I'd like to knock down a few walls, put in a little kitchenette and one of those stackable washers and dryers…."

"That's a good idea," I said.

"You think so?"

But I hadn't really heard her. I was amazed by how she was handling her life, baffled and envious, not angry like I'd been in the immediate wake of Daniel's death. Kathleen could move on. She was strong; she was resilient. She didn't know that Robert Saenz was out, walking free in the world—but would she have acted any differently if she did?

"Curtis?"

"Yeah," I said faintly, trying to focus on her words. I was noticing that she'd let her hair grow long, that there were a few gray hairs at her temples. She looked trim, healthy. I let my gaze drift across her face—skin so pale it was almost translucent, that slight bluish vein visible on her forehead. I was aware of how rumpled I looked after a day on the road, the soda stain that bloomed on one cuff.

"Of course, Jeff says most of the house should be gutted. But he doesn't have an understanding of the bones of the house, of the architecture. You should see where he lives—you will see it, if…" she trailed off. "How long are you planning to stay, exactly?"

I cleared my throat. "There are some things…" But I couldn't go any further. The full weight of the day descended on me, like a heavy cloak of X-ray armor.

Kathleen stared at me. "What is this about, Curtis?"

I couldn't answer. Despite days of rehearsing the words in my head, I couldn't actually say them.

"I'm glad you're here, and Olivia," she said, when it was clear I wasn't going to contribute. "But I can't have it like it was, where you refuse to talk to me. That was killing me. I can't do it. I can't put in all the effort."

"No," I said, my voice thick. "I don't want you to. You won't have to. I'll—" I stopped, as if I were trying to find my place in the script.

Kathleen waited, her posture uncomfortably straight, chin slightly forward, bracing herself for the bad news.

"Tomorrow," I said. "I'm hardly thinking right. Maybe we could have this conversation tomorrow."

She nodded, tucking a loose curl behind her ears. "Tomorrow, then."

"Tomorrow, then," I said, and she nodded.

That was all I had—one more day.

olivia

I woke up surrounded by white blankets, white pillows and a yellow bedspread, and couldn't for the life of me remember where I was—what city, what hotel. Then I spotted the row of boxes with Mom's handwriting and sat up, groggily.

I'd plugged in my cell phone last night and left it charging on the nightstand, but it took me a moment to realize why I was awake. There was an alert on the screen, a message from Sam.

So? Did you make it? Did you talk to your mom?

Sam. Only a day ago we'd been standing in front of the automotive shop, kissing. I brushed my fingers over my lips, reviving the memory. It had been beautiful and sweet, but now it felt sad, like a long-ago dream, the details already fading. I wrote back:

Not yet. Today, I promise.

I cracked open the bedroom door. Maybe this was my best chance, while Dad was still in the basement, sleeping. The

door to Grandpa and Grandma's room—Mom's room, now—
was open, the bed already made. I paused on the stairs, listening to the sounds of my mother in the kitchen, achingly
familiar. The refrigerator door opened and closed, something
was whisked in a bowl. And she was humming. Funny how
I'd forgotten that, as if the memory itself had climbed into
her Volvo and left along with her physical body.

Mom had always hummed—when she was scrubbing the
bathroom floors, sanding down a piece of furniture, staring
into the open refrigerator while she planned our groceries
for the week. It was a trait she had shared with Daniel, but
now I wondered: Had her humming influenced him, or had
his humming influenced her? Mom wasn't necessarily on-
key most of the time, and she would get stuck on one or two
lines of a song, usually an advertisement or, between October
and January, a Christmas song, and she would hum it until
we went insane—*Santa baby, slip a sable under the tree, for me....*
But sometimes she and Daniel would join forces in a humming duet. Once, I remembered, Daniel had been riding in
the passenger seat and I'd been in the backseat, and the two
of them together had hummed their way through *Yellow Sub-
marine*, laughing and cracking each other up.

Standing there on the stairs, I tried very hard to remember Mom humming after Daniel died. There must have been
some time, at least once, maybe when she was ferrying me
from school to the therapist, or when she was reupholstering
our old couch...or had that been one more thing that died,
along with Daniel?

But when I rounded the corner and came into the kitchen,
she was still humming, stirring something at the stove. "Hey!"
She looked torn, as if she wanted to drop the spoon and give
me a hug, but settled instead for a little air kiss as I passed.
"How does a vegetable frittata sound?"

I eased into a chair at the table. "I should warn you that my body may not be capable of digesting anything that doesn't contain vast amounts of sugar or salt."

Mom glanced at me, concerned, and did some quick whisking in the bowl on the counter. "That bad?"

"No," I said, feeling stupid for a joke that had fallen flat, and feeling defensive on Dad's behalf. "Not that bad at all."

"Well, anyway, your dad's just gotten into the shower. He must be exhausted, driving all that way."

"Hey! I drove part of the way."

Mom glanced again in my direction, wounded. I wasn't planning these little jabs, but maybe there was an unconscious part of me that wanted to hurt her, because they just kept coming.

"You didn't tell me you had your license," she said.

"I don't. But remember, I told you that Dad let me drive in Utah, when we were on the salt flats."

"Oh, that's right," Mom said. She flipped something in the pan with a spatula and stood staring down at it, as if without her attention it would burn. And maybe it would—that was a perfectly good reason for her not to look at me. But I couldn't help feeling the awkwardness of the moment, the way nothing I said came out exactly right, the flash of disappointment on her face when I'd evaded her kiss.

This was the time, I realized. I just had to come out and tell her, find a way to get the conversation going. We would get into our rhythm, that mother-daughter patter we'd once had, that intimate, confessional space. The trouble was that I'd gotten so used to being just with Dad. He and I kept up a constant, running shtick of sarcasm and puns and double meanings. It was our defense mechanism: laugh at ourselves, joke about our failures, crack wise, and nothing in the world could hurt us. Now, with Mom, it was like we had to find our footing all over again.

"Want to pour us some juice?" Mom asked, and I slipped off the chair to comply. This should have been a simple task, but the refrigerator was one of those fancy ones designed to blend in with the cabinetry, and I first pulled open a cupboard and stared blankly at a row of canned food. Mom laughed, and I quipped, "Oh, you didn't want me to make it from scratch?"

Finally, I poured orange juice into two tiny glasses. "So, Mom…"

"So," Mom said soberly, as if I'd said something profound.

"I wanted to tell you that—" I froze, hearing a door open and footsteps approaching on the wood floor.

"Oh, your dad's out of the shower. You want to get him a glass, too?"

I stood again, numbly. I'd blown it. The thing to do was to blurt it all out in one fell swoop. *Dad was on the roof of the cafeteria and maybe going to kill himself and there were bullets in our car.* Why was that so hard?

"What were you going to say?" Mom asked as Dad entered the kitchen, holding a bundle of dirty clothes. He was dressed in jeans and a long-sleeved polo, his typical off-work uniform.

"Good morning," he said, and just stood there awkwardly, as if he were waiting to be invited any farther into the room. But at least he was *here,* not avoiding us entirely like he had done when Mom visited in Sacramento. I took pity on him and handed him the glass of juice.

"I just wanted to know the agenda," I said. It took my parents a moment to react, as if I had communicated with them in Morse code, and they were counting out the dots and dashes. "For today. I wanted to know what we're doing today."

Dad looked at Mom.

"Well!" she said, bustling back into motion. "Breakfast,

obviously. And then I figured I'd show you around Omaha, if you wanted to see the shop...."

Dad and I took seats at the table, and Mom fussed around, delivering hot slabs of frittata onto our plates. I looked at Dad, waiting to follow his lead. This trip had been his idea, after all.

"Of course," Dad gushed, and I almost laughed, his enthusiasm felt so fake. *Of course! We absolutely want to see the place where you spend all your time when you aren't spending it with us.*

"Liv?" Mom was waiting for me.

"Um, yeah," I said.

"Great. I told Stella I would be taking today off and maybe tomorrow, and then we'll see from there, I guess. We can take a little drive around Omaha, find a spot for lunch and then tonight Uncle Jeff and Aunt Judy want to have us over for dinner. Sound good?"

"Sure," I said.

"And if there's anything else you want to see, in particular... I mean, if you need anything, we can go shopping, or I could take you by the high school. It's only a mile or so away."

"Why would I want to see the high school?"

Mom shrugged. "It's where I went to school."

I looked at Dad again, but he had set down his clothes on an empty chair and was digging into his breakfast as if he hadn't eaten in a week. When I thought about it, he really hadn't eaten much on our trip. He'd picked at all of our meals and then snacked in between on the odd handful of chips, washed down by giant-sized cups of whatever he'd found inside gas stations.

Still, I thought it was strange that he wouldn't even glance at me, even as I kept my eyes on his face. We were both hiding our secrets, but I had the feeling that Dad's were darker than mine, and more monumental than I could begin to imagine. I felt a little shiver, like a pinch on the back of the neck. A part of me was scared for him, wrestling with that dark thing I couldn't even begin to name. And a part of me was scared for myself, too.

curtis

For our grand tour of Omaha, Olivia rode shotgun and I sat in the backseat like a banished toddler. The sky was a lazy blue with intermittent clouds that lay low on the horizon. As she drove, Kathleen pointed out items of interest—the historic buildings, the parks with walking trails, a new yarn store that offered weeknight knitting lessons, a café with seventeen blends of espresso, a Whole Foods.

"Mmm-hmm," Olivia said, stifling a yawn. She glanced into the side-view mirror, which was angled so she had a perfect shot of me. I gave her a sloppy grin, and she returned it uncertainly.

Look around, Olivia, I willed her. *See how happy you could be here.*

We were nearing the Old Market district of Omaha, an artsy area with galleries and museums and cobblestone streets. Kathleen rambled on, with the hyper-enthusiastic voice of an HGTV host, "And this building used to be an old grain mill of some sort, but now it's being converted into condos. I have a client who just bought in to the building, so I got a peek inside. It's the most amazing space—a little cavernous, maybe...."

I had seen pictures of Kathleen's store on the website, which I'd browsed every so often, marveling at what she'd accomplished. She'd borrowed some money from her brother up front to be a co-owner in the business, a buyer and creative partner who sometimes worked on special pieces for commission. The store exhibited the old-meets-new style that represented her journey as a designer. When we'd first moved to California, the ink on her art history degree still drying, Kathleen had started as a clerk in an antiques store and worked her way up to being a sought-after buyer for a number of dealers around the Sacramento area. It had always amazed me, when I'd accompanied her on a Saturday driving from one estate sale to another, how Kathleen could home in on one particular vase on a cluttered folding table and know something about it—the country of origin, the year, the maker, the materials, the sort of glaze, the technique. "This is an example of Japanese cloisonné, early nineteenth century," she would murmur. Barely able to restrain herself, she would pull me to the side, out of earshot from the seller, "Those are Windsor chairs, James Chapman Tuttle, late 1700s...." Although I could never distinguish between the finer details she noticed, I found something incredibly sexy about her brain—the sheer amount of data she had accumulated, her mind a glossary of names and dates and pictures.

When we bought our downtown house, it had become the canvas for her mind and the spark that unleashed more genius within. Motivated at least at first by our meager budget, she switched her focus to "reclamation—" finding hidden beauty even in pieces that had been left curbside. An old chicken cage became a coffee table with compartments for the kids' books; a massive headboard was split into four hinged sections and used as a divider between our kitchen and dining room. She'd sold a similar piece to an admiring friend, and then began to take special projects on commission, refurbishing a buffet for a downtown coffee shop, furnishing an upscale boutique near the convention center.

"I can't wait for you to see this," she said now, pulling her Volvo into a space behind the row of buildings. "We could enter through the back, but I really want you to see it from the front, to get the full effect."

I followed as we made our way down the alley onto a side street, a strange trio. Kathleen was wearing cargo pants, short boots and a black cardigan, her hair upswept in a clip. Sunlight caught a few of her silver strands. Olivia, wearing her standard head-to-toe black, stumbled in her combat boots as she tried to keep up with Kathleen. In my least dirty pair of jeans, I trailed so far behind that outsiders wouldn't have recognized me as part of the group. It's just a mother-daughter outing, I thought. This is what they'll do without me; this is what they'll look like when I'm not around.

The words SEEDS & SUPPLIES were stenciled across the second floor of the brick building, the sort of retro throwback that Kathleen loved. A smaller sign hung over the double entrance doors: *Absolutely Interior.* Kathleen opened the door, ushering us in with a grand sweep.

"Mom—wow," Olivia said. "I mean, *wow.*"

"It's fabulous, Kathleen," I agreed.

She beamed. "You like it?"

"It's fantastic." I touched her on the shoulder, tentative, more of a "well done" pat than anything else, but the familiarity of that shoulder sent a sad thrill through me. What were we, other than skin and sinew and bone?

"Wow," Olivia said again. "Seriously, wow. It's a good sign, isn't it, that I'm speaking only in palindromes?"

It was a former industrial space, reclaimed itself, reinvented. The ceiling was at least thirty feet high with light fixtures dangling like stars from black cords. Although the space was vast, burgeoning with merchandise, the store didn't feel crowded. Furniture was grouped in cozy arrangements, with startling displays of color and ingenuity—shining dark wood mixed with painted wood, creams and teals and chartreuses, burgundies and silvers and golds.

"We've actually been contacted about renting out the space for events, cocktail parties, that kind of thing." Kathleen's face was flushed with pride. "Not that it's exactly easy to move everything out of the way for a large group. And the fear of a spilled glass of wine has kept us from fully entertaining the idea."

Olivia's eyes were slowly roving from piece to piece, trying to notice everything. "The whole world should be this beautiful," she said.

It was the sort of occasion where a person should be able to quote a significant line of poetry—but I had nothing to give. "It's just fabulous," I repeated. "Well done."

"Kathleen! Kathleen's family!" A woman was striding toward us from the back of the store. I recognized Stella instantly from one of those long-ago Omaha summers—a little heavier, a little more brassily blonde, still Kathleen's physical opposite. She wore a purple dress, knee-high boots and oversize gold jewelry that clanked when she moved.

"This is Stella," Kathleen said. "Stella, this is my daughter, Olivia. And I know you met Curtis—"

"Years ago, more than twenty, but who's counting?" Stella breezed in, extending her hand to Olivia, then me. "Kathleen is a genius, isn't she?"

Kathleen laughed. "Don't let Stella fool you. She has every bit as much creative genius, but she's the more valuable partner because she can sell *anything*."

Stella linked arms with Kathleen in a chummy way. "Speaking of which…I know you're officially taking a few days off, but there is something I wanted you to look at, if you can spare a minute."

"You don't mind, do you?" Kathleen asked. "Why don't you look around? Maybe you could pick out something for your birthday, Liv."

"My birthday isn't until September," Olivia objected, but Stella was already leading Kathleen away.

"Let's wander," I said. We did so carefully, Olivia's fingers tracing picture frames, a gold-and-black world globe, the print on a tufted floor cushion. There were probably twenty customers in the store and a few employees in simple black dresses and flats. At the stainless steel counter in the middle of the store, someone was choosing fabric swatches; another employee was wrapping a large box in brown butcher paper. I'd glimpsed this world on the website, but the effect in person was more impressive. It was almost mind-boggling what Kathleen had achieved in three years. I'd filled my days with teaching, with Olivia, with the nagging back-burner thoughts of Robert Saenz, and in that time Kathleen had been creating this entire world out of nothing.

Although I wasn't sure we were supposed to occupy the merchandise, Olivia and I settled onto a bright yellow sofa. I wondered if Kathleen had worked on this piece, or been involved in its selection. This was a color she loved, the yellow lemony and rich; I could imagine her hand-picking the paisley buttons between the tufts of fabric. Years ago she had taken apart a secondhand sofa on the back patio, just to see how the upholstery worked. Olivia had been seven or eight then, old enough to be bribed with a few dollars to help with the task, to collect and sort the disassembled parts.

Without thinking, I said to Olivia, "Maybe you could get

a job here, some kind of summer sales associate, that kind of thing."

"What am I going to do, telecommute?" she asked sharply.

"It's just an idea," I said, backpedaling. "I think you would be really good—"

"Is that what this is all about?"

"This isn't all about anything."

We stared at each other, Olivia's eyes narrowed into icy slits. "You're lying to me."

My throat felt tight, as if its walls were closing in. "How am I lying to you?"

"It's a lie of omission, then."

I didn't say anything. My list of omissions was massive and growing longer every second.

"This is about me moving here permanently, isn't it? That's why you brought Daniel's remains with you, because we're not going home again."

"You went through my suitcase?" My mind reeled, thinking of the gun. But no—it had been with me the whole time. "I really don't think you had any right to—"

"Really? After everything you've put me through, I'm getting a lecture?"

I took a deep breath, calming myself. Of course she was right. I leaned in closer, but she shifted away to the very end of the sofa. "Olivia…"

"You know what's going to happen," she accused. "You've been holding all the cards. This is some stupid plan you've had all along."

I didn't stop her. I couldn't say *There's no plan*. I looked around, willing Kathleen to appear, needing her brightness, her optimism, her eternal belief that somehow things could be better.

Olivia wiped at her eyes angrily. "I can't believe that you're doing this to me."

I tried to say "All I wanted..." but she drowned me out, saying what she'd never said before, even though it was the line teenagers all over the world had said to their parents. Daniel had said it to me, and I'd said it to my father. I'd heard my students throw it around when they couldn't go out on the weekend, when they didn't get the phone they wanted, when things were in some vague and indefinable way "unfair." But not Olivia, no matter how much I'd deserved it, no matter how the circumstances had called for it.

"I hate you," she said, her breath ragged, her words coming out in gasps. "I hate you for this. I hate you for everything."

Maybe I'd been waiting for it, all this time. Maybe, in a way, it was a blessing. She could let me go. I reached for her again, and she didn't pull away. She let her gaze drift down to my hand on her leg, as if it were an alien thing, the hand of a stranger, a pervert. I pulled back just as Kathleen approached, her smile fading instantly. She looked at me, indicting without the facts—although if she'd had them, it would have been an indictment all the same.

"What is it?" she asked, the words dangling like a lifeline neither of us could catch.

The store hummed around us. Olivia wiped her eyes carefully on her sleeves, but a smudge of black mascara left a dark shadow on one cheek.

"You know what I want, Mom? You know what I think would be really great?" she asked, her voice rising dangerously.

Kathleen's eyes darted between us nervously, as if she were afraid to ask.

Olivia was undeterred. She had a brilliant, bogus smile on her face, and I felt my heart clench as if it were caught in a vise. Whatever she said, it would be something I deserved.

But I didn't expect what she said next, when she turned that horrible smile on me, her eyes bright with tears.

"I think the only thing missing from this happy reunion is a trip to the zoo."

olivia

Once, when I was a kid, I'd thought about running away. I'd taken a vintage train case, something Mom had picked up at a yard sale, and crammed it full of things from my room—dolls and toys and a blanket and my toothbrush. Mom had interrupted me when I was sitting on top of the case, trying to get it to close. "What's this?" she'd asked, spotting the edge of my blanket where it was spilling out of the suitcase. "Are you planning a picnic?"

I wasn't sure exactly what she thought when she saw me crying in her beautiful store, on top of her beautiful couch, but again she played along, true to form. "Why not? That sounds like a great idea!" she said. "We haven't been to the zoo in—what? I don't know. Years."

I didn't volunteer the information, but I could have told her the exact year of our last visit down to the day. It had been part of our family Christmas trip—Dad and Mom holding gloved hands, Daniel boosting me up at the exhibits to get a better look. We had been a zoo-going family; Daniel and I had been to the Sacramento Zoo and the Oakland Zoo and the San Francisco Zoo—we'd seen monkeys and sloths and giraffes and pandas and penguins. Now that I was older, the realization that these animals were in captivity—that they had not *chosen* to live on this patch of land in San Francisco or Oakland or Sacramento or Omaha—put somewhat of a damper on the experience. Still, I wanted to see the zoo again—to feel happy and carefree as a kid. Somehow, a visit to the zoo felt like the one thing I absolutely wanted at that moment.

"Really? We can go?"

"Of course. We can do whatever you want," Mom said.

As we drove, I avoided looking at Dad in the rearview mirror, even though I could feel his eyes there, boring into me. At a traffic light, Mom leaned over and smoothed the top of my hair, which was sticking up in stiff peaks where the hairspray had dried. "Maybe we can eat at that little café at the zoo," she offered. "It's overpriced, but…"

"That would be great," I said. "Wouldn't it, Dad?"

"That's fine," he said amiably, still watching me in the mirror. I had the feeling that I could ask him for anything at that moment—a tattoo, a body piercing, a keg of beer— and he would have gone along with it. Not that I wanted a tattoo, a body piercing or a keg of beer, but I wouldn't have minded watching him wallow in his guilt. I felt whiny and stubborn and unreasonable, like a real teenager for a change. Even though it was cold, I rolled down the passenger-side window and threaded my fingers through the crisp air. In the backseat, Dad must have been cold, but he didn't mention it.

Mom was telling us about a woman from Seattle who had visited the store and commissioned a half-dozen pieces to be finished by the end of summer; just this morning an order had come in from one of the woman's friends, and she and Stella were over the moon. Dad asked about the pieces, and Mom mentioned a new wood-staining process. The way they kept up a steady stream of small talk, it was as if we were a happy family on a sitcom, the kind where the *D* word would never be discussed, because it simply wasn't in the trajectory of the characters.

"That's really great, Kathleen," Dad said.

Mom said, "Thank you, Curtis, I appreciate that."

I glared out the window. It was all so fake. They might have been reading from a script called How Not to Let Your Divorce Royally Fuck up Your Child. Why else would they be calling each other by their names? They had probably planned this whole stupid trip together months ago as a way of manipulating me. They'd known what I wanted—friendly, happy parents, and were just waiting for me to fall into line.

We made our way directly from the zoo entrance to the café behind the Wild Animal Pavilion. Dad picked up the tab for our burgers and fries, and Mom studied the zoo brochure, pointing out the Orangutan Forest and the Gorilla Valley.

Stop! I wanted to scream. *If you're getting a divorce, then just come right out with it.* Had they just been dancing around the issue, silently agreeing not to mention it in my presence? It *was* strange that they'd never discussed it with me, despite three years apart.

And if they were getting a divorce, it explained just about everything—from our crazy road trip to Dad all but admitting he was passing me off to Mom. Was that what he was thinking when he was on top of the cafeteria, looking down—that he had only one more cord holding him to the world, and it was time to cut himself free? Or had it been Mom's doing, arranged in a clandestine phone call? She'd wanted this from the beginning, from that awful day we'd sat in the living room and I'd picked Dad's side.

For a second I felt the wooziness that typically preceded a major hyperventilation attack, and then I realized I wasn't scared, not at all. I was mad.

"We're taking a few of our pieces to a show in Minneapolis

this fall," Mom continued, picking apart her hamburger, and Dad nodded, sucking it all up. "The great thing is that we've taken on a few interns, mostly unpaid, but they're able to help us out and learn at the same time…." Mom's face was practically gleaming from happiness, or maybe just from the glow of a pendant light over our table. Then she must have noticed that I wasn't returning her smile, because her lips wavered.

Did she really need to rub her success in my face? She didn't need to prove how much she didn't need us—not Dad's advice, not my companionship. In fact, if I'd been there all along, if I'd packed up my stuff three years ago and come east with Mom, maybe she wouldn't have been successful at all. Her whole life would have been consumed with me and my *teenagerness,* my needs, my five million irrational fears and my rational ones, too. There would have been no time for her to woo clients or construct fabulous pieces or plan trips to Minneapolis. She'd been a million times better off without me, but now Dad had had enough, and it was time for the big trade-off. Clearly I'd failed there, not holding him together the way I should have, not being able to keep him from going up on that roof, not being reason enough for him to come down on his own. He would be better off without having to worry about me and everything I was worried about.

It was a fairly shitty thought, but it was true: both of my parents would be happier without me.

"You okay, Liv?" Mom asked.

"Did we come to the zoo to sit in a restaurant, or what?" I demanded, standing up with my half-full tray. I waited outside so they could have that parent talk, where one parent says, "Did you say something to her?" and the other says, "No, but I think she knows."

I took off ahead of them, leading the way through the Lied Jungle, which claimed to be the world's largest indoor rain forest. It was difficult to stay angry and disappointed and anxious when there were gibbons swinging past, branch to branch, and pygmy hippos near the water's edge. I hadn't realized it was a Saturday until I had to elbow myself into position for an unobstructed view of the Cat Complex. Coming out of the Bear Canyon, I was nearly trampled by a horde of seven- or eight-year-olds moving in a pack, and the human-to-stroller ratio did seem completely skewed. I peered into the strollers to see sleepy babies inside, blissfully sucking on fingers or pacifiers or the giant rubber nipples of their bottles. Nothing had gone wrong for them yet—not that they knew.

Dad and Mom were close by; every now and then I turned around, and Dad bumped straight into me, or I overheard Mom say "Look over there! A lemur!" But somehow, I felt desperately alone. If Daniel had been there… No. If Daniel were alive, he would be twenty-three, and that would be way too old to wander through a zoo on a Saturday, even to humor his little sister. He'd be off in London or Tokyo, giving a concert that I would later see on YouTube.

I pressed on, determinedly, my feet beginning to ache in my combat boots, not that I would have mentioned this fact. We passed the okapi, the gazelles, the zebras, the warty pigs, the bongos, the swift herds of antelopes. I could pretend, too. I could act as if this were a happy family outing, and we were just normal Omahans enjoying a normal Saturday at the zoo.

Mom caught my arm in the Simmons Aviary, using her free hand to point out the magnificent plume on a crowned crane. It *was* sort of beautiful—a tiny golden crown perched on top of a not-so-special bird head. I reached into my pocket for my cell phone to take a picture, but Dad jumped in like some kind of photographing superhero, insisting he would get a picture of both of us. Instead of getting a picture of the crowned crane, I ended up with a picture of Mom and me standing a foot apart with a not-very-special tree in the background.

I tried to corner Mom while we waited in line for the women's restroom, but unlike lines for women's restrooms the world over, this one moved too quickly. "So, what's next?" I asked.

"Hmm, what do you think?" She pulled the folded brochure from her pocket. "Maybe the Desert Dome? They've got iguanas, a meerkat…"

"I meant after the zoo," I said pointedly. "After today. After tomorrow. What's next?"

She looked at me as if I were speaking her language, but in a different dialect or with such a strong accent that it took a while for my words to make sense. "Um, we're heading to dinner," she said. "Uncle Jeff and Aunt Judy can't wait to see you again."

"Mom—"

But I was at the front of the line, and a stall became free, and I lost my chance. When I came out, I waited at the sinks for Mom, but she must have peed extremely fast, because I found her waiting outside on a bench with Dad, their heads bent close together. They were planning the hand-off, trying to figure out how to make it seem spontaneous, or worse— trying to figure out how to make it all look like *my* idea in the first place.

We ended our Fake Family Day with dinner at Uncle Jeff and Aunt Judy's and me still in a bad mood. Even their house made me angry. They had one of those massive, modern, sprawling homes that had a separate space for everything—a music room, a play room, a living room, a family room, a den, a dining room—so that it was sort of like walking through a beige mausoleum. Each room looked more or less the same, which must have driven Mom nuts—tan walls, stone floors, a light brown couch, a cream-colored throw.

Aunt Judy threw her arms around me at the front door. I hadn't seen her since Daniel's memorial service, and it surprised me that she was still so much taller than me. Had I not grown at all since then? She'd played basketball in college and had the kind of body that was all hard angles, so that she didn't so much hug a person as box out everyone else. She gushed, "You know, if you're still here a few weeks from now, Chelsey will be home for the summer. It would be so nice for you to catch up!"

A few weeks from now. Apparently, everyone was in on this conspiracy, except me. I forced a smile. It would have been awkward to see Chelsey, anyway; she was closer to Daniel's age, and other than bumping into her online, we hadn't seen each other for years.

Uncle Jeff lifted me completely off the ground, swung me around for a bit like a child on an amusement park ride, and deposited me back onto my feet. He was over six feet himself, broad-shouldered like Grandpa had been. "You're getting so big," he said. "Course, big is a relative term around here."

Everyone laughed.

I noticed that no one hugged Dad; it was two quick handshakes, and that was that. Friendly but frosty, the way you said hello to someone you had purposefully been avoiding until you couldn't avoid them anymore.

Aunt Judy poured wine for the adults and directed me to a massive side-by-side refrigerator in the garage, which was stocked with twenty kinds of soda in long-necked bottles. Who in the world drank all of this? Had it been a last-minute purchase for my benefit, or stocked for Chelsey's return home from the University of Iowa? Maybe Chelsey still had pool parties and movie nights with her high school friends. If I were being dumped in Omaha, we would probably get to know each other. But right now, if she walked through the door and caught me snooping in her refrigerator, she might think the house was being robbed.

The evening was filled with awkward conversation, reminding me of our long-ago family therapy session, with each of us going around the circle and stating our piece. Uncle Jeff talked about a new commercial development on the north side of town. Aunt Judy was coaching a traveling girls' basketball team and had a number of trips planned for this summer. Mom rehashed the same tidbit about the woman from Seattle who loved her work, and then it was on to Dad and me. Dad said that teaching had been challenging this year, and he was glad for a little break. Everyone jumped to murmur agreement, and then the conversation fell flat, like a fart at a cocktail party. True, I knew very little about cocktail parties, but it did fit what I knew about farts. Uncle Jeff got up to open another bottle of wine, and Aunt Judy went to check on the dessert. When they came back, they were smiling so hard it might have been family picture day at Olan Mills.

It was my turn.

"What about you, Olivia?" Uncle Jeff asked.

I wondered what they wanted to hear first: that I had filled at least a dozen notebooks with things I was afraid of, that I was once again failing P.E., that although I was sixteen years old, I didn't even have my driver's permit, that I'd lost my virginity to someone who didn't even know my name, that yesterday I'd kissed someone who I wouldn't at all mind kissing again. And to top it off, neither of my parents particularly wanted me.

Mom smiled at me encouragingly, her teeth stained pink from the wine.

Aunt Judy winked at me. "Oh, she's probably got a million secrets, just like any teenager. Chelsey was the same way at that age."

I took a long slug of my grape soda and said, "Actually, my life is fantastic, in an illusory sort of way."

No one had anything to say to that.

curtis

When we were finally back at the house—at Kathleen's house—Olivia yawned dramatically and announced she was going to bed. Since the confrontation in Kathleen's store, I'd been on the alert for a major blow-up, but instead, Olivia had been operating on a slow simmer, like a teakettle not quite coming to a boil.

"Hey," I said, catching her arm as she started up the staircase. "I want to say good-night."

Kathleen had walked ahead of us with a Tupperware container of leftovers, and I could hear her boots clack on the kitchen tile.

Olivia squirmed out of my grasp. "That's all you want to say?"

I swallowed. "I want to say that I'm sorry I haven't done a better job of things."

She stared at me, and I waited for the apology that didn't come. *I don't really hate you, Dad.* Would I have apologized if the tables were turned? Was she waiting for me to apologize?

I reached for her again and gave her a quick, tight hug. "I love you," I whispered.

"Yup. Night, Dad," she said, breaking free again.

I watched her walk upstairs, steadying herself with a skinny arm on the banister. It wasn't a real goodbye, but I hoped she would remember the hug, the I love you. Someday, I hoped at least she would remember the moment.

I found Kathleen in the kitchen, taking our breakfast dishes out of the dishwasher. "Ready for that talk?" I asked.

She nodded, surprised.

By mutual, tacit consent we went down to the basement and sat down on the mattress of the pull-out couch, pushing aside my rumpled bedding.

I ran my palms over my thighs, suddenly nervous as a teenager.

Kathleen said, "I need to know why you're here."

This was the moment. I don't know how I'd envisioned it—maybe over a glass of wine, a toast to old times' sake. I still felt somewhat waterlogged from the wine at dinner, although its warm effects had worn off.

"Kathleen." I looked at her, *really* looked at her—this woman I'd met all those years ago, when she was still a girl, really, when I'd been so fascinated by her. She had saved me; she'd taught me to believe that another life was possible, a good one. She'd had our children; I'd loved the feel of her pregnant body, so lovely and round, her belly reverberating with tiny movements as the baby shifted and stretched. If I could go back and do the same things again with the guarantee of different results, I would have.

"Curtis," she said, pleading now. "Tell me."

All the anger was gone, all the reproach, all the long silences that had grown between us, that I had allowed to grow. We were just two people, the same two we'd been all those years ago. I took her hand. "Kathleen, I want you to take Olivia."

"Of course," she said, not even hesitating. She didn't say I told you so. She didn't remind me that this was what she'd wanted from the beginning, that she had known it would be for the best. "But why, Curtis? What is it?"

She didn't say: *What the hell is wrong with you?* But it would have been a fair question.

I only told her what she already knew, in whole or in part, things that were true enough without being the real truth. I told her that I was barely making it through the school day, could hardly juggle work and home. I said that Olivia needed a female influence in her life more than ever. She needed to be challenged and pushed and encouraged, and I wasn't sure I was up to the job.

Kathleen listened to me ramble, watching closely. She had always been a good listener, silent when silence was called for, but ready to speak—to pronounce a verdict, to share sympathy—when needed. When I finished, she cleared her throat and said, "Maybe both of you need to move out here."

I blinked.

"I'm serious. Maybe that's what needs to happen."

"That's not what I was suggesting." I'd tried to say it gently enough, but she flinched. I could see her trying to rally, trying not to be hurt. Since Daniel, she'd had to keep her guard up. I'd caused that. I'd pretended she was brittle, a hard shell of the woman I loved, someone who could put one foot in front of the other and move right on with life, as if a chasm hadn't opened up between us. But it wasn't fair; I was the one who had been brittle, not allowing myself to feel anything but hate. Kathleen had been waiting, warm to the touch, for me to reach out to her. It was my fault for not reaching.

Her voice trembled. "I would love to—"

I cut her off. I knew what it must have taken, for her to make the offer. "Not now," I said, heart pounding. *Not ever.* I laced her fingers with mine, brought her hand to my lips.

I thought I had forgotten about beautiful things, but what

happened next was the most beautiful déjà vu in the world, the most perfect goodbye.

We had followed a dutiful protocol, those long ago summers when I had stayed at her house. I'd worked construction jobs by day and come back, exhausted, to find Kathleen waiting for me. But we were rarely alone; Owen and Barbara were there, or Jeff, who was out of college and engaged to Judy but still living at home to save for their wedding. All day long, on top of the roof I was helping to shingle, the sun burning against the back of my neck, I'd thought of Kathleen—the nearness of her when we sat side by side in front of the television, her parents in the next room; the coy rub of her calf against mine under the kitchen table.

Every night I had spent on the pull-out couch in that basement, I'd imagined sneaking up two flights of stairs to her bedroom, sliding beneath her sheets to where she was waiting. Out of respect for her parents, in her parents' house, I had never done more than entertain the idea. At Northwestern, we'd tumbled in and out of each other's beds, leaving notes for roommates or hanging scarves on our doorknobs, telltale, shameless signs. In Omaha, the waiting became unbearable. When we couldn't stand it, we'd take my Datsun out on the pretext of shopping for one thing or another, complete the errand in warp speed and drive down to a spot Kathleen knew near the river, where my car was hidden from the road. Usually we made it out to the blanket I kept in my trunk, but sometimes we just slid into the backseat, all hands and elbows, half-clothed, laughing and fumbling. Once, we'd stopped at a McDonald's afterward to cool off, and I ordered us soft-serve vanilla cones. Sitting across from each other in a booth, I'd asked her to marry me, and she'd said yes. There wouldn't be a ring for another six months or so, and I'd be teased relentlessly for my lack of romance—*In a McDonald's, Curt? And she still said yes?*—but I knew I couldn't have lived with myself if I hadn't asked her, and she hadn't said yes, right at that moment.

But once—only once, the summer of our impulsive engagement—we had made love inside the house. She had appeared at the bottom of the basement stairs, whispering, "Shhh, Curtis." Until she pulled the nightgown over her head and stood in front of me naked, I'd thought I was in a dream. She straddled me, her body creamy-white and so beautiful I moaned into her throat. We were quiet, but we didn't rush. Afterward, we lay side by side, smiling, our bodies coated with a sheen of sweat. *It will always be like this,* I had promised myself. *This will be our forever.*

But it was even better this time, maybe because it had a final quality for both of us, maybe because we were both people who liked closure, who wanted to bring things full circle. The mattress on the pull-out bed was as bad as it had been back then, and creaky, too. I thought once of Olivia all the way up on the second floor, but we weren't as quiet as we'd been when we were twenty.

Kathleen was still beautiful, would always be. I ran my hands slowly over her, neck to toe, her body waiting and welcoming. We had changed in all the expected ways in thirty years, but we came together more gently, weighted down with everything that had happened between us. It was an underwater reverie, a fearless exploration. We fell asleep wrapped in each other's limbs, Kathleen's head on my chest. I dreamed that I was tangled in her hair and didn't want to find my way out.

When I woke, Kathleen was gone and the house was quiet. I fumbled for my cell phone. Four-thirty. Maybe she had wanted to sleep upstairs, to be close in case Olivia needed her, or maybe she was bound by that old sense of propriety, of what could and couldn't be done under this roof. Or maybe it was something else entirely—she'd gone upstairs because we were done with each other, and that was the gentlest way to say so.

From my suitcase, I removed the box of Daniel's cremains and held it for a long moment. It was only right that he stay here—not alone in our house in Sacramento, not at the mercy of whatever happened to me in Oberlin. I looked around the basement for the right place, somewhere it wouldn't be discovered right away. And then I took out the letter I'd written in Lyman and left that, too.

I hadn't really unpacked, so it was easy to zip my bag and carry it upstairs in a single trip. I winced at the sound of the engine starting in the driveway, but no lights came on upstairs from where Kathleen and Olivia were asleep, and there was no movement behind any curtains. Nevertheless, I waited for a long moment before raising my hand in a grateful goodbye.

olivia

Mom was at the kitchen table when I woke up, still wearing a pair of flannel pajamas. I could tell something was wrong—her hair looked particularly wild, as if she hadn't even run a hand through it since waking. She stood when she saw me, retrieved a mug from the cupboard and poured me a cup of coffee.

"Thanks," I said, sitting down. "But I'm going to need a pound of sugar and a cup of half-and-half before I can drink this."

Mom didn't say anything.

"What is it?" I asked. It struck me that the house was too quiet; there was no sound of another person waking up, moving around. Dad could still have been down in the basement, zonked out, mouth open—but somehow I knew he wasn't. "Where's Dad?"

She passed me a piece of paper, something that had been ripped off a notepad. The note was in Dad's handwriting, but I had to read it several times before I understood.

> *Please understand that I had to take care of some things.*
> *You'll hear from me soon.*
> *Love you both—Curtis (Dad)*

I stared at the note for a long time, turning the paper over to look for the rest of the text. It bothered me that he hadn't even used a full sheet of paper, and he obviously hadn't done a rough draft first and then a final draft, taking his time to make it neat and polished. His signature was mashed up against the edge of the page. Had he been that desperate to get away, that he couldn't even be bothered to write a proper note? Obviously—otherwise, he would have bothered to say a real goodbye. I remembered his hug the night before, uncomfortably tight, and how I'd wriggled my way out of it. He'd known, of course. He'd been saying his real goodbye then.

I set the note down on the table and looked at Mom. "Now what?"

She blinked.

"Oh, is this where you pretend you weren't in on it from the beginning?"

"I'm not sure—"

"Really, Mom? I figured it out," I said, putting air quotes around the words. "The Great Kiddie Transfer of 2013."

"Olivia!" She looked genuinely hurt, which hurt me, too—because I knew it must have been true.

I gave the coffee cup a little shove of rejection, causing liquid to spill over the rim and onto the tablecloth The coffee was absorbed by the creamy fabric, fanning out in a murky, brownish stain. "So, what? He just called you and said, I'm sick of living with this kid, it's your turn. Right? Did he tell you I'm so awful he just couldn't take it anymore? Or did you two set some kind of date from the beginning, some kind of your-turn, my-turn agreement, an equal division of labor?"

Mom put one hand on top of mine and then grabbed the other one, too, squeezing both of them tight. "Of course not! Don't even say something like that. And you're forgetting that

I wanted you here from the beginning. We both wanted to be with you."

I looked up from the coffee stain and met Mom's eyes. "You knew he was going to leave me here."

"No."

"Mom! I know you probably think you're protecting me or something, but you're not. I'm old enough to know what's going on. This is my life, too."

Mom looked as if she were going to be sick. "I didn't know anything. We had a long talk last night, and he said that he was just so overwhelmed—"

Since Mom was still holding my hands, I wiped my nose on the shoulder of my sweatshirt. I hadn't even realized I was crying, but the snot was flowing like a toddler's, dripping dangerously close to my lip. *I'd done this*—I'd overwhelmed Dad, probably with all my stupid fears and my failing P.E. grade and the fact that I was always hanging around instead of giving him space. Why wouldn't he want to be by himself?

"Just a second," Mom said, and left the room. I wondered if she was going to return with something Dad had left for me, maybe a box that held all the secrets of my childhood and would explain everything for me, the way it might happen on television. *Your father wanted you to have this,* she would say, and somehow everything would be okay. Instead, she came back with a new box of Kleenex, ripping off the strip of cardboard along the perforated edge. I took the tissue as permission to cry like an idiot, so I did.

"I didn't want him to leave," Mom said, wiping her own eyes with a tissue. "I told him you were both welcome to stay here as long as you wanted, even permanently."

"You did?"

"Of course."

I'm not sure why, but this made me cry even harder—deep,

ugly sobs that required a small stack of Kleenex. Finally, catching my breath, I asked, "Did he take all his stuff? I mean, is he really gone, and not just out for an oil change or something?"

Mom nodded. "I saw the note when I came downstairs. I looked in the basement, and everything's gone. His suitcase, his clothes. He even stripped the sheets off the hide-a-bed and put the couch back together."

"Where did he go?"

Mom shook her head, and I saw what I hadn't seen before. She looked unbearably sad.

"He didn't tell you where he was going? I mean, last night, when you had the heart-to-heart about dumping me off here, he didn't happen to mention where he was going to go?"

"Liv! When you say *dumping* you here, you have to know that hurts."

"Well, what did he do—just turn around and drive back to California?"

"I don't know where he went. He just needed some time alone, I think. That's what he told me, that he was going to take some time to figure a few things out."

"So he could be going back to California. He could be going anywhere." I had stopped crying and started to shiver, not because it was cold in the room, but because all of a sudden I felt cold from the inside out. What was Dad doing? What was his plan? "I'm going to call him. I have to talk to him."

Mom wiped her eyes with the heels of her palms and gave me a shaky smile. "I've already called him three times this morning. It goes right to voice mail, so his phone must be off. But look—it'll be okay, honey. He said we would hear from him, so we'll just have to wait."

It seemed like such an obvious thing to say, the kind of thing you might say to a child who needed to be pacified at the dentist's office. *Just wait and be a good girl, and I'll give you a sucker later.*

"But aren't you worried about him? I mean, he just went off alone, and no one in the world knows where he is. He's basically unstable—" This last part just slipped out, not the way I'd been planning to mention it.

Mom's eyebrows shot up. "He's *unstable?*" she parroted.

I backpedaled. "Well, you know. Not *unstable* unstable, but…"

"What does that mean?"

I bit my lip. Suddenly, I had the very shitty feeling that I should have told her earlier—not just the first night when we'd arrived, and not from a phone call on the road. I should have called her when I was standing on the asphalt near the cafeteria entrance, squinting up to look at Dad on the roof. I wasn't sure where to begin, now.

"Olivia?" Mom was leaning so close, I noticed that she had tiny red lines in the whites of her eyes, either from crying or not sleeping, or both.

I shrugged my shoulders, which felt unconvincing, so I also shook my head. If I protested again, I knew, it would just be a trifecta of foolishness. "I mean, I thought we had been doing fine, but he…" I trailed off.

"Olivia? I'm not kidding. If there's something you need to tell me…" Mom's voice held a warning note. We hadn't lived together in so long, and the time we'd lived together after Daniel died had been so strange, so I'd almost forgotten that it was Mom who was the taskmaster, the more demanding parent. Daniel and I used to be able to get away with things from time to time with Dad—not because he didn't care but because he honestly didn't seem to notice. Once I'd let Dad take the rap for a glass that Heidi had knocked down—a glass I'd left sitting on the edge of the coffee table without a coaster underneath it. Hearing the crash, Dad had simply said, "You know, I think that was the glass I was drinking out of after dinner." While Mom went on about his carelessness, I'd done nothing more than listen, guiltily.

Now she placed a hand on each of my shoulders and said, "You need to tell me what's going on."

I took a deep breath, and I told her about that day at school—or at least, almost all about that day at school. I mentioned that I was in the bathroom at the time my name was paged over the intercom, but not that I was in the bathroom because I'd been cutting P.E. It seemed like the sort of detail that would get in the way of the real story, not to mention cast significant doubt on the narrator. I told her that Dad had come calmly down the cafeteria stairs with the principal, but didn't mention that he'd walked right past me, looking dazed and disoriented at first, before giving me a big, sunny wave as if I were his first visitor at the mental institution.

Even without these details, it was a frightening enough story, and Mom kept saying, "Oh, Liv" and "Honey." She wrapped her arm around my shoulder, her hair tumbling against mine. I felt the tears on her cheeks mingle with the tears on mine. This was the way she'd held me when I was younger. This was how she'd held me the night Daniel died.

I pulled back to look at her. "There's more. But it might not be anything at all...."

"What?" Mom demanded. When my eyes drifted downward, she put a hand on my chin and angled my face upward, so we were eye to eye. "What else?"

"I didn't want to worry you," I said, and it was true. Maybe there was no good way to deliver bad news, or even potentially bad news. How was this any better than a phone call in the middle of the night, like the one that had disrupted our lives? *Here, Mom. Your life has been going pretty great, and now I'm going to hand you this live grenade, and see how that changes things.*

But what choice did I have? Was there really any other option, at all?

I tried to keep my voice steady. Once the words were out, I knew, I couldn't take them back. "Mom," I told her. "I think Dad might be planning to kill himself."

curtis

The streets had a cinematic quiet to them, or maybe I was attaching cinematic importance to my own actions—the lone warrior, heading into battle. I had threaded my way back to the freeway before dawn, feeling a touch of envy for them, those sleeping Omahans, secure in their single-family homes.

There was no *should* or *should not,* there was no choice to be made. If there had been a moment to make a decision, it had been that night when the phone rang, startling me awake. I'd been sleepwalking since then, haunting my own dreams. I was awake now, blood thrumming through my veins with purpose.

By tonight I could be in Oberlin, knocking on the door, the Colt in my hand, my finger on the trigger. Would Robert Saenz know me? Would there be a flash of recognition when I announced my name, before the flash of the revolver?

When Robert Saenz had pled out, he'd taken away my day in court. There had been no judge behind the bench, no American flag on one side, no Ohio flag on the other, no bailiff keeping a stern eye on the crowd. I hadn't had the pleasure of seeing Saenz in an orange jumpsuit, his wrists handcuffed, his legs shackled, his movements reduced to an awkward step-shuffle. There had been no witnesses, no medical reports, no police testimony. I hadn't taken the stand or looked Robert Saenz in the eye; I hadn't told him who it was that he'd killed. In my mind, I wanted to spill before him a thousand pictures and plaques and trophies and certificates, a million words, nineteen years of memories. "This is Daniel," I had wanted to say, daring him to look away.

Would there be time to tell him these things, or would I have to shoot before I could get the words out? I had the element of surprise on my side, because Robert Saenz would have no idea I was coming. He'd never apologized, never owned up to anything more than causing a traffic accident, never expressed remorse that a human being had been killed because of him. There had been no statement read at his sentencing, no letter tearfully penned from prison. Would he tell me, surprised, "I did my time," because he considered the matter of Daniel Owen Kaufman to be closed? Or maybe, "I done my time"—why credit him with the proper use of grammar?

Afterward, I didn't plan to run. I was no hardened criminal, determined to hole up in one-star motel rooms until my money and options ran out. It would be a pleasure to offer myself up to the Oberlin Police Department, arms raised above my head in surrender. "I'm your man," I would say.

Twelve hours—if I could stay awake, if the weather held—until I could say "I took out that dirty son of a bitch for you. You're welcome."

olivia

I had been hoping that Mom had some kind of crazy explanation for the bullets beneath the driver's seat, or that she would think the story of Sam switching the bullets with batteries was hysterical, and we could have a good laugh together. There was only the slimmest of possibilities at this point that everything had a clear, logical explanation—but I clung to it, until I saw Mom's face go white and drained, as if all her blood had decided at that moment to pool elsewhere.

"Mom? Say something."

"I need to think about this, Liv. Why don't you leave me for a minute, let me figure this out."

"Are you sure?" I asked, but Mom's posture was rigid, her spine frozen into place. I backed away from the kitchen, went upstairs and took out my Fear Journal. I sat on the bed with my legs tucked under the comforter, willing all my thoughts to spill out. But it's hard to write clearly when you're shaking or crying, and I was doing both. What the hell was Dad up to? What had he done, in the hours he'd been gone? What was he going to do?

It was nice to believe that the past was the past and we had moved on, but if I didn't know it already, I knew it for sure

now: that was a big fat lie. Everything in our lives came back
to one event, one night. No matter what else happened in our
lives, we'd lost Daniel. All we'd lost was him, and the rest of
us had crumbled. There was probably a physics rule to explain
it—topple one domino, and the rest went, too.

Daniel—you idiot. *If you hadn't been walking by yourself, late
at night, headphones jammed into your ears, would any of this be
happening right now? Couldn't you have just been the charmed kid
forever, the one who never did anything wrong, especially nothing as
stupid as getting killed by a toppled speed limit sign?*

I picked up my cell phone and called Dad's number. I didn't
even hear a ring, just his voice mail greeting. "Dad," I whispered. "I'm sorry for what I said. I'm so sorry. Can you just
come back?" And then I waited.

Eventually I heard Mom's feet on the stairs, followed by
the sound of the master bathroom shower running full blast.
I entered her bedroom, stepping over the clothes she had just
been wearing, which were scattered on the bedroom floor as
if she'd been undressing as she went.

"Mom? You okay in there?"

She used to check on me the same way, when I was a kid
sitting too long on the toilet with a book in hand. *You okay in
there, Liv? You haven't fallen in or anything, have you?*

"I'm fine," she called, her voice rising with the steam.
"You're going to need to pack up your things. We should be
on the road as soon as we can."

I wasn't sure I'd heard her. No—I'd heard her; I just wasn't
sure that anything made sense anymore. "What?"

The water stopped, and Mom reached a dripping arm to
retrieve a bath towel. A second later she stood in front of me,
the towel fastened around her chest. Her curls, momentarily
flattened by the water, were sending fat droplets of water to
the floor.

I leaned against the doorway for support. "Where are we going? I thought you said you didn't know where Dad was."

Mom's eyes were bright, a steely blue. "I have an idea," she said, moving past me to the bedroom. She pulled open a dresser drawer and began removing some clothes. "I'll explain more when we're on the road, okay?"

I looked away as she shimmied out of her towel, feeling sick and disoriented, the way I'd felt as a kid when I'd wound the chains of a swing into a circle and then spun out, the world a dizzy blur around me. Just over a week ago, I'd been living what passed for a normal life in California. I felt a desperate longing for a bowl of orange mac-and-cheese from a box, shared with Dad in front of a Friday night movie marathon. "Um, Mom, hello? You have to tell me what you're thinking. I'm about to have a panic attack here. And I've been told—by you, actually—that I'm not a very fun person to be around during a panic attack."

Mom grabbed me by the shoulders, her chin level with my nose. "No, you're not. We don't have time for a panic attack. You hear me, Liv? This is serious."

I swallowed hard, forcing the words out. "Where, Mom? Where are we going?"

"Oh, honey," she said, brushing my forehead with her lips. Her hair fell damp around my face. "We're going to find him. We're going to bring him home."

curtis

The road through Iowa was familiar to me, even the names of exits, the signage for Casey's General Store and Cracker Barrel. Kathleen and I had made the drive from Northwestern to Omaha each May, then returned again at the end of August. Those summers had been a happy, languid interval between our busy semesters, a break before real life began. On our way to Omaha, we were loaded down with dirty laundry; on the way back, the Datsun had bulged with supplies Kathleen's parents had gifted us with for the next semester—toilet paper and laundry detergent and ten-dollar rolls of quarters for the washer and dryer.

Except for airport layovers, I hadn't been back to the Chicago area since the morning after our graduation from Northwestern, when Kathleen and I had packed up the rest of our belongings, crammed them into my Datsun and headed for Omaha one last time. At that point, our wedding was only two weeks away, and we had a new life planned for us, one that didn't include anything or anyone in Chicago.

Now, everything on the road seemed familiar to me. I tried to fight down a rising tide of memory, but it was like containing a bout of food poisoning. The closer I came to Illinois, the more the past punched its way into the present. Illinois was Chicago for me, and Chicago was the seat of my childhood, the place I'd escaped. In my Chicago, there was no Michigan Avenue, no Magnificent Mile, no Cubs games or waterfront or expensive shopping or overpriced slices of deep dish pizza. Other than the two trips to Oberlin—the one with Kathleen when Daniel was alive, the one I'd taken by myself after Daniel had died—I'd managed to avoid even a layover there. Not that I would have bumped into my father at the airport; he was poor and drunk, and the parameters of his life were strictly limited to a radius of three or four blocks. Still, even the slimmest of chances, even the snowball's chance in hell that I would run into my father, had kept me away.

And here I was—on my way back, alone, with a gun, about to settle a score.

I hadn't thought of this neighborhood in years. My childhood was best seen through a dirty lens from a thousand yards away, where it might have some American-dream, rags-to-middle-class resonance. I took the familiar exit as the drizzle that had started earlier became a steady rain, then a downpour. The old house surprised me by still being there, by still standing. The overall neighborhood had improved over the years, from one housing boom or another, from gentrification, from young couples forgoing rent in high-rises for an old house that could be gutted and redone, top to bottom. But this particular two-bedroom house, with its tiny shared bathroom, its unreliable toilet, its thin walls, hadn't been updated; even through the rain, I could see that the roof was missing some tiles, and the gutter over the front porch was sagging, weighted down by leaves and debris.

I sat there for a long time, probably freaking out any of the nice young couples who happened to glance out their windows, noting the presence of a middle-aged man in a dirty

Ford Explorer with California plates. I sat there for a long time, my toes growing numb inside my shoes, remembering the last time I'd visited, when I'd promised Kathleen I would never return.

It was the one and only time she'd met my parents, a trip that served both as an introduction and a goodbye, a neat two-fer trick. After that visit, I'd effectively ceased to be their son. After that, when the subject of families came up, I said my parents had died when I was in college and brushed off the onslaught of sympathy by saying it was a long time ago.

But Kathleen had insisted she meet them, and it had seemed only fair—after spending two summers with her parents in Omaha, the excuses I'd given her about my family had worn thin.

"How bad can they be?" she'd teased.

"Trust me—bad."

"You never even *call* them," she'd said more than once, accusingly. "Don't they want to know what you're up to? Don't you want to know if they're okay?"

Kathleen couldn't understand that the answer to both questions was *no*. How could she? Her parents called each Sunday night, and she dropped everything to chat with them for an hour. I couldn't imagine a world where my parents cared about my classes, knew the schedule of my upcoming papers and projects, wanted to fill me in on everything from the new neighbors to how many bowls full of berries they'd picked from the bushes in the rear of the property.

"My family is nothing like yours," I promised her. We'd been lounging on her bed at the time, her back against the wall, feet in my lap. I was rubbing each foot slowly, toe to heel, and Kathleen had moaned contentedly.

"They can't be so bad, if they had you."

"Yes, they can."

By then I had known that I wanted to marry Kathleen, and this seemed the only fair thing to do—to let her meet my family before I asked her to marry me, to give her all the facts before she made a decision, an informed consent. We'd made the drive on one of the last days of our spring semester—short in distance, long in every other way. Kathleen had grown quiet as we'd neared their neighborhood, where dogs barked behind chain-link fences and groups of young men leaned against storefronts, watching us. We parked in front of the two-bedroom house, walked up the cracked concrete steps and knocked, ignoring the bell that had been broken for as long as I could remember.

My mother had opened the door, and she stared at us from the entry without saying anything. I had phoned that morning to let her know we were coming, but for all the recognition she showed, we might have been visiting from the local Kingdom Hall. It's possible that my mother had been born this way—slow, dazed, dull—but equally possible that life with her husband had made her this way. I'd never known. She wore a shapeless dress that was dirty along the hem where it grazed the floor, and her hair was pulled back from her face and gathered in an oversize clip. I knew she was in her late forties, but still someone could have convinced me she was at least sixty.

"Hello, Mom," I said. "This is Kathleen."

"Oh, it's so nice to meet you finally," Kathleen had gushed, but my mother answered with only a polite "hello" before turning away.

We followed her through the narrow hallway, lined with nicotine-yellow walls. I felt Kathleen's slight intake of breath as she tried to adjust to the smell.

"They're here," my mother announced, rounding the corner into the den, and my father heaved himself to his feet from the couch.

He was a tall man, but wider than he'd been three years ago. I'd been home only occasionally, since I spent summers in Omaha and qualified for holiday housing on campus through my work-study job. My father had the kind of body that might have been athletic in his youth—although I had no memory of him this way—and was still somehow powerful and strong, though outsized. When he held out a hand to Kathleen in greeting, his gut came between them, as solid a mass of tissue as a thirty-pound tumor. In the other hand he held a highball glass. His smell was rancid and sour. My mother, easily two hundred and fifty pounds herself, almost disappeared behind his bulk. But she could be invisible even when she was the only person in the room; she had perfected this art, and employed it whenever necessary, like an animal camouflaging itself in the wild to avoid a predator.

Kathleen tried again. "It's so nice to meet you..." But her words were lost. This wasn't a house where we observed social conventions and shared niceties. My own father, while giving Kathleen an appreciative up-and-down glance, hadn't bothered to greet me.

"What do your parents do, Kathleen?" my father asked gruffly, as if this was a standard opening question for meeting your only son's girlfriend. When he spoke, alcohol fumes leaked from his mouth.

"My dad's a builder," Kathleen squeaked, caught off guard.

"Oh, yeah? What does he build?"

Don't answer, I thought, but it was too late to stop where this was going. Dad fancied himself a builder, too. I'd heard him refer to himself often enough as a skilled carpenter, but what he meant was that he was a laborer, capable of moving things from one place to another, able to operate some tools, but not with anything close to proficiency, as the run-down nature of this house surely proved.

"Um, residential, some government buildings, things like that," Kathleen said modestly. Owen had done well for himself; he had a good reputation, which, combined with a genial nature, opened up some fairly lucrative opportunities.

"Government buildings?" Dad wheezed. "So he's got his hand in that, huh?"

I cringed. This was the sort of thing that delighted my father, because it confirmed his understanding of how the world worked—that some people got the perks, and the rest of the world got shat on. It went without saying that he was one of the ones who was shat on, and he accepted no responsibility for this fact. It didn't matter that he was drunk more often than sober, that he had lost so many jobs for being insubordinate or obstinate that he was lucky to find intermittent work as a day laborer, that he basically lied and bullied and connived his way through life. No—for my father, the blame clearly lay with the people who had it all, who owed him something. This was the sort of thing he went on for hours about, using the recliner in the den as a bully pulpit from which he had tried for eighteen years to indoctrinate me. I'd managed to escape through good grades and a high school counselor who took me under his wing; if Mom had escaped, it was only by adopting a convenient sort of deafness.

Kathleen released an uncomfortable laugh. I could feel her eyes on me, pleading for me to guide her through this conversation. She'd been asking from the beginning, from that first date at the bowling alley with a basket of fries between us, what my family was like, what my childhood had been like. I'd managed to dodge most of her questions by supplying only the barest of facts—that money had been tight, that my parents were mainly involved in their own lives, that I'd more or less needed to raise myself. I'd been casual about it, turning the questions back to her, as if it wasn't a big deal, as if maybe I'd even preferred it that way.

From a framed photo on her dresser, I had learned that Kathleen's family visited a cabin at a lake each summer. They owned Jet Skis and kept them tied to the dock during their two-week stay. In my mind, all of it—the cabin, the lake, the Jet Skis—had taken on mythical proportions. Our families weren't just different in their obvious financial statuses, but in general health and happiness, too. Even if my family had rented a cabin on a lake each summer, it wouldn't have been the same. My father would have sat on the recliner there, or the couch, or even the end of the dock, gesturing with a bottle in one hand, the weight of an unfair world on his shoulders. My mother would have stayed indoors, smoking.

He wasn't finished grilling Kathleen; in fact, I could tell that he was only warming up. I'd been gone so long that he might have fallen out of regular practice. With only my mother as his verbal and physical punching bag, he had probably been storing up. He took a long sip of the amber-colored liquid in his glass and asked, "He works pretty hard, though, your dad?"

"He works very hard," Kathleen said cautiously, unable to tell where this was going.

"Not everyone understands hard work anymore," Dad continued, taking another swallow. He savored this swig, rolling it around in his mouth like a delicacy, rather than whatever had been cheapest at the only liquor store within walking distance. I saw what was coming and wished I could have prevented it or at least given Kathleen fair warning, but I was paralyzed, almost fascinated by this glimpse of my father in action. "You take my son here, I can't figure he's had an honest day's work in his life."

Kathleen laughed again, probably thinking this was a joke. When my father's hard grin didn't change, she bristled. I let her take my hand, although my skin had gone clammy to the touch. "I don't know if he tells you, but Curtis works incredibly hard," she began.

Dad's laugh stopped her. His eyes were pitiless. "Nose in a book. Not what I call work, exactly." Behind him, my mother smiled as if we were discussing something as banal as the weather. Maybe she wasn't following the conversation; maybe she'd drifted to whatever world she visited when Dad started in.

I gave Kathleen a look, but she couldn't stop. It was her basic sense of justice, of what was good and right and fair. Kathleen picked up trash on the sidewalk, she openly scorned cheaters, she stood up for the underdog. "He does work, though, besides going to school. He has two—"

I squeezed her hand sharply, trying to convey the pointlessness of the situation, and she stopped, midsentence. I'd worked harder than my father could ever understand, bussing tables through high school, weeknights at one place and weekends at another. "Women's work," my father had called this. I hadn't kept a cent of the money at home, where he could get to it. I'd deposited my checks and threw away the receipts. Northwestern was paid for by scholarships, loans, working four afternoons a week as a physics lab assistant and bartending weekends, an off-the-books gig I'd picked up even though I'd barely been eighteen at the time. Mostly the bar catered to a young crowd, college students who had inherited disposable income from their parents, or older men who threw down big bills to impress twenty-year-old girls. But sometimes I served men at the bar who reminded me of my father, men who were garrulous and unhappy, beaten down by life and unable to do anything about their situations, except raise a finger to get my attention, one more time. I could no more understand their lives than my father could understand mine.

I'd only intended our visit to last a couple of hours, figuring we would arrive after lunch so my mother didn't have to be troubled to sort through the refrigerator for cheese and lunch meats that hadn't passed their expiration dates. I also figured that by early afternoon, my father would have polished off a few beers but not yet started his serious drinking of the day, which typically began during the evening news, escalated through unfunny sitcoms and peaked during the late show. By the time he was sloppily, angrily drunk, screaming insults and throwing dishes and twisting my mother's arm behind her back, I hoped that Kathleen and I would be back on campus in my dorm room or hers, making pasta from a box—*if* she still wanted to be with me.

But that day Dad was in rare form. Maybe he'd been planning his invectives from the time I'd called to inform Mom of our visit. I'd expected the slights directed toward me—shaming me was basically his pastime—but since I'd never dared to bring a friend to our house, I wasn't prepared for the way he went after Kathleen. Poor Kathleen. So trusting, so eager to make a good impression, she was nothing more than a slab of meat in front of the jackal's cage.

"You're a student at the college, too?" my father had asked. *The college*—as if it didn't have a name, or he didn't know which college it was. Another slight.

Kathleen nodded. Maybe she didn't want to encourage him in the conversation; maybe she hoped a nod would suffice.

"You study science, too?" The word came out with a sneer. I wasn't sure what my dad knew about science, if maybe he had an image in his mind of my sixth grade project for the science fair, presented on a tri-fold piece of cardboard from a box that my mother had brought home from her job in the school cafeteria. No matter what was on the front—all the hours of research, the carefully stenciled letters—the back of the box had said Charmin. It was a toilet paper box. Dad had ridiculed it just as much as my classmates.

"No," Kathleen said, hesitantly. "I'm an art history major."

"What's that?" My father looked genuinely confused, and I suppose it was possible he'd never heard the two words paired that way. *Art* he probably knew, and *history,* too—not that he'd had any use for the former, and the latter was a set of facts and figures that had benefited him in no way.

"Well…I mean, I'm studying the different movements of art…." Kathleen stammered.

I was an asshole for not jumping in at that moment. That's what I should have done. I should have asked, "What are *you* working on these days, Dad?" and let him regale us with the stories of the sleaze of his last foreman, of so-and-so who had been chosen for a job that should have been his. Or maybe I could have asked about the Bears, which had long been the sole passion in my father's life, along with alcohol. Da Bears and da bottle.

"The different movements of art," my father echoed. He turned around to face my mother, the only audience member who had ever been fully on his side, no matter what the argument or issue. "Weehee! Did you hear that, Lorene? The movements of art!"

"It's very nice," my mother said, still smiling, still somewhat dazed. I wasn't sure if she'd ever heard of art history, either, but I imagine there were things all the time that my mother heard that she simply filtered out, sorting them into a massive and growing pile of things she would never need to know or care about.

"It's— I mean, like neoclassicism—" Kathleen stuttered, and I took her by the arm, guiding her slightly behind me.

"The movements of art!" My father hooted. "I guess I'm too uneducated to know anything about the movements of art! I'm more concerned with the movements of my bowels. That's what I think about art, too, come to think of it!"

Kathleen made a little whimpering sound, and I told her over my shoulder, "We're leaving, don't worry." To my father, I said, "Dad, that's enough."

My father did a strange little dance in front of us, dipping from one side to another, the arm with his glass extended as if he were leading an invisible partner. It was probably the most exercise he'd had in a while, the longest he'd stood without leaning against something. "This is who my son picks!" he whooped. "An aaaht history major!"

I nudged Kathleen and, with my hand at the small of her back, we retraced our steps through the stale air of the den into the hallway.

"Aww! Did I offend you?" my father jeered. "Are you too high and mighty to be in this house? My son, the scientist, and his girlfriend, the *artiste?*"

I ignored him. "We'll never come here again," I told Kathleen, even though I wasn't sure there would be a "we" after this. But it was just as much a promise to myself: I couldn't let myself go there again. It had never been *home,* and it wouldn't ever be now.

My mother came huffing behind us, frazzled. "Do you have to go? I was hoping you would stay for dinner, so we could get to know your friend a little better."

We were outside by then, Kathleen halfway down the sidewalk. I caught my mother by the shoulders and said, "I wish you could get to know Kathleen. She's wonderful. You'd love her. But we can't stay in this house another minute."

It was as if my words had shaken free a sudden lucid moment. Her eyes widened. "If you'd come earlier," my mother pleaded. "Next time come earlier in the day, when he's just waking up. He's better then."

I'd said this to her a dozen times during my adolescence, testing the waters: *What if we left? Couldn't we find somewhere else?* I tried it again, one last time. "Mom, you don't need to stay here. Can't I help you find a place to go?"

Before my eyes, she reverted to her dazed state, as if she couldn't fathom what I was talking about, or why in the world I might suggest such a thing. Leave? Never. Why?

Dad was still yelling when we got into the Datsun, something unintelligible and angry, a final goodbye. I didn't look at Kathleen, who was bent over, sobbing in her seat. We drove for a few blocks, past the run-down homes, the cars up on blocks in driveways, the battered strollers abandoned on front stoops. Before our freeway exit, I pulled into a restaurant parking lot and cut the engine. Kathleen was still sobbing, her face hidden by her curls.

"I'm sorry," I said, finally. It had been stupid to bring her, cruel to force my father on her. I wasn't apologizing for my father's behavior so much as for my entire life, for not growing up in a decent neighborhood with decent parents who held down decent jobs. But most of all, I was sorry because I had lost Kathleen—hadn't I? She wasn't looking at me; her gaze was fixed on a metal trash bin, as if it were the most interesting thing in the world.

"I'm sorry," I said again, daring to put a hand on her thigh, just above her knee. "Kathleen, I never should have brought you—"

She whirled, her face puffy, black smudges of mascara like animal tracks around her eyes. "Why did you?"

I shook my head, bracing myself for the impact of her words.

"Was it to get back at me or something?"

"To get back at you?"

"For having the family I have. You've been saying that all

along, only I didn't really understand what you were getting at. How my parents are wonderful, my brother wonderful, our house wonderful, our life *wonderful*. And all along you were just making fun of them, you were just resenting me for it!"

"Kathleen, I wasn't making fun of you. And I love your family."

"But you could have told me! You knew what this would be like! How could you let me walk in there, thinking I was going to have some normal kind of meet-the-parents moment, when you knew? You knew!"

"You're right," I told her, fingering the keys in the ignition. "I knew what would happen. Well, that's not exactly true. I knew it would be awful, but it's always a different form of awful. Something new sets him off.... But it's always the same, too—he's always drunk, there's always some kind of score to settle, he wants to get the last word in, he wants to win, and she makes excuses for him."

Kathleen looked at me, wiping away tears. "How long…?"

"Has he been a bully? Been an alcoholic? Let's see…how old am I now?"

She softened, pity creeping into her voice. "You mean, you grew up like that? All alone in that house with them?"

"I wasn't always there. I had school nine months out of the year, and I worked, and I figured out how to leave." I didn't tell her that I arrived to school before anyone but the janitor, and stayed late for homework help even though I didn't need it. On Saturdays I sat at the library until it closed, and when I was home, I stayed locked in my room as much as possible. Summers—until I was fourteen and old enough for my first job—had been endless. I had already removed myself from that scared boy who had shut himself in the closet with a flash-light, reading, sometimes humming to himself to drown out the sound of his father's voice. It had been three years since

I'd slept in that house, although sometimes I still woke in the middle of the night, the noise of a door slamming somewhere in the dorm bringing me to consciousness in a cold sweat.

My hand was still on her lap, and Kathleen curled her fingers around mine. "You don't have to apologize. I should. You tried to tell me, but I didn't understand."

"But I could have tried harder. I just wanted you to really know what you were getting into. With me. If we were…" Red-faced, I backtracked from the word *married*. "If we were together down the road, it would just be me. There wouldn't be any family on my side, no one to support us in any way if we needed it." This thought had been occurring to me more often lately, the more serious Kathleen and I became, the more entangled our lives and future plans. I hadn't just been deprived of a childhood, but any children I had would be deprived of grandparents, of cozy family meals, of presents at Christmas, of Grandparents' Day at school.

She nodded slowly, then said, "I don't want to go back there."

"We won't."

"I mean, ever."

"Ever," I agreed.

"I don't want them to be a part of our lives."

I grasped this like a life preserver and let it pull me to the surface. *Our lives.* "They won't be."

Kathleen dabbed at her eyes, smearing her mascara further. "Or our kids. I don't want him talking to our kids, not ever. Not even on birthdays and Christmas. No phone calls. No letters."

There was a strange tug in my chest, as if something long anchored had broken free inside me. "Kathleen," I pressed my thumb and forefinger to her chin, angled it gently so we were facing. "We don't have kids."

She laughed, a bubbly sound that meant she was still on the verge of tears. "I meant, when. *When* we have kids. Or if. Maybe I meant *if*."

"I like when," I said and kissed her.

By the end of the summer, we were engaged. I kept my promise, not sending an invitation to our wedding, not sending the announcements of Daniel's birth or Olivia's. But I had called my mother a few times a year, to find out if she was alive, to tell her I was alive, too.

It was painful to remember that last visit, in a strangely physical way, as if I'd directly defied doctor's orders and over-exerted myself, opening the old wound again. It was best to keep going, to start the car and drive away, to continue on the way to Robert Saenz. There was no expiration date on the promise I'd made Kathleen.

And then, although there was still plenty of daylight left, the light over the front porch came on—a bare bulb, the way it had always been; no fancy fixtures for us Kaufmans, no needless expense on decoration, when that money was better spent on a bottle of Wild Turkey. The light wasn't on a timer, because nothing in that house was automated. Someone in-side had flipped a switch.

There was no other way to see it, except as a summons.

olivia

For the second poorly planned road trip of my life, I was basically already packed, since I hadn't bothered to unpack when we'd arrived in Omaha. It was nearly nine by the time we were on the road, but so cold that Mom had to blast the heat in her Volvo until my teeth stopped chattering. It was basically summer in California, but just over forty degrees here. The sky was an ominous gray, the sun completely hidden behind wispy clouds.

Mom spent the first twenty minutes of the drive on the phone to Stella, saying vague things like, "Maybe a few more days…" and outright lies like, "it's just so good for us all to be together."

When she finally hung up, I turned to her, peeking out from beneath my hoodie. "Are you going to tell me what's going on, or am I supposed to be picking up clues?"

Mom inhaled sharply and exhaled, the air coming in a quick burst through her nostrils. "This is not how I imagined we would have this conversation. Actually—I didn't ever imagine we would have this conversation. Your father promised me…"

"You're killing me here. Is there a plain English version I can listen to, rather than this cryptic parent-speak?"

"Okay. Look, this is going to be strange for you, so you'll need to hear me out. I'm talking about your grandparents."

I watched my mother watching the road and tried to decide what was worse—that Dad had cracked up, or that Mom was well on her way to Crazyville and taking me with her. Either that, or I had sustained a serious head injury and was stuck in a nightmare loop in the middle of my coma. Funny how that seemed like the best option.

"Mom," I said carefully. "Are we talking about dead people?" Grandpa and Grandma Eberle's funerals had been years ago, although not so long ago that I didn't remember them. And I'd never even met Dad's parents, who had died long before Daniel was born, although the details had always been spotty in my mind—cancer for him, heart disease for her, or the other way around? Either way, I had exactly zero grandparents to call me on my birthday and spoil me rotten with silly little gifts on Valentine's Day and Easter.

The look on Mom's face suggested that whatever she'd eaten for breakfast hadn't agreed with her. "Olivia, listen to me. Your grandparents—your dad's parents—aren't dead. They live outside Chicago."

I pressed my hands to my temples.

"Liv, I'm sorry. There's a very good reason why we didn't tell you this sooner. In fact, if you want to blame someone, blame me. I made your father promise…. Aren't you going to say something?"

"I'm pretty sure that sooner or later I'm just going to wake up, and I'm not going to waste energy trying to figure out this nightmare."

"Liv, really—"

"You've been hiding my grandparents from me?"

"Believe me, it's been for your own good. Look, I'm going to tell you something…"

I stared out the window, trying to listen, although my mind kept getting hung up on one simple fact. Somehow, I had grandparents who were alive, who lived near Chicago. My living family, which, as far as I had known, included only my parents, an aunt and uncle and a cousin, had just grown by two.

"For your own good," Mom was saying, and I realized that she'd mentioned this several times already. Apparently, I didn't just have living grandparents—I had living grandparents who were so awful, they were more monster than human, more tyrants than grandparents. Mom used the words *alcoholic* and *abusive* and *passive-aggressive* and *better to believe they were dead than to ever have even the slightest contact with them.*

"But they're alive?"

"As far as I know, yes," Mom said. "That's what I'm figuring. Your dad must know more."

"He's never mentioned anything to *me*." Of course not— they were supposed to be dead. Maybe this was where I'd taken my cue about Daniel: *we don't talk about dead people in this family.*

"No, he wouldn't have. Your father spent a long time trying to get away from them, to make a better life. It was one of the things we agreed on from the beginning, that they wouldn't have any contact with you kids."

It was too much to process. "But I share genes with these people?"

Mom flinched. Did she have any idea of the host of new fears she'd dumped in my lap? I reached down to my backpack.

"I made him promise," Mom continued, her hands clenched on the wheel. All of Iowa was whizzing by—cornfields and tractors parked beside barns and little towns and American-made cars—and we were on our way to Chicago, to pursue my probably crazy father who might be visiting my previously dead grandparents with a potential gun.

"What are you doing?" Mom asked, because I was starting to get really panicky now. I dumped out the contents of my backpack on the floorboard. Pens, some lose pieces of gum, a novel I'd brought along but hadn't opened, a half-eaten and most likely now stale candy bar, but no Fear Journal.

"Where...?" I closed my eyes, remembering. That morning, I'd gone downstairs, read Dad's note and come back upstairs to write everything down in my Fear Journal. Except I couldn't; the words wouldn't actually come. And then I'd thrown everything in my suitcase and zipped up my backpack, leaving the Fear Journal on my bed, beneath the comforter. It might as well have been on the moon for all the good it could do me now. From the woozy, unsteady place that was my mind, I thought, *This is what it's like to operate without a safety net.* I managed to squeak out, "My Fear Journal."

"Are you sure? It must be there somewhere."

"Of course I'm sure!"

"We can buy another one, maybe when we stop for gas again," Mom offered.

It wasn't that simple, of course, but I couldn't expect her to understand. The comfort was in the ritual of the book, in the fact that I could look back over my old fears and see how, one way or another, I'd avoided or survived them, and know that the same thing was probably going to happen with whatever new fear I was about to record. It wasn't the notebook itself that was special—*that* could be replaced. It was everything else. "I don't know if I can do this," I whispered, soft enough so that Mom might not have heard me even if she wasn't in the middle of a complicated litany.

Her hands were clenched on the wheel, knuckles white. "I told him he couldn't ever see them again, not if he loved me. I didn't want them to know anything about our lives together, or about you and Daniel."

"So my monster grandparents don't even know I exist?"

"I don't think so."

"What about Daniel? Did they know about him?" This had to be one of the most awful things I could imagine. Even a monster would have loved Daniel.

Mom shook her head. "Olivia, I can't even tell you how awful they were...I mean, you couldn't even imagine."

"Maybe I could," I said. "I watch HBO."

"Since when do you have HBO?"

"That's the worry here? That Dad and I have a subscription to HBO?"

"Never mind," Mom said. "You're right. But if these people had been involved in our lives, in your life, in any capacity... no, I can't even imagine it."

I stared miserably out the window. As quickly as I'd inherited two more living relatives, my world had shrunk again, since these living relatives had turned out to be horrible and defective. Fascists, maybe. Child abusers.

"And Dad was okay with that promise?" I asked finally. "I mean, he didn't want to get in touch with his parents at any point? Not even to brag about how wonderful his kids were and all that?"

Mom spoke more quietly now, and I had to strain to hear her over the sound of tires on asphalt and wind whipping past our windows. "That's one of the things I was worried about, after Daniel died. I mean, your dad seemed like he was really losing it. And I thought—if he turns into the kind of guy his father was—if somehow he couldn't fight off that grip of genetics..."

"Dad's no monster, though."

"No, but still—"

I felt angry on his behalf. "There's no *but*. Dad's not a monster. He's not even close to being a monster. He's my dad. He's wonderful. He's just... Right now..."

"Okay, Liv. I'm sorry. You're right—he's not a monster. He's this wonderfully complicated man who's just doing what he thinks is right."

I stared at her. It was the nicest thing I could remember her saying about Dad, if not exactly a confession of love. "Okay, then. But why do you think he's going to Chicago? Why would he want to see his parents, if they were so horrible?"

It took Mom a while to formulate an answer. "I guess…it just seems like unfinished business."

"Unfinished business? Like a score to settle?" I thought of the bullets under his seat, and the gun I'd never actually seen, but could picture now, real as the road in front of us.

"No, I don't think…no. Nothing like that."

"You could try to be more convincing, for my sake."

Mom's smile was grim. "We're just going to concentrate on getting there, okay? We're going to make sure nothing awful happens."

Exactly how would we do that? To calm myself, I started reciting these new fears silently, so I could remember them for later, when and if I was ever reunited with my Fear Journal. At the same time, I was remembering the advice Dr. Fisher had given me, about sorting fears into categories—things that had happened, or were likely to, and things that were just plain ridiculous. I hoped all of this was ridiculous, an absurd and someday funny series of jumping to conclusions. But if any of this were true, we needed to stop him—it was as simple and complicated and horrible as that.

And then, just when I thought it couldn't get any worse, it began to rain.

At first, it was just a few drops on the windshield, brushed away intermittently with gentle whisks of the wipers. Traffic slowed, wheels swishing against the asphalt in an almost peaceful way, like the sound of a miniature home water fountain.

It's not that I believe in omens, necessarily, but I don't like to overlook possibilities. Every single day since Dad and I had left Sacramento, the weather had been the stuff of storybooks: blue skies, fluffy clouds—"cumulus," Dad would say if he were here, but of course, he was not. The sky had been so intensely blue over parts of Nevada and Utah that it had looked fake, like a black-and-white film that had been colorized with an unrealistically strong palette.

Just outside Des Moines, the rain got serious. Traffic slowed, headlights came on. When we passed trucks, or they passed us, giant whorls of water crested up against the Volvo.

"We aren't really going to drive in this," I shouted, because the sound of the rain had drowned out the possibility of a normal speaking voice.

"We're going to be fine," Mom called back. "You've been in California too long. People in the Midwest drive in rain like this all the time."

Maybe I had been spoiled without *real* rain—northern California had been in a "drought condition" for as long as I could remember—but this was ridiculous. It felt like a sign from the heavens—*Stop this trip! Turn back immediately!* "This is beyond rain, though! It's a postapocalyptic downpour," I protested.

Mom shook her head. "Postapocalyptic? I forgot how funny you are."

Funny? I stared at her. Who could joke at a time like this?

"Look at all the other cars on the road," Mom said, as if this were reassuring, rather than cause for further alarm. Apparently, the other drivers were just as stupid and stubborn as we were, and they weren't going to be deterred by a few tons of water.

"Oh, I see. Everyone else is doing it, so why can't we?" I checked off the reasons on my fingers. "Diminished visibility, slick roads, windshield wipers breaking, the possibility of sliding off the highway into a ditch and not being discovered until tomorrow since it's dark and no one would be able to see our overturned car or hear our weak cries for help." *The possibility of not getting to Dad in time.* I had worked myself into a breathless frenzy. I tried to instruct myself as a therapist would a patient: *Relax, breathe, think of happier things.*

"Well," Mom said carefully. "Those things may be true. But still—your father is out there, and we need to get to him."

She was right, of course, and I was a scared, selfish brat. Dad was heading off to find his monster-parents, and we were just going to have to battle the Storm of the Century like good little soldiers. I fished my cell phone out of my backpack and called Dad's number. I listened to his outgoing message and I hung up, not sure where to begin.

"Let's just get there, okay?" Mom said, gently. "I'll be careful, but let's just find him."

I bit down on the cuff of my sweatshirt. There was simply nowhere to look—out the window was like watching a bleak forecast on the Weather Channel, and closing my eyes didn't make what was outside the window any less real.

There was really nothing to do but pray—even if I wasn't the sort of person who prayed, or at least not with any specific expectations. Saying a prayer was like writing another journal entry, or talking to a family therapist, or just letting out all my thoughts. I never could shake the general self-centeredness of it, that I was throwing all my troubles and problems onto God when there were way more important issues in the world like war and famine and clean sources of drinking water. As crappy as my life sometimes seemed—even right then, with the windshield wipers waving back and forth like spindly skeleton arms, and my father doing who-knew-what—there was always someone who had it worse, who needed prayers more than I did.

Still, I prayed. I prayed about the rain and about Dad continuing solo on the trip we'd started together. I prayed about whatever it was that he thought he had to do and wherever it was that his journey would take him, a desperate, middle-aged pilgrim without a Mecca or a shrine to St. Thomas à Becket. I prayed about the all-too-real bullets that had been taped beneath his seat, and the all-too-possible gun that I had never found.

While I prayed, a shiver ran down the length of my body, from my scalp to my toes, cold in the tips of my combat boots. I figured that wherever he was going, Dad's trip was a lonely one, with a dark destination. But I prayed I was wrong about that, too.

curtis

"Oh!" my mother said when she opened the door. She looked the same as she had twenty-nine years ago, because twenty-nine years ago she had been a prematurely old woman—with wide, cushiony hips and flabby arms, a limp, frowzy perm and deep pouches of sleeplessness under her eyes. She peered over my shoulder, as if a small army might be lurking on her sidewalk. "Well, come in, then," she said, leaving me to close the door behind myself. "Let me just get my coat."

"Mom," I called, causing her retreating figure to halt in the middle of the narrow hallway. It was literally narrower than when I had lived here—the walls had grown inward. I wasn't imagining this; as my eyes adjusted to the gloomy interior, I noticed boxes stacked against the wall, almost floor to ceiling. They were, predictably enough, liquor boxes—sturdy, small, with two holes for handles, labeled with the names of vodka manufacturers. "Wait a minute. What's going on?"

She turned, facing me. Her face was relatively unlined, any creases filled by excess fat. It was a recognizable face, of course, but I was relieved not to see any trace of Daniel or Olivia there. "You got my note, then," she said.

"No, I don't think so. What note?"

"I sent you a letter last week. To California."

I shook my head. "I haven't been in California. I've been traveling with Li—with my..." I let that thought trail off, unfinished. "What was the letter about? Are you moving or something?"

She stared at me. "If you didn't get it, how did you know to come?"

My mouth felt dry, my lips cracked. I wanted to push past her to the kitchen, to take a long drink of water from one of the chipped tumblers in the cupboard next to the sink. On the other hand, I wanted to leave while I could, before I got sucked in any further. I'd had this sense of inevitability during my childhood, that I was in the grip of forces I couldn't control—Dad's drinking, Mom's apathy, the amount of food in the refrigerator, the fact that I'd grown too tall for my pants, or that I would need ten dollars for one field trip or another at school, and it would take a movement of heaven and earth for me to come up with it. Now I felt that vise again, like Dad's warm grip on my neck, steering me toward something I didn't want to do. I'd given my mother our Sacramento address years ago, careful to stress that it was *for emergencies only*. Apparently, there had never been any emergencies—until now.

"Where's Dad?"

"I was just going to see him," she said, and at the table at the end of the hall, I saw that she had her purse and a brown overcoat ready.

I felt the long ago, familiar relaxation, the tension seeping out of my body. He wasn't here, then. Maybe I should have known; the house was dark and stale-smelling, but quiet, not possessed by the raving evil spirit that was my father.

"It's good you came," my mother continued, struggling into her coat. She had a bit of trouble getting her second arm into the hole, and I stepped forward to help her. It was a surprising sentiment for her to express—it hadn't occurred to me that she would think it was good to see me. Then, as if to clarify, she added, "This way I don't have to take the bus."

My mother didn't seem the slightest bit disturbed by the state of my car, where the wrappers and empty plastic bottles from my day on the road layered the floorboard. Buckling herself into her seat, she simply rested her steady, orthopedic shoes on top of the mess and stared straight ahead, purse clutched on her lap.

I started the car, then waited, idling, for her to speak. It had been a strange fact of my childhood that my mother was omnipresent and yet not truly there, an empty shell of a person whose personality was marked by placidity. "Oh, no," she'd said, when my father inevitably threw something against a wall, and then rushed to pick up the shards. "That's a good boy," she'd said, when I announced my scholarship to Northwestern, as if she had observed me picking a piece of trash out of the gutter.

Now, in the same mild tone, she said, "Your father is at Mercy."

"Mercy Hospital?" I echoed.

"Yes, fourth floor," she said, as if this explained everything.

The rain had settled to a light mist, but the roads were wet enough to send up gray splashes that further blurred visibility. I was grateful for the swishing of the windshield wipers, which somehow covered the need for conversation. We nearly reached the hospital before I got the story, word by painful word, out of my mother. She seemed annoyed to have to tell any of it to me—repeating, several times, that it was all in the letter. The only logical solution, clearly, was to drop her off at Mercy, drive back to California, read the letter and return only when I was able to join the conversation.

My father, it turned out, had quit drinking cold turkey six months before. His liver had held out a surprisingly long time. When I'd thought of him, only very occasionally through the years—fighting back the urge to share good news, to rub success in his face—I'd imagine him wasting away, his days becoming rapidly numbered. One way or another, I figured a tragedy was headed his way—a drunk driving arrest, cirrhosis, a cancer eating its way through his body. The only surprise was that it had taken so long.

Even though he'd stopped drinking, the damage had been done, and Dad had begun to go into "septic," Mom said—which I took to mean septic shock, *sepsis*—an infection that meant his organs could shut down, that death was a very real possibility. It went without saying that he was not a candidate for a liver transplant—but Mom revealed this with a sharp huff of breath. Did she think this was an injustice, as my father himself probably did? *If I'da been a rich guy, you can bet they woulda sliced me open right then. They woulda cut it out of me right there.*

Mom insisted we could walk together, that she didn't need to be dropped off at the door. I took her elbow as we made our way through the parking garage, feeling a proprietary sense of care for her. I did the math in my head and realized Mom was nearly eighty years old. She had a lumbering, uneasy gait, which may have been from her weight or any number of ailments—a bad hip, a bum knee? We took the elevator down from the parking garage, entered the hospital lobby, and made our way to another bank of elevators. Mom pushed 4 and stepped back.

I asked, "What about all the boxes?"

Mom was watching the lighted display over the doors, which indicated that we were moving from floor one to floor two. "What boxes?"

"At your house. In the hallway, there were all those boxes stacked up."

We stopped on the second floor and a young woman in blue scrubs entered the elevator and pushed the 3 button.

"Those are all your things. I boxed them up for you."

"My things?" I asked, as the elevator started again. "What do you mean, my things?"

Mom turned her gaze to me, as if I were the one who needed things explained slowly. "Some books, sheets from your bed, clothes you'd outgrown. Those things."

I was floored, imagining that the boxes full of my outgrown, secondhand jeans and T-shirts had been sitting in my parents' front hallway for close to thirty years, waiting for me to come back for them. "When did you...?"

The young woman in scrubs exited the elevator, and a trio of women around Mom's age got on, sniffling and arguing. One of them pressed 1, and I said, "This elevator is going up to four," which caused them to turn and noisily exit. Mom made a little clicking sound with her tongue, as if this were an unfortunate occurrence.

I tried again. "When did you pack up all of those things, Mom?"

"Oh, not that long ago. When I learned that he wasn't coming home. I'll have to move out soon."

The doors opened onto the fourth floor and Mom took off ahead of me, rounding the nurses' station, moving with an efficiency that belied her age and general health condition. The nurse behind the desk looked up, registering our entrance, and then back down at her computer monitor. After passing through a complicated maze of hallways, we arrived at 471-A. Mom stopped, seeming to brace herself. Written in dry erase marker on a whiteboard outside the room was the label KAUFMAN, C. followed by the names of his a.m. and p.m.

nurse and the doctor in charge. I winced, seeing his name, my namesake.

"Don't go surprising him, now," Mom said, but I wasn't sure what she meant by this. I wasn't intending to pop around the curtain that separated us with my hands held out, like a performer at a child's birthday party. Surely my presence itself would be a surprise—even if it hadn't been for my mother. She entered before me, plopping her purse down in a chair next to the bed. I could see my father's feet pointing up beneath a blue hospital blanket, and then his entire body shifted beneath the covers, registering Mom's presence.

"How are you feeling?" she asked.

His answer was a painful wheeze, as if it took a great amount of energy for this single word to exit his body. "Tired." I'm not sure I would have picked his voice out of a lineup.

"I got a ride with Curtis," Mom said, and after a long beat, while this information must have sunk in, my father rasped, "Curtis is here?" This time the voice was more familiar, with that hard edge my name always had in his mouth. How many times over the years had I thought about changing my name, becoming a person who didn't resemble my father, even on paper?

I had been standing between the open doorway and the curtain, not wanting to go any farther. The full effect of this mistake was upon me. I should have been heading toward Oberlin, doing what I'd set out to do. This detour brought back all the misery of my childhood with the new complications of one sick parent and one about to be homeless. My father's voice, even altered by age and illness, still sent a chill through me. As a child, I had found reasons to stay in the bathroom after dinner, even though I knew from experience that the cheap latch lock could be broken, and Dad could force his way inside. As a child, I'd suspected that my mother didn't love me the way

other mothers loved their children—the mothers of my classmates, the women who lived on our street and watched their
children play from the front stoop. Those women would have
protected their children from raised fists, from flat, stinging
slaps with the palm of a hand. As an adult, watching Kathleen
with Daniel and Olivia, I'd known this was true.

Now my mother gave the curtain a little jerk, revealing me
where I was standing.

The man lying in the bed was definitely my father—the
head of dark hair now reduced to thin gray wisps that stuck
to his scalp. His eyes were a cloudy version of the same blue,
his face more bloated. He'd had his nose broken a few times
during my childhood in the occasional bar fight, and it looked
misplaced on his face now, crooked, a large bump on the
bridge, an oxygen tube forced up inside one nostril. This
observation allowed me to note the rest of the tubes—an
IV hooked to his arm via a needle in the back of his hand, a
catheter bag strapped to the side of the bed, a series of wires
disappearing beneath his thin pajama top that led to the elec-
trodes attached to his chest. These might have been—unless
I was reading too much into things now—the exact pajamas
he'd owned during my childhood.

He squinted up at me. "Curtis?"

It hadn't occurred to me until then how I'd changed, but
of course I had. I wasn't a boy anymore; I was a man, and a
middle-aged one at that. The years since Daniel died hadn't
been kind—the grief, the stress, the anger. Not to mention
I hadn't showered that morning in my quest to leave quietly,
and I was wearing a wrinkled shirt that hadn't been washed
since Sacramento.

I took a step closer. "Hello." I braced myself, because surely
the barrage was coming: *Where the hell have you been?* And
What have you done with your life? And *Why are you here alone?*

Did she leave you, that artsy-fartsy girlfriend you brought to meet us? Surely he had years of pent-up anger waiting to be released on me, like air from a ruptured tire.

Instead, he propped himself up on one elbow, breathing hard, and said in a funny whistle that sounded as if it came from his nostril, rather than his throat, "My son."

olivia

We stopped for gas, and for the millionth time that week, I used a public restroom stall that failed to meet cleanliness standards for anyone, anywhere. But somehow, it hardly bothered me now. *Clumps of toilet paper on the floor? Wadded up towels in the sink? Strange smear along one wall? Bring it on, world. I've got bigger problems.*

Mom handed me a spiral notebook and a two-pack of pens when I came out of the bathroom. "You probably won't need this at all," she said, almost shyly. "It's just in case…."

Just in case all hell broke loose and I had time to write it all down? But I took the notebook gratefully, and once we were back on the road, I separated the plastic front from the cardboard backing to free the pens. I would be ready, just in case.

The closer we got to Chicago, the more ridiculous this whole plan seemed to me. I'd called Dad's cell phone a dozen more times and each time it went right to voice mail, but for all we knew, his battery was dead and he had spent the day driving around Omaha and was even now back at the house, wondering where the hell we were. Mom seemed so certain, though, so determined to press on, despite torrential rain and all sorts of other odds stacked against us.

"Do you think maybe we should call the police or something?" I asked finally, after turning the words over in my mind.

Mom looked horrified. "And say what, exactly?"

"I don't know...at least, they could put out some kind of APB for a white man in a green Explorer with California plates, who may or may not have a gun and may or may not decide to use it when he sees his monsterlike parents...." It sounded stupid even to me, and I was used to my own stupidity. Was Dad even in the Chicago area? Was I right about him having a gun?

Mom was quiet, probably because she was becoming used to my stupidity, too.

"Let's say we don't find Dad," I continued, after a few more miles had ticked by. The rain had slowed considerably, but the roads were still wet, and the sky had changed from rain-darkness to regular evening-darkness. "What happens to me?"

"What do you mean? As far as...?"

"As far as my life goes." It seemed like a fair question for an unfair situation. How could all of this be happening now, when I was only a year away from graduating high school—once I made up those two years of P.E., anyway—and starting my own life? I had no idea what that life might entail, and it was certainly not as prearranged and deliberate as Daniel's post-high school life had been, but there must be *some*thing waiting for me. I thought about Sam Ellis in Lyman, who had probably packed up his display table for the day. Even his vague and not too promising plans were better than what I had.

"We don't need to make any decisions right now. We've got at least until the end of the summer, and then..."

"What decisions? I mean, if something happens with Dad, there's not really a decision to be made, is there?"

Mom was quiet, and I thought she might let the question

just hang there, but finally she said, "I'm not going to force you to do anything you don't want."

I laughed. "Like pick one parent over the other, you mean? I think I already had to do that."

Mom drove on, her lips pinched into a tight line. "I wish it could have been different," she conceded finally.

I must have been feeling particularly hurtful or especially honest, because I didn't let this go. "Well, it could have been different. If you'd stayed, that is." My heart was thudding; where was all this sincerity coming from?

"It would have been different, but it would have been worse," Mom said, obviously choosing her words. "We would have become the kind of parents who couldn't even tolerate each other's presence. We would have yelled at each other and smashed things. I would have become a person I couldn't stand to see in the mirror. I pushed as hard as I thought I could, and if I had pushed harder, your dad would have hated me and probably himself. So, yes, I could have stayed, Olivia. But I hope you understand when I say that I just couldn't, either."

With my tongue, I caught a tear that had squeezed out of the corner of one eye and slithered down my cheek. "But we needed you," I told her, my voice cracking. "We still need you, Dad and me. It's not like we have anyone else in the world. I mean, you have everyone in Omaha who knows you! And plus, Dad's a *man*—he considers other teachers his friends because he happens to see them outside of work once or twice a year. If I hadn't stayed with him, he wouldn't have had anyone."

Mom reached into the door well and pulled out a pocket-sized pouch of Kleenex. It really was amazing how prepared she was for a spontaneous multistate road trip, even without a few days to prepare. She worked two tissues free and handed one to me.

"Liv, I really believed that if I left—if *we* left—it would force your dad to do something, to make some kind of change in his life. He was just stuck. I thought if I wasn't there, he could finally move on."

Not for the first time, I felt like the frayed rope used for a game of tug of war—Mom pulling from one side and Dad pulling from the other. "Well, that didn't happen," I said, knowing I was twisting the knife a little harder. "You gave him almost three years, and now, look."

Mom blew her nose loudly and reached for another tissue. She said something that sounded like "damn," but it couldn't have been—because the apocalypse would really have to be upon us for my mother to swear.

"What did you say?"

Through her tears, I detected just the tiniest hint of a smile in Mom's voice. "I said, damn it. Damn it, Liv. We're going to find your father and set this all straight."

curtis

Looking at my father in his hospital bed, I realized how connected they were in my mind—my father, my son. They had always been linked. Because of the horror that had been my childhood, I'd tried to love Daniel even more—with a love tainted by all the ways my father hadn't loved me. Everything I'd done right over the years had been a stab at him. *Look what I can do without you. Look what I can do better than you.*

Still, my father seemed convinced that I had come to see him in his final moments, as if I'd simply been waiting in the wings for the right opportunity to appear. The effort of communicating with me exhausted him; he sank into an instant, deep sleep and then woke a few minutes later, demanding to know who I was. A minute later he was asleep again, his chest rising and falling irregularly.

He was dying—a nurse confirmed this for me in the hallway. He was in the final stages of liver disease, and would soon be moved to a hospice facility. One day soon, I realized, my mother would come to visit him, and the bed would be empty.

"I understand you're his son," the nurse said, patting my arm sympathetically.

I recoiled, unable to accept that fact even now. I'd never changed my name, after all—it seemed more trouble than it was worth. But a name was all I was willing to share with him, as if we were two John Smiths, linked by a random label. To the nurse I said only, "I thought he had quit drinking."

Again the sympathetic smile. "The trouble is, once the damage is done, it's done."

This made sense. The part of me that was still a teacher—that should have been preparing lessons for Monday, like it was any ordinary weekend—stored this in my mind for a future lesson, like a public service announcement. *The drinking you do today causes harm you can't undo tomorrow.*

"Will you be back in the morning, Mr. Kaufman? You could meet with his doctor, and there are some papers that need to be signed…."

I shook my head, absolving myself of all responsibility. "No, I can't sign anything. I don't know my dad's wishes. His wife—my mother—knows about all of that."

The nurse stepped back, a look of faint disgust on her face. What kind of son won't help his father in his final moments?

I'm not really the son, I wanted to say. I was an imposter, a fraud, an apparition that had appeared out of a Chicago mist and would disappear into it again. As a child, I'd wished I'd been adopted, chosen by some loving couple or other, instead of born as a mistake into a family that had never wanted me. He hadn't been a father, so I wasn't really his son. I was free to simply walk away on my own.

Mom was there suddenly, her mass filling the doorway. "He's asking for you," she said simply.

I looked at my watch, making the calculations. The stop in Chicago had put me hours off course. I'd be arriving in Ohio too early on Monday, when Robert Saenz was dreaming his sweet just-released-from-prison dreams. I had planned on day-light. I had planned on seeing the look on his face.

I stepped again into my father's hospital room, maneuvering around the curtain and the cart at his bedside. He was propped into a sitting position, still wheezing from the effort of movement. His abdomen was oddly extended, as if a tumor or pregnancy lurked beneath the thin pajamas.

I had a sudden flashback of Kathleen in the hospital for Daniel's birth. It had been a twelve-hour labor, culminating in screams and spasms that ripped through her body, as if we were on the set of a horror film. Where she'd gripped my arm, raised red welts had appeared. Later, when the doctor was attending to Kathleen, when Daniel had been cleaned and weighed and measured, the nurse handed him to me. I'd looked at his tiny body, bundled in a blue blanket, and thought: *my son.* The next thought had been of my father, who hadn't crossed my mind in years. What had he been like at my birth? Had there been even a single moment of fatherly pride when he glanced at me, his heart expanding like a balloon slowly inflating inside him? Had he promised to be the best father he could be, to give his son a good life? Or had he been in a bar across the street, bitching about hospital bills and the cost of diapers and all the ways my birth was going to set him back?

He looked so helpless in the hospital bed now, exhausted as if he'd been running for miles, but the specter of my father as the strong man, the villain, had loomed large over the years of my own parenthood. When Daniel had spilled a tumbler of milk at dinner, I ordered myself: *Don't react like your father would.* Instead, I righted the glass, swabbed up the mess with a wad of napkins and set a new cup of milk in front of him. When Olivia screamed as a baby—which she did almost constantly, with the lungs of a trained opera singer—I didn't scream back at her, or leave her to cry. I'd bundled her up and brought her to the car for long drives in and around Sacramento, trying out one CD after another to lull her into silence. Her hands-down favorite was *Crosby, Stills & Nash,* but she didn't always fall asleep; sometimes, when I looked in the mirror, she had seemed to be *listening* to the music.

That was my parenting guide, then: whatever your father did, do the opposite. I didn't spank—although Kathleen had, now and then. I encouraged them in school; when Daniel showed promise on the piano, I gave myself over to the thousands of hours of practices, recitals, the drives from one venue to another, the financial sacrifices. When Kathleen and I went out, I ordered a glass of wine with dinner and stopped there. Not that I didn't trust myself—I had in my father the best possible deterrent from the life of an alcoholic—but I couldn't take a sip without seeing my father and his omnipresent bottle of whiskey. It had been his hand at the end of my arm, holding the tumbler between finger and thumb.

"You came to see me," my father whistled, a repeat of the conversation we had already had. I neither confirmed nor denied this, just stared down at him. His hand, the skin papery thin like the husk of an onion, rose and fell on his bed sheet. He might have been trying to reach for me, but I didn't move closer. "I didn't know if you would. I didn't think I deserved that much."

"I'm not sure you do," I said, loud enough for him to hear, soft enough so that my voice wouldn't travel to the hallway.

The man I had known all those years ago would have taken that statement as a challenge. He wouldn't have hesitated to crack me across the face with a fist that was always ready to fly, that somehow did not require a big windup. He might have pulled me by my hair, even coming away with a small clump in his fist. But the man in the hospital bed made no move at all, except to give me the faintest of smiles.

"That's my boy," he whispered, and closed his eyes.

My mother was standing beside me, I realized, and had probably been standing there since I returned to the room. She reached out to adjust the bedding, pulling a sheet over my father's chest, closer to his chin. There was something genuinely tender in her touch, not just efficient and practical. "I think it's just too bad," she murmured. "It's too bad you never got to really know each other."

My throat was too tight for words. I *had* really known my father, but I knew that he hadn't ever known me. He hadn't bothered. He'd never intended to be a father; I knew because he had said this, yelled it, sneered it, sighed it. He hadn't wanted a child; over the years he'd accused my mother of tricking him into becoming a father. If abortion had been a legal option at the time, he would have insisted on it, I was sure. He would have driven my mother to the clinic and waited in the car, taking regular sips from a flask. He had probably made sure, one way or another, that it never happened again.

But there I was—the child he never wanted.

Although it grew harder to tell over the years, as my father's body became more and more ravaged by alcohol and general bad health, I was clearly his son. I had the same brown hair, now growing thin; the same blue eyes, pale skin, cleft chins. We each topped six feet—although he looked shorter in the hospital bed, as if age had compressed his height.

Mom was wrong—I had known him, as much as a child can know a parent. I knew him in the clinical sense—as the person who had half carried, half dragged him, one of his arms draped over my shoulder, to bed at night. I had wiped up his vomit while Mom murmured that it was a shame he was so sick. I had known him as the man who fought and was thrown in jail and somehow bailed out, who came out of the precinct not even slightly chastened, claiming he had been the victim, it was a setup, and he was going to catch the son of a bitch.... I knew him as the man who didn't bring me to school or pick me up, who never attended a single parent conference, who wasn't there on senior scholarship night, who never once told me I was a good kid, that he was proud of me. A man who had let me graduate college and get married and live an entirely new life without ever expressing the smallest interest in who I had become.

As I'd seen it when I was in high school, I had two choices: to leave or to stay. To leave was to escape, to make my own way in life. To stay was to know that one of us would kill the other. He might go for me in a drunken rage, a lashing out spawned by nothing, or I might go for him, finally so disgusted by his very existence that one more second of life with him was intolerable. It wasn't even a question; I left in the nick of time. I had started to dream about it, to fantasize about the details—my hands around his neck, my hands at his back, pushing him down the stairs.

It wasn't too late, I told myself now. If my mother would leave the room, it could be done in only a few seconds—a pillow over his face, pressed down. Why not? By buying a gun, by taking this trip, I had crossed that line already, the one that divides right from wrong. I was planning to kill one man; what was one more? My father's eyes were already closed, his eyelids a pale, babyish purple. He didn't deserve it any less just because he was weak, just because he was close to that end without my help. But the fight must have gone out of me, or maybe I was just saving the fight for something else, for the cause that mattered more.

"How long are you going to stay?" Mom's voice shook me from my dark reverie. It was easy to forget she was there, like forgetting the color of the wallpaper.

"Not much longer," I said.

My father's eyelids fluttered open again. He held my gaze, and I didn't look away. Now was the chance—too late—for him to know me. I was a man now, and I'd become a man without his help. I was not only his equal, but his superior— the stronger man, not the boy who hid in the closet with a flashlight, who shut himself in the bathroom and prayed that the lock held. Without saying anything, my father seemed to acknowledge this. The look he gave me approached respect.

"You have a boy?" he croaked. It took me a moment to understand his question, and not only for the diminished quality of his voice. I nodded hesitantly, not correcting the present tense. What was the point? *My son—the grandson you never knew anything about—is dead.* It seemed like blasphemy to introduce Daniel that way, as a person who was no longer alive.

"That's good," he said. "You can do right by him. You can do what I never did."

This time when he closed his eyes, he seemed to sink directly into sleep, his chest immediately, unevenly, rising and falling. I watched the machines by his bedside, their silent, blinking vigilance. Oxygen and fluids were pumped in, the unwanted fluids pumped out. My father would be dead soon. I couldn't summon sadness, exactly, but his words were already echoing in my mind, like a fatherly blessing, a benediction. *Do right by him.*

When Mom stepped around the curtain and into the hallway, I followed her and took her by the arm. "What will you do when he's gone?"

She didn't seem fazed by the question. Her expression, as always, was impossible to read. Would his death be a relief, or a mere change of circumstances? "I have a friend who lost her husband. We'll just live together when he goes."

I wondered about the friend, and wondered about the house

or apartment where my mother would be living. In all respects, it had to be a better situation. I wished I could ask if she wanted to stay with *us*—but *us* was a family that no longer existed, in a place that no longer existed.

"What's the name of your friend?" I asked and then turned on my phone to record the information along with my contacts. My phone beeped frantically, alerting me to a dozen missed calls and a number of voice mail messages, a few from Kathleen, the rest from Olivia. I turned off the phone again.

"Do you have to go?" she asked, and I looked at her closely. Was she asking me to stay?

"There's something I have to do," I said carefully, but my mother's eyes had wandered down the hallway again, looking at nothing. *She's done with me,* I thought. *I've been dismissed.* She wasn't the brute that my father had been, but she hadn't been a loving mother, either. She wasn't anything like Barbara had been with Kathleen, like Kathleen had been with Daniel and Olivia.

I squeezed her hand, which was surprisingly strong. I thought of all those years of her standing behind a plastic dome in an elementary school cafeteria, her gloved hand reaching out with a scoop of cole slaw or a handful of chicken nuggets. "Mom," I said, taking her other hand. I wanted to shake her, to make her focus, to see me right in front of her. I was gripping her too tightly; I only succeeded in sending a brief flash of pain across her face. She flinched, and I relaxed my grip. It was the last time we would see each other. "Mom, I just want to say that…" My throat constricted, and I stopped, because she was looking away again, over my shoulder.

But then she turned to me, her eyes watery blue. "I love you, too, Curtis," she said.

olivia

It was dark by the time we reached Chicago. At least, the massive highway billboards kept informing us that we were in the Chicago area, but we spent at least an hour in stop-and-go traffic on the rain-slick freeway, the sort of rush-hour mess that really shouldn't exist at night, on a weekend.

Mom took a random exit, and we went inside a Burger King to use the bathroom. There were two stalls, but only one had a working latch. Mom went first, and when I came out, my hands only half-dry from an ineffectual air dryer, Mom was sitting in a booth with her cell phone against one ear and her free hand jotting down an address on a napkin.

When she hung up the phone, she said, "I was right. They haven't moved. I mean, all those years, and they're still in that run-down house. I don't know if I've ever heard anything so depressing." She folded the napkin neatly and stood. "Think I'll grab a burger to go. You want something?"

I shook my head. How could I eat with all this uncertainty?

In the car, Mom plugged the address into her cell phone and passed the phone over to me so I could navigate while she took quick bites of her burger.

"I knew it was somewhere around here," she said, executing the turns as I called them out.

"We're not going to call first?" I asked.

"We've been calling," Mom pointed out. "It's not like he's dying to return our calls."

"Not Dad," I protested. "I think that we should call them. Grandpa and Grandma, I mean."

She crumpled the wrapper from her burger and said, "Don't do that. Don't call them Grandpa and Grandma. They aren't your real grandparents."

"That's right, they're my fake grandparents."

"Olivia. Look, tomorrow or whenever this is all over, you can ask me questions or yell at me, or whatever you want. Tonight, let's just get to your dad and make sure everything's okay."

"That's why I thought we should call. To make sure everything's okay."

Mom slowed for a turn. According to the directions on her phone, we were 1.3 miles from our destination. "I'm not hoping for a friendly chat."

My heart was hammering around in my chest cavity as Mom made a final left turn. We were on a residential street, with houses close together on small lots and cars parked along the curb on both sides of the street. "This place has really changed," Mom mused, straining to see in the dark.

"Changed good or changed bad?"

"Oh, changed for the good. It used to be a lot of falling-down houses and chain-link fences."

There were still a few of those around, I noted, but the cars parked in driveways were decent-looking minivans that could fit a whole soccer troop in their backseats, next to the occasional sporty hybrid. Mom was scanning for the house number on one side of the street, but I was craning my neck for a glimpse of our teal-green Explorer, without any luck.

"There it is!" Mom pointed to a house that was basically falling in on itself. She slowed directly in front of it, and since no one was behind us, we stopped to stare. A bare bulb over the porch illuminated, but barely, a rusty screen door, sagging porch steps, a concrete walkway from the curb that was so cracked and uneven it was an invitation for a stubbed toe, or worse. A lone shutter hung from a small window, and I wondered if its mate had fallen into the shrubs below, where it was even now rotting away into nothing.

I fought back a lump of vomit that was lurking at the back of my throat. Someone I knew—my father—had lived in this house? Suddenly, this all seemed like a very bad idea, another wrong turn on this crazy road trip. If I clicked my heels together three times, would I end up back where we'd started? Dad wasn't here. Maybe we'd read this whole situation wrong, and Dad hadn't been here and wasn't going to be here, and yet, *we* were here. Unannounced, uninvited, unexplained, about to barge in to the most unwelcoming house I could have imagined.

"Let's go," I whispered frantically, and Mom, misunderstanding, said, "Geez, Liv. We can't just leave the car in the middle of the street. Let me find a place to park."

We had to drive for a few blocks before we could find a spot that could accommodate a Volvo station wagon, and then we hiked back down the street, with Mom urging me forward. How was she so fearless? If Dad really was in their house with a gun—even if it was unloaded—I was more and more convinced with each step that it wasn't the place for me. But Mom was determined, clutching her purse strap with one hand and me with the other. Soon we were back in front of the brokendown house, standing on the cracked concrete at the curb.

"I don't think anyone's home," I said, trying not to whimper. Right then my mind was flooded with about a billion things I wanted to write in my Fear Journal, like *dark spaces* and *roofs caving in,* not to mention the sudden memory of my ninth grade English teacher reading from *The Fall of the House of Usher.*

"There's a light on inside," Mom pointed out.

"But it's late. They're probably asleep. Maybe we should come back in the morning." *Or never.*

"This will be the first time I've interrupted their lives in almost thirty years," Mom said. "I guess they'll just have to live with that." She led the way up the walkway, paused at the screen door hanging slightly open and reached around to rap, hard, on the front door.

Nothing. I felt relief wash over me. In maybe twenty minutes we could be at a decent hotel, tucked into clean white sheets, watching *House Hunters.* We would call Dad again, and I would leave a longer message repeating how sorry I was for saying that I hated him, and maybe telling him a joke or two so he would know everything was okay. Or I would just say "Love" and wait for him to call back with "Elephantine."

Mom knocked again, harder.

There were footsteps inside the house.

"I'm going to throw up," I whimpered, but there was no time. The door swung inward, and the woman standing there, looking lumpy in a few layers of cardigans, smiled as if she were used to strangers appearing on her doorstep on a rainy night.

"Hello, Kathleen," my grandmother said. "And this must be your daughter."

curtis

By the time I delivered my mother back to her house, it was after eight o'clock. I was exhausted, but too pumped full of adrenaline to stop now. I couldn't imagine stopping at a hotel room, pacing anxiously within four walls. No, sitting in a hotel room wasn't going to cut it. I couldn't stop—I needed to keep going, to drive as fast as the Explorer would take me, straight through the night, even if I arrived in Oberlin hours before daylight.

I'd forgotten how long it took to get around Chicago. More than once traffic came to a complete stop, and I banged my fists against the steering wheel in frustration. I was driving toward Robert Saenz and away from my father at the same time. I was fulfilling my childhood fantasy, the one where I packed my troubles in an old backpack with a broken zipper and never, never came home again. I'd managed to make that escape as an eighteen-year-old and stay away for more than half of my life. My father was dying, and that should have made me happy. How many times, in how many ways, had I imagined the moment? Take your pick: falling off a bar stool and hitting his head. Picking a fight with the wrong person, someone who could actually fight back. Drinking himself to death, plain and simple. I had prayed for acts of God, like tornados or lightning strikes. I would have been happy with a beam falling at a construction site, and my father being squashed like a little bug beneath its weight. Ironically enough, I'd prayed for a car accident, something quick and simple and final. If the world had any fairness at all, it would have been my father and not my son who was killed by Robert Saenz, by the truck clipping the sign, and the sign bearing down upon him.

But the world wasn't fair. Daniel was long dead, and my father was still all too much alive, living out his last few days—hours?—with a small staff catering to his needs, with my mother worrying over the position of his bed pillows. My father had the luxury of making final pronouncements, of handing down advice and apology, of saying goodbye. Daniel, who deserved that and more, had never had a chance.

You can do right by him.

What the hell did he know? What right did he have?

I released my hold on the steering wheel, suddenly aware that I was gripping it with a painful intensity. *Relax,* I ordered myself. The traffic thinned, Chicago was finally behind me, and I still had another five hours to go.

It was small consolation that there would be few people on the road other than the tired, possibly drugged truckers pushing against time to make it to their destination for the night. Robert Saenz had been one of these men on his way home that night, too tired and doped up to know that he'd killed someone.

I kept myself busy by flipping through stations, catching a song or two before the music buzzed into static. In Sacramento, our house was cluttered with CDs. Daniel's room held hundreds, and I'd burned myself copies over the years, labeling them with a Sharpie. Why hadn't I brought more of them with me? God knew there was room.

I got gas near Gary, Indiana, and gave in to my need for caffeine—although it meant I would be stopping more often en route. The girl at the register, her hair a series of gelled spikes, was absorbed in a magazine and jumped, startled, as I entered.

"Is it pretty cold out there?" she asked, taking the two dollars I slid across the counter.

"I don't know," I admitted, and she glanced at me quickly, then down to the cash register, fingering my change.

Was it cold? Hot? Wet? Dry? Did it matter? In my mind I was miles away, already lacing my way through Oberlin, past the conservatories and the brick buildings on campus, past front porches and picket fences. I was only dimly aware of what was actually happening around me.

"Okay, then, you have a good night," the girl said, depositing the change in my open palm. I fingered it idly, as if I'd lost the ability to count, to name things.

"You have a good night, too," I mumbled.

Outside, the sky was made even darker by the absence of stars, obscured by a low gray haze of cloud cover. Even the stars have gone, I thought, senselessly—and realized I was barely hanging on to sanity. I wasn't the father of Daniel and Olivia anymore. I was no longer Mr. K, the goofy teacher who posed for his yearbook photo in a white lab coat, holding a beaker of green liquid. I wasn't the young man who had fallen in love with Kathleen. I was now a desperate man, or his shadow. Suddenly I remembered a hand-painted sign that Kathleen's father had hung in his garage: *When you get to the end of your rope, tie a knot and hang on.* I was at the end of the rope. I had tied a knot. I only had to hang on a little longer.

Every few miles—and I knew, because I was watching for the reflective mile markers with an almost religious fervor— I found myself thinking about Olivia, or about Kathleen, or about Olivia and Kathleen, the two of them finding my note. Olivia would be hurt and furious, although maybe not surprised. What had Kathleen known, what had she suspected? Only last night we'd made love as if it would be the last time, as if the world had ended and we were the only people left. Kathleen, Olivia—I had to force them out of my brain, like physically slamming a door. *Think about Robert Saenz,* I reminded myself. I remembered his mug shot—the disheveled hair, the dead eyes, the slight upward tilt of his chin: What the fuck are you going to do about it? *Remember how he killed Daniel and drove away.*

If I could, I'd get a punch in first. I don't think I'd ever thrown a punch in my life, although I'd been on the receiving end often enough as a kid. But I needed my fist to land squarely on Robert Saenz's upraised chin.

"That's for Daniel," I imagined myself saying as Saenz fell backward, a twin to my childhood fantasy—my father falling backward, felled by my powerful blow.

Funnily enough, it was Dad's voice that kept popping into my head: *Do right by him.*

Yes, but I'll do right by you, too, Dad.

Kill one, let the other die.

Indiana passed in a dark blur of asphalt and semis and road signs. I stopped once for coffee, stopped twice to piss against fences that seemed to border nothing. When I passed the giant sign welcoming me to Ohio, it felt as if a bell should have sounded, one loud enough to be heard by the whole world. I sat up straighter, drove faster, resented when I had to stop again for gas. A sprinkling of rain fell, spattering the windshield. I finally knew the answer to the cashier's question back in Gary—it was cold outside and growing colder. Here and there the ditches were dotted with the crusty, stubborn remains of snow heaps that hadn't received the message about spring.

I took the exit for state route 58 toward Amherst/Oberlin, forcing myself to keep to the speed limit; that was all I needed, a speeding ticket this close to my destination. I could imagine the conversation with the officer. What's a guy from California doing out here after midnight? You have business in town, buddy?

I had moved beyond tired to a strange place where adrenaline kicked in, defying normal human powers. I'd heard stories of men who lifted cars off of trapped victims, who scaled impossibly high fences to escape a charging animal. I could feel a pulse thrumming in my fingertips, my neck, my thighs. Was he asleep already, passed out, dreaming his last dream?

I tapped the gas and eased up, tapped and eased, tapped and eased.

Soon, it would all be over.

olivia

Stepping into that house was like stepping into a television set from the 1970s, complete with wallpaper and shag carpeting and the widespread use of brown. It was hard to pin down the exact smell that assaulted my nostrils as we walked through a dark hallway—not pets exactly, not cigarettes only. The walls had a dingy, yellowish quality; if I bumped my shoulder against any wall, I might come away smudged. As we followed my grandmother—my *grandmother!*—through the house, it occurred to me that this was what life would smell like if nothing was ever washed and if no window was ever opened to let in a bit of fresh air.

"Would you like something to drink?" my grandmother asked as we came into the den.

Mom and I glanced around, taking in the bare walls, the ancient television console, a sagging plaid couch.

"No—thank you, though. I'm so sorry to barge in on you like this, and so late at night." Mom's smile was uncertain. Her eyes kept flitting around to the corners of the room, as if worried that something evil was lurking in a dark recess.

My grandmother settled her cushiony weight onto the couch, which sighed in mild protest. Mom was right, I realized—it was hard for my mind to form the phrase *my grand-mother,* let alone the word *Grandma.* But what else could I call her—Mrs. Kaufman? If I'd passed her on the street, I wouldn't have thought she was any relation of mine. Her face was broad, her features somewhat hidden by folds of extra skin and a thinning perm that framed her face like dandelion fluff. She stared at me vacantly. If I didn't know better—and I didn't— I would say my grandmother was pleasantly stoned.

"You look like your father," she said, and I realized that while I was scrutinizing her, she'd been scrutinizing me, too. I was worried that I was making a bad impression for a first-meeting-of-the-grandmother. Never in my life had I felt so out of place for wearing all black. In this house, the land that time forgot, there was no such thing as a pair of skinny jeans, and combat boots were to be worn only in actual combat.

"I do?" I blurted. I'd honestly never been told this. It was Daniel who looked more like Dad, or really, like a blend of Mom and Dad, if you took their very best qualities and melded them together. Once Daniel had told me that I fell off a truck at the farmer's market and had been rescued by my well-meaning "parents." He'd apologized for it later, but when I looked at myself next to the rest of my family, it had made a sort of sense.

My grandmother nodded and continued, "Yes, when he was a boy."

Oh. This was either a strange compliment or an outright insult. I couldn't think of anything else to say, not even some-thing witty or ironic or at least marginally funny, so I settled for, "I'm Olivia."

"It's nice to meet you, Olivia." Her smile was empty, the action of a robot programmed to give automatic responses.

Mom shot me a look that said, *Shut up and let me do the talk-ing.* She cut right to the point. "We're looking for Curtis."

"Well, you just missed him. He left a few hours ago."

"He was *here?*" I blurted again, like the kid in class who wasn't paying attention and needed everything repeated. Yes, I was that kid. But I had to hand it to Mom. I'd figured we were on the wild-goose chase to end all wild-goose chases, and she'd been right all along. It turned out I did have a secret set of grandparents, and it turned out that my father had indeed come to visit them.

"Yes." For the first time, a real emotion—surprise, puzzlement—passed across my grandmother's face. "He was here earlier, to bring me to the hospital."

"To bring you to the...?"

Mom looked at me again, and I let the rest of my question drift away, although this took a tremendous effort on my part.

"Well, I thought you would know, because I sent the letter. My husband has been in the hospital, and Curtis took me to see him."

Mom absorbed this information silently, although it must have made about zero sense to her, too. What letter? What was he in the hospital for?

"I did think it was strange that he came alone," my grandmother said. It sounded like an insult to me, but Mom let it pass.

"We're supposed to meet up with him," Mom explained. "But somewhere along the way, our plans got mixed up. Did he say he was staying in town tonight?"

My grandmother looked back and forth between the two of us, her gaze suddenly more focused. I tried to keep my face as neutral as possible, although I felt like screaming. It was bad that Dad had dumped me in Omaha, and it was bad that he had come here, but it was much, much worse that he hadn't stayed here. There was a long pause while my grandmother considered us, as if we might not be family at all, but some kind of secret agents or saboteurs who were out to destroy her son.

Mom said, "Please, Lorene," her voice tender, as if she were talking to a small child.

Lorene Kaufman, I repeated to myself, trying to give the words meaning. My grandmother.

"I don't know," she said finally. "He said he had to go, and he hugged me real tight."

Mom swallowed. "But he didn't say anything in particular...?"

It looked like there was nothing else for us to learn, and Lorene Kaufman was ready to usher us back into the Chicago night, but still we waited. I glanced at a clock on the wall, the hands marking time behind a plate of cracked glass. Finally my grandmother said, as if she were just remembering, "He said there was something he had to do."

"Something he had to do," Mom echoed.

My grandmother nodded and pushed herself to a standing position, a hand on the armrest of the couch for support. There was no mistaking the message: *We're done here.*

curtis

The closer I got, the more I itched to pull over, take the Colt out of the spare wheel well, load it with the cartridges I'd taped under the driver's seat and ride with the gun on the seat next to me, where I could see it, where it would keep being real. It wouldn't be long now.

Oberlin was still the same sleepy town with the blinking traffic lights, the towering trees with limbs that arched over the road. On my previous visits it had been snowing, and now a light, stinging rain hit with little pings against the windshield. Maybe the weather was always bad in Oberlin, like a dark cloud hovered directly over its city limits. The streets were quiet, the town hunkered down for the night.

On my phone, I'd looked up the address of Jerry Saenz, Robert's brother, and used satellite imaging to zoom in on 1804 Morgan Street—a white house with turquoise shutters, a gravel driveway and a detached garage. Jerry had taken in his brother after the incident in North Carolina; he'd even assigned him a route for his trucking company. I was banking on the fact that Jerry had taken him in again, that Robert Saenz was right now sleeping under his roof. If not, I'd keep going until I found him.

The possibility that he could be so close—only a few blocks from where he'd killed Daniel—sickened me. He'd killed my son and gone to prison, and in the logic of the justice system, he got to go right back to where he'd come from, as if he were simply completing a loop, closing a circle.

Morgan Street was something people in Sacramento couldn't imagine—no sidewalks, quarter-acre front lawns, no fences clearly delineating the neighbor's space from your own. If you had a kid, this would be the place to throw a ball after dinner, with a few other kids from the block joining you, baseball gloves at the ready. It would be criminal, I decided, to live here and not throw a ball with your kid on summer evenings. I would have done this with Daniel every single night if I could have torn him away from the piano. I noted the mailboxes along the road—some of them cutesy, with hand-painted vines snaking up the posts, and little flowers and butterflies and frogs painted on the mailboxes themselves. *Happiness lives here!* they screamed. I read the names as my headlights illuminated them: The Severins. The Omgards. I slowed in the 1800 block, although I had no intention of stopping yet.

There was nothing fancy about 1804 Morgan Street, which had grass from curb to porch, rather than expensive concrete or stone work. A commercial flatbed truck was parked in the driveway, Saenz & Co. Short Haul printed on its side in block letters. I felt a crushing hate, like a weight on my chest. Wouldn't I be doing the world a public service if I prevented Robert Saenz from ever, ever getting behind the wheel again? Someone else should have done this years ago—his brother, a police officer, the district attorney, a relative of the woman who died in North Carolina. Jail time didn't work—and who was there to monitor him, constantly, from getting behind the wheel? No one had stopped him from taking the corner too fast and clipping the speed limit sign that killed Daniel; I was the only one who would stop him from doing it again.

I looped into the countryside and back into town, slowing again as I passed 1804. The house itself was dark, except for a single light on the porch. I took a quick inventory: the same white siding that used to be sold on Sears infomercials; dark trim around the windows; an empty planter box; those bright, out-of-place shutters; plastic chairs stacked seat-to-seat on the front porch, out of commission until summer arrived. I allowed myself to look at the apartment over the garage, my heartbeats reverberating like a snare drum.

Robert Saenz was up there—I knew it. Of course he was— would anyone plunk their two-time murdering parolee brother in the main house? Above the garage, he was out of earshot and eyesight.

At the end of Morgan Street, I turned left, heading back through town. There were few other cars on the road, although I passed students walking closer to campus, their collars up, wearing the sort of knitted hats that my students in California had worn to be cool, rather than to protect against the cold.

I realized with a jolt that I had passed the spot. It was unmarked, a stretch of sidewalk along a road like any other, where people walked every day, not thinking that someone— that Daniel Owen Kaufman—had died there.

I was flooded with déjà vu; it was this moment—or close to it—that I'd envisioned from the roof of the cafeteria, looking over the campus where I'd spent the better part of twenty years. I'd seen myself in Oberlin, making things right, making things final.

At the same time, it was as if I was reviewing my life in a selective editing mode. The phone call in the middle of the night. Skip. Daniel's body at the morgue—that pale scar on his abdomen. Skip. The box with his *cremains,* so insubstantial. Skip. The night I'd followed the stranger in the parking lot and ended up in the bar. Skip. Kathleen packing her clothes, leaving not even a single pilled sweater or flattened pair of slippers behind, her message clear.

Skip.

The gun in my hand, Robert Saenz dead on the floor.

olivia

"Where are we going?" I panted. The second my grandmother had closed the door behind us, Mom had taken off at a sprint for our car. For a moment I thought she might have been worried about parking her Volvo on a public street in a not-so-fantastic part of town, but even when the car was in view and clearly fine—stereo, hubcaps and windows all intact—she hadn't slowed her pace.

"Hurry up!" she called over her shoulder.

I would have liked to point out to her that my combat boots were not exactly ideal running shoes, mainly since each boot weighed approximately five pounds, and running down the street in them was a little like trying to swim with a block of cement on each foot. Why hadn't I ever considered this before? It would be absolutely impossible for me to swim in these boots. If one of my million water-related fears ever came true, I would sink like a stone.

Mom started the engine while I was still a half-block away, and the second I slid into my seat, she was already pulling away from the curb.

"Whoa," I said, yanking my door shut. "Um, hello, I don't even have my seat belt fastened yet."

"All right, Liv. Get out your phone. I can get us back to the freeway, I think, but I want to make sure we're taking the shortest possible route."

I stared at her, not understanding. "Home, you mean?" Even as I asked it, I realized I had no idea what home I might be referring to, or what exactly we were going to do when we got there. Omaha or the long haul back to California?

"Not home," Mom said grimly. Her jaw was set, her hands on the steering wheel at ten and two, and she was leaning forward, as if the weight of her body alone could propel each turn. The Volvo stuttered along, accelerating too hard one moment, braking too suddenly the next.

I stopped myself from blurting out something about being tired, and wanting to stop at a hotel so I could shower and brush my teeth and pee without worrying about the million contaminants on the seat of a gas station toilet. I was hungry and overwhelmed. In less than a day, my dad had left with only the crappiest of explanations, I had discovered living grandparents who were less than outstanding and now Mom was going to get us killed in the dark on our way to who-knew-where.

But there was something in Mom's voice that made me shut out the whiny, self-absorbed Olivia and give her all my attention. I groped around in the dark for my cell phone. The red warning light was on; I had less than twenty percent battery life, but at least it was something. "Okay," I said, trying to keep my voice level and calm, like an air controller with a lost pilot. "Where to?"

"Ohio," Mom said automatically. "Oberlin, Ohio."

Oberlin? My hands were shaking so hard, I could hardly navigate the screen on my phone.

Even though I had worn only black for as long as I could remember and had spent serious time chronicling the ways a person could die or be dismembered, I wasn't at all interested in visiting the place where Daniel had died. The fact that my brother had died in Oberlin meant it wasn't even in the top million places I wanted to visit.

I waited for Mom to explain it to me—why we were headed to Oberlin, why she thought Dad might go there. If I didn't know better, I'd think she and Dad were both off their meds—swinging without warning to the manic side of the pendulum. Her eyes looked wild, dancing in her sockets as if she were tracking something on the road in front of us, rather than following the road itself, which was long and dark and increasingly lonely the farther we got from Chicago. The night opened before us, shrouded in an inky, ghostly black.

Finally I whispered, "I don't feel so good."

Mom's eyes flashed at me. "What, like you're going to throw up?"

It had felt more like passing out than throwing up, but once she said the words, throwing up seemed like a very real possibility. Everything inside me was being turned upside down and inside out—like some strange disease where my internal organs suddenly began leaking through my skin. I pressed one hand against my stomach and the other against my mouth.

Mom reached around her seat with one arm and located an empty Walmart bag. I held it a few inches from my face, even more nauseated by the smell of the plastic.

"What is Dad going to do in Oberlin?" I asked, my words escaping into the bag. The initial wormy feeling of nausea had passed, but it was way too soon to say I was out of those woods.

Mom shook her head back and forth several times, as if it was too awful to say, or she was trying to shake the thought right out of her head.

Still, I needed to hear her say it. "Mom? What's Dad going to do? What's going to happen in Oberlin?"

Mom hesitated, choosing her words carefully. "Olivia, will you promise not to take this the wrong way?"

Well, shit. Was Oberlin the home of some other long-lost relative, another person I may or may not want to know? I whimpered, "What?"

"I need you to shut up, okay? I need you to just shut up."

So I did.

And we drove.

curtis

I left Oberlin, circling the countryside while I waited for daybreak. A few miles out of town, I followed signs to a twenty-four-hour truck stop. The face in the bathroom mirror looked familiar, like I was seeing a distant cousin, someone from my childhood. I forced down a fried egg sandwich and a cup of coffee, all the while giving myself these little internal pep talks, my mind a coach on the sidelines, calling plays to my body. *Sure you're tired, but you can't stop now! You've got the target in sight!*

There were two other cars in the parking lot when I emerged, and I figured they belonged to the waitress and the cook, the only other humans around. Still, I kept an eye out as I popped the trunk of the Explorer and fished around until I located the Colt in its wad of T-shirts. From my suitcase, I removed the little pouch, the bag where I'd stowed the press clippings about Daniel's recitals, his death and his killer. Since there was time to kill—*a joke, Curtis, a fucking hysterical joke!*— I spread out the clippings one by one on the passenger seat and studied them in the dim glow from a nearby light pole.

All the before pictures, where Daniel was alive and well, smacked of happiness. I couldn't feel that anymore, though.

Now each smile was a sting, a slap in the face. The last one had been taken on Daniel's summer home from college, when he'd been teeming with confidence, eager to tell us everything he'd learned. Kathleen had snapped the picture when he was playing the piano, a new piece, something he'd composed. His eyes were half-closed, dreamy. He would always be that way now—twenty, dreamlike, an angel.

I hoped he couldn't see what I was about to do, but still I wanted him to know I'd done it.

It was strange how a man like me, who was not powerful at all, and certainly not powerful enough to keep my son from dying, could feel formidable with a gun in his hand. That was the attraction of a gun, the allure. If the waitress from the truck stop came outside at that moment and saw me with the Colt, she would only need a glance—not even a shot fired— to regard me in a way she hadn't before. She would fear me.

Some men wanted this kind of respect, I figured. I just wanted to kill Robert Saenz, that son of a bitch.

In order to reach the bullets, I had to bend over awkwardly, my head butting against the steering wheel. I was proud of myself for thinking of this hiding place, almost a *MacGyver* move, a place where Olivia would never have looked. I seized a corner of the duct tape between my thumb and forefinger and gave it a little yank—too hard, apparently, because the bullets popped free and hit the floorboard, scattering. *Damn.* I forced the seat back, giving myself enough room to bend forward, my hand feeling along the dark floorboard. I lifted one of the cartridges, then snapped on the overhead light and bent down for a closer look.

I held the bullet to the light, understanding coming slowly, thickly, like breaking through a dense northern California fog.

What I held in my hand wasn't a bullet at all.

It was a battery.

olivia

I kept quiet for a long time, watching the road before us. Mom was thinking, her lips set in a flat, grim line. I could have kept pestering her out of pure selfishness, just to have her say something, even if it wasn't true at all.

I don't know how long we stayed that way, alternating between long stretches of darkness and brief bursts of civilization. Right then I would have preferred to be on the scariest roller coaster in the world, with the biggest drop, the fastest turns, than where we actually were.

The road had almost lulled me to sleep when Mom said, "He never accepted that it was an accident. He just couldn't let it alone. He was obsessed with it—with that guy."

I sat up. The name came to me quickly, even though it had been years since Mom and Dad had argued in the kitchen about the plea deal, the reduced sentence. But there it was: Robert Saenz, as if I'd studied the name for a test and simply filed it away until needed.

"But that man—he went to jail," I said, fighting the nausea that rose as I spoke. "Or prison, or whatever. He was punished."

"Right, but your father fought for a longer sentence. There

had been a previous DUI, another accident where someone died."

It took a while for this to sink in. "How did I not know that?"

"You were only twelve. You had enough to worry about."

"I can't believe you didn't tell me. I can't believe Dad didn't tell me." It felt as if something inside me had deflated. Not just a lung, because that was so typical, but maybe my liver, or my spleen or some other vital organ—withered up like one of those Shrinky Dinks Mom and I used to bake in the oven on rainy days. Now I wouldn't have been surprised if my entire body just collapsed.

"Really, Liv, would it have mattered? Wouldn't it have just made everything worse?"

I could only force a laugh. "Worse than what?"

To this, my mother had no response.

When I had allowed myself to think through the sequence of events, of what had happened to Daniel that night, I'd thought of it as an accident, a random, horrible thing—a speed limit sign falling over and my brother in its path. I had rarely thought about the man in the truck, the guy behind the wheel. He had been locked away, doing his time. Was it possible Dad had been thinking of nothing else?

I tried not to look at the speedometer as we hurtled through Indiana, on a collision course with our fate, whatever that was. For once in my life, my melodrama didn't exactly seem melodramatic. It seemed a huge understatement.

Maybe Dad had reached his destination already and was trying at this exact moment to kill the man who had killed his son. I shivered. This was *real* fear, not the random worries that had plagued me over the years, not the endless list of things—scalding hot radiators and pendant lamps and infected paper cuts and the plantar wart that was surely awaiting me if I went barefoot in the girls' locker room. This was real, *genuine:* What if Robert Saenz had a gun with actual bullets, and poor Dad was left helpless because of what Sam and I had done, as if he'd brought a knife to a gunfight? More helpless, even— a search of his luggage hadn't revealed a knife. I wanted desperately to call Sam Ellis and dump the whole problem in his lap again, to see what new solution he had.

"I didn't see it earlier," Mom was saying, more to herself than me. "I thought he meant his father—I figured that had to be it."

I felt my face go hot. "He told you something, didn't he? And now you're not telling me?"

Instead of answering, she reached into the back pocket of her jeans and handed me a folded sheet of paper, dense with writing. "After I found the other note, I went downstairs and just sat there for a while, thinking, And then I saw the box— the one with Daniel's ashes, up on a high shelf. This letter was sitting on top of it. I didn't want to show you—I'm sorry, I didn't want you to be even more worried. It sounded like he was saying goodbye, and my first thought was that he was talking about his father. But he must be talking about that man—the one who hit that sign."

I held the letter for a long moment in the darkness, before turning on the overhead light. Mom and I both winced, blinking at the sudden brightness. I read the letter once through quickly, then twice more, slowly. The words swam before me. *All my rage was focused in one direction...it's too late to convince myself of any other alternative.... If you had known what I was planning, you would have talked me out of it.*

"But he's in prison," I repeated. "The man who killed Daniel is in prison. So, what exactly is Dad going to do?"

"I don't know," Mom said. "I'm trying to think. It hasn't been long enough—his sentence shouldn't be up already. Has your dad been talking to anyone lately? Maybe the D.A, or something?"

I shook my head. If he'd been talking to anyone, Dad had done a pretty decent job of keeping it under wraps. Life had been normal enough. But then again, there was the day he'd gone up on the roof of the cafeteria, when I'd recognized him first by his brown loafers, dangling down. I'd been so wrapped up in my own petty fears that I wouldn't have known if there had been a phone call or a letter. Suddenly, I remembered the little zippered bag in Dad's suitcase, the one Sam had opened, spilling the contents on the motel bed. We'd been looking for a gun, and once I knew for sure the bag didn't contain any kind of weapon, I'd more or less forgotten about it. "Well," I said. "I did find all these newspaper clippings...."

Mom looked at me sharply, and the Volvo drifted slightly off the road. She jerked the wheel, bringing us back. "What do you mean?"

"I don't know. I didn't read through everything. But he had this collection of stuff—" a *memorial,* I remembered thinking, trying not to show Sam how wounded I was "—and it was all about Daniel. Like, newspaper clippings and pictures and things." At least, that's how it had seemed to me at the time, but Robert Saenz's name had been there, too. *Driver Under the Influence, Police Say* and *Man Who Killed Sacramento Prodigy Sentenced.* I swallowed hard. The tidy stack of photos and clippings wasn't just a tribute to my dead brother but an obsession with the man who had killed him.

Dad had been obsessed with bringing Daniel's killer to justice.

One way or another, he must have found his chance.

curtis

I stared at the batteries for a long time, letting them roll back and forth in my palm. Five of them. My first thought was of Zach Gaffaney and our quick exchange in the dark outside his trailer. But I'd *seen* the bullets—I'd looked in the cylinder, unloaded them, taped them beneath the seat myself. So there were only a few possibilities—the Ellis brothers, Sam, Olivia or even Kathleen.

If it had been Olivia…

Would she have thought one was meant for her, or Kathleen, or me? It was hard to argue, having driven cross-country with the sole purpose of killing Robert Saenz, that I wasn't a danger to society. But I never meant to be a danger to my daughter; I couldn't even conceive of the idea. Whoever had switched out the bullets had believed I was capable of something, had seen something in me that I could barely see in myself until now—until this moment.

There was no time to execute a Plan B, even if I had an alternative. Maybe I could have called Zach Gaffaney, although I'd promised to lose his number, to ask what he knew about gun laws in Ohio, about the best places to buy ammunition.

I'd figured on having a loaded gun, on taking all the shots I needed.

And then I remembered.

I fished into the pocket of my pants. I'd been carrying one bullet with me since our breakdown outside Lyman; that just-in-case for a case I couldn't imagine at the time.

One bullet, one shot—like Russian roulette.

But that should be all I needed. If I couldn't kill Robert Saenz with one bullet, then I wasn't worth anything.

The first light was breaking by the time I was back in Oberlin. I slowed to a crawl down Main Street. The streets were still quiet, but a diner was open; inside, a few patrons sipped coffee and read newspapers. An empty plastic bag blew past the spot where Daniel had died. I nearly jumped when a station wagon pulled out of the gas station. For a frightening moment, it looked like Kathleen behind the wheel. But that was just the sleeplessness at work—coupled with the understanding that I was about to become a cold-blooded murderer—because it was a newer model Volvo with an Ohio plate, and Kathleen was hundreds of miles away, unaware of what I was going to do.

I turned again onto Morgan Street, every sense alert. Down the street, one of Jerry Saenz's neighbors walked from his front door to a spot halfway down the lawn. He glanced up as I passed, and in the rearview mirror I saw him bend to retrieve the paper. What constituted big news in Oberlin—an athletic championship for a local high school? A ribbon cutting at a new drugstore? A visiting lecturer? I could imagine the headline tomorrow, in a giant font: Murder in Oberlin. Maybe a subheading: Man Exacts Revenge on Son's Killer. But it might not be that at all. It might be California Man, in Wake of Mental Breakdown, Kills Oberlin Resident.

It didn't matter. Or it did—but only to me.

There was no sign of life at Jerry Saenz's house. A glance revealed that the upstairs apartment was dark, the curtains still pulled. The sun was rising a clear and brilliant yellow on the horizon, but it was possible no one was awake inside the house yet.

I parked down the street, watching 1804 Morgan in my rearview mirror. I was definitely too far away to take a shot—to risk my single bullet—but even if I'd been a trained sniper, that wasn't my plan.

I needed Robert Saenz to know exactly what had hit him and who had fired the shot. I suddenly remembered a slogan from a long-ago history class, maybe as far back as junior high school: *Don't fire until you see the whites of their eyes.* That was from the Revolutionary War, probably, but it applied here, too. I wanted Robert Saenz to see the whites of my eyes. When he had killed Daniel, it had been random—I knew that. It might have been any person walking down the street, but it just happened to be Daniel, my son, who was in that place at that exact time. When I killed Saenz, it was going to be deliberate in every way, and I wanted him to know it, to feel the difference.

I started as the front door opened, and a man came out, wearing jeans and a bulky winter coat. He had a baseball cap pulled low, the brim shielding his face. Curly dark hair stuck out like wings on either side of his head. I remembered Robert Saenz's disheveled hair from his mug shot—curly on the sides, the top flattened. Hat hair.

My first instinct was to shrink lower in the seat, hiding from view—but this was pointless, because if he was far enough away that I couldn't make out his facial features, then I was far enough away that he couldn't make out mine. I reached for the Colt, held it without knowing exactly what I would do.

The man—Robert? Jerry?—crossed the sidewalk to the

driveway and unlocked the door to the truck. He stepped up, started the ignition. I squinted hard, trying to decide who it was. The truck, leaking gray puffs of exhaust, reversed in the driveway and backed onto Morgan. While I pretended to be reaching for something on the passenger seat, it passed me.

I straightened, watched as the Saenz & Co. truck slowed at the end of the street, turned left and accelerated, heading out of town. He was getting away.

I tucked the Colt into the console and followed.

olivia

We stopped for gas just past Toledo. It was freezing outside and not much warmer in the bathroom, where my reflection in the mirror was clouded by a long exhale. That girl looked like me, moved like me, and somehow didn't seem to be me at all.

At the pump, Mom was listening to the slow, steady *glug, glug* of gasoline.

"How much longer?"

"Maybe another hour, especially if I can keep going eighty."

I leaned up against the side of the Volvo and watched the numbers roll, the dollars increasing much faster than the gallons. This was getting to be quite the expensive trip my family was taking, I thought—especially when you factored in a new transmission and all the unseen costs of whatever my dad was about to do.

Mom leaned back next to me, both of us ignoring the mud splattered against the side of the car. She looked exhausted, like an older, less healthy version of the person who had been standing in her driveway to greet me just two days ago. I wondered who we would be by the end of this trip, if either of us would even resemble ourselves.

"You want me to drive?" I asked.

Mom snorted.

"Don't say I didn't offer," I told her, relieved.

She put an arm around me. I held back at first, then rolled my head to the side so I could rest against her. Somewhere in this state, my dad was driving around with a gun, looking for the man who'd killed my brother. For just a moment I thought I would be okay if we stayed right here, at a gas station off the Ohio Turnpike with Mom's arm around my shoulders.

"I missed you," she said.

"I missed you, too."

"Just the little things, you know? Even the stupid stuff, the day-to-day things. I miss seeing you every day. Hearing your funny observations. Laughing at your jokes."

"I tell very few jokes," I said shakily. I was in a fragile place. Instead of a flesh and blood heart pounding away in my chest, it felt as if I had nothing more substantial than one of those construction paper hearts that kids make on Valentine's Day. One false move, and my little red heart might rip right down the middle.

Mom laughed an in-spite-of-herself laugh. Like, *nothing is really funny right now, but I'm going to cling to this one tiny moment.*

I tried to make my voice sound normal, although I was on the verge of crazy blubbering. "But when you think about it, we probably talked more than most mothers and daughters who live in the same house. If I had a joke to tell, you probably heard it."

"I know. And I loved our talks. I loved hearing your voice, your wit…but of course, it wasn't enough. And I always felt like we were holding back, like you weren't telling me all the bad things, and I wasn't telling you how lonely I was, because we both wanted the other person to be happy."

I didn't say anything, because she was absolutely right. I'd babbled on every week about dumb stuff, about what Dad and I had made for dinner, about having to study for a test, about the competition on one reality show or another. I basically spent the week gathering these little scraps of information so I would have something to fill the silence, the void that was created by all the things we wouldn't say. Somehow, in the middle of all that talking, I never told her about losing friendships and being lonely, about failing P.E., about how awful it was to lose my virginity to a stranger on someone's bathroom floor.

"Now, no crying," Mom told me, using the sleeve of her fleece sweatshirt to dab at my eyes. And then she dabbed at her own, which were sparkly with tears. We smiled at each other madly for a moment, and then Mom replaced the gas pump with a clunk, and we got back into the car.

When this nightmare with Dad was over, I promised myself, I would tell her everything I'd left out, every single thing.

And then maybe, *maybe,* things would be all right.

curtis

The road was still slick; at the left turn, my tires did a half-second spin.

Calm down. You can't blow it all so close to the end.

I followed the Saenz & Co. truck at what would have been a safe distance in Sacramento, with a few hundred other cars on the road. On this flat horizon, against the open Midwest sky, the Explorer was way too obvious. If Robert Saenz—or could it be his brother, Jerry?—looked in his rearview mirror, he would have seen me a quarter mile behind, leaning forward in my seat as if I were about to burst through the windshield. I kept the same pace, wishing I had some kind of GPS display on the dashboard; where exactly were we headed?

The calm resignation I'd felt leaving the truck stop had disappeared. That had been the calm before the storm. Now adrenaline was rushing through my veins, masking again my exhaustion. How many hours since I'd slept? Back in Omaha, a world away, Kathleen and Olivia were barely beginning their day, one more of many days without me.

The road widened into two lanes; apparently, we'd joined up with a state highway. I couldn't afford to wait and see. For all I knew, Saenz & Co. was heading to Canton, to Akron, to whatever was farther south. I couldn't hang back any longer, waiting to find out. I pulled into the left lane and accelerated, trying to draw even with the truck. This wasn't an easy task, since it was traveling at a good speed, and the Explorer, rebuilt transmission or not, felt like a rattling ton of tin at anything over seventy. I had to be patient several times, holding back so that I could pass slower-moving vehicles on the road—the occasional town car, a few semis lumbering along with heavy loads. It was a difficult task to keep one eye on the road and one on the Saenz truck, a feat better suited to a movie scene with a stuntman driving, the eye of the cameraman from the backseat making all the necessary observations. All I could make out was the back of the driver's head, the dark rim of hair.

Robert Saenz's head, Robert Saenz's hair.

What was my whole life now if not a chance?

I said his name out loud, letting the words fill the Explorer's airspace. It was strange to *say* the name—to have the freedom to voice my thoughts when the syllables had been inside me for so long, pounding like a heartbeat, pulsing like a deep wound.

I drew up on the left, trying to match the Explorer's pace with his, nose to nose. The driver was looking down, then straight ahead, then—as my whole body tensed—he turned his head.

It wasn't Robert Saenz.

This must have been Jerry, a younger version of the man from the mug shot, with a face that was thinner, healthier, a mouth that settled naturally into a smile, even as he shot me a surprised glance.

I eased back immediately, foot off the gas. Jerry Saenz turned, looking repeatedly over his left shoulder and back to the road. He tossed up an arm in an angry gesture, but I had fallen back. My grievance wasn't with Jerry. He'd taken in his killer brother and essentially provided the weapon that had killed my son, but I didn't want to hurt him—not directly, anyway. If I had only one shot, I was going for the killer himself.

A car honked behind me—the Buick I'd passed earlier, catching up. I slid back into the right lane, heart pounding. An older woman in the passenger seat swiveled to fix me with concerned blue eyes.

She would be another one, I thought. She would see my mug shot in the paper and ask her husband, "Wasn't that the man who was driving so strangely? Weren't those California plates?"

I took the first right turn I could, then swung around in a wide arc and retraced the route to Oberlin. Jerry Saenz had seen me, but he wouldn't understand the significance until later. The encounter would mean nothing to him now, would be only a tiny odd blip in an otherwise normal day.

I was back on track. Robert Saenz would be alone now, waking up in his room above the garage. I said his name, like a chant, all the way back to town.

olivia

As we drove, the sun came out. Most of the clouds from yesterday were gone, and the day was more beautiful than a day had any right to be. Maybe even that was some kind of omen—a beautiful day for the last day of life as we knew it.

"So, how are we going to find Dad, if we don't know where to look?"

Mom said, "Oberlin's tiny, Liv. I mean, *tiny.* If he's there, we're going to find him. And as soon as businesses are open, I'm calling the D.A. and the police department. They'll know for sure what's going on with Robert Saenz, if he's been paroled, or what."

I had a vision of us stopping pedestrians in Oberlin and asking if they had seen a white man, six-one, late forties, probably two hundred pounds after all the junk food we'd eaten on the trip. But most of the men I'd seen in the Midwest fit this description, at least roughly.

Out the window was farmland, white houses and big red barns, trailers cropping up here and there out of nowhere, the occasional cow or horse behind a barbed wire fence. It was all so peaceful and so wrong. If a genie appeared right now with the promise of three wishes, I would ask to go back in time. Not just to the day that Dad went up on the cafeteria roof, but to the night when Daniel died. I'd insert myself in the scene, intervene in some way—which was just the sort of thing that never worked out in time travel movies. It was like stepping on a butterfly in the past; the reverberations could be huge. Maybe I'd even find myself in a different sort of crazy situation, a new nightmare for which I was solely responsible.

Besides, not *everything* that happened after Daniel died had been bad. For some reason, I remembered Dad and me eating our TV dinners in front of old reruns. Dad could do a voice that was a dead ringer for Mr. Ed's: *I wish that guy would just leave me alone. It's not natural for a man to be so attached to a horse.* If I could keep some of those moments and still have Daniel alive and Mom with us, I'd climb into a time machine in a second.

We both jumped when we saw the first sign for Oberlin, and Mom gave the gas pedal another steady push. When we met up with Dad—*if* we met up with Dad—I would have all kinds of questions for him. But I had to take advantage of this moment with Mom. I pinched my eyes shut, as if I were making a wish, and said, "Tell me about your road trip with Dad, the one you took to California."

Mom looked startled. "Where did that come from?"

"I just want to know. Before we get there, and before it's too late and I never have a chance again."

Mom considered this. I was grateful that she didn't say *Of course you'll have another chance to ask me anything you want!* For once, we were on even footing. "But what's there to say?"

"Nope, that's not good enough. Dad tried to buy me off with that."

"It was just so long ago. I can't imagine it's interesting. Are you sure you want to hear this?"

"Mom, come on."

"Well, okay." She paused for a few seconds, probably calling it all back. "We had our trunk loaded with all this junk from college, and then all these wedding gifts we'd unpacked from their boxes to make more room, and we'd rolled the breakable things in our clothes. It was pretty tricky to unpack when we got to Sacramento, because when we picked up a flannel shirt, a drinking glass would come rolling out of it." She smiled a little. "See? I tried to warn you, not interesting."

"No, it is. It's fascinating. Keep going."

Mom sighed. "We didn't have much money, so we only stayed twice in hotel rooms, and we spent the other night in the car. That was somewhere in Utah outside Salt Lake City, and your father woke up with a massive crick in his neck, so we stopped and bought a bag of frozen corn for him to hold against his neck, and then we threw away the corn at a rest stop somewhere in Nevada." She was smiling faintly. "I haven't thought about that in a long time."

"And you were happy," I said.

"And we were happy," she confirmed. "I don't think I'd ever been so happy."

"And then Daniel was born," I prompted, continuing the story.

"Well...I mean, years later. Five years, almost exactly."

"And you were happy," I said again.

Mom's smile was broader now, her face relaxing, although her hands were still clenched on the steering wheel. "We were so happy. I wish you could have known your brother then, Liv. He was such a serious little kid. The second he could speak, he had a million questions about everything, and he was always very skeptical about our answers. Sometimes I heard him asking your father the same things he'd just asked me, like he was checking to make sure we had our stories straight. This was before he started piano, of course—after that, he had a one-track mind."

"And then you moved," I prompted.

"Then we bought that crazy old little house. I fell in love with it the second I saw it, but I really had to work on your father to convince him. Where I saw potential, he saw serious amounts of hard work." She had a faraway look, as if she were chasing the memory.

"And then you had me."

"And then we had you."

"And you were happy?"

"Of course!"

I looked out the window.

Mom glanced at me. "Why did you say it like that? Was there any question we were happy?"

Because after Daniel, you didn't need me. Because I've never heard anyone say a single bad thing about Daniel, ever, and it stands to reason that there's no point in improving on perfection. I bit my lip, holding this back. *Because when Daniel died, I should have somehow taken his place and become the wonderful daughter to replace the wonderful son—and I didn't. I became the messed-up kid who was afraid of her own shadow and who had failed P.E., twice.*

"Of course we were happy," Mom repeated, stung. "You had a very happy childhood."

"I don't remember," I whispered, which was mostly true. It was as if the world of after, with all its awfulness and emptiness, had somehow obliterated the good of before.

"Well, *I* do. By the time you came along, Daniel was already in school, so you and I were home a lot during the day. That's before I had my little studio, so sometimes I propped you up in your car seat in the garage, and you watched me paint things."

"And inhaled the fumes..." I murmured.

"You remember!" Mom looked less frazzled than she had before, her face open and happy. "When you were a little older, we'd finger-paint out there. Once for your dad's birthday, we made him a giant card on a canvas tarp that had to be twelve-by-twelve. You stamped hundreds of wet handprints all over it, and it was so runny with paint that it took days to dry."

"What happened to it?"

"It's probably still out there, all rolled up in a corner. It turned out not to be very practical for long-term display."

"What else did we do?"

"Well, you used to come with me to estate sales way out in the boonies, all over northern California. We'd just pop in some music and sing along until we got there. This is when I discovered that you loved Peter, Paul and Mary."

I laughed now, grudgingly. "Did I have a choice?"

Mom sang, slightly off-key, "'Puff the magic dragon, lived by the sea…'"

I picked up the next line, giggling. "'…and frolicked in the autumn mist…'"

"'In a land called Honah Lee,'" Mom finished.

"I can't believe you let me sing such druggie songs when I was just a little kid."

"Oh, please. Druggie songs. I still maintain that it was a song about a magical dragon in a kingdom by the sea." She continued humming a verse or two, and I tried to figure out if I actually remembered these trips, or if I only did because Mom was re-creating them for me.

"What about Dad?" I asked.

"What about him?" My question had startled her.

"Back then, was Dad happy, too?"

"Of course he was. We had this perfect little family, like we'd always wanted. You should have seen how proud he was of you, how much he loved having a daughter. I used to worry that you weren't ever going to learn to walk, since he insisted on carrying you everywhere, hoisting you onto his shoulders or swinging you so that your feet didn't even touch the ground."

I didn't remember him carrying me, but I remember sitting on his lap in front of the TV, the evening news on low. He always smelled vaguely of chalk dust and the chemicals used in the science labs. At some point I had become too old for sitting on his lap, and too old to want that, either. At some point I'd pulled away from his kisses and rolled my eyes when he said, "I love you."

"But I wasn't good enough." I couldn't stop myself from saying it.

"What are you talking about?"

It felt as if I had something stuck in my throat, or maybe my throat was closing all on its own, like the onset of anaphylactic shock, apropos of nothing. I'd learned about that years ago and dutifully recorded it in my Fear Journal. I forced the words out: "If I were enough, then we wouldn't be here."

"I don't know what you're talking about."

I took a deep breath. "If I were enough, we wouldn't be here right now. Dad wouldn't be in Oberlin, living out some stupid-ass revenge plot. If I were enough, you two would have stayed together for my sake. If I were enough, the world wouldn't have stopped the second Daniel died. If I were enough…" I couldn't finish, I was crying so hard.

"No," Mom said, crying, too. "No, no, no…"

She wanted to pull to the side of the road, but I wouldn't let her. I'd been following the little red dot on my GPS that showed our car moving closer and closer to our destination. It was like watching a horror movie, and not any one horror movie in particular, but *all* horror movies, where you knew something bad was going to happen, but you just couldn't look away.

And then the battery in my phone died.

We counted off the miles using Mom's odometer, our dread mounting: eighteen miles. Sixteen.

Mom said, "He probably just wants to scare him."

And I said, "Right!" because it was the only thing to say.

The man who bought a massive container of chicken noodle soup from Costco when I was sick, and then brought a bowl to my bedside—he wouldn't kill another person. The man who had given me all those piggyback rides—he wasn't a killer. The man who had been Mr. K, who had stayed after school almost every day to help his students understand their homework—he couldn't hurt anyone.

Fourteen miles, eleven. I needed to throw up. No, I needed to use the bathroom again. No, I needed to call Sam, to call anyone, to get some advice.

I looked out the window at the neat Midwest grids of land—a farmhouse here, a barn there, a truck traveling along a frontage road there. It was all so isolated. You could scream here, and no one in the world would hear it. You could fire a gun, and—

"Why are you slowing down?" I gasped. "Go faster!"

"This is our exit," Mom said, pointing to a sign I'd missed. "Didn't you say Highway 58?"

I was about to burst out of my skin, like a piece of overripe fruit.

And then we saw the sign: Oberlin Welcomes You.

curtis

S uddenly, I knew exactly what I was going to do.

There was an unsettling disconnect between my mind and my body; my body kept moving forward as if pre-programmed, and my mind was watching the whole thing from a distance, where it could safely call the shots.

I sped through the streets. It was past seven now; my detour through the Ohio countryside and back had cost me precious time. The day had fully arrived, ushered in with a golden sunlight that glinted off the asphalt.

I said it, hummed it, sang the three syllables: *Rob-ert Saenz*.

The Explorer fishtailed for a wild moment as I took a hard turn onto Morgan. It didn't matter who saw me, what anyone said or thought. Saenz was in my sights, and everything else had disappeared. For all I knew, the rest of the world had fallen into a sinkhole, and this little plot of land was the only thing left standing.

This time I didn't circle the block and park at a distance, or slow down to stare out the window and consider my options. Instead, I swung the Explorer into the driveway and jerked to a stop in the space that had recently been vacated by Jerry Saenz in the Saenz & Co truck. I waited a moment, watching. There was no movement inside the house, no face peering at me from behind a curtain. I fixed my eyes on the apartment above the garage. He was there, hungover, still in bed—I was sure. I heard the words in my head, as if I'd actually spoken them: *Do you know who I am? Does the name Daniel Kaufman ring any bells?*

I stepped out of the car, the Colt tucked into my waistband. Maybe even the sight of it would give Robert Saenz a massive coronary. That was fine, too. It was *when,* not *if.* It was *when,* not *how.*

My shoes crunched against the gravel where the driveway ended and a stone pathway began. The area around the bottom of the steps was filthy with cigarette butts, smoked to nubs. Add this to Robert Saenz's list of crimes—littering, abuse of the environment. The stairs leading along the side of the garage up to the unit seemed to be an afterthought and not entirely up to code. Saenz & Co. was in the hauling business, not in construction. The entire staircase creaked under my weight, and the railing was less than stable. Left alone, Robert Saenz might just take a header down these stairs one night, without any help from me—but I wasn't going to wait for that.

The time to consider my actions had been before. Minutes before, driving back into town. An hour before, loading a single bullet in the parking lot of the truck stop. Two days ago, when I was in Omaha with Kathleen and Olivia, when I could have taken one last stab at making things right. Almost a month before, when I'd received the letter, and things had started to spiral out of control. Years ago, when I'd made the decision—consciously? unconsciously?—that what had happened to Daniel was going to define my life.

Now there was nothing to do but raise my fist and pound on the door, a sound so loud against the crisp quiet of the morning that it might have been a gunshot itself. I was about to try the handle, then force myself in if needed, shoulder to the door, when the doorknob turned, and the door opened inward.

Robert Saenz, wearing a stained white T-shirt and a pair of gray sweats, was standing in front of me. He ran a hand over his face roughly, as if he were rubbing himself awake. It was the same face I'd seen in the Oberlin newspaper, the same face on the booking jacket that the police officer had pushed across the conference table at me. It was hard to see him in real life and not remember that mug shot—his face bloated and large in the foreground, a height chart climbing the wall behind him. Now he was older, hair shorter and graying around the temples, his eyes bloodshot. His stomach was a hard ledge beneath his T-shirt.

I said his name—not a question, just a recitation of his name out loud as I'd been reciting it inwardly.

What surprised me more than anything was the expression on his face. This man had killed two people, I had to remind myself. He had done time in prison—scenes from an episode of *Lock-Up!* flashed in my mind—but he didn't look hard-bitten or criminalized. He didn't reach out and push me down the stairs—which he could have done without much difficulty—or slam the door in my face or reach out to throttle me with his bare hands. Instead, he looked resigned. He looked horribly tired.

I said, "You don't know me, but I know you. I've been waiting for this moment."

He took a step backward and raised a hand, chest-high, as if to stop me. "Okay. Now hold on."

"Daniel Kaufman was my son," I said, my voice breaking on his name.

Saenz ran a tongue over cracked lips, his dead eyes sparking with life. "What do you want from me?"

All the language had been sucked out of my brain. Where words had been, carefully rehearsed, was only a raw jumble of feeling. My hand went to my waistband, to the Colt, and his eyes tracked my movement.

"I want you to say his name."

"Look, I don't know—"

"His name was Daniel Owen Kaufman."

"Okay. So I'll say his name, and then you'll leave?"

This was the moment—my one shot. I tugged at my sweatshirt, bringing the Colt into view. "I'm here to make things right," I said.

Robert Saenz's eyes locked on the handle of the gun, but then his gaze shifted ever so subtly to something over my shoulder.

Behind me, at the foot of the rickety stairs, someone said, "Uncle Bobby? What's going on?"

olivia

We sped through Oberlin, craning our necks out open windows, scanning the horizon frantically for a green Ford Explorer with California plates, for any sign of Dad. We passed brick buildings, open green spaces with towering pieces of public art and signs for pizza and twenty-four-hour Laundromats.

Daniel lived here, I reminded myself. As much as I fought it, I couldn't stop the next thought: *Daniel died here.*

And then: *I can't let Dad die here, too.*

"He's not here. We're never going to find him," I moaned.

"We haven't been up and down every street yet."

"Maybe he's not even here, because maybe Robert Saenz isn't even here."

Mom brushed this aside. It was still too early to contact anyone on the phone, to learn anything about a release from prison, terms of parole. "Plan B," she said, pulling into a gas station. Before I could protest, she left me in the car, the engine running. Madness—it was all madness. Maybe I could slide across the center console, plunk myself in the driver's seat and leave my parents and all this lunacy behind. Angling my neck out the window, I saw Mom inside the store, gesturing with one hand to the clerk behind the counter.

A few seconds later, she was back, clutching a scrap of paper with a few crudely drawn lines. "His brother lives here in town." She tossed the map into my lap, and I picked it up, trying to determine the orientation.

"You don't need the map," Mom said. "Just look for Morgan Street."

curtis

"Uncle Bobby?" the voice repeated uncertainly.

I turned slowly, the gun still tucked in my waistband. The voice belonged to a girl in jeans and sneakers and an oversize Oberlin High School sweatshirt that dwarfed her body. She had one foot on the first step, one hand on the unsteady railing. She was young—fifteen? Sixteen? *Olivia's age.* I forced the thought away.

"Tell her everything's okay," I ordered, my voice low.

"Everything's okay, Katie," Robert Saenz called. "Why don't you go back inside?" He was cool, much cooler than I would have been if the roles were reversed, if it were Olivia standing at the foot of the stairs.

"Who are you?" Katie asked, not moving. "Do we know you?"

I looked again at Robert, who called down, "Don't worry, Katie. Everything's okay. Don't you need to leave for school soon?"

She squinted up at us, assessing the situation. "I'm coming up there."

"Don't come up here, Katie," Robert said.

"You don't need to come up here," I repeated. It was my

PAULA TREICK DeBOARD

Mr. K voice, coming from deep within me. It was the tone I used with my students—friendly but firm. "I'm just here to talk to your uncle."

"Then I'm going to talk to him, too," she said, reminding me more and more of Olivia with each second. She took a few steps and stopped again, watching me. Closer, I could see that her hair was still wet from a morning shower, combed flat but with the ends beginning to curl up as they dried. The sunlight glinted off some metal in her mouth: braces, the colored bands alternating purple and blue.

I couldn't let this girl be involved. In all the thousands of times I'd played this scene in my mind, it hadn't included anyone other than him and me.

That was how it had to be now.

I surprised Robert Saenz with a one-handed shove against his chest, and he took a staggering step back into the apartment. All I needed was to get him inside, the door locked behind us. There would be only a few minutes. Oberlin was a small town, after all. I remembered the police sergeant telling me that a paramedic from Lorain County had been on the scene of Daniel's accident in less than three minutes.

But then, two things happened.

Katie, frozen on the step below, screamed.

And in the driveway, a car screeched to a sudden stop. I only vaguely registered this out of the corner of my eye; Robert Saenz had regained his footing and was launching himself in my direction.

"Say his name, Saenz," I sputtered. "Say his name before you die."

But then a car door slammed, and someone yelled, "Dad! No!"

olivia

The Explorer was in the driveway, and Dad was standing at the top of a flight steps over a garage, his eyes wild.

There was no time to be afraid. Even though I was shaking and bawling and breathing through my own snot, I pushed fear away and bolted out of the car.

Mom was right behind me, her car door slamming. "Curtis! No! Get down here!"

At the bottom of the steps a girl was screaming. She stepped back to let us pass, probably believing we had control over Dad, as if he was a psych patient on the lam and we had been charged with bringing him back.

When I reached the middle of the stairs, I had a clearer view of Dad, who had stepped inside the apartment. The gun that Sam and I hadn't been able to find was in his hands. It wasn't a large thing, but somehow that made it even more terrifying. He held the gun out before him, aiming into the dark, gaping hole of the apartment. For a split second he shifted his gaze down the steps, to where I stood.

I flinched, as if he'd shot me with that look. I wanted to

know, to believe deep down, that my dad couldn't kill any-one. He wouldn't, I was absolutely sure, kill *me*.

"Curtis," Mom called, her voice oddly calm, as if she were negotiating a hostage release. "Why don't you come down here, so we can talk?"

Dad didn't say anything, but I'd lived with him long enough to know that his silence was itself an answer. Aiming a gun at the man who killed his son might not have been right, but I could see that it was his only answer at that moment, and he believed it was right.

I wiped my sleeves over my eyes to get rid of the tears. "Dad! Please. You have to come with us now."

"Get them away from here, Kathleen," Dad called, gestur-ing with his free hand.

"What's going on?" the girl at the bottom of the steps called, her voice strained with panic.

Mom turned. "Call 9-1-1! Right now!"

The girl hesitated, then dashed off in the direction of the house, looking back over her shoulder.

"Curtis," Mom tried again.

"Dad! Please! Put the gun down!"

Dad looked down at us, like for just a moment he was con-sidering it. And then another man was visible, hooking an arm around Dad's neck.

In that split second between seeing and reacting, between realizing what was happening and being able to voice a scream, the man dragged Dad into the apartment.

"It's not loaded!" I screamed, although I wasn't sure this was true. It had seemed such a simple thing at the time, such a clever solution: switch the bullets for batteries. Attention, America: We have solved the issue of gun control. Now, I knew that Dad could have bought more ammunition, and that a police officer charging up these stairs wouldn't care if the gun was loaded or not. Sam and I hadn't solved anything.

Mom was right behind me as we raced up the steps. The screams coming from my own mouth were unintelligible, like speaking in tongues with the spirit inside you. Except that what was inside me was my whole life, spilling out in an animal's yell. The staircase rocked beneath our feet—*death by falling off a wobbly staircase*—but I figured that the collapse of the stairs might even be a blessing right then. It was the least of our worries.

I reached the top first, elbowing my mom out of the way, a feat that surprised me as much as it would have surprised my P.E. teacher in my former life. It was dark inside the apartment, and there were heaps of clothes and shoes and food wrappers on the floor. Dad and the man who must have been Robert Saenz had fallen to the ground, where they writhed on the carpet like a two-headed, eight-limbed beast. Dad still had hold of the gun and was ramming it against Robert's ribs, but it seemed like a shaky hold at best.

"Don't! Don't—" I screamed, but Dad pulled the trigger. The gun clicked, but nothing happened.

Robert freed his hands and got them both around Dad's neck in a choke hold.

"It's not loaded!" I screamed again, this time at Robert. "Let him go! He was just trying to scare you!" More than anything, I wanted this to be true. I *believed* it. I lunged for that thick arm, trying to pull it off Dad's neck. The hold was way too tight, and I couldn't budge his grip even slightly. Dad's face was turning a violent reddish color, his eyes bulging. If I didn't know who he was, I wouldn't have known him at all.

Mom was on top of Robert's legs, trying to pin him into place. Her hands were struggling to get the gun from Dad's grasp, and all of a sudden the gun was pointed directly at her.

I heard myself scream *OhmyGodohmyGodohmyGod,* scream-ing and screaming because I could see how this was going to end, with the gun loaded and discharging, the way guns did, and the bullet entering my mother's chest, splintering through skin and bone to organs, to the spongy insides that make us everything we are.

But as it turned out, that's not what happened.

Mom wrestled the gun away, and she leaned back on her haunches and aimed at Robert Saenz, who was still choking my dad, and said, "Let him go. Let him go, and we'll put an end to all of this."

"Please, *please,*" I begged, grabbing on to Robert Saenz's legs, as if I could distract him. He kicked me, his foot con-necting with my shoulder, and I tried again. I knew only the barest of facts about Robert Saenz at that point, but I would learn more later, when the newspaper published a giant feature that was fascinating and horrible at the same time, spilling the guts of our family for the entire world to read if they wanted. Robert Saenz, the article would claim, had been the family's bad seed, the one who always needed bailing out. He had fa-thered a child, a boy who was about my age, but never visited the kid or paid a cent of child support, so the term *father* could be used only as a technicality. He had taken drugs for more than half his life, beginning when he was younger than me.

But I didn't know any of that then.

At that moment, he was the man who had killed my brother, the man who was going to kill my father. *Asphyxiation, broken windpipe, broken neck.* "Shoot him!" I cried. Would I have said this if I had time to think and plan and be rational?

Maybe.

His hands still on Dad's neck, Robert Saenz turned to look at Mom.

Out of the corner of my eye, I could see her shaking, the gun in her hands wavering.

I had wasted years of my life being scared of little things when I should have been saving all my energy for this moment. My screams felt like a prayer, like a reckoning with God— *Don't don't don't let Dad die.*

And then Dad's head hit the floor with a sickening thud. He didn't move. I could hear sirens now, and realized I had been hearing them for the past minute, only now they were closer, surrounding us.

Robert Saenz was reaching for the gun when Mom pulled the trigger.

And then the whole world went black.

curtis

At first, I thought I was dead.

Someone was leaning over me, asking questions, but the questions didn't make any sense. I didn't know where I was, or who had a gun, or why someone was screaming. All I knew was that I was out of breath, my windpipe burning. Was it still Monday? Was it still morning? Were we still alive?

"He meant business, all right," a paramedic said. "You're going to have some pretty serious bruising there. Can you say something for me?"

I rasped, "Olivia."

"Is that the girl who was here? We took her outside. She's waiting by the ambulance."

"Kathleen?" My throat ached like the mother of all sore throats. I tried to sit up and slumped back again, dizzy.

"Whoa, now. Is Kathleen the...? Uhh..." The paramedic turned, talking to someone else in the room, a person who was a blur to me. "Kathleen—your, ah...wife—has been taken into custody."

Through my general fogginess, I realized that the screaming was coming not from me or Kathleen or Olivia, but from

Robert Saenz. Another paramedic was kneeling over him, and his shirt was drenched in blood. His screams were awful, but he was alive. The paramedics were discussing the best way to transport us; their gurneys were too wide for the garage steps.

Seeing Robert Saenz on the floor, blood seeping through a tourniquet on his arm, his face white with pain, I felt it all leak out of me—the hatred, the anger I'd stored for months and years. All that energy spent, all that time lost. He was just a man, just a human. I tried to get a full breath through my bruised windpipe, felt a beautiful, painful rush of air pour into my lungs. I knew that Daniel was still dead and that was still horrible—but it was long-ago horrible, his loss receding in front of me like a mirage on a flat stretch of highway.

"I can walk," I insisted, forcing myself again to sit up. I needed to see Olivia. I needed to see Kathleen.

Assisted by two paramedics, I made my way down the rickety staircase. Each breath seared my lungs, and the timing of my steps was off, as if my feet were getting the message long after my legs. During my long, stumbling descent and walk to the ambulance, I locked eyes with Olivia, who was wrapped in a navy blanket.

Forgive me, forgive me, I begged her silently.

I was at the hospital for several hours, processed and observed and finally released into police custody. The consensus from the emergency room staff was that I was lucky—my bruises and a slight abrasion on my neck would fade to nothing in a week. There really wasn't a way to measure the damage I'd caused.

Olivia held my hand while we waited; she answered my questions woodenly. While I had been passed out on the floor, Kathleen had fired at Robert Saenz, shattering his right wrist. He'd been reaching for the gun, trying to wrest it from her grasp. The single bullet had chambered, the shot hitting its mark.

When the police arrived, she'd set the gun at her feet and kicked it over to them. She'd told the police that it was her gun, that she'd learned that Robert Saenz had been paroled, that she'd driven all the way from Omaha with me in hot pursuit, that she deserved all the blame.

"Why?" I whispered to Olivia, who only shook her head.

It was the holiest kind of crime: a mother seeking revenge for her dead son. It would make the *Oberlin News Tribune,* the *Cleveland Plain Dealer,* the *Akron Beacon Journal.* It would show up on the CNN crawl.

But the Oberlin Police Department had plenty of questions for me.

It was the second time I'd sat across a table from Sergeant Springer, a manila folder open on the table between us. This time the name wasn't SAENZ, ROBERT but KAUFMAN, KATHLEEN. In the time since I'd seen him, he'd been promoted, grown a beard. I had been demoted; I was no longer the righteous grieving father, but the son of a bitch involved in the disruption of an otherwise calm Monday morning.

I corroborated Kathleen's story, as I'd heard it from Olivia in the emergency room. Poor Olivia, waiting in the lobby with the most wanted signs, no doubt cataloguing a host of new fears. Or maybe she was asleep in one of the uncomfortable vinyl chairs. We'd been transported from the hospital to the police station in the back of a patrol car, and she'd dozed off instantly. I'd been in the room when she was questioned, but she'd declined to do anything more than make a short statement—essentially the same statement Kathleen had made, and which I'd parroted, dazed.

Sergeant Springer's stare bored into me, as invasive as a cavity search. "I gotta say, Kaufman, you gave me a bad feeling, all those years ago. Something just wasn't right."

I watched him, waiting. I wasn't about to say anything that didn't absolutely need to be said.

"Sure, you were this grieving father, and you had my complete sympathy. But something about you was just—off."

I swallowed.

"And Robert Saenz, well, it's not like he didn't have his share of demons, you know?"

I knew. Apparently Saenz had refused to talk—his upstairs apartment had contained a pharmacy's worth of painkillers, obtained on fraudulent prescriptions. The baggie of white stuff by his bed was likely meth.

"But for you to show up here again, all these years later..." He shook his head slowly.

There were a million things to say, but none of them would help. I fidgeted in my chair with the wobbly leg, thinking of Olivia, wanting to hold Kathleen.

"Maybe you can help me with this, Kaufman. We've got your wife's statement that she shot Saenz, but something isn't sitting right with me. Katie Saenz swears it was you and not your wife who arrived first, and Jerry Saenz says he saw a man matching your description this morning on his way out of town."

I raised my eyebrows but said nothing.

Sergeant Springer sighed. "You're a strange one, Kaufman. I wasn't wrong about that."

The stress of the past day—of the past week—was upon me, and I fought to keep my eyes open.

"Maybe this was just a case of things going horribly wrong," he said finally. "Is that what you're trying to say?"

It was.

★ ★ ★

Olivia and I spent that night in a junky motel outside of town. The Oberlin Inn—the best and only hotel in town— had seemed impossible, considering. I went into the bathroom to wash, and noticed the bruises on my neck, the raised welts of Robert Saenz's fingers. He was a killer, but he was just a man, about as flawed as they came. And the same was true of me.

Olivia was already asleep, fully clothed on top of the covers, when I came out of the bathroom.

That night and for weeks afterward I woke up in a cold sweat, my sleep plagued with nightmares. It was always the same, up to a point. I was getting out of the Explorer, heading up the rickety staircase to Robert Saenz's apartment over the garage. But what happened next was always a different, awful version of reality, and I was always powerless to stop it, until the moment I realized that Olivia was shaking me awake.

"Dad, you're dreaming," she said, and I reached out a hand to her, wanting reassurance that she was alive, my flesh-and-blood daughter and not a dream apparition.

In the end, Kathleen was charged with possession of an illegal firearm and pled guilty, avoiding a trial. She was sentenced to three years, including time served, and with the possibility of early release for good behavior. It worked somewhat in her favor that, after firing the single round from the Colt, she had been the one to rip off her sweater and fashion Robert Saenz a makeshift tourniquet out of her sweatshirt. She had handed over the weapon willingly, had offered up a full—though admittedly false—confession.

This time the Kaufmans had managed to get the attention of the Lorain County District Attorney himself, not an assistant. We had one meeting after Kathleen's sentencing, and Harold

Emsinger looked me straight in the eye and pronounced his verdict: "This was a gift."

He was flanked by an American flag on one side and shelves lined with thick legal books on the other. He had the weight of law and order, of precedent and justice, behind him. But what he said next was more along the lines of mercy. "The question, Mr. Kaufman, is what is your family going to do with this gift?"

It wasn't as if I could talk man-to-man with Robert Saenz afterward, to discuss the various decisions we'd made in our lives, and how we'd both ended up in his upstairs apartment, tussling over a gun loaded with a single bullet. If he'd succeeded in getting the gun away from me, I have no doubt he would have used it—and as far as I could see, that made us equals. After he completed his physical therapy, Robert Saenz would have limited use of his right hand, which had been patched together with pins and screws. His muscles would be too weak to form a solid fist.

I didn't search for him online, or make any phone calls, or return to Oberlin again—but news filtered down from her attorney to Kathleen and from Kathleen to me that Robert Saenz was in rehab, battling his addiction. There wasn't much time to think about him now, which was strange, since I'd essentially spent five years of my life doing nothing but thinking about him.

A single gunshot fired in an upstairs room had changed that. It had changed everything.

We weren't allowed to visit Kathleen for the first few months of her term, and she mostly used her phone calls for legal matters or business arrangements. She'd had to give up— at least for the time being—her interest in the Omaha store. Olivia wrote her long letters, and Kathleen responded immediately, as if they were keeping up a continual conversation—a private one.

In the first letter I wrote to Kathleen, I said: "If I were you, I wouldn't ever forgive me."

Her response came back: "I haven't."

Then I wrote every day, letting her hear every thought in my head, even the smallest bit of minutiae. I always said I was sorry. I always promised I would make it up to her.

When I could finally see her, on the first day she had visitation rights, she looked almost the same—her hair a duller version of itself, her skin so translucent that I could see the little blue vein on her forehead. "Prison pallor," she said, shrugging it off. She also claimed to have gained ten pounds, because her choices were "starches or starvation."

Olivia and I took turns in the room with her, giving each other privacy. When I was with Kathleen, I could tell she was wary of me, her eyes regarding me with a deep intensity. "You can trust me," I told her. "I'll spend the rest of my life proving it to you."

When it was Olivia's turn, I waited in the hallway, queuing with a sad collection of relatives visiting other prisoners. I wanted to know their stories; I wanted them to know ours. Olivia always brought Kathleen something—a pencil sketch, a poem, a handwritten copy of lyrics, letters that were sealed and dated, so Kathleen would have something to open at regular intervals.

I had nothing to offer except myself and my endless gratitude.

I didn't go back into the classroom, but I found a job developing curriculum for online courses, and when things settled down with Olivia, I started studying up on antiques. When

Kathleen got out, I was going to be her partner in business—a good partner, an enthusiastic one.

We had to list the house in Sacramento as a short sale and sell the cars, and I had to pull out a little money from my retirement fund to tide us over, but if we spent wisely, we could make it. I borrowed some books from the library, and Kathleen made me lists of what to look for, and when I could, I scoured the Ohio countryside for estate sales in our new-to-us twenty-year-old Toyota. Olivia, when she could, came with me.

On one of those spring days, almost a year after our trip from Sacramento, we followed signs along a winding path and ended up at an old farmhouse, wares spread across the lawn.

The sky was the kind of blue that hurt your eyes. *Daniel would love this,* I thought—for the first time in a long time. He would; he had always loved spring, and the endless blue sky of a California summer. Remembering Daniel used to make me angry about his death and depressed because I had failed him. But as Olivia and I picked our way through the washboards and vases and bassinets, I remembered him with a smile. This was a happy, good moment—and there would be others, many happy, good moments to come.

"What do you think about these chairs?" Olivia called.

I ran my hands up and down the chair legs, studying their bones. "I think your mom would love these," I said, trying to figure out how we would get both of them into the car at once.

"She will," Olivia promised me. "She absolutely will."

olivia

As you can imagine, I had one hell of a college admissions essay.

Or, I would have, if I'd actually earned my P.E. credits and graduated on time with the rest of my class back in Sacramento—which didn't happen.

After Mom's sentencing, Dad and I drove back to California to pack up our house and load everything into a U-Haul, which we drove first to Nebraska, to drop off most of our things at Grandpa and Grandma's old house for long-term storage. Then we continued on to Marysville, Ohio, where we rented a single-wide trailer not far from the grounds of the Ohio Reformatory for Women.

Dad and I both went to counseling sessions, separately. My counselor, Dr. Munoz, was a tiny man who stood about even with my nose. He had glasses and a carefully trimmed beard, and he wore comfortable-looking orthopedic shoes, as if he had just come off a shift in the E.R.

In the beginning, I told him, gearing up for the story, *there was a boy named Daniel. But now he's gone.*

"Daniel was your older brother," Dr. Munoz prompted.

"He was," I agreed. I sat very still for a long time in my chair.

Finally Dr. Munoz asked, "Did you want to tell me something about Daniel?"

I smiled and said, "Only that I loved him. And that now, I've moved on."

He smiled back at me. "Then let's not talk about Daniel. Let's talk about Olivia."

I told him about the classes I was taking, and how I'd decided that maybe, somewhere deep within me, there was a writer. I told him about some friends I had made, and how on the weekends I'd been going to arts festivals and things like that. I told him that I didn't wear black anymore, or at least, not head-to-toe. I told him about Sam Ellis, who had finally sent me one of his creations. I knew what it was, instantly, even before I'd freed the snow globe from its packaging. It was the great tragedy of my own life, two people in a car heading down a lonely road, our troubles buried beneath a light sprinkling of snow. I wrote him a long letter, thanking him, but I was smart enough to know that Sam wasn't pining for me, and that I shouldn't be pining for him, either.

"And what's that?" Dr. Munoz said, pointing to the notebook in my lap. It was the book Mom had bought me at the gas station somewhere between Omaha and Oberlin, when I'd realized that I'd left my Fear Journal behind.

"Oh, it's just a list I've been making," I told him, blushing. The Olivia Kaufman who had worn all black and obsessed about falling ceiling tiles wouldn't even recognize the things in this book. "I've been writing down some good things— you know, all the things I have to be grateful for. It turns out there's really a lot."

When Dr. Munoz smiled, the corners of his eyes wrinkled. "It sounds like you have a solid grip on things, Olivia," he said.

I ended up taking my GED, proving wrong the guidance counselor at Rio who had told me it was impossible to get past high school without passing two full years of P.E. It did prove impossible to attend community college in Columbus without getting my driver's license, though. After everything else that had happened, I was hardly scared at all to get on the road in our little junker Toyota, giving the car some gas to speed past the tanker trailers in the slow lane.

By the time Mom was out, I planned to have my general ed courses completed, and after her year of parole, we would be moving back to Omaha. Uncle Jeff and Aunt Judy had been "unfailingly decent"—Dad's words—in keeping the house for us. I was going to apply to the University of Nebraska-Lincoln as my first choice, casting a wider net around the Midwest as backups.

Sometimes I entertained the idea of applying to Oberlin, too—if only to give someone in the admissions office a shock: Not *that* Kaufman, surely.

Dad found hundreds of ways to show me he was sorry. He helped me study for my political science quizzes, he scouted sources for my English research papers, he drove around Columbus with me, helping me find interesting buildings to sketch for my art class. And he said it, too—about a million sorries before I told him that it was enough, that saying it over and over again wouldn't change what had happened.

Sometimes at night, when we were sitting in front of our ten-inch TV that got three channels, it almost seemed like the old days again, when it had been just the two of us in Sacramento. We made biting comments about poorly written sitcoms, and sometimes we even cracked jokes.

Once, he slipped and said "Love," and I said, as if I'd had the word ready for a long time, "Eventually."

And that's how it would be—eventually.

★ ★ ★ ★ ★

acknowledgments

The first thanks goes to my families, the Treicks and De-Boards, and their extensions—the Battses and Cervanteses and Kranzes and Wills, the Visses and Boons and Cefres, and the Davenports and Ayalas and Youngs—for their love and support. Special shout-outs to John DeBoard, my biggest fan, Beth Boon and Sara Viss for reading early drafts, Beth Slattery for the give-and-take critique every writer needs, and Kelly Jones for reading late into the night and then meeting me for an emergency lunch. (I so needed that.) Love and thanks to the extended Stonecoast/University of Southern Maine community of faculty and writers, especially Paige Levin. (We're only "eight away," you know!)

Every writer needs a group like the English Girls—Mary Swier, Cameron Burton, Alisha Vasche, Jenna Valponi, Amie Carter and Michelle Charpentier—and I'm so blessed to have these women as friends. I'm also grateful to others who listened to my ramblings, especially when they had little choice in the matter: my Wexford's trivia buddies, my comp students, and the members of the Writer's Guild at San Joaquin-Delta Community College.

The team at Harlequin MIRA was amazing—Erika Imranyi championed this book from its inception, and Michelle Meade helped me to see through to the heart of the story and make the book in every way better. I loved that Michelle seemed to feel the same way about the Kaufmans that I did: that they were real people we just needed to understand a bit better. Much appreciation also to my agent Melissa Flashman at Trident Media Group, who has proven to be both a sounding board for my scattered ideas and an invaluable resource for my panicked questions. Alanna Ramirez Garcia—good thoughts are still coming your way.

Since *The Mourning Hours* was published, I've heard from readers across North America (especially—oh, my goodness!— readers in Wisconsin). Thank you for allowing my little book into your lives. To the booksellers and bloggers and librarians who eat, sleep and breathe books—I'm proud to be your kindred spirit.

As I was researching this book, Craig Macho gave me a much-needed, slightly terrifying, after-hours crash course on firearms. Any errors in that regard are solely mine. Other research was conducted along I-80 in a madcap version of Curtis and Olivia's road trip—from Oberlin, Ohio, back to California with a few interesting detours en route. Will and I were thrilled to connect with Dawn Cordes, Jim and Nancy Kwasteniet, Joel Hood, and Sean and Laurie Covington along the way. I like to think my parents were there in spirit (rather than at home in California) as we crossed the plains and crested the Rockies— my dad grumbling at the frequency of the bathroom stops, my mom insisting we brake for every brown historical marker.

On that note, much love and gratitude is owed to my forever road-trip companion and coconspirator, Will DeBoard. There are crazy ideas I haven't even had yet that I already know you'll agree to, take on and stand behind. This book— like all our adventures—wouldn't be possible without you.

*Turn the page for a gripping excerpt
from Paula Treick DeBoard's first novel,
THE MOURNING HOURS.
Available now from Harlequin MIRA.*

one

Everything you needed to know, Dad said, you could learn on a farm. He was talking about things my mind, shaped by Bible stories and the adventures of Dick and Jane, could barely comprehend—the value of hard work, self-sufficiency, the life cycle of all things. Well, the life cycle— I did understand that. Things were always being born on farms, and always dying. And as for how they came to be in the first place, that was no great mystery. "They're mating," Dad would explain when I worried over a bull that seemed to be attacking a helpless heifer. "It's natural," he said, when the pigs went at it, when the white tom from Mel Wegner's farm visited and we ended up with litters of white kittens.

Nature wasn't just ladybugs and fireflies—it was dirt and decay and, sometimes, death. To grow up on a farm was to know the smell of manure, to understand that the gawky calves that suckled my fingers would eventually be someone's dinner. It was to witness the occasional birth of a half-formed calf, missing eyes or ears, like some alien-headed baby. We couldn't drive into town without seeing the strange, bloodied remains of animals—cats, opossums and the occasional skunk who had risked it all for one final crossing. By the time we got Kennel, our retriever-collie mix, we'd had three golden Labs, each more loyal than the last, until they ran away during thunderstorms or wandered into the path of an oncoming semi headed down Rural Route 4. When Dad had spotted him at the county shelter, Kennel had a torn ear, a limp in his back left leg and ribs you could spot from a hundred yards away—the marks of an abusive owner.

Even humans couldn't avoid their fates. Sipping lemonade from a paper cup after the Sunday-morning service, I weaved between adult conversations, catching little snatches as I went. A tractor had tipped over, trapping the farmer underneath. Cows kicked, and workers were hurt. Pregnant women, miles from any hospital, went into early labor. Machines were always backfiring, shirtsleeves getting caught in their mechanisms. This was to say nothing of lightning strikes, icy roads and snowdrifts, or flash floods and heat waves. This was to say nothing of all the things that could go wrong inside a person.

So we were used to death in our stoic, farm-bred way. It was part of the natural order of things: something was born, lived its life and died—and then something else replaced it. I knew without anyone telling me that it was this way with people, too.

Take my family, for example—the Hammarstroms. My great-great-grandpa had settled our land and passed on the dairy to his son, who passed it to Grandpa, who passed it on to Dad, who would pass it on to Johnny. Dad and Mom had gotten married and had Johnny right after Dad graduated from high school, leaving Mom to get her degree later on, after Emilie and I were born. I'd always thought it was extremely cool that our parents were so much younger than everyone else's parents, until Emilie spelled out for me that it was something of a scandal. Anyway, when Johnny had been born, Grandpa and Grandma had moved to the in-law house next door, where Dad and Mom would someday move, when it was time for Johnny and his wife to inherit the big house. This was simply the expected order of things, as natural as the corn being sown, thinned, watered, fertilized and harvested. Everything that was born would die one day. I knew this, because death was all around me.

There was Grandma, for one. I was too young to have any concrete memories of her death, although I'd pieced together the facts from whispered conversations. She'd been standing in her kitchen, peeling apple after apple, when it happened. A *pulmonary embolism,* whatever that was. A freak thing. I couldn't walk into Grandpa's kitchen without thinking: *Was it here? Was this the spot?* But life had gone on without her. Grandpa stood at that sink every morning, drinking a cup of coffee and staring out the window.

The first funeral I remember attending was for our neighbor Karl Warczak, who'd collapsed in his manure pit, overwhelmed by the fumes. An ambulance had rushed past on Rural Route 4, and Dad and Mom had followed—Mom because she had just completed her training as a nurse, Dad because he and Karl Warczak had worked together over the years, helping with each other's animals, planting, harvesting, tinkering with stubborn machinery. By the time they'd pulled in behind the ambulance, Dad had said later, it had already been too late—sometimes, he'd explained, the oxygen just got sucked out of those pits.

Mom had lain out my clothes the night before the funeral— a hand-me-down navy wool jumper that seemed to itch its way right through my turtleneck, thick white tights and a pair of too-big Mary Janes with a tissue wadded into the toes. She'd always been optimistic that I would grow into things soon.

During the service I'd sat sandwiched between Mom and Emilie, willing myself not to look directly at the coffin. The whole ashes-to-ashes, dust-to-dust thing made me feel a little sick to my stomach once I really thought about it, and so did Mom's whisper that the funeral home had done "such a good job" with Mr. Warczak. It was incredible that he was really dead, that he had been here one minute and was gone the next, that he would never again pat me on the head with his dirt-encrusted fingers. There had been such a solemn strangeness to the whole affair, with the organ music and the fussy bouquets of flowers, the men in their dark suits and the women in navy dresses, their nude panty hose swishing importantly against their long slips.

"It is not for us to question God's perfect timing," Pastor Ziegler had intoned from the pulpit, but I remember thinking that the timing wasn't so great—not if you were Mr. Warczak, who thought he could fix the problem with the manure pump and then head inside for lunch, and not for his son, Jerry, who had been about to graduate from Lincoln High School and head off to a veterinary training program. The rumor had been that Mrs. Warczak's cancer was back, too, and this time it was inoperable. "That boy's going to need our help," Dad had told us when we were back in the car, riding with the windows open. "It's a damn shame."

"Why did it happen?" I'd asked from my perch on top of a stack of old phone books in the backseat. I could just see out the window from that height—the miles of plowed and planted and fenced land that I would know blindfolded. "Why did he die?"

"It was an accident. Just a tragic accident," Mom had said, blotting her eyes with a wad of tissue. She'd been up all morning, helping in the church kitchen with the ham-and-cheese sandwiches that were somehow a salve for grief. When we'd parked in our driveway, she'd gathered up a handful of soggy tissues and shut the door behind her.

"Oh, pumpkin," Dad had said as he sighed when I'd lingered in the backseat, arms folded across my jumper, waiting for a better answer. He'd promised to head over to the Warczaks' house later, to help Jerry out. "It's just how things go. It's the way things are." He'd reached over, giving my shoulder a quick squeeze in his no-nonsense, farmer-knows-best way.

Somehow, despite all the years that passed, I never forgot this conversation, the way Dad's eyes had glanced directly into mine, the way his mustache had ridden gently on top of his lips as he'd delivered the message. He couldn't have known the tragedies that were even then growing in our soil, waiting to come to harvest.

All he could do was tell me to prepare myself, to buck up, to be ready—because the way the world worked, you never could see what was coming.

THE FRAGILE WORLD

PAULA TREICK DeBOARD

Reader's Guide

MIRA®

1. Was it surprising that Kathleen was able to move on with her life while Curtis couldn't seem to move past his anger? What causes parents to react differently to tragedies in their family?

2. Would you be able to forgive a person who caused serious injury or death to a loved one—even if that act was unintentional?

3. Robert Saenz, although a fictional character, could be all too real. Curtis believes the judicial system has failed where Robert Saenz is concerned. What might be an appropriate punishment for an action—however unintentional—that has such deadly consequences?

4. Curtis doesn't seem to believe he could ever cause harm to Olivia or Kathleen, although of course, his actions could have a devastating effect on their lives, as well. Does this lack of awareness come from a callousness or insensitivity to others, or is he simply blind to everything but his desire for revenge?

5. Consider Olivia's many fears throughout the book. Do these fears seem like a natural reaction to her circumstances, or a sign of a more serious issue? In what ways can fear affect a person?

6. Why does Kathleen take more responsibility than she deserves for what happens at the end of the book? Why doesn't Curtis intervene and publicly take responsibility?

7. When Curtis and Olivia say "Love… Eventually" at the end of the book, do you believe them? Can things work out for the Kaufmans, moving forward?

The Fragile World is as much a story about loss and grief as it is about love and the strength of family. What was the inspiration for this story and the characters in the books?

The Fragile World wasn't inspired by any one event, but my heart goes out to families who have experienced a heartbreaking tragedy or loss. In this story Curtis needs to hold someone accountable for his son's death; it's the only way he can make sense of his new world. It's a dark but very human impulse, and I wanted to follow him down that path to see what this would mean for the rest of the family. Ultimately, people do deal with tragedy in different ways, but I always want to believe that healing is possible.

Your previous novel, The Mourning Hours, is told from the point of view of a young girl named Kirsten. In this novel, sixteen-year-old Olivia is one of the two main perspectives. What draws you to writing from the eyes of a younger narrator?

I can't say that this decision was a conscious choice from the beginning, but after I had the idea for the book, I tried to just let the characters speak to me. I found Olivia's voice to be an interesting contrast to her father's and really enjoyed writing her scenes. Between my time as a student and my time as a teacher, I've spent twelve years in high school, so I feel oddly comfortable entering the mind of a young person.

Also, I suspect that at heart I am very immature. ☺

A big part of *The Fragile World* takes place on the road. Did the confined setting present a challenge as you wrote or was it helpful?
I come by my love of road trips honestly—my parents carted my sisters and me around the country every summer of my childhood. I made my peace with that feeling of confinement and used it as a springboard for creativity. Plus, the world outside the window always amazes me—there's a stark beauty in even the most unvaried setting. In a practical sense, Curtis and Olivia's road trip brought them away from the world they knew into a new realm of possibilities. Unfortunately, they didn't get to do all the really cool things along I-80, like visit the world's largest stuffed polar bear in Elko, Nevada, or the landlocked lighthouse in Gretna, Nebraska.

Curtis, Kathleen and Olivia go through an extremely emotional journey throughout the course of the novel. While experiencing moments of utter despair, there are also beautiful moments of joy and acceptance. By the end of the story, they've all grown immensely, yet there seems to be a lot of healing left to do. What do you hope readers will take away from watching the evolution of these characters?
Deep down, I'm skeptical of fairy-tale endings and happily-ever-afters. What I'm more interested in is how people move on after tragedies—how they go about their everyday lives, and how they continue to love each other, even in the midst of a complicated situation. The Kaufmans are working through a

devastating loss in their various ways, but I hope readers see a family that still cares deeply for each other.

Do you read other fiction while you're doing your own writing or do you find it distracting?

I read constantly, whether I'm actively writing a story or not, and I've come to the point where I realize that my current "to read" list is long enough to last the rest of my life. Reading is my first love, and I can't stay away from it for any prolonged period of time. I do tend to compartmentalize the facets of my life—when I'm writing, I give it all my focus. But every night, I find time to curl up with a book.

Can you describe your writing process? Do you outline first, or dive right in? Do you have a routine? Do you let anyone read early drafts, or do you keep the story private until it's finished?

As I was writing *The Fragile World,* I had a rough outline of the book in my head—although not on paper. In general, each day I have more or less an idea of what I want to accomplish with a particular scene, so I start from there. One of the interesting things that happens as you write a story is that the characters almost become real people—they say unexpected things and make surprising decisions, and that might change a key scene or the overall direction of the story. Sometimes these little detours make all the difference, so it's crucial to listen to that instinct.

Until I reach a point where I feel comfortable sharing the story, I tend to keep my writing to myself. When there's something (like a sticky plot point) I'm trying to wrap my mind around, I'll talk it through with a trusted friend—a sort of writer's therapy session. I do have a small group of readers I can count on for honest feedback when I'm ready to share, and I'm immensely grateful to them.

What was your greatest challenge in writing *The Fragile World*? What about your greatest pleasure?
I split my time between writing and teaching college-level composition, so it's always a challenge to stay on top of each discipline. But I've found that these parts of my life are complementary; writing is my solitary escape, and teaching gets me out of my head and allows me to interact with others. I've found that when I'm working on a longer manuscript, I have to take pleasure in the small victories—the scenes that come together well, the breakthroughs in character or plot that suddenly open up in my mind. But the ultimate gratification comes from connecting and sharing with other writers, whether professionals or beginners.

In *The Fragile World*, Olivia is working through a number of fears—some realistic, and others very unlikely to happen. Were you able to relate to any of her fears?
I've had many fears in my lifetime, but most of them, like a fear of the dark, I've basically outgrown. The one fear that persists is claustrophobia; no matter the situation, I am very aware of the amount of space around me. On a trip to Barcelona, my husband (who is afraid of heights) and I ill-advisedly climbed the very narrow, winding steps to a spire atop La Sagrada Família. We laugh about it now, because that's all we can do. But neither of us was laughing at the time.